"SHARRH! SHARRH SHIP, SIX O'CLOCK!"

Michael Chamoun was on the bridge of a ship, only his name wasn't Chamoun and the ship was like nothing he'd ever seen afloat on Merovin. It was a *space-going* vessel, the memories that weren't Chamoun's were clear on that. On other things, too, though the body he was in was damaged beyond repair, dying on that bridge amid the smoke and the sirens.

He knew he was an electronics specialist in the Merovin Defense Force, and he knew they were up against an enemy they weren't prepared to handle—the sharrh! The sharrh—who weren't just a legend—were very real and very near and very sure to win. . . .

**C.J. CHERRYH invites you to enter
the world of MEROVINGEN NIGHTS!**

ANGEL WITH THE SWORD *by C.J. Cherryh*
A Merovingen Nights Novel

FESTIVAL MOON *edited by C.J. Cherryh*
(stories by C.J. Cherryh, Leslie Fish,
Robert Lynn Asprin, Nancy Asire, Mercedes Lackey,
Janet and Chris Morris, Lynn Abbey)

FEVER SEASON *edited by C.J. Cherryh*
(stories by C.J. Cherryh, Chris Morris,
Mercedes Lackey, Leslie Fish, Nancy Asire,
Lynn Abbey, Janet Morris)

MEROVINGEN NIGHTS

FEVER SEASON

C.J. CHERRYH

DAW BOOKS, INC.

DONALD A. WOLLHEIM, PUBLISHER

1633 Broadway, New York, NY 10019

DAW Book Collectors No. 722.

First Printing, October 1987

1 2 3 4 5 6 7 8 9

PRINTED IN THE U.S.A.

CONTENTS

MEROVINGEN NIGHTS

FEVER SEASON

MEROVINGEN

FEVER SEASON

C.J. Cherryh

It was fall in Merovingen, nasty fall, when old Det approached his winter ebb: snows fell to the far north, up far above Nev Hettek, and the river that reached Detmouth, at Merovingen, was a sullen, quiet river. The bog up on the Greve widened, the water lay in stinking pools up there and on the north side of the lagoon, where river-weed rotted and small fish that had thrived there in the early stages dried out and fattened the bugs and the vermin. Merovingen of the Thousand Bridges, poised on its pilings and shored up precariously above the waters, smelled it when the breeze came off the mudflats, a stink predictable and faithful as sunrise. The skips and poleboats moored a little lower, that was all, at pilings that showed water-stain a handspan up, and had a little less current to fight in the winding Gut, and up on Archangel.

Then Merovingen began to think toward winter, from the uppermost levels of the wooden city, where the hightown wealthy lived in splendor, to the middle tiers where merchants began to haul winter goods out of warehouses, to the lowest levels where the canalsiders and the skip-freighters and the bargemen began to think in much more basic terms—like bartering for socks and sweaters, or a paper of blueangel, to fight the fever and ease winter aches in the cold nights ahead.

Fall, when the days varied between balmy warmth and treacherous chill, and fog wrapped the town about at night, hazing the lights that shone, making the lightless world of the canals beneath the bridges dark indeed.

That was the rhythm of things. It always had been. And Altair Jones, sixteen and on her own since she had been barely able to handle the skip pole on her own, found herself strangely out of step. She smelled the change in the air, and blood and bone, she felt the sense of take-hold and take-cover in her gut: time to store and hoard and time to think what little of all she owned in the world she could possibly trade— time to work hard and save the tiniest coppers, and think protective.

But for the first time in her life she was comfortable, for the first time in her life she had not one extra sweater, but three, had shoes, and two changes of socks, had a full tank of fuel, the skip's ancient motor in prime condition, the hull painted, had a couple bottles of good whiskey in the number one drop bin, and full store of food, besides a candle and cookstove and all. For the first time in her life she had everything she could think of to have. And the feeling both- ered her, a kind of karmic something-wrong that would not let her alone even in broad daylight and got worse by dark.

She brooded on it—brooded on it increasingly as the nights grew colder and the putting-away started . . . canaling was her life, dammit, even after she had pulled one Thomas Mondragon out of a canal and got herself tangled in hightowner affairs. Out of which she stayed as much as possible.

Except she tied up at Petrescu most every night now, left her skip to the watching of old Mintaka and Del Suleiman and Mira and Tommy, who had tie-up rights there nowadays . . . all friends, all folk she would trust with her life (and had) so that she knew that there was nothing going to go missing off her boat, and nobody going to mess with it or come up Tom Mondragon's stairs past that hour that honest canalers took to their hideys and slept.

She climbed up the stairs to the second level and Mondragon's door, gave the knock and waited for him.

The lamp was lit in the front room. Which was his way of saying it was all right, he had no visitors, he was waiting for her.

She heard him inside, heard his whispered: "Jones?"

"Yey."

She would not answer that if she had trouble with her. He took a quick peek by the tiny garde-porte and then opened up the door, let her in; and she stepped quickly into the light and the warmth, pulled off her battered river-runner's cap while he was locking the front door again.

A handsome man, pretty as the Angel Himself, as Retribution, who guarded the town from His post on Hanging Bridge. Mondragon never let on to folk where he was really from: Falkenaer was his ordinary story, a Falkenaer offspring of the Boregys . . . and maybe that was true, somewhere back of it all, there being nowhere else on Merovingen that hair came that blond, or skin that fair—Jones' own short, straight hair was black as was the rule in Merovin, her skin dusky, her eyes dark as canalwater. But Mondragon's real home was Nev Hettek, up river, where Adventists were the rule and Revenantists were the exception. His real connections were less with the Boregys he pretended to be related to than with Anastasi Kalugin the governor's son. His skills as a spy were another thing he did not let on about, and he was always nervous about opening doors.

Why he kept opening his to her she wondered about every time she saw him like this, handsome and gold as the Angel Himself, and fine, fine in all his manners. She would have understood if he had sort of drifted away and come less and less to the lowtown; she would have understood if he had found some hightown woman to take up with—she would have wanted to gut that woman, but she would have understood it was natural: Lord, he was what he was, and she had herself all braced for it, just—someday—he was going to find somebody else.

But he more than took up with her on his get-abouts on the

canals, where he *needed* someone with brains, someone who could watch his back, someone who would keep her mouth shut: he said it was safer she should come sleep at his place and tie up down below—he would let her know if things got unsafe, as they well could. But meanwhile there was a soft bed to be had and breakfast in the mornings: his hours were like hers, late.

The bed in question had him in it. And there was no other woman: Jones had kept an eye on that the way she kept an eye on his place and his whereabouts—for his safety's sake. Not that she would have stopped it. But she would have been madder than hell.

He tipped her chin up and kissed her, gave her a hug before he went and blew out the light in the sitting-room. "Good day?"

"Fair," she said. Which was what she generally said.

She shared a bedtime snack with him in the little brick kitchen, backstairs, while water heated, and she had her bath (Lord and the Ancestors, she was getting so she *smelled* the canal-stink she had never smelled before, and she took her clothes to laundry right along with Mondragon's, every Satterday). She wrapped up like him in a robe he lent her before they headed up the front-hall stairs to his upstairs bedroom and the brass bed with the fine smooth sheets.

Then he made love to her the way he had from the first, fine and gentle, and worked the aches out of her bones and the canal cold out of her gut before he fell to sleep the way he usually did, on his face, one leg tangled with hers and one hand on her shoulder, which she liked, except sometimes he got heavy and sometimes he had bad dreams and scared hell out of her—

Karl! he had yelled once in her ear. And rolled over and fought to get clear of the bedclothes while she scrambled to get clear of him.

Another time he had yelled *No!* and shoved her right out of bed, thump! Which had waked him up. *Jones*, he had said then, *Jones?* And put his head over the side of the bed, asking anxiously whether she was all right.

Sure, she had said, from flat on her back, *why not*?

He never told her what he dreamed about, but she had developed a certain consequent wariness when he took to mumbling in his sleep.

As he did this night, waking her from a sound sleep. "Stop it," he murmured into her ear, and: "No. O God, no more—"

She tried just to unwind her leg, but he jerked away, *he* rolled aside, and went, thump! over the side.

"Mondragon," she exclaimed. "Mondragon!" But *she* was not going to put her head over the edge of the bed looking for *him*. She got up on her knees to look, in the light of the always-burning night-lamp. "Ye all right?"

"God," she heard, softly uttered. And saw him lift his head. He levered himself up on the mattress rim and hung there on his arms with a terrible bemazement in his eyes.

"I didn't push ye," she said, afraid he would think that way.

"God." He lowered his head against the mattress and crossed his arms over his neck; but then he got up and helped her straighten the covers and got back into bed.

Lay down by himself then, face up and staring at the ceiling. So she edged over and put her arm over him. He patted her. And shivered. She felt it go all through him.

"Sorry," he said. "I'm sorry."

"What was that 'un?" she asked. And when he said nothing: "Dammit, Mondragon, ye could *say*, ye know?"

"It's just a dream. I'm sorry. I'm really sorry, Jones. You don't have to put up with this. I'll go sleep on the couch."

"You don't. Ye ain't going anywhere. Ye want t' make love t' me?"

"God, Jones, what do you think I am?" He shivered again and drew a long breath. "Damn."

"Want I should make love t' you?"

"Couldn't hurt," he said after a moment. "But it won't do you much good."

"Hell if it don't." She edged on over a little and started massaging tight muscles. "You c'n go on to sleep, I don't mind." She gave him a kiss at the pit of the throat, which usually made him react. It did. His arms came up around her, he pulled her down, and for a long time just held her like that, skin against skin, so tightly it all but hurt.

"You ain't going to sleep," she said.

"No," he said.

And did nothing for a moment. Just held her. Then: "Jones," he said. "I don't want to hurt you. I don't want to hurt you."

"Well, that ain't real likely. You want to go to sleep or you want to do something or you want to tell me what that all was?"

He rolled her over. He was halfway rough, and all too quick, and she sighed and put up with him collapsing on her: she hugged him, and wound her fingers into his hair and tugged at it gently.

"Mondragon, ye want to tell me? Ye want to say what that's about?"

"No," he said, and moved his hand on her stomach, gently, sleepily as a child with a doll. Then: "Prison," he said. "Sometimes I dream about prison, Jones. You don't want to know about that. Sometimes I'm there, that's all."

Nev Hettek's prison was bad. She knew that much. They said things about that place she never would ask him about and he would never want to tell.

"That's past," she said. "You ain't never going back. You're here. Ain't no way you're going back."

"No way," he murmured.

But after a little while he said: "You can't ever get too safe, Jones, you can't ever get too safe. Don't take chances. I wish you'd get off the water. At least after dark."

"My best trade is after dark." Now it was her heart beating hard and fast and her muscles going tight. *Damn, mama, you told me, didn't you? Damn man gets me into his bed and here it comes. Off the water, he says. Off the water!*

"You're running too late," he said.

"Takes a while. Just takes a while. I had a barrel pickup. I told ye."

"Down there in Megary territory. Dammit, Jones—let Moghi

hire somebody else for those runs. You don't need to do that kind of work any more."

"The hell!"

"You don't. You can work the evenings, if—"

"You can swim next time. Hear?"

"All right, all right." He rubbed her shoulder. "Forget it. You were late; I worried; is that any wonder?"

She thought about it. Decided not. She heaved a sigh and rested on his chest, fingers winding in his hair, which was longer than hers, and curly and fine. And sighed again, dredging up the bad news she had saved for going out the door in the morning. "Well, I got a late 'un tomorrow. One of Moghi's. Mondragon,—" She felt him draw a breath and stopped him with a hand on his mouth. "Right down the Grand and back, ain't no problem. I just got this load to get—"

"Moghi's load," he said, and took her by the arm. "Dammit, it's Harbor, isn't it? Isn't it?"

"Listen, friend, I been getting along right fine before you come into my life."

"Jones, let's not be so damn touchy. Let's use a little sense. For God's sake, you're *not* just any damn canaler, you're tangled up in my business, and what am I going to do if somebody grabs you some night and gives me a choice I haven't got? I just haven't got too many ways to turn, you understand me? And you're putting me at risk, you ever think of that?"

She did not like that kind of reckoning. It backed her against the wall, and took away *her* choices. And left her nowhere, because there was nothing else to be but Jones, and a canaler, and a skip-freighter with her own boat; there was nothing else she ever wanted to be, because nothing else made any sense.

Nothing else was worth anything. She had had her days of sitting at tie-up because of Mondragon's business; and waiting for bad news or worse news, with her gut in a knot. And watching canalers pass who were a hell of a lot happier, with a boatload of crates or barrels and a partner or so to help, not to be off about uptown in a lace-cuffed shirt and fancy boots and risking his damn neck for Anastasi damn-him Kalugin.

She had done one cross-town race when a hightowner body turned up floating: she had been mortally sure it was Mondragon. And she had never forgotten that feeling in her gut that morning.

Talk about 'held hostage,' mama, lookit this man. Lookit what he does to me.

She saw Retribution Jones sitting—Lord, right over there in Mondragon's chair, hat pushed back on her head, her bare foot swinging the other side of the chair arm. *See*, her mother said. *Told you so.*

She scrambled off Mondragon, rested her elbows together under her, and stared at the chair, but her mother was not there to argue with.

Only the feeling in her gut was.

And the other feeling, that was Mondragon's hand stroking her shoulder, Mondragon leaning on his elbow by her and trying to have his way by confusing hell out of her.

"Sorry," she said. "Some things I ain't going to trade."

"I'm not asking you to give up the boat. I'm asking you to give up those damn smuggling runs! I'm asking you to use your head, dammit! and not put us in trouble."

"Not put *us* in trouble! Who was doing all right before some fool man got himself throwed in the canal in front of her boat, and *then* she gets him safe and he gets himself caught again—"

He stopped what he was doing. Then he rolled onto his back and was very quiet.

Damn.

Damn the man. Hurt his feelings, she had. And he hurt her gut.

She slumped down on her arms, bowed her head against the tangled sheets and bit her lip till it hurt as much as she hurt inside.

My, we're touchy, Mondragon.

She had said worse to him. But when people got too close they hurt each other, that was the way of it.

"I can't change," she said. "Mondragon, you been in prison. Where ye trying to put me?"

Silence, a long time. Damn, that was *really* the wrong thing to have said. It hurt too much. They could not help it with each other.

"Jones," he said quietly, then, "I only want you to be safe."

"Locked up. Same as walls."

Another long silence. Finally he snaked his arm under her stomach and turned over against her, holding her tight. "Jones," he said, "Jones, Jones, Jones. Just be careful."

"Ye been in here too long yourself. You been sitting in these walls and messing 'round with that damn Anastasi and that Boregy. Time you got the feel of a boat again, time you worked up some callus on your hands, work up a sweat, feel old Det move under your feet—"

"I wish, I really wish I could."

"Run with me tomorrow night. We got a Falkenaer ship in. We just go out there and make a little deal, Moghi's got 'er all set. Ain't no way there's going to be trouble. Ye want people t' believe that ye're Falkenaer, right? Ye got business ye don't want people t' know. So ye smuggle. *Ever'body* knows a smuggler's got secrets he don't want people messing into. Answers all their questions. Smart, right?"

More long silence. She felt him sigh, and his hands caught hers. "Jones, I've got business tomorrow. I *will* have. For a few days."

"What d'ye mean business? You been sitting on your rump in this place for a month, ye—"

His hands squeezed hard. "Tomorrow I won't be. I've got to go uptown. Tomorrow. Maybe late. Maybe more than tomorrow. I don't know. I haven't got a choice. Understand?"

"Ye wasn't going to tell me!"

"I was going to tell you in the morning. I swear."

"Oh, *sure*."

"I'm not lying. I swear."

"What's he want?"

"I don't know. *See* him. That's all the message I got."

"Anastasi?"

"Yes."

"Damn him."

"I don't want you running late. I don't want to worry about where you are. I'd like you to go to Moghi's, rent the Room,—"

"Well, I can't do that, can I? I got a run to make." He frightened her. He was good at that. So was Anastasi Kalugin, the governor's son, who had them both any time he wanted to take them. And so, equally well, the Sword of God frightened her. It was in town again. Maybe it had never left at all. It aimed at upsetting everything. It aimed, Mondragon had said, at whatever would cause the most trouble and give it the most power. Mondragon should know: he had been one of them. Which was his value to Anastasi Kalugin, who hoped to outlive his brother and his sister and be governor of Merovingen someday.

Of course Anastasi's sister Tatiana had other thoughts. Maybe so did Iosef Kalugin, who was not through being governor.

There were a lot of people she and Mondragon had reason to worry about. There were a lot who had reason to worry about them. And who might, some dark of the Moon, try to do something about it.

"Forget the run," he said.

"I can't do that!"

"Moghi'll understand. He can find somebody else. You give him enough money, he'll understand well enough how it is."

"Oh, sure, I back out on him this time and I make him go use some other skip and then what do I get next time? What's he going to do next time he wants a load carried? Call me? Hell, I might be busy. *I* might have some reason to hide out. *He* might just find himself another skip that don't come with problems, mightn't he? And the word might just get around Jones ain't real reliable, Jones don't need the work that bad—"

"Moghi will understand!"

"Moghi's who we got to go with if we got to have help. You want I make 'im mad at me? You want I go back on a promise with 'im? I dunno how you do business uptown, Mondragon, but canalside, ye don't back out on a thing and then come asking favors. You could've told me—"

"I didn't know it, dammit."

"Well, now it's too late, ain't it?"

"It's not too late. Tell him you have a friend in trouble, tell him it's life and death, hell, wouldn't you, if you had to? How's he to know the difference?"

"Because I ain't never give my word an' lied, that's how! Because if you was in trouble uptown I'd come, but you ain't asking me to come with ye, ye ain't got any intention of it, and *I'll* have my skip tied up here about while Moghi gets the idea I might need help an' sends somebody to follow me— How'd that look, huh? I *got* no choice. I go with you, or I make that run."

"You *can't* go with me. It's uptown. I'd have to leave you at a tie-up at Boregy and it's not safe—"

"Well, ye got it, then, don't ye? I make the run. I'll tell Moghi he *better* keep an eye to you. An' he'll do 'er. Won't make no noise, either."

"Not a bad idea," Mondragon allowed. "Not really a bad idea."

"Ye want Del to take you up?"

"No. I'll pick up a poleboat. I don't want Del mixed up with this." She sighed. And thought that she knew now why he had asked her here every night. It hurt, even if it was good of him. Trying to keep her safe, that was all. Keeping her inside walls as much as he could.

Her gut hurt when she reckoned that.

So, damn, you didn't think it was your looks, did you?

Shut up, mama. He ain't no fool. Never was. But he was looking out for me, wasn't he? We're friends. An' he don't mind making love to me.

"Fine," she mumbled aloud, to what he had said. "Fine."

"Is it fine, Jones?"

"Yey." She turned over in the circle of his arms and faced

him, nose to nose. "Hey, I'll be careful. I'll slip out there and back, I got the fuel, ain't no way I'll make a mistake. I'll watch real sharp and I'll use the engine, all right?"

"Don't get caught. For God's sake don't get caught. It could get political real fast and I'm out of trade-goods. Hear?"

"I hear ye. I hear ye real good. If *you* get in trouble, ye hail any boat, hear, *any* boat in the Trade. Ye tell 'em Moghi's. Ye know that."

"I know."

"Deal, then." She snuggled closer. Wrapped her arms around him and shut her eyes. She was still worried, but sleep when it came, came fast and deep, on the exhaustion of a heavy cargo and a long run—honest work, well, mostly. In *her* dreams the water moved, the bed had the motion of the waves, the pilings glided like black ghosts. Like all her life on the water. It was stable ground that was the dream.

Tea in the morning, biscuits—Mondragon *could* cook, if he had a whole kitchen to do it in, and pans enough to outfit any three boats. Eggs. Sugar for the tea.

Then it was dress and get ready: the canals woke up early as they went to sleep late—canalers dozed during the day as they got the chance; and there was no way she could ask old Min or Del to watch her skip for her while trade slipped away. She pulled on her pants, pulled on the faded red sweater and put a blue one over it, figuring what the morning was going to be out there, and made up her mind to be thoroughly cheerful in the parting at the door.

So he was going to risk his neck.

So he would be fine, he always was, he had a cat's luck and an eel's ways when trouble was on him.

He gave her a hug at the door, and a kiss on the mouth— *He don't need to do that, now, does he, mama?*

She kissed him back, feeling the fool, her, in her canaler's rough clothes and him still in his robe. Lazy man. Going back to sleep after he had seen her off.

Sleep until he had to keep his own appointments.

"Damn," he said, "wear socks. It's cold out there."

"Working feet is warm. Wet socks is damn cold, lander. My feet'll be fine once I get to poling."

"Makes me cold to think about it. Here." He fished a small heavy purse out of his pocket and pressed it into her hand. "For Moghi, for whatever you might have to do."

"Lord an' my Ancestors, Mondragon, I *got* money. I got all I need—"

"Take it. Hear?"

"Won't." She shoved it back at him, shoved it back so hard, and him not taking it, the purse dropped and hit the floor, scattering bright gold bits.

Gold, by the Ancestors. All of it gold.

"Lord, Mondragon, what're ye trying t' do?"

"You can take it, is what." He bent down and picked it up and slapped it hard into her hand. "You can damned well take it and put it on account with Moghi—"

Get off the water. You don't have to work. You don't have to take the late runs.

"I ain't doing no such thing!" she yelled. And tried to give it back. Dropped it again when he would not take it. "Mondragon, ye don't buy me off! I ain't taking any more money."

"You damn well take it!"

"Won't!"

"I'll stop over at Moghi's and leave it, if I have to. It'll just cost me a stop. Waste my time. Put me late."

"Ye're always giving me money, Mondragon, and I ain't earned it! Ain't no way I earned it, I damn sure ain't earning it in no bed, and you can take it an'—"

"Jones—"

" 'Day." She jerked the door open and walked out into the fog and the chill, across the second-level walk, down the stairs where the ghosts of slips waited, with friends.

Damn man.

What c'n I do with 'im?

Damn weather. Ain't much moving till noon, that's sure.

*But fine weather if we got fog again tonight, running out to
that ship in Harbor.*

Down to the canalside, bare feet sure on the slick boards.

The fog was lifting by the time Mondragon set foot out his
door—quietly dressed, in dark blue trousers, black sweater,
a heavy jacket and a navy knit cap pulled down low. He
locked the door and set the small trip—he varied it: this time
it was a sliver of wood that an opening of that door would
crack without notice. He had taken similar precautions with
doors inside, that were always set a certain way, with trips
that were not standard Sword teaching. He had learned certain things in prison. Some of the inmates of Nev Hettek's
notorious hellhole *had* been professional thieves, waiting
execution.

He turned up his collar against the chill and took a second
good look around with a single glance. No weapon on him at
the moment but a riverman's knife. He had left the uptown
clothes at Boregy. He came and went into that house by the
servants' entry. Like any good riverman with business with
the highest banking interests in Merovingen.

God knew why. Boregy wanted it that way, that was all.
Layers upon layers of duplicity: give out that he was a
relative pretending not to be, but showing uptown, which let
people think that he was in fact a Boregy with foreign connections. Boregy wanted folk to perceive his coming and
going by the servants' entry as elaborate subterfuge designed
to fool the town authorities, and his coming and going in
society and in Merovingen-below alike as the actions of a
Boregy spy (possibly really a cousin) living frugally in mid-
town because that was where the Boregys wanted him, but
socializing uptown because he *was* Boregy and thought no
one knew about his other life. All of which mess was his
cover: he was a *Kalugin* spy, which had nothing at all to do
with banking, and a great deal to do with Boregys, in a very
non-commercial way. Which Boregys of course knew, the
Sword presence in Merovingen knew, and he was sure Tatiana

Kalugin knew, and probably Iosef the governor as well, which meant that anyone who had a motive to kill him knew.

The only ones in town who did not know what he was and who he worked for were the ordinary folk he met on the walkways, the merchants and tradesmen and canalfolk and craftsmen that *were* Merovingen. Which was the way it had to be—because Merovingen would never tolerate the things its leaders and would-be leaders were up to. Merovingen was upset enough about the Nev Hettek trade mission. There was muttering in the bars and taverns waterside, that it would be no wonder if some foreigners turned up floating some morning.

There were the beginnings of whisperings about Tatiana Kalugin: he had seen to that. It was too good to let pass, the intimation that the governor's second heir had been sleeping with a Nev Hettek trade minister. Tell old Mintaka a romantic secret and it was end to end of Merovingen by nightfall for sure.

But people gave Tatiana benefit of the doubt: That Nev Hetteker better count his change, was one way they put it. Meaning Tatiana did nothing that did not involve profit to herself, and the very fact she had done something so blatant meant she was after something. It puzzled people. It puzzled them enough they had rather gossip about it for a while. Which was where things stood.

Till the news got down to the canals about the census that old Iosef had requested—still a rumor, nothing had gotten to the lowest tiers yet. But there was assuredly a point-past-which-not with the rank and file in Merovingen . . . something the Kalugins instinctively knew; and which maybe the Sword, for all its fine calculations, did not entirely figure into its plans.

It was even possible that old Iosef had thrown out the census for a bait, to get the town stirred up. Which made it a more difficult atmosphere for the Sword, in some senses.

Far *better* to be a Falkenaer in public eyes, than Nev Hetteker. Hanging Bridge had seen more than one lynching, so accounts ran.

Better, he thought, as he rounded the corner of Foundry

onto Grand, and had one of the widest views in Merovingen, the whole Grand Canal spread out in front of him from Ventani to Ventura, all the skips, the barges, the busy main artery of Merovingen—better if he could do what Jones wanted: throw over everything, take to the water, live his whole life on one of those skips. Free.

But that was not a choice he had.

It never would be.

He had no idea what Anastasi wanted of him. But he knew the way things were tending. He knew that there were too many sides to this, and too much danger, and too many enemies.

There were several enemies he would as soon eliminate— had offered to; but Anastasi said no. He thought about arranging an accident to Magruder and Chamoun on his own, something Anastasi could not readily trace. But that had hazards as grievous as letting these people go. And if he had a hope in the world it was that Anastasi would live to be governor, and find him for some reason . . . still useful, and not an embarrassment. God knew he had no hope with Tatiana and none at all with her new friends.

He had helped one man into a governorship: Karl Fon, up in Nev Hettek. He had been Karl Fon's close friend and comrade in arms—until Karl Fon found it necessary to bury his affiliations with the Sword of God and become a staunch and conservative Adventist moderate. So Karl used him for a scapegoat; murdered his own father and Mondragon's whole family, and framed his boyhood friend for all of it.

Karl Fon was horrified to learn of his friend's true character. Of course.

Damn him to deepest hell.

Mondragon sneezed, suddenly and violently. Morning chill. He realized an ache in his bones, which he attributed to the cold and to, God help him, falling out of bed like a fool. Prison and old wounds made him hate the winters. He felt a violent chill when the same morning wind that began to blow the mist away got under his coat and up his sleeves. He had half decided to walk over to Boregy, but that turn of the corner on Foundry decided him: it would be a hell of a lot more comfortable to get out of the windy upper tiers, go down to canalside and hail a poleboat. No sense courting a cold.

Jones would not thank him for that. Damn, if he had felt his throat this prickly last night he would not have shared a bed with her.

He thought of Jones, barefoot in this weather, like every other skip-freighter down there, and shivered.

HEARTS AND MINDS

Chris Morris

Three months had passed since Mike Chamoun found the dead man, gutted like a fish, aboard his boat, and the worst hadn't happened—yet.

No one had come to Boregy House, where Chamoun was living with Cassie Boregy, his new bride, to accuse him of murdering Dimitri Romanov, who had been the most feared and influential agent that Nev Hettek's Sword of God had in place here in the stronghold of its enemy, Merovingen. *Second* most feared and influential man in Merovingen, Chamoun amended on his way to the Revenantist College for his catechism lessons: Dimitri Romanov, the Sword's tactical agent in place, was a) dead and b) no match for Chance Magruder, or else Romanov wouldn't be dead.

It was probably Magruder—His Excellency, Nev Hettek's Ambassador and Minister of Trade and Tariffs in Merovingen—who'd arranged Romanov's death. Then arranged to keep Michael Chamoun's name out of it, the young man told himself for the hundredth time as he slipped unremarkably through the sparse traffic across the high water bridge that led, if you didn't mind cutting across the Signeury, straight from Boregy House to the College, where Chamoun's uncle-in-law, the cardinal, waited to make a good Revenantist out

29

of a heretical Adventist from Nev Hettek who'd married his niece, Cassie, for mercantile reasons.

Married to Cassie Boregy, even on a five-year contract, Michael Chamoun had a certain degree of immunity from the laws all lesser folk of Merovingen-above and -below obeyed. The Boregys were inextricably linked to their patron, Anastasi Kalugin, son of Iosef who ruled Merovingen with a rusty iron hand. Aging, Poppa Kalugin was preparing for the future of his dynasty: watching and waiting while his three children— Mikhail the Craftsman, Anastasi the Advocate Militiar, and Tatiana the Terrible and only daughter—vied for position.

Soon the old man would die, and even if he designated a successor, the war for power here would break into the open. If the war between Nev Hettek and Merovingen didn't break out first, helped along by Nev Hettek's agents provocateur in Merovingen, a "terrorist" group called the Sword of God, of which Dimitri Romanov, dead on Chamoun's boat, had been a member.

Of which Chance Magruder was another. Of which Michael Chamoun was a third, brought in here at great expense and under painstaking cover for the express purpose of marrying into the Boregy family, as close to Anastasi Kalugin as the Sword could get.

Or as close as it had thought it could get, until Chance Magruder found a way into Tatiana Kalugin's bed. Certainly it was Chance who was protecting Chamoun from involvement in the investigation of Romanov's death. Probably it had been Magruder who'd ordered the hit—a disagreement between rival Sword factions. Magruder wouldn't say— wouldn't admit it to Chamoun.

And that worried Michael. It worried him every day. It worried him at night in bed with sweet Cassie Boregy, the girl he'd married for the Cause, who loved him with an innocent love he didn't deserve. It worried him especially when he was out of Boregy House, abroad in Merovingen as he was now, crossing the treacherous heights of the Signeury where the Kalugins had total and autocratic control. There were fates worse than pretending to convert to Revenantism to legitimize his marriage.

There were dungeons in the Justiciary; interrogation cells, it was whispered, in the Signeury itself. To land in one of them, you only needed to make a Kalugin nervous. And Mike Chamoun had already done that, in spades.

His booted feet slapped hollowly on the cold stone of the Signeury's outer walk. The Grand Canal was on his left, the rock of the Kalugin's administrative fortress on his right. He was taking the long way around because his skin crawled every time he crossed the private bridge to the Justiciary. He didn't want to end up there. He prayed he wouldn't.

So he went the long way, and he went his circuitous way among the Boregys who'd taken him as a son-in-law, and he went his own way less and less frequently these days.

It had been a good plan, the plan of Karl Fon, Nev Hettek's governor, and Chance Magruder and others of the veteran revolutionaries who'd come to power in Nev Hettek. It had been a plan to open diplomatic and trading relations with Merovingen, to infiltrate and conquer, to start a war on Nev Hettek's terms.

The plan might have worked, even with young Mike Chamoun as its fulcrum—worked although so much depended on a poor boy from Nev Hettek. A boy who knew little of society matters and less of destabilization strategies mounted by governments but knew very clearly when he and his Nev Hettek family were caught in a trap lethal to all if complete obedience was not given. . . . It might have worked, but for a traitor named Mondragon, an ex-Sword agent under the protection and in the employ of Anastasi Kalugin and Vega Boregy.

Vega Boregy, the father of the girl named Cassie whom Chamoun had married, had called Chamoun into his marble study, the very night of the 24th Eve Ball—mere hours after the wedding and the merger had been announced, and the Sword disrupted the proceedings. There, in that room, Mike Chamoun had met the fabled traitor, Mondragon, for the first time. And Mondragon had fingered Chamoun as Sword of

God, fingered him before Boregy's eyes, declaring Chance
Magruder another Sword agent, and Dimitri Romanov a third.
Then the two men had demanded from Chamoun the most
impossible things: a Sword connection, a conduit to Karl Fon
back in Nev Hettek . . . *a conduit other than Chance
Magruder*.

If Magruder knew the truth of it, Magruder would say that
Chamoun had doubled, been turned by the enemy back upon his
masters, the Sword of God, Karl Fon, and Magruder himself.

But Magruder didn't know. Chamoun had found no way to
tell him. Magruder was sleeping with Anastasi Kalugin's
mortal enemy, his sister Tatiana. Anastasi had sent Karl Fon
a message, through Mondragon and Boregy, and via Michael
Chamoun, that he'd be willing to help an adversarial Sword
faction—against Magruder and Tatiana.

The whole convoluted mess was beyond Mike Chamoun's
capacity for understanding, except in very simple terms: he
knew he was a traitor twice over; he knew Anastasi would
have him killed if he failed to run his messages to Megary
and back; he knew Mondragon was in no better a position and
would cut out Chamoun's heart at the slightest balk. He knew
Magruder would kill him quicker if Chance ever found out
that there was a faction of the Sword now working hand in
glove with Anastasi Kalugin—against Magruder personally—
and that this arrangement had been facilitated by one Michael
Chamoun, thrice-compromised agent of the Sword of God.

He knew, because Magruder had promised Chamoun, on
the night of the 24th Eve Ball when the Sword had attacked
Nikolaev House, killing Kika and wounding her sister Rita,
that Magruder would "take care of Romanov," the assumed
culprit. So the gutted corpse on Chamoun's *Detfish* shouldn't
have been a surprise.

But it had been. Magruder wasted no motion, no energy,
no emotion. Magruder was here ostensibly to protect Chamoun—or had been. Thus, upon first seeing the corpse,
Chamoun had thought that Magruder couldn't have done
it—wouldn't have done it. Filleting Romanov and leaving
him on the Detfish just wasn't Chance's style.

It was a warning, since it hadn't been a frame-up. And there was no reason Magruder would send Chamoun such a warning, unless Chance had known, somehow, about the meeting with Mondragon and Cassie's father—known even while the meeting was taking place.

But he couldn't have; he just couldn't have. Magruder had been closeted with Tatiana all that night, while Chamoun stumbled through a strange city alone, looking for the slaver's stronghold called Megary and a Sword contact he didn't know by name or face, only by password and location to be sought and used in the direst emergency.

That night had been such an emergency. It still was one, in the heart of the young Adventist commoner from Nev Hettek thrust suddenly into a strange culture among his Revenantist betters, a pretender and an enemy in their midst.

Mike Chamoun stopped suddenly, having walked blindly all the way around the Signeury and over the bridge to the Revenantist College. Stopped before the wide and intimidating stairs to wipe the back of his velvet sleeve across his mouth. It came away damp with sweat, even though the day was cold with the surety of autumn and the promise of winter to come.

Up the stairs, on either side, were impossible statues: whales bearing wheels of fire, tails in each others' mouths; great, many-armed women with ornate crowns; the effigy of an angel with a sword, much smaller than the one guarding the harbor or the bridges. That sword, the sword of retribution, was partly drawn.

The angel's name was Michael, according to the ancient lore Chamoun was now learning by rote—the only part of it which made sense to his stubborn Adventist soul. His new wife and her family and all of these believed in karmic debt and punishment befitting all crimes, meted out by an angry and nit-picking universe, as if God and all his minions were accountants of the soul.

Michael Chamoun believed that the enemy sharrh, the aliens who'd destroyed all tech on Merovin and isolated the world from the stars, would come again. All Adventists knew that punishment had already come once, with the arrival of the sharrh and the destruction they'd wrought. Adventists knew that the sharrh would come again, by which time mankind on Merovin had best be ready to fight to the death. Under that imperative of doom, all lesser imperatives paled. There was no right but the right of preparedness for the awful day of battle coming; there was no wrong but the possibility of failing to be ready to defend Merovin.

Two philosophies, incompatible, at odds. Mike Chamoun, caught between them, was now expected to mount these seemingly endless stairs each day and learn the Revenantist catechism of unending punishment on earth for misdeeds done in previous lives.

And in current lives. If his tutor at the College, Cassie's uncle the cardinal, should find out about Romanov, or Magruder, or even that Mike Chamoun was Sword of God, not all the Boregys in Merovingen could protect him from swift and didactic Revenantist retribution.

Before his eyes once more rose Romanov's shade, as the corpse did daily, haunting him. Romanov's death had been a warning, he knew. But he wasn't really sure from whom, and thus he didn't know why.

Trembling and sweating on the College steps in the chill wind, Mike Chamoun bit his lip and forced his legs to begin climbing. *Into the monster's den, fool,* he told himself, blinking dead Romanov's ghost away. *You're no safer anywhere else than here. Not now. Not ever.*

At that moment, if Chance Magruder had appeared, swinging down those steps as if he owned all of Merovingen, above and below, Chamoun would have told Chance all about Romanov and Mondragon and Vega Boregy and Megary: about the whole mess that Chamoun was in. He'd have thrown himself on Magruder's mercy and taken his chances, just to be freed of Romanov's ghost.

But Minister Magruder wasn't there, so Chamoun couldn't. He could only climb the stairs and pull the silken rope that rang the College doorbell. Which was a good thing, in its way. Throwing himself on Magruder's mercy was a fine and honorable thought, but a foolish deed. His Excellency Chance

Magruder, Minister of Nev Hettek Trade and Tariffs and strategic officer for the Sword of God in Merovingen, had no mercy, none at all.

Halfway into today's lesson, Cardinal Ito Tremaine Boregy still couldn't keep his mind on the student or the ritual, although this was a private lesson and his pupil was his nephew-in-law, Mike Chamoun.

He said to the student, an Adventist to his irredeemable core, "And now, m'ser, we shall begin to contemplate the rules of conduct as they are known to the lower tiers. The Revenantist theology that makes us relevant to the everyday lives of Merovingians." The cardinal walked to his blackboard, chalk in hand.

The single student's eyes followed, his young sharp-faced head turning slowly above its mud-colored velvet as if Chamoun were no more than a puppet.

Ito noticed that he had chalk dust on his claret velvet sleeve, and brushed at it absently as he said, "A religion must have something to offer its proponents and practitioners, day by day. It must prove itself in the world. It must, in short, ring true. In the language of the streets, Revenantism reaches its finest moment."

Ito began to write:

1. *What goes around, comes around.*
2. *Play today, pay tomorrow.*
3. *Evil is as evil does.*
4. *What you give is what you get.*
5. *No bad deed goes unpunished, if not in this life, then in the next.*
6. *No one gets out of here alive.*
7. *Be here now until you're there then.*
8. *The punishment fits the crime.*
9. *God doesn't give free throws.*

>   *10. The only thing worth saving is
>   your soul.*

And when he'd finished writing, he added, "To these axioms that sustain the lower classes, we have added the unwritten one, for men like yourself—foreigners, skeptics, unredeemed of every sort: *A mind blown is a mind shown.*

The student shifted in his seat. Cassie Boregy's husband was a creature of mercantilist opportunity, as well as an Adventist sloth from Nev Hettek. His sharp features, so clearly un-Merovingian in their virility and their boldness; the gleam in his unrepentant eyes; the set of his shoulders—all showed this was a man in need of humbling. Nowhere in Vega Boregy's newest pawn (and affront to the laws of God) did Ito Tremaine Boregy see anything more than a piece of walking karma.

But that was precisely the reason Ito had undertaken the boy's conversion personally: Michael Chamoun could be a manifestation of Instant Karma, the only sort that worried Ito, a cardinal, not a mere priest.

Ito was a pragmatic man, and he knew trouble when he saw it. Instant karma was the sort that tumbled ruling houses into the sea, and why Vega couldn't see beyond his own aristocratic nose into the danger that this youth represented was beyond Ito's understanding. Therefore, in some way or another, the youth's presence here was an act of God.

Not the little, mean god who tortured the waifs in Merovingen-below, keeping them poor and hungry, but the great God of the noble houses, who determined fate by more temporal means: the quality of one's maneuvering, the depth of one's ruthlessness, the insight of one's planning. This was the real meaning of karma: do unto others before they do unto you. Because they would. And did, daily among Ito's flock, the well-heeled and the conscienceless.

For these, Ito devised expiative punishments: fines payable to the College that, when paid, negated a sin before it became karmic debt. Ito was the best fundraiser in the College, and his sense of the monetary value of a piece of potential karmic evil was unsurpassed.

Therefore, he'd taken on the conversion of Michael Chamoun, and he was going to do it right. When he finished with Cassie's husband, the boy was going to have the fear of God—or at least of the Revenantist College—in him. And Vega would have a son-in-law broken to his will.

The young man was looking at Ito blankly, as if his face were carefully arranged to show no emotion. Doubtless, the hidden emotion was hidden for a reason: outrage, amusement, or skepticism could not be tolerated here.

Well, the lesson Chamoun would learn today would wipe all his carefully contrived sophistication away.

"Come up here, my son." Ito walked to his desk, over in the corner of the small, red-linened room. The youth stood up and came to the other side of the desk, away from the blackboard whose instructions meant nothing to him yet. Beside the desk, catty-corner, was a long couch, which Chamoun would soon need.

The young man awaiting instruction stood easily, not understanding enough to be worried. This would soon change.

"Now, m'ser," Ito explained in a silken voice, "you are about to receive the sacrament of the inner circle. This is a privilege not available to most." Ito reached behind him and from the sideboard took a small, covered silver tray. He put it on the desk and lifted its lid. On the platter were three wafers, each topped with a fillet of deathangel that had been augmented with certain other psychotropic drugs. Once the boy had eaten them, he was going to be devoid of will, though completely conscious—a good student at last.

And that student was going to get the lesson of his life—of his lives.

"Take the sacrament and devour it," Ito said formally.

"Yes, m'ser Cardinal," Chamoun agreed meekly, and took the first wafer in hesitant fingers.

When the Adventist youth had choked it down, Ito felt a thrill of relief. Even one would do the job. "Now the next," said Ito, watching the widening pupils and the loosening muscles of his prey.

Automatonlike, without a blink or a hesitation, Chamoun ate the two remaining wafers.

"Go sit on the couch with your hands on your knees," Ito commanded. The drugged youth obeyed without question.

Knowing the boy would remember only what he was told from this moment onward, Ito sat on his desk and crossed his legs in less than cardinal dignity as he said, "Now, Michael Chamoun, look at your feet. Stare at them even though you feel your body rising. And do not be afraid, for you are floating to the ceiling. You are floating through it. Your mind and your limbs are under my control . . ."

Slowly, repetitively, Ito shook his subject loose from the temporal lock of the here-and-now. The young man's body sat limply on the couch, fingers spread on knees. His unblinking eyes stared at his shoes so that, eventually, tears streamed down his face.

Chamoun could neither speak nor move without a command from Ito, such was the power of the hypno-sacrament.

". . . you are floating high in the air, floating through time and space. And now, you are beginning to drift downward. As you descend, you must keep looking at your feet because it is your feet which will take you back, back, back into a life of yours which you will now remember. This previous life of yours will be the one most pertinent to your life among us in Merovingen; it will be the life whose karma you are discharging here. It will be the life that teaches us both what we need to know about you, Michael Chamoun. Nod if you understand me."

The boy on the couch nodded through his tears.

"Close your eyes, now, Michael Chamoun. When you open them, you will see your feet in the shoes of a previous life. Around you will be the greatest moment of that life, and you will tell me everything you see and everything you know which is relevant to your karma and your purpose here."

Chamoun seemed to quiver; then his eyes closed.

Ito started counting the seconds absently, seconds he knew were necessary to wait before he asked the youth questions.

In those seconds, his own mind drifted to a cardinal's temporal concerns. The Janes had dumped something in the water, and that something had changed even the smells of the canals. Fever season was upon them differently, this year, and a Jane priestess had shouted from a bridge that there would be no plague. It felt, it seemed, like chemical warfare of some sort, and everyone in the College was worried.

They were even more worried because, at just the wrong moment, old Iosef Kalugin had decided to show his teeth—a reaction conceived during the aftermath of the Ball's disruption by Sword of God terrorists, no doubt. Iosef had clamped down with every governmental agency he controlled, policing everything—including the power-hungry militias of Anastasi and Tatiana; overseeing all of Merovingen personally as he hadn't done for years. Making changes and issuing decrees. Overstating the importance of the opening of Nev Hettek's trade mission in Merovingen, for instance (and the importance of Nev Hettek's ambassador), without even consulting the College for guidance. Iosef had begun decreeing right and left.

He had decreed, among other things, that a census be taken. A census of every living soul in Merovingen. A census of all citizens. A census of all foreigners-in-residence and foreigners visiting. He had decreed that all Nev Hettekers must have alien-identification cards and that every one of those must get their cards at Nev Hettek's new embassy. He had done this (Vega Boregy and his patron, Anastasi Kalugin were sure) at the behest of Tatiana Kalugin, to further advance her new lover, Chance Magruder.

But the cardinals did not think that was the reason. Iosef had done what he had done to throw a wrench in all his children's plans. And to demonstrate once again that absolute power rules absolutely.

The results of this—a census, a numbering of the Janes and Adventists and Revenantists in town—were unforeseeable. There would be, for the first time, a list of who was who, and where. Nev Hettek's new embassy would have a head count of all the Nev Hettekers in Merovingen; Chance Magruder, if

Vega was right, would have an unconscionable advantage over other Nev Hettekers, if he wished to do them harm.

And the Sword of God faction that Anastasi and Vega had fallen in with would be at the mercy of the Nev Hettek Ambassador, unless they refused to be counted. Either way, there was potential here for renegades and infighters, for evil of the first order. And the College didn't like it.

This boy, this spy, this asp whom Cassie Boregy had married, might be of some help, if the College could account him loyal. Thus, the sacrament that no other Boregy had ever received.

A secret sacrament, unknown outside the College—except in the interrogation cells, where its power was used not to explore previous lives and previous transgressions against the law of God, but current lives and current transgressions against the ruling Kalugin hierarchy.

"Michael," Ito said gently, "you will listen only to me; you will hear only my voice." The cardinal, pulling his long nose, caught a glimpse of a man much older than he felt in the mirror behind the desk. He looked away from himself; a man is no older than he feels; a cardinal is no weaker than the call of duty upon him; God would work through Ito Tremaine Boregy, if God there were. If not, the College was strong enough, and worthy enough, to take the place of a Deity.

Long ago Ito had decided that, if there had been sharrh, there must have been God. He wasn't sure either existed any more, but he had overseen enough regressions of the sort Michael Chamoun was now undergoing to know that there was . . . something.

Something behind the pageantry and ritual. Something behind the crowd-control axioms and the customary reverence that allowed some men to rule over others. Something inherent in a social order that validated its tendency to make some men slaves, some masters; some rich, some poor. As something more than mindless chance decreed that one child was lame and blind from birth, and another hale and destined for high estate.

Ito had sired an infirm child, and drowned it on the spot.

His status among the College cardinals would have been undermined if he had not: such horrid karma could only be Retribution for crimes unexpiated, of a degree that a cardinal should not be subject to. Therefore, it had not happened. The wife and the child both died to make that fiction true.

And now, before him, was the piece of trash to whom Vega had decided to marry Cassie. Sweet Cassie, who should have been Ito's wife, by rights. What was forty years, between great houses? The blood-tie was thin enough; the benefit should have been clear enough. And the cardinal needed a young wife of high estate right now, to replace the one he'd had to murder, because of her imperfect child.

But before negotiations could be consummated, in came Chamoun, with Magruder backing him, and the deed was done in such a hurry that there was no time to object. No way.

Ito began gently guiding the helpless psyche of Michael Chamoun down from its perch above its body. Down and down and down, into the body and into a previous time.

Chamoun went rigid as Ito told him to raise his eyes from his feet and look around. Then the boy's face contorted, his hands came up to shield his eyes, and he screamed: "Sharrh! *Captain, look out! Sharrh ship, six o'clock!*"

And he fainted. Keeled over before Ito could ask the first of many prying questions, designed to compromise and ensnare the young husband of the woman who should have been the cardinal's wife.

Michael Chamoun was on the bridge of a ship, only his name wasn't Chamoun and the ship was like nothing he'd ever seen afloat on Merovin. It wasn't a yacht; it wasn't a riverboat; it wasn't a seagoing vessel.

It was a *spacegoing* vessel, the memories that weren't Chamoun's were clear on that. On other things, too, though the body was damaged beyond repair, dying on that bridge amid the smoke and the sirens and the emergency lights blinking while panels of electronics shot sparks and other men who could still move screamed for breathing apparatus and emergency procedures.

The lower half of his body's face was gone; the pain was a white blanket. The edges of his vision were dark and that dark was encroaching toward the center. As if looking through a telescope, he could still see, though. He could see clearly through a pinhole in the middle of his failing sight. *He could see the stars!*

He saw them as Michael Chamoun had never seen them, clear and bright and oh so close. There were so many, and among them, the enemy sharrh. He could see those too, because he was staring close-up at a targeting array. He was lying on his stomach across a smoking control console as his blood shorted circuits beneath him.

He had a vocabulary, in this body, that knew the names and purposes of all these things. It knew the crosshairs and the changing numbers below and beside certain moving stars, stars that maneuvered as no star should be able to. He knew his name was Michael, here, too—but everyone called him Mickey. He knew he was an electronics specialist in the Merovin Defense Force, and he knew that they were up against an enemy they weren't prepared to handle.

He knew the patrol ship around him was dying, and that everybody on it—the men he'd shipped with, the friends who made up his extended family—was doomed. The sharrh weren't just a legend, then, one of his minds told the other.

The sharrh weren't just an anomalous sea story, the mind of Mickey corrected the mind of Michael. The sharrh were very real and very near and very sure to win.

There was nothing berthed on or near Merovin with the kind of firepower, let alone the numbers, to give the sharrh a run for their money. The mind of Mickey, fading, was full of sorrow for a job undone, and regret at not being able to protect what he so dearly loved—the colony below. The mind of Michael tried to tell the mind of Mickey that it was all right, not to grieve, that there'd be life left when this was over.

The mind of Mickey mourned, *But the sharrh will win. We can't fight them, not with these weapons.*

The mind of Michael consoled, *But life will go on; civilization will survive—planetbound, but alive.*

The mind of Mickey didn't think there was any civilization worth mentioning without the stars. The mind of Mickey was a rover's mind, a soldier's mind, a mind that couldn't grasp what Michael was trying to tell it.

So Michael lied to the mind of Mickey, saying that the Adventists would make mankind on Merovin ready for a second confrontation with the sharrh—and that this time, man would win. Lied even as, through Mickey's eyes, he saw the targeting array shiver with sharrh ships like pox popping out on a sick child's face—too many sharrh ships for the damaged display to handle. It went blank, and so did the mind of Mickey, wiping out the changing numbers and the unchanging stars.

Michael Chamoun heard a voice groaning, and another voice speaking unintelligible words. And he heard another sound, like the rushing of air from a vessel—or from lungs. He heard the rending of metal and the rending of flesh. He heard a soul leave its body and other souls screaming their last breaths as a ship broke apart under them, leaving them abandoned in a sea they couldn't swim.

Then there was just quiet, and the pinprick stars on a field of red, and one voice droning over and over, "Michael, come back. You hear only my voice. You respond only to me. I will count to three, and at the count of three, you will open your eyes . . ."

The voice had been saying that for ages, Michael realized, and tried not to listen. He wasn't Michael, he was Mickey, and Mickey was a dead sergeant in the Merovin Defense Force who wanted to sleep forever, who didn't want there to be an afterlife because he'd failed in life and helped lose everything dear to him: a war, a society, a freedom . . . the stars.

The stars were what Michael Chamoun first saw when his eyes snapped open as if Ito Tremaine Boregy had strings attached to his eyelids. The stars danced in his field of vision, nearly blocking out the soft suede boots of his Merovingian outfit, the boots Cassie had given him.

Then he saw the boots and he could feel his hands on his

knees, his fingers digging remorselessly into his own flesh.
He could feel his heart pounding, very much alive. He could
hear the thunder of his pulse in his ears. And he could hear
Cardinal Ito telling him he wouldn't remember any of this.

But he already did. He remembered everything. He looked
up into the eyes of the parchment-faced Revenantist cardinal
and said, "I was there. I was there in the first battle against
the sharrh! I saw it! I was a part of it." Somehow, he got to
his feet and his legs held.

He took two steps, hands outstretched, toward the cardinal.
Then he faltered and suddenly his arms went around the old,
sepulchral monster and Michael Chamoun was sobbing un-
ashamedly: "Thank you, Cardinal. Oh thank you, m'ser!
You've given me more hope than I've ever had before—more
strength, more . . ." He broke off when he felt the old man
stiffen.

They backed away from one another. Chamoun, trying to
hold his fear and awe and the strange joy welling up in him,
tried again: "I never really believed in reincarnation, m'ser,
but you've made a convert out of me! I'm so grateful. I've
got to—"

"You will do nothing," said the cardinal in a thundering
whisper. "You will tell no one of what you think you remember. You don't remember anything, m'ser. You had an aber-
rant vision, nothing more. You're a foreigner. The drug was
too strong for you. We use it to mold the hearts and minds of
the gullible, to teach humility and obedience. We don't use it
to reinforce specious hopes of confrontation with an apocry-
phal enemy. We don't use it to reinforce Adventist rebels in
their sinful work!" Ito's eyes were blazing, coal black in his
lined white face. "Do you understand what I'm telling you,
Adventist?"

"Uh . . . yes, m'ser. I'll keep what I learned to myself."

"You didn't learn anything, you fool." Ito strode around
to the other side of his desk in a flourish of velvet. From
behind it, with both fists resting on it, the cardinal said
forcefully, "This ritual is forbidden to the masses; it's not to
be discussed with anyone, not even Vega Boregy. On pain of

Retribution of the personal sort—overseen by me. What you thought you experienced had more to do with your expectations than reality. In your previous lives, Adventist slime, you were no doubt a stableboy, a petty thief, or a murderer. There was never any Merovin Defense Force, and if there had been, a soul as poor as yours could not have been among them. As likely you were the Angel with the Sword—the true Michael. Now get out of here, and come to your senses. Your lessons are suspended for one week as punishment. If, at the end of that week, I don't like your demeanor when you return here, they'll be suspended permanently. And we'll see how long your precious marriage lasts after a College cardinal has deemed you officially Irredeemable. Now, out!''

Chamoun let the tirade roll over him, only half listening. His head danced with the images he'd encountered during the regression: with the vision of the patrol ship's bridge; with his memories of the stars and the culture he'd been a part of, which called the stars its own.

It had to be real. It had to be true. He'd never have dreamed such a thing—never had in all his life. Ito was just angry because it was an Adventist past-life that Michael Chamoun had found himself living. A life that had ended abruptly, ended in darkness, but ended with honor.

Chamoun never remembered slipping out the door of the cardinal's office, or through the College halls, or down the stairs.

Then the cold wind came in off the canal and slapped him across the face, and he remembered the death of Mickey. Spinning toward the light. Nausea at the speed. But spinning toward the center of the universe, free among the stars. He didn't know where the Revenantist creed would take its adherents, but he'd learned something very precious: to him and his kind, eventually, were given the stars. His—or Mickey's—dying soul had sped toward a central point in the universe, past starfields and through comets' tails, as if drawn by a magnet. The Revenantists believed that if they lived righteously and died enough, they'd be reborn repeatedly, until they got it right. Then, having expiated all sins, they'd be reincarnated on some other human world, a world less blighted, a world that was not a prison.

But Michael Chamoun now knew, in the depths of his heart, that the prison doors would open with his death. He'd be like Mickey, free among the stars. Mickey had been relieved when, after the ship shook apart under him, the pain shook apart too. And there had been the traveling.

Unseeingly, Chamoun headed homeward, forgetting to take the long way, going around the Signeury on the inner side, where the bridge to the Justiciary was, thinking things through.

There *was* life after death, and there was rebirth, not just the racial memory or wishful thinking that Ito had told him he'd experienced. Mickey was a part of him, or Michael could never have imagined the smell of burning insulation on melting wires, of overstressed circuitry, and the sound as the air rushed from the screaming, rent hull of the ship. . . .

Mickey was a part of Michael, who was a part of the Adventists, who remembered their responsibility to the people of Merovin, who knew what Merovin needed to do before it was too late . . .

Thump! "Hrrmph!"

"M'sera Kalugin! I'm so sorry. I didn't see you. Lost in my thoughts. . . ." Desperately, Chamoun clamped his mouth shut. He'd walked straight into Tatiana Kalugin, and she wasn't alone. With her was Chance Magruder, and the Ambassador was frowning at him.

"M'sera Secretary, I believe you met our newest Boregy, Michael Chamoun, at the Twenty-Fourth Eve—"

"Your protégé, you mean, Chance," said the tall Kalugin woman with the canny eyes. "Yes, I recall him. Good evening, m'ser Chamoun. What had you so absorbed in your thoughts?"

"What am I doing here, you mean?" Chamoun spoke without thinking. "I was at my catechism lesson. Cardinal Ito is teaching me, and he . . ." Ito had warned him not to tell.

Chamoun looked desperately at Magruder and the dangerous tableau before him came into sharper focus, wiping away the memories of Mickey and the warm, exultant feeling that had buoyed him ever since he'd awakened from the trance. He made a motion with his right hand, a conference signal Magruder had taught him; then another that meant, 'I need help.'

But Magruder didn't appear to notice. He stood in the whipping wind with a Merovingen cloak billowing around him so that he seemed twice mortal size. The dusk put shadows under his eyes and deepened the bars of flesh around his tight mouth. His colorless eyes measured Chamoun for a long moment as a gust whipped up and past.

Tatiana grabbed her hair at the nape of her neck to keep it from blowing in her face and looked from Chamoun to Magruder, understanding that something was wrong here—or at least that something was keeping Magruder rooted to the spot.

Then Chance said, "Have you heard, Mike, that Iosef's decreed a census? Tatiana and I have been trying to wrestle with the logistics of it all day."

"I—yes, I've just heard."

"So that's why I forgot about meeting you here," Chance said smoothly. And turned to Tatiana: "This young m'ser's up to his hips in Boregy intrigue, m'sera Secretary. And I've been paying too little attention to his problems, with which I've promised to help. Plus, we've got to get him his paperwork for the census. . . . So if you'll excuse me—"

Tatiana Kalugin scowled at Michael Chamoun. "You know, m'ser, you're stealing my favorite alien advisor. Don't keep him too long. Ambassador, our dinner can't be postponed. We've got to determine just how many teams we need to send out to convince the people to be counted in the census. Perhaps you can press the young m'ser into service—in my name, of course. Getting the aliens to register is, we think, most of what my father is interested in." Her humorless smile cut through the last of Chamoun's confusion.

"Yes, m'sera Secretary, whatever you say. I'd be honored to help in any capacity. It ain't—it isn't any kind of imposition. All I'm doing is taking these lessons at the College—" He waved vaguely behind him.

At that, mercifully, Tatiana chuckled. "Anything to get away from your Uncle Ito, eh? Well, Chance, see what you can make of this boy before dark. But I can't do without you tonight."

Without another word, and without waiting for an answer from Magruder, Tatiana Kalugin swept by Michael Chamoun in a gale of cloak and perfume and female warmth and august will.

Chamoun slumped, jamming his hands in his pockets, his eyes unable to meet Magruder's. But he had to ask: "Did I screw up bad?"

"Not bad, Mike. Maybe good, who knows?" His hand clapped Chamoun on the shoulder roughly. "Come on, let's go to the Embassy. When we're on Nev Hettek soil, we can talk."

A warning. The Nev Hettek soil to which Magruder referred was on the Spur at Government Center, among the militia's buildings, where if anyone decided a Nev Hetteker enclave was suddenly a security risk, that enclave could just as suddenly cease to exist.

Chamoun had never been there. He hadn't exactly been Chance Magruder's confidant, the last months.

He had a feeling, by the way Chance was eyeing him, that this was about to change.

If it did, Chamoun would find some way to tell Magruder about Mondragon and Vega Boregy, about the messages he'd been running to Megary and the betrayal he'd been forced into. And about the regression he'd experienced under Cardinal Ito Tremaine Boregy's ministrations—about Mickey and the Merovin Defense Force. About seeing the unclouded stars.

"Whatever you're not telling me," Magruder said after he'd listened to the young Sword prattle on about a revelation gained through regression into a previous life as a space patrol officer, "now's the time. Ito can't hurt you, unless you go against his direct order and tell Vega about the cardinal trying to turn you into some kind of psychic zombie—and we might be able to use that against the College, later. C'mon, Mike—give. You've been avoiding me. Why?''

"Avoiding you?'' The young agent looked around at Magruder's fancy-assed office in the new embassy, full of ormolu furniture and paintings on linened walls. He shifted on the brocaded settee and Magruder saw a furtive look flash over his face.

Chamoun was in worse trouble than you could get from eating deathangel and taking a mental trip at the hands of a psychwarring priest. Magruder could feel it.

"M'ser—Chance, you've been hard to find and they've been watching me, and every time I tried to get near you— when I really needed you—you were sleeping in with that Kalugin woman, so I couldn't get to you. Didn't dare, what with the risks—'' It came out in a rush that ended as suddenly as it had begun.

"You bet,'' Magruder said easily, wandering to the mantle beside bookshelves that Tatiana had filled for him. "We've both been walking our own tightropes. Women are tough to run; you're finding that out.'' *Whatever it is, Det-man, you spell it out or I'm going to start considering you part of the opposition.* "How's yours?'' He turned on his heel and faced the youth sitting on the whale-armed settee as if he might slide off.

"My what? Oh, my . . . woman. Cassie's fine. It's not that.''

"And Rita Nikolaev, your secret love? Seen her since the incident?''

"I—m'ser, did you . . . kill . . . Romanov?''

So that's it. Well, here we go. "Nope. Said I would, I know. Somebody else beat me to it. That's what's bothering you? He turned up in the Grand, pretty decomposed, and that's all anybody knows about it—''

"No it ain't. He was dead and gutted in my cabin, is what he was. Where we found 'im, and tossed his ass overboard.''

"Grammar,'' Magruder reminded Chamoun mildly, to hide his shock. "I see. And you would have told me sooner, but I wasn't available, right?''

The youth nodded stiffly.

Kid, don't do this. Whatever you're into, it won't mean squat compared to what I'll do if you so much as look sideways at me. I've got too much on the line here now to risk you blowing everything. A dead husband wouldn't be insurmountable; we'll just create you a brother to administrate your holdings here . . .

"Me and the boathands, we did well enough. Nobody knows. But if you didn't kill him, then who?"

"That's to the heart of it. Who? I dunno." Magruder ran a hand along the mantlepiece and lifted a humidor's lid. Another present from Tatiana, whom he didn't trust as far as he could throw the Signeury. He picked two smokes, rolled them in his fingers against his ear to test their dryness, and offered one to Chamoun.

"We'll find out, Mike. Next time, use your emergency fallbacks sooner—"

"I . . . did," said the young Sword agent as if the two words were an agony to articulate.

"You did? You went to Megary? By yourself? Why wasn't I informed?"

Chamoun shook his head miserably. "M'ser, I just did what I was told, and the Swords there did the rest."

"Anyone in particular who was helpful?" Who the hell had aced Romanov? And why? And how deep did this go? He stared at Chamoun's open face, at the green eyes wide with palpable fear.

The youngster said, "They weren't giving names. But they were giving hard times. Bastard named Baritz was one. I didn't see no al-Banna, even though that was where all the loose Sword talent was supposed to be."

"All right, that's enough. Let's drop it. I'll work on finding out the hows and whys of Romanov's death—if it was an inside move, we'd *better* find out about it. Meanwhile, I've got something I need your help with—"

Young Chamoun didn't look relieved, as Magruder had expected. He looked positively distraught. He looked constipated. He looked like somebody had just slammed a door on his tail.

But then, he had a cushy berth, a slick young wife, all the money he could dream of, and, thanks to the Sword of God, a hell of a lot to lose. You couldn't blame him for being nervous that the Sword would play him too openly. He could find himself swimming for his life in the general direction of Nev Hettek as quickly as he'd found himself the captain of the *Detfish*, putting in to port here with Sword-given prospects and an arranged marriage on his horizon.

"I want you to do what Tatiana suggested: help with the census matter," Magruder said implacably. "I want you to put together a team of . . . four . . . Nev Hettekers—not all Sword, for God's sake. I'll get you names. Some of them can be Merovingians of Nev Hettek descent, as long as they're good at the local dialects. We'll be working with Tatiana to make sure that her father's decree is obeyed—that everybody registers."

"Is that—good for us?"

Us. The Sword of God. "I think it sucks, but I can't let on. Old Iosef sprang this damned trap on everybody—probably to tame his wild children; maybe to put a leash on me. You've seen the trick, I guess, or you wouldn't have asked that question."

"Uh . . . well, if everybody's registered, then they—the government—know how many we are, and where. Whoever doesn't register is an outlaw."

"That's right, Michael. And though I can use the list of Nev Hettekers to prune the Sword factions, I already *have* such a list: it's the Kalugins who don't. But we've got to help, or appear to be helping. It's possible the whole thing will fail. Merovingen-below won't like the idea of queuing up and taking a number. But you come around here tomorrow, and we'll put together a team for you. It'll look good for your family—the Boregys—to take a leading part."

"All right, sir. That's if you'll square it with the College—in case I'm not really suspended for the next week—until further notice."

"Fine." Chamoun hadn't lit his smoke. Magruder lit his ostentatiously and exhaled a blue cloud with obvious satisfaction.

Still, Chamoun didn't move. Magruder prodded: "Something else?"

"No, m'ser. But—"

Magruder threw Chamoun matches. The youth caught them and lit the smoke, his eyes darting everywhere but Magruder's face.

"What if," Mike Chamoun said, "Romanov's faction was . . . is hooked up, somehow, with Boregy House?" His voice was trembling.

"Then you've warned me," said Magruder casually. "I'll check it out." The youth was probably seeing enemies everywhere. Romanov gutted on the *Detfish*—it was a wonder the youngster hadn't cast off and been headed home to Nev Hettek by morning. "Give your wife my best—and your best." Magruder had other things to do, and a meeting with Tatiana for which he had to change clothes.

Merovingian etiquette was a pain in the ass, time consuming and foolish. But Tatiana called the shots here, literally and figuratively. Magruder was surviving on her patronage.

And that thought made him look up at Chamoun, poised halfway to the door like a dog who didn't know whether it was going to be beaten or petted next. "Mondragon part of your problem, son?" Not that wild a guess . . .

Chamoun stared at his feet. "Sir," he said, shedding the patois so many had spent so long drilling into him, "I gotta talk to you. About Vega Boregy and Mondragon, and what's goin' on out at Megary."

The tone of Chamoun's voice and the words he spoke told Magruder that he wasn't going to like what Chamoun said next, and that when he got to Tatiana Kalugin's dinner party, if he managed not to be late, the census was going to be the last thing on his mind.

But then, he already knew what he wanted to do about the census. What he didn't know was what he was going to do about whatever compromised position this Chamoun had gotten himself into. But he'd do something. That was why he was the Sword's strategic officer in Merovingen. And its action officer, whenever he decided action was called for.

He said to Mike Chamoun, "Look, sonny, whatever mess you're in, we can turn it to our advantage as long as you tell me everything. There's nothing Mondragon can do we can't counter. Just trust in the Sword, and the Cause." *And put your life in my hands willingly, Chamoun, because that's where it's been all along.* "We're here to win the hearts and minds of these Merovingians," Magruder continued with a feral grin when Chamoun didn't respond, "and we're going to do it if we have to put the fear of sharrh in heaven into 'em."

Chance had promised Michael that he'd "be part of the Sword's tit for tat," whatever that was going to be. Some sort of retribution for the census decree, Magruder had alluded. And while Chance had been talking, it occurred to Michael that both Cardinal Ito and Chance Magruder had used the phrase "hearts and minds" to him that night.

But now it didn't matter. Now he was coming up the water-gate stairs into Boregy House, and he could hear Cassie's tinkling laughter as he made the main floor landing.

He couldn't wait to see her. He couldn't wait to tell her about his wonderful previous life . . . not just because Mickey had been a warrior against the sharrh and a hero, but because he, Michael Chamoun, had *had* a previous life.

There was nothing more wonderful he could share with his new bride than the revelation that he, too, believed in reincarnation. Now they wouldn't have to avoid the topic of religion so carefully, now they could share even more together.

And although Ito had warned him not to tell anyone, not Vega Boregy or any of his ilk, surely that prohibition couldn't extend to Chamoun's wife. . . .

Cassie was in the blue room, a formal parlor, and there were other voices emanating from it. One of the liveried Boregy servants minced up to Michael and took his cloak, damp with the chill mist of imminent winter. So exhilarated by his spiritual revelation was Michael Chamoun that he smiled at the retainer, who blinked in surprise.

Normally, the Boregy servants made Chamoun so nervous and guilty that he tried to ignore them. In Nev Hettek, his parents had been barely better off than any of these menials, until the Sword had lifted them out of poverty for reasons of its own. . . .

In the blue room, when the servant opened the door for him with a flourish, announcing him as if he were a stranger because there were non-family members within, was a sight that nearly drained the joy from Chamoun's soul.

Sitting around an inlaid card table were his lovely wife Cassie, all peaches and cream in a low-cut blouse; Rita Nikolaev, the woman whose body called to Chamoun in a way Cassie's never could—a woman forbidden by every law of Sword and common sense; and the pale duelist known as Mondragon, traitor, ex-Sword, master spy.

"What are you doing here?" Chamoun blurted before he could stop himself. And then held his ground. He was a Boregy man, master of this house more than Mondragon. He had a right to know.

Cassie said, "Michael?" and pushed back her chair, a flush rising in her cheeks. "We're having a game of cards, please join us."

Cover the lapse, she would. Decorum was all to these people. Somehow, he found himself sitting at that table, one of his knees brushing Rita Nikolaev's, her dark hair rinsed with something that made it glow red as a beating heart. Somehow he found himself making small talk and picking up his cards and then, finally Cassie asked him, in front of both the guests, "Is something wrong, Michael? You look . . . pale."

"Not as pale as our friend Mondragon," Chamoun snapped. But it was true. Mondragon's handsome head seemed greasy; his skin was waxen; his eyes were red-rimmed.

"Not feeling my best tonight, Chamoun—you're observant. But then, we knew that."

We. Mondragon and Cassie's father, Vega Boregy, were

thick as thieves; together, they'd compromised Chamoun and tried to use him against Magruder. Chamoun didn't need to be reminded of that. At that instant, Rita Nikolaev shifted and more of her thigh touched Michael Chamoun's than could have, by accident.

So he said, to answer his wife's question and put Mondragon in his place and impress Rita, whose every breath was a wonder and a miracle, even under a high-necked blouse of the sort Chamoun's wife should be wearing, "Nothing's wrong, Cassie—not wrong at all. I was going to wait until we were alone to tell you, but . . ." He looked to his right, at Rita; then to his left, at Mondragon. Then at his wife again.

"Oh, come *on*, Michael. We're among friends. Tell us. We've been bored to tears all night, playing this stupid game—and losing all our allowance to Thomas." Cassie Boregy's sweet young face turned pouty. "Tell us."

And he was glad to, by then, because he saw the smirk dancing at the corners of Mondragon's lips and he wanted to wipe it away at any cost. "Tatiana Kalugin personally chose me to head a team of four people who'll be preparing the citizens of Merovingen-below to register for the census."

Thomas Mondragon's face went even paler. His eyes, opaque, stared steadily at his hands. Cassie beamed with delight, gave a squeal of joy, and came rushing around the card table to embrace him. Rita Nikolaev said in her throaty voice, "We're coming up in Merovingen society at a rapid rate; your karma must be excellent, m'ser Michael."

"Oh, please, Rita—Michael's *family*," Cassie insisted, her arms still around his neck. "We don't need to be so formal."

"But we do need," interjected Mondragon, "to get Rita home before the hour grows later. Tell your father, Cassie, that I'll drop by again. And thank you for a pleasant evening."

There was an interval of coat-getting and leave-taking and all the while Chamoun measured the stiffness in Mondragon's spine with satisfaction. Got the bastard, that time. Scared the snot out of him. Chamoun knew he might pay for this moment of pleasure later, if he were called to Vega's office, where the scheming of the house was usually done. But now, it was sweet to see Mondragon so pale, as if he'd taken ill.

If Chamoun found out that Mondragon had put a hand on Rita Nikolaev, he'd be worse than ill, Sword cover or no Sword cover. And then Chamoun remembered that he'd finally been able to warn Magruder of what was afoot in Boregy House, and the glow of well-being that had followed him ever since his lesson at the College suffused him once again.

He was even able to say farewell to Mondragon and Rita as if he meant it. He was bold and brazen; he kissed Rita Nikolaev's hand.

Which irked Cassie, but not for long. Up in their aqua and peach bedroom, with its high bed and its deep quilts, he waited until she was brushing her hair before he began casually, "Cassie, you'll never guess who I was in a previous life . . ."

"Don't tease me, Michael," she said with a sad little frown he could see clearly in the mirror. "I know you're just converting for me . . . that you don't believe any—"

"But I do. Ito put me in a trance so that I could experience a previous life, and I was this warrior in a space battle against the sharrh. It was so real. I was there. It was glorious. And I died—"

"What?" Cassie tossed her brush to the vanity and came to stand before the bed. "You what? Ito what?"

"Don't act like you've never heard of a regression before. Surely—"

"But I haven't." Lines appeared on her forehead, and then smoothed. "You'd better tell me everything, Michael, from the beginning."

And when he was done, she was lying in the crook of his arm with tears streaming down her face. At first he didn't understand her tears, but she said, "Ito was trying to do something terrible to you, Michael, but he did something wonderful instead. Instant karma of the best sort. You were meant to be my husband and bring this wonderful news to me. Oh, Michael, you remember a past life. How I wish I did."

"You can."

"No, I can't."

"I remember how to do it. I remember what to say. Just get some deathangel, and we'll do it together."

She sprang up and straddled him. "You will? You promise? Oh, it's so wonderful. Wait till I tell—"

"You'd better not tell anyone, at least not your father or his friends. Not now. Or they won't let me help you find your past lives. Promise."

"I promise."

"Good," said Chamoun. "If it's so important to you, we'll do it tomorrow if we can get the deathangel."

"It's not as important to me as you are, husband and lover—Officer of the Census," whispered Cassie as she brought her lips down to cover his.

And the pleasure of that was so intense that it almostly completely blocked out the phantom he kept remembering, the vision he'd seen as he shook Mondragon's hand in farewell: Romanov's ghost, hovering over Mondragon's shoulder, in the stairwell that led to the watergate.

There were some who'd never be counted in the Merovingen census—some who never should be. And Michael Chamoun had just chosen his side publicly in whatever was coming. It was the side of Tatiana Boregy, by default. By Magruder's ultimatum. And, if Cassie and the rest of the Revenantists were right, by karmic debt.

Whatever the truth of it, Chamoun had a feeling Cassie's father was going to be about as pleased as Mondragon had been to hear his news. But he didn't have to sleep with Cassie's father.

And he didn't have to go out into the mist tonight, as pale Mondragon had just done, with Romanov's paler shade following close behind.

So he took his warm wife in his arms and closed his eyes and pretended that she was Rita Nikolaev, the forbidden nymph of his dreams, while about him Merovingians went on their secretive missions through the dark, cold night.

FEVER SEASON
(REPRISED)

C.J. Cherryh

The wind was blowing a steady mist as the Boregy launch approached Nikolaev's slip on Rimmon Isle, a mist that spattered on the windshield and fractured the harbor lights beyond the shadow-shapes of Boregy crewman. Rita Nikolaev chattered steadily about the weather and the winter, and asked Mondragon whether he was used to weather like this.

Of course. Because he was Falkenaer, to the Nikolaevs as to most everyone. Mondragon dragged his eyes back from the dark beyond the side-windows of the launch, his mind having wandered toward a certain Falkenaer ship and a small skip that might be out there on this unfriendly water, that bucked and pitched the powered launch and rattled cold mist on the canvas weather-canopy. A very small skip and a woman working solo tonight in the wide waters of the harbor, because she was damned stubborn and a damned fool.

"Very much so, m'sera. The Isles have very little to stop the wind."

So he had heard. He had little more notion than she did, what the Falken Isles were like.

"Why do people *live* in such a place?"

"M'sera, because people are born there." He did not intend to be rude. He was aware of her sitting closer than the cabin space demanded, was aware of her trying to draw him out, perhaps for her own reasons, for Nikolaev's, who knew? Perhaps she was even Anastasi's, testing him, or being perverse, or trying to snare him romantically.

Who knew that either? He was exhausted. A day of back-and-forth between Boregy and Nikolaev had had him out in the weather more than he had planned: and the cold and the damp had gotten into his bones.

He still did not know what reception he had waiting at Nikolaev. He had thought he was through—take a briefing from Vega Boregy, do an errand, see the Nikolaev daughter home, deliver the packet that he had tucked under his cloak, which contained, not coincidentally, a mortgage that Honesty Rajwade had yet to discover had been sold to Boregy and thus to Anastasi Kalugin; a minor thing, the purchase of a soul—Anastasi traded in things like that. Mostly he had spent his day trying delicately to make contact with a very nervous younger cousin of Rosenblum, who had gambling debts; and who was willing to do anything to evade the wrath of his creditors.

Foul and filthy business. But it led into the Justiciary offices where Constancy Rosenblum held a post. And ultimately to Rosenblum's willingness to work after hours making copies of documents, securing a flow of information that Rosenblum *thought* was going to an agent of Tatiana Kalugin, and the blacklegs.

Let him commit himself. Then what Rosenblum found out he was into would be only one more lever against him. God help the poor bastard. Mondragon sneezed again, heard Rita Nikolaev chide him about night air, and wrapped his cloak about him as the launch nosed its way into the Nikolaev slip.

Beside a black hull that cast back the light in faint glistening, and towered over them.

" 'Stasi's still here," Rita said, clutching his arm for steadiness as they got up. "Won't you come up to the house, Tom, have a little brandy?"

"Thanks, no, I have to get back."

He saw her ashore. He stood there wrapped in his cloak

while Nikolaev servants with lanterns came and retrieved m'sera and wended their way in a snake of lights up the steps that led to the Nikolaev mansion, on the edge of Rimmon Isle. He turned then and slipped into the shadow under the bow of the black yacht, and walked around the slip to the gangway, while the launch throttled up and backed, on its way back to Boregy without him.

He came up onto the high deck of the yacht and met challenge from the watch, instantly. But he had the right pass, a face and a voice they knew; and their orders let him below very quickly, into the companionway and into the warmth of Anastasi Kalugin's own shipboard quarters.

It was all red cushions and blue carpet and fine wood inside. Electrics burned, powered from the ship's generators. The man who owned it all was hardly more than thirty-five, pale-skinned, with a black, close beard. He did not resemble his auburn-haired sister Tatiana in the least; was probably not like his elder brother Michael either; Iosef Kalugin had had no wives, just offspring. Two too many of them. Anastasi wore a loose-sleeved tunic, black, with rubies at the collar; plain black trousers and boots; red embroidery on the belt, but minimal, everything a shade under flamboyant. It was his style in Kalugin. Or here. Or wherever he held court with his own adherents.

Anastasi had one servant, his doctor, Iosef—same name as his father. Which probably gave him a certain pleasure. And Iosef stayed during all interviews, a shadow in the peripheries: Mondragon had ceased to be anxious about him, only knew that he was there.

"Do you have it?" Anastasi asked.

"I brought everything," Mondragon said, and carefully took the packet from under his cloak, knowing that Iosef's hand was momentarily out of sight. He handed the papers over. "The Rajwade papers. The others. I finally made contact with Rosenblum. I'll get to him again Monday next. He says he'll have something by then. He's a very nervous man. He thinks he's working for your sister."

Anastasi laughed, shortly. "Sit down. Iosef, Mondragon would like a brandy."

Anastasi never asked. He assumed. Mondragon sank into the nearest chair and studied the far wall, the floor, answering Anastasi's questions. He took the brandy when it arrived, felt the ache of last night's fall in his back and his neck and wished to hell he was home in his own bed.

Which he would get to only when Anastasi was satisfied. *If* Anastasi was satisfied. He mumbled answers and thought of Jones and the weather out there, that was the main thing gnawing at him. It was a damned small boat. The engine had always been chancy. He drank and he felt the brandy sting his throat like fire. "Yes, ser," he said to one question. "No, ser," to another.

When he was away from Anastasi he had his doubts whether this man would survive. The odds were high against him. When he was in the same room with him he had no doubt that Anastasi would survive. Anastasi's stare and his questions were alike, razor-edged, quick, his presence full of a force more than ordinary. Anastasi affected him in a way that he had at first not understood, until he realized it was an old feeling Anastasi roused in him, the same projection of assurance and cold sane efficiency that Karl Fon had projected. The same game. The same promises.

Mondragon's skin crawled.

The wind came down across Rimmon Isle and the bay was white-capped, the skip pitching like a living thing as Jones came up on the dark bulk of the Falkenaer ship. No standing up on deck in this blow: she used the engine and managed the tiller sitting down, the tiller bar tucked under her arm, the other hand gripping the deck-rim, while the rain soaked her to the skin and she wished she did have socks on.

Filthy weather. But it was dead sure there were no black-legs out here tonight on patrol. Good as fog for her business.

The Falkenaer ship loomed up like a wooden wall—a ship of sail, like all its kind, lean and sleek and full of foreign mysteries, come in from the high seas and all around the Chattalen.

But it was a bolt of Merovingian lace and two bolts of Kamat's best in the oilskin packet in the bow, a few kegs of Hafiz' whiskey, and a sizable keg of salted fish—Lord knew what kind and Jones asked no questions, if the painted lords of the Chattalen or wherever else wanted to sample a dangerous delicacy like deathangel and risk the hereafter: rich folk took damn strange chances for their amusement, and she took hers for credit with Moghi—monetary and otherwise. It was brandy and Chattalen silk supposed to come back again, duty free. And everybody was happy. Even the lords of the Chattalen, who would pay plenty for a taste of Merovingian fish and a moment of life-risking bliss.

She let go the deck-rim and pulled a whistle up to her mouth, blew once loud and shrill, reckoning on the wind to carry it to the ship and no one out here to hear it except those that should.

And sure enough a light showed on the Falkenaer's deck, toward the stern, where they were tied up at the deepwater wharf. Thank the Lord and the Ancestors, no crossed signals, no need to do more than snug in among the pilings and wait for the Falkenaer to send a few men down to the dockside: easier for them to do than for her to try to steady the skip enough to offload and take on cargo from a sling.

She eased the skip around the stern, close, but not too close, and gave it all the room it needed as she came around toward the pilings in the dark, where the big ship heaved and groaned at its moorings.

Then it was fast work—cut the engine, scramble down into the well while the boat pitched in the chop, run out the boathook and snag herself a hold on the rope-buffered pilings. Damn! Bang into a piling hard enough to rattle her teeth, and a wave over the side that sloshed about under the deck-slats.

She got the hold all the same, wrenched the heavy boat closer and closer and snagged the buffer-ropes with the barrel-hook in her left hand until she could lay down the pole with the right and get a special line snubbed about the barrel-hook handle. Damn sloppy tie-up, but it was hard enough to get anything close to the waterside steps with the surge coming in like that and carrying her head up dangerously close to the underside of the dock.

She heard a whistle sound faintly. She answered it, and in a little while heard a still fainter hail from the direction of the stairs that gave the deep-sea sailors access to Merovingen's water-transport. Or the use of their own dinghy on Merovingen's waterways, if they had a mind to.

Now came the serious dealing. She took a good bight about the piling with a main-tie, then stood up and kept track of the up and down pitch with a hand on one of the support beams overhead, seeing men on the stairs, faintest shadows in the deeper shadow of the big ship's hull.

This was the dangerous part. There was always the chance of someone trying to take advantage and claim the goods defective or outright steal them. Or her. There were slavers, mostly rivermen, never Falkenaers. Moghi generally made the deals himself, and he had this time.

"You Moghi's?" the query reached her across the water.

"That I am," she answered back.

It was a damned long fussy business, them getting their goods overside, down the stairs, her working in close: the waves and the water depth made the pole useless and it was a matter of hooking along the overhead without cracking one's skull or cracking the skip's seams on the pilings. She was warm enough when she finished, sweating and drawing the dank air in huge gasps.

"Ye're alane on that 'ere boat?" a sailor hailed her.

"Hey, she's just a little run. You want I help ye with them barrels?" Bravado. She ached right down to her gut; but she made fast in good order. "I got ever'thing in the list, got 'er writ fair."

"Cold night," a sailor said. "F' a gel alane."

"Shut up," said another, female. "He an't been th' same sin' we et th' wooly." General laughter. "Ye offload, we onlade. Yey?"

"Fair deal."

"Ne, ne," a young man said, and skipped aboard, landing on the bow and making the skip rock and Jones reach for the barrel-hook at her belt. But he kept his distance, held up a hand. "Shulz's me name. 'At's Finn, wi' th' mouth. She ain't bad. But the wooly wa' better." He picked up a barrel and passed it off the bow. More general laughter.

"She don' talk much," someone said. "Hey, canaler, ye got a tongue?"

"Hell, no, I'm just letting this man unload my boat while I catch my breath."

"Got a bottle for a cozy."

"No, thanks. I'm sure ye're right fine, but I ain't buying t'night. I got a long way back and Moghi don't hold with it. Sorry."

"Hell, Finny-gel, we're stuck wi' ye." More laughter. And, thank the Lord and the Ancestors, they started loading on their own barrels. Jones drew a quieter breath.

"Aft, aft, some of that, ye deepwater sailors, leave me a walk: I got to push this skip in the canals, and I got to have free walk for'ard."

"Gotta be Finn's own sister," one complained. "Bitch, bitch, bitch."

Damn, it was a heavy load. She felt the skip riding lower than before, fussed with the trim, ordered a shift in the barrels. And the Falken sailors shifted them.

"I don' like how she's riding either," one said. "Hell, gel, gi' up a few barrel."

"Damn Moghi can't count," she muttered. But there was that big boat up there, that big fine ship that could glide like a seabird in the wind, and she felt a twinge of envy. It was no small amount of pride that made her say: "Hell, I'll make 'er, no worry."

"That's all I know," Mondragon said, "all Vega knows. Chamoun announced it tonight. It wasn't a situation where we *could* ask questions—his wife was there. And Rita Nikolaev. I'd suggest you ask Ito Boregy what went on. I'd suggest a real caution with Chamoun. And Vega should keep a nightwatch on him . . . before he wakes up with his throat cut some night. *I* think Magruder is trying to lever Vega away from you. He's putting pressure on me.''

"What sort?'' Anastasi asked.

"Threats. Not half as attractive as what you pay me. Like protection. He can't outbid you. I think you should know that.''

Anastasi smiled. "You want me to know that.''

"I'm quite faithful.''

"What about Chamoun? You said you'd bought him.''

Mondragon glanced down, thinking that there was coin to use, that in Vega's eyes Cassie was expendable. He thought of Jones. And did not want to make any suggestion involving Cassie. There was very little edge left to this Sword. Very little nowadays. And he reminded himself that he could lose everything by caring for anything. But the edge was gone, that was all. He did not know where or when. "I don't know. I don't like what's going on. I'm going to talk to Vega. If all else fails I'm going to talk to Chamoun. Maybe one of the cardinal's sessions. Who knows?''

"You keep in touch with me about that.''

"Chamoun was still high when he said it. Eyes dilated. Voice up. I don't know who talked to him, I don't know when he got this assignment, I don't know why the cardinal let him out in that condition. Or whether someone else got to him. All this came up at the last minute. I haven't had time to trace it.''

Anastasi nodded, thinking, and looked at him, so much like Karl Fon in that little mannerism it caught at his gut.

"Do that,'' Anastasi said.

The skip plowed its way through the chop, logy as a three-day drunk. She took a little water, but very little: Jones kept her bow to the waves and chewed a piece out of her lip every time a gust rocked the boat.

Then the engine sputtered.

She hit the engine-box with her fist. "Dammit, not now!''

Second sputter. Same with her heart. If the engine died and she lost way, there was no way to keep from going broadside to the waves, which meant water and more water and the bottom of the harbor.

She throttled up a little, knowing that tank was going to go down fast at that rate, but the sputters smoothed out.

More water over the side.

Damn.

Damnfool stunt.

She twisted round, still fighting the tiller's tendency to go off to starboard, got the bottom of the engine-box open and reached in by feel and started working the hand-pump, moving fuel over from the second tank, a rig that had cost her a goldbit, and worth it all now, in the dark, in the wind.

There were oars. That was well and fine, but the skip was too wide for one rower. Took two.

Dammit, Mondragon ain't ever going to know, is he? Damn grease slick'll wash out to sea and they ain't never going to find the boat.

Sputter.

Sputter. Up with the throttle again, hope to hell there was no clog in the line. Sometimes it was the filter-screen did it, picked up some damn bit of weed. Sometimes it was the damn intake. And she was running out of hands.

Put the pin in to hold the tiller steady on, never mind the damn water coming in, never mind the fuel drain. She felt after the stick she used and poked at the filter through the access while the engine went on sputtering and water washed over the port side.

Engine was running hot. She felt it. She could not tell whether there had been anything in the intake. Maybe it was just the load.

She pulled the pin out to free the tiller and took it under her arm, fighting the skip to avoid another wash.

You lose my boat, Altair, I ain't thanking you.

Damn, mama, I know, I know.

What in hell're you doing out here?

Good question, mama.

Man stung you in your pride and look what ye gone and done, look what damnfool thing ye did.

She thought that over awhile. Having bitten her lip till it bled.

Ain't a bad old engine, mama. He's still running.

Listen to me, Altair.

Yey, mama. I hear ye. That's Ramseyhead up there. I think she's going to hold.

Hear me?

Yey, mama. Your daughter's a fool. But I ain't going to lose this boat.

You got to be a fool, Altair, be it for something worthwhile.

Yey, mama. He is. Most-times. —Damn!

A Rimmon yacht was out and underway, dark and sleek, needing no sails, and low enough to make the bridge at Ramseyhead, which meant low enough to make Fishmarket and Golden and any bridge between Ramseyhead and Archangel, where boats like that had to do their turn and come about again.

She thought she knew which one that was.

She had seen it ride down a skip once, the night the Signeury had come under attack. Folk said after tempers cooled, well, she's a big boat, she don't see too good.

But the master of that black ship didn't damn well care—not a spit and a damn did he care.

Mondragon, she thought, clinging to the tiller. *Mondragon's there. With him. I hope.*

Oh, damn, going up to the Signeury tonight. Going up near Boregy. And the Justiciary, and wherever.

Maybe he's home by now, instead. Safe in bed. Wondering where in hell I am.

Can't go no faster, Mondragon. I ain't going to get t' Moghi's much before dawn.

"Easier," Anastasi had said, "if certain people come aboard . . . rather than having you out knocking on doors."

Certain people meant Vega Boregy. And Cardinal Ito Tremaine Boregy. And Chastity Rajwade, cloaked and muffled and carrying a sword she very possibly could use. Mondragon flinched at the latter presence: it was one more person to whom his cover became transparent.

"My cousin," Vega Boregy said of Mondragon.

But Rajwade, a long-faced, sober woman with enough jewelry on her collar to have bought a hundred lives, quirked a brow and said: "Of course. How nice—" in a way that said she believed none of it. There was something predatory in her, something that said blackmail was nothing and what she wanted was all-important.

At the moment she had her hand on Vega's, on his hip, and looked at Mondragon at the same time as if she were wondering what his price was and what it bought. While Mondragon wondered, knowing that Vega had sheltered in Rajwade before a Sword attack killed his cousins and put him as acting head of Boregy, whether Chastity Rajwade had been the shelter and what the Rajwade mortgage that Boregy had handed to Anastasi really meant, in terms of *who* was going to end up head of house in Rajwade.

But that was not the question at hand. That was not something he was privy to, and he reckoned that his uneasy peace with Boregy would be better served by silence. "M'sera," he said at that introduction, with all courtesy. He was all right for the moment. He had drunk enough to numb him and soothe his throat, not enough to fog him, no matter the lack of sleep: stark terror could keep a man awake.

Jones was back at Moghi's by now, surely. Or at tie-up under Petrescu, wondering where in hell he was. But he could not help that. He gathered his wits, such as he had left, and added up the questions he had for Vega and for the Cardinal, regarding one Michael Chamoun.

"That's got 'em," Jones said. She saw the last of the barrels off at Moghi's landing, and staggered in for hot tea. It was all she could do. There was just no more strength in her, not without the tea, not without the bit of bread and fish and eggs that Jep set in front of her.

"Damn late," Moghi commented, coming out of his office to stare at her, hands on hips, a huge man.

But he got real quiet when Jones looked up at him and scowled.

He knew what the weather had been.

"You got full count on them barrels," she said after a moment. "You owe me, Moghi."

"Bed's upstairs." The Room, Moghi meant. Safest bed in Merovingen, and no callers. "No charge. Boys take care of your skip."

"Ney, got to find Del. Seen 'im?"

"No. Ain't."

"Unnnh," she said, and polished off the eggs and tea with a few gulps.

It was a damned long push over to Petrescu. She made it. But Del and Min were already gone, and if Mondragon had come home last night he had gone out again. Not unusual. She tied up and curled up in the hidey with mama's pistol under the rags at the back end, because in Mondragon's vicinity a body never knew.

It was going to be one of the steamy days after the cold of the night before. That was the way of autumns in Merovingen. And she was grateful for the warmth.

A PLAGUE
ON YOUR HOUSES

Mercedes Lackey

A piece of plaster bounced off Raj's nose, accompanied by a
series of rhythmic *thuds* from overhead. By that sure token he
knew, despite the utter darkness of his 'bedroom' that it was
around oh-six-hundred and dawn was just beginning.

He reached over his head and knocked twice on the wall.
He was answered by a muffled curse, and the pounding of
Denny's answer. He grinned to himself, and began groping
after his clothing.

Thudathudathudathuda—pause—(Raj braced himself)—
thud. A series of plaster flakes rained down. A professional
dance-troupe had the studio above their 'apartment' from
dawn to about ten hundred. From ten hundred to eighteen
hundred it was given over to classes—noisier, but less inclined to great leaps that brought the ceiling down. From
eighteen hundred to around third watch—

Nobody on Fife talked about what went on then, and
nobody watched to see who went in and out. Raj knew,
though; at least what they looked like—thanks to Denny's
irrepressible curiosity, they'd both done some balcony-climbing
and window-peering one night. A dozen or so hard-faced men
and women had been there; and it wasn't dancing they were
doing. It was some kind of hand-to-hand combat, and all of

71

them were very, very good. Who they were, why they were practicing in secret, that was still a mystery. Raj smelled 'fanatic' on them, of whatever ilk, and kept well clear of them.

Then from third watch to dawn Rat's old acting troupe had the run of the place, which meant less ceiling-thumping but a lot of shouting. ("Jali *deary*, do you think you *might* pay *less* attention to Kristo's *legs* and a *little* more to your *lines*? *All* right children, *one* more time, from the *top*.")

Raj had learned to sleep through it all, though noise generally made him very nervous. It was friendly shouting, for all the mock-hysterics.

Being directly below the studio was one reason why this place, technically a three-room apartment, was cheap enough for two kids to afford. Now Raj hurried to pull on his pants and shirt in the black of his cubbyhole bedroom, wanting to be out of it before the other reason evidenced itself. Because the other reason was due to start up any minute now——

Right on time, a hideous clanking and banging shook the far wall, as Raj pulled open his door, and crossed the "living room," the worn boards soft and warm under his bare feet. He stood blinking for a moment in the light from their lamp; after pitchy dark it was painfully bright even turned down to almost nothing. He reached over and turned the wick-key, and the odor of fish-oil assaulted his nose until it flared up; then he unlocked the outer door and slipped down the hall to the bathroom shared by most of the apartments on this level. That incredible ruckus was Fife Small Boat Repair. It started about now, and kept up till second watch, and sometimes later. There was another apartment between them and the repair shop, but it didn't provide much in the way of sound-baffling. Fortunately (for him) the tenant of *that* place was deaf.

Denny still hadn't turned out by the time Raj got back, so he pulled open the door to the other "bedroom" (just big enough for a wall-hung bunk and a couple of hooks for clothes, and identical to Raj's) and hauled him out by the foot. There was a brief, laughing tussle (which Raj, by virtue of his age and size, won) and Denny betook himself off to get clean.

There weren't any windows in their home, so there was always the oil-lamp burning up on the wall. It was a curious blend of cast-off and makeshift; the brass base had once been good, and still could be polished to a soft golden gleam, but the chimney had been constructed out of an old bottle with the bottom cut out. That lamp came with the place. So had the wood-stove—another makeshift made of the metal base of an old chair and a metal barrel with stovepipe and door welded on. It sat in a half-barrel of sand for safety's sake, and gave them a bit of heat and a place to cook. The 'main' room was a little bigger than both the 'bedrooms' put together; all of it bare wooden-floored and sooty-walled, but warm and without drafts, and too many floors below the roof to get leaks when it rained. On the wall opposite the oil-lamp and next to the stove was a tiny fired-clay sink—scarcely big enough to wash a cup in, much less them; but it had a safe water-tap that was fed from the tanks on the roof. Everything else was theirs, and compared to the little Raj had owned in the swamp or what Denny had had in the air-shaft, it was paradisiacal. They now boasted a couple of cushions to sit on, a vermin-proof cupboard for food, and a second cupboard for storage (it currently held two tin plates, two mugs, two spoons, a skillet and a battered saucepan, and assorted odds and ends). They also owned their bedding and three changes of clothing, each, and a precious box of a dozen or so battered, dirty, (mostly) coverless books. The last were Raj's property; some bought at second-hand stores, most gifts from Rat, a few from Denny. He knew the ones Denny gave him had been stolen; he suspected the same of Rat's—but a book was a book, and he wasn't going to argue about the source.

All that hadn't come out of nowhere. Word had gone quietly upriver with a Gallandry barge that Raj and Denny still lived—and a special verbal message had gone to Elder Takahashi from Raj as to why they weren't coming home again. Back down again just as quietly had come a bit of real coin—not so much as to call attention to the recipient, but enough to set them up comfortably. With the coin had come another verbal message to Raj from his grandfather. "You salvage our Honor," was all it had said—and Raj nearly cried. Granther had clearly felt that Angela had impugned the Family by her activities with the Sword of God—he had said as much when he sent them into exile. There was honor, and there was Takahashi Honor, which had been something special even before Ship days. All Nev Hettek knew how dearly the Takahashi clan held their Honor.

And now Granther had said with those few words that he felt Raj had redeemed what Angela had besmirched.

That—that had been worth more to Raj than all the money that had come with it.

Raj hoped that the rest of what he was doing was worthy of that Honor—although he was fairly well certain in his own mind that it would be. Honor required that debts be paid, and he owed a mighty debt to Mondragon. So hidden under the books was his secret, beneath a false bottom in the box. Pen, ink, and paper; and the current 'chapter' of Mama's doings, back in the Sword days. When he had five or six pages, they went off to Tom Mondragon, usually via Jones. He was up to when he'd turned ten now; how much of what he remembered was useful he had no idea, but surely there was something in all that stuff that Mondragon could turn to a purpose. Something to even up the scales of debt between them—

Raj boiled up some tea and got breakfast out—bread and cold fish, bought on the way home last night. Denny bounced back in the door, fighting his way into his sweater.

No one would ever have guessed, to see them side by side, that they were brothers. Raj strongly showed his Japanese ancestry, taking after his mother, Angela. Straight black hair, sunbrowned skin fading now into ivory, and almond-shaped eyes in a thin, angular face made him look both older and younger than his sixteen years. Had he been back with the clan, nobody would have had any trouble identifying which Nev Hettek family *he* belonged to, for Angela had been a softened, feminized image of Elder Takahashi as a boy. Whereas Denny, round-faced and round-eyed, with an olive complexion and brown hair, looked like a getting-to-be-handsome version of the Merovingen 'type'—and not a minute older than his true age of thirteen.

"Need t' get clothes washed t'night," Denny said, gingerly reaching for his mug of hot tea, "or t'morrow."

"Spares clean?" Raj asked around a mouthful of bread, inwardly marveling at the fate that had brought him full circle to the point where he and Denny actually had spare clothing. Of course things had been a great deal better back at Nev Hettek—but no point in harkening over that. To go back home would put the entire Takahashi clan in danger, and with the worst kind of enemy—Sword of God. In no way was Raj ever going to do that.

"Yeah. I'm wearing 'em, dummy."

"So'm I. Tomorrow, then. That's my day off; 'sides, I gotta see Tom tonight." Washing clothes meant getting the bathroom after everybody else had gone to work; clearing it with the landlord and paying the extra three pennies for a tub full of hot water besides what they were allowed as tenants. There was an incentive to Raj to volunteer for laundry-duty. Denny was still kid enough to tend to avoid unnecessary baths, but Raj used laundry-day as an excuse to soak in hot, soppy, soapy water when the clothing was done; soaking until all the heat was gone from it before rinsing the clean clothing (and himself) out in cold. After five years alternately freezing and broiling in the mud of the swamp, a hot bath was a luxury that came very close to being a religious experience for Raj. Hence, Raj usually did the laundry.

" 'Kay. I'll clean the damn stove."

"*And* the lamp."

"Slaver. *And* the lamp. Whatcha seein' Mondragon 'bout?"

"Dunno. Got a note from him at work yesterday. Just asked me to meet him at Moghi's, 'cause he was calling in favors and had something for me to do."

"Hey, c'n I come 'long?" Denny never missed the opportunity to go to Moghi's or Hoh's if he could manage it. Unlike Raj, he loved crowds and noise.

Raj thought. "Don't see why not, he didn't say 'alone,' and he usually does if that's the way he wants it. Why?"

"Gotta keep ye safe from Jones, don't I?"

Raj blushed hotly. He'd had a brief crush on Jones; *very* brief. It hadn't lasted past her dumping him headfirst in the canal. He hadn't known she and Mondragon were pairing it at the time. Denny still wasn't letting him live it down.

He hoped profoundly that Denny never found out about Marina—he'd rather *die* than have Denny rib him about her. He much preferred to worship her quietly, from afar—without having half the urchins Denny ran with knowing about it. He still didn't know too much about his idol—the only reason he even knew her name was because he'd overheard one of her companions using it.

Oh, Marina—

Enough of daydreaming. "Get a move on, we're going to be late," he replied, while Denny chuckled evilly.

There had been plenty of gossip among the other clerks today, and because of some of it, Raj made a detour on the way home—to Kamat.

So here he was at Kamat's gatehouse, facing the ancient doorkeeper through its grate. He was glad that it was nearly dusk; glad his dark sweater and britches were so anonymous, glad beyond telling that the shortsighted doorkeeper of House Kamat couldn't see his face. It took all his courage to pretend to be a runner with a message to be left "for m'sera Marina." He moved off as fast as was prudent, eager to get himself deep into shadows, once the folded and sealed paper was in the doorman's hands. His heart was pounding with combined anxiety, embarrassment, and excitement. Maybe— well, probably—Marina would get it, if only when the head of her household demanded to know "what this is all about"—

And—Ancestors!—they'd want to know what it was about, all right. Because it was a love-poem. Anonymous, of course, so Marina would be able to protest honestly that she had no idea where it had come from, and why. And Raj's identity was safe. He'd written and erased it twenty or thirty times before it seemed right. And the only reason he'd found the courage to deliver it was because today he'd finally found out just *who* she was.

M'sera Marina of Kamat. *The* daughter of the house. Not above Rigel Takahashi—provided that the hostilities between Nev Hettek and Merovingen could be overlooked—but *definitely* above the touch of Raj Tai.

Raj had buried Rigel Takahashi quite thoroughly, and not even for the sweet eyes of Marina Kamat was he going to resurrect the name he'd been born to. But even if he couldn't touch, he could dream—and perversely, even if she were never to learn who her unknown admirer was, he wanted her to know how he felt. So he'd spent three hours struggling over that poem.

Just two weeks ago it was, he'd seen her. At Moghi's, with a couple of companions. Until then his daydreams had been confined to something just as impossible, but hardly romantic.

The College. Lord and Ancestors, what he wouldn't give to get in there—but he had no money, and no sponsor, and the wrong religious affiliation on top of it all. Not that he gave a fat damn about religion anymore, but in no way was he ever going to pass for Revenantist. He didn't know the creeds, the ceremonies, the doctrines—

But he was young enough that sometimes, sometimes when the day had gone really well, it almost seemed possible. Because a long-buried dream had surfaced with this new life. Raj wanted to be a doctor; a medic, anyway.

The patrons of Mama's drug-shop had teased him about that—but right along with the teasing they'd asked his advice, and taken it too. That perfect memory again; he remembered symptoms, treatments, alternatives, allergies—he'd helped old May out in the swamp, later, with her herbs and her 'weeds,' dispensing what passed for medicine among the swampies and the crazies.

Of course, since seeing Marina for the first time, she'd crowded out that particular daydream more often than not.

He wondered if he'd see her tonight at Moghi's.

His feet were chilled as he padded along the damp wooden

walkways. He couldn't get used to shoes after five years without them in the swamp, so he generally went as bare of foot as a canaler. The temperature was dropping; fog was coming up off the water. The lines of the railings near him blurred; farther on, they were reduced to silhouettes. Farther than that, across the canal, there was nothing to see but vague, hulking shapes. Without the clatter of boot-soles or clogs, he moved as silently in the fog as a spirit—silent out of habit. If the walkway-gangs (or the swamp-gangs) didn't hear you, they couldn't hassle you. Breathing the fog was like breathing wet, smokey wool; it was tainted with any number of strange smells. It held them, fishy smell of canal, smell of rotting wood, woodsmoke, stink of nameless somethings poured into the dark, cold waters below him. He hardly noticed. His thoughts were elsewhere—back with the inspiration for his poem.

Oh, Marina—

She tended to show up at Moghi's pretty frequently. Of course Raj was under no illusions as to why. Tom Mondragon, naturally—hell, Tom even had Rat and Rif exchanging lustful jokes and comments about him. Raj wondered hopelessly if *he'd* ever have—whatever it was that Tom had. Probably not.

His feet had taken him all unaware down the walkways and the long, black tunnel-path through Fife to his very own door, almost before he realized it. He started to use his key, but Denny had beaten him home, and must have heard the rattle in the lock.

" 'Bout time!" he caroled in Raj's face, pulling the door open with Raj standing there stupidly, key still held out. "Ye fall in th' canal?"

"They kept us late," Raj said, trying not to feel irritated that his daydream had been cut short. "There any supper? It *was* your turn."

"There will be. Got eggs, an' I promise not t' burn 'em." He returned to the side of the stove, cracked an egg into the pan, and began frying it with studious care as to its state. "They give me tomorrow off too, like you—somethin' about a Falkenaer ship—ye got anythin' ye wanta do? After chores, I mean.''

"Not really," Raj replied absently, going straight over to the wall and trying to get a good look at himself in the little bit of cracked mirror hung over the sink. Denny noticed, and cocked a quizzical eye at him as he brought over a dented tin plate holding Raj's egg and a slice of bread.

"Somethin' doin'?"

"I just don't see any reason to show up at Moghi's looking like a drowned cat," Raj replied waspishly, accepting the plate and beginning to eat.

"Huh." Denny took the hint and combed his hair with his fingers, then inhaled his own dinner.

"Hey, big brother—y'know somethin' funny?" Denny actually sounded thoughtful, and Raj swiveled to look at him with surprise. "Since ye started eatin' regular, yer gettin' t' look a lot like Mama. An' that ain't bad—she may'a been bird-witted, but she was a looker.''

Raj was touched by the implied compliment. "Not so funny," he returned, "I gotta look like somebody. You know, the older *you* get, the more you look like Mahmud Lee. In the right light nobody'd ever have to guess who your daddy was.''

Denny started preening at that—he was just old enough to remember that Lee had been a fair match for Tom Mondragon at attracting the ladies.

Then Raj grinned wickedly and deflated him. "It's just too bad you inherited Mama's vacuum-brain too.''

"Hey!"

"Now don't start something you can't finish—" Raj warned as his brother dropped his empty plate, seized a pillow and advanced on him.

Denny gave a disgusted snort, remembering how things had turned out only that morning, and threw the pillow back into its corner. "No fair.''

"Life's like that," Raj replied. "So let's get going, huh?''

*   *   *

Moghi's was full, but subdued. No clogging, not tonight; no music, even. Nobody seemed much in the mood for it. The main room was hot and smokey; not just from Moghi's lanterns, either. There was smoke and fog drifting in every time somebody opened a door; which wasn't often, as it was getting cold outside.

Lanterns tonight were few, and turned low. Customers bent over their tables, their talk hardly more than muttering. Dark heads under darker caps, or bare of covering; no one here tonight but canalers. Raj looked around for the only blond head in the room, but had a fair notion of where to find him. Mondragon preferred—when he had a choice—to sit where he could keep an eye on everything going on. Pretty paranoid— but normal, if you were ex-Sword. Raj had been known to choose his seats that way.

There he was—black sweater, dark cap, golden blond hair that curled the way the carved Angel's hair curled. Not surprisingly, Mondragon was ensconced in his usual corner table. But as Raj and Denny wormed their way closer, Raj could see that he was looking—not quite hungover, but not terribly good. Limp-looking, like it was an effort to keep his head up and his attention on the room and the people in it. Minor mental alarms began jangling.

Still, if the man wanted to binge once in a while, who could blame him? Gallandrys had plenty to say about him, not much of it good. Raj picked up a lot just by keeping his mouth shut and his ears open, doing the accounts they set him and staying invisible. What he heard didn't exactly seem to match the Tom Mondragon that had given two dumb kids a way out of trouble when it was more logical for him to have knifed them both and dumped them in the canal. He had a feeling that someday he'd like to hear Tom's side of things. He also had a feeling that if that day ever came, it *would* be when Mondragon was on a binge. If he ever lowered his guard enough.

Mondragon's table had a candle over it, not a lamp— candlelight was even dimmer than lamplight. The two boys moved up to the side of that table like two thin shadows. Raj had brought his week's worth of recollections, neatly folded into a packet. Maybe it was the dim light—but they stood beside the table for nearly a minute before Mondragon noticed them. Raj bit his lip, wondering if he'd offended Mondragon in some way, and the man was paying him back with arrogance—but, no; it was almost as if he was having such trouble focusing that he could only tend to one thing at a time. As if he *really* wasn't seeing them until he could get his attention around to the piece of floor they were standing on.

When Mondragon finally saw them, and invited them to sit with a weary nod of the head, Raj pushed the sealed packet across the table towards his hand. Mondragon accepted it silently, then stared off into space, like he'd forgotten they were there.

Raj sat there long enough to start feeling like a fool, then ventured to get his attention: "M'ser—"

Now Mondragon finally looked at them again, his eyes slowly focusing. He did *not* look hungover after all; he looked tired to death and ready to drop. "You asked *me* to come here, remember? There something you want us to do?"

"I—" Mondragon rubbed one temple, slowly, as if his head was hurting him; his eyes were swollen and bruised-looking, and there were little lines of pain between his eyebrows. "There was—I know there was a reason—"

This was nothing like the canny Tom Mondragon Raj was used to dealing with! Alarmed now, Raj took a really hard look at him, eyes alert for things May had taught him to take note of, and didn't like what he saw.

A thin film of sweat stood on his forehead; his green eyes were dull and dark-circled—and Mondragon was fair, but he'd never been *this* white before. His hair was damp and lank, and not from the fog, Raj would bet on it. And his shoulders were shivering a little as if from cold—yet Moghi's was so warm with closely crowded bodies that Raj was regretting he'd worn his thick sweater! And now Raj was remembering something from this morning and the gossip among the other clerks at Gallandry—a rumor of fever in the town. Maybe brought in on that Falkenaer ship. Maybe not.

Raj's bones said whatever was wrong with Tom had its roots *here*—because Raj's bones had once shook with a chill he'd bet Tom was feeling now.

"M'ser, are you feeling all right?" he whispered under cover of a burst of loud conversation from three tables over.

Mondragon smiled thinly. "To tell you the truth, boy—no. Afraid I've got a bit of a cold, or something."

He broke into a fit of coughing, and his shoulders shook again; and although he was plainly trying, not all of his iron will could keep the tremor invisible. Raj made up his mind on the instant.

"Denny—go find Jones. Get!"

Denny got. Mondragon looked at Raj with a kind of dazed puzzlement. "She's probably on her way. What—"

"You're drunk—act like it!" Raj whispered harshly. "Unless you *want* Moghi to throw you in the canal for bringing fever here! I don't much imagine he'd be real happy about that."

He rose, shoved his chair back, and seized Mondragon's arm to haul him to his feet before the other could protest—or react. And that was another bad sign; Mondragon had the reactions of any trained assassin, quick and deadly. Only tonight those reactions didn't seem to be working.

Raj had always been a lot stronger than he looked—with a month of regular meals he was more than a match for a fevered Tom Mondragon.

"Now, m'ser Tom," he said aloud—not too loudly, he hoped, but loud enough. "I think a breath of air would be a proper notion, ne? 'Fraid m'ser Moghi's drink is a bit *too* good tonight."

There were mild chuckles at that, and no one looked at them twice as Raj half-carried, half-manhandled Mondragon out the door. Which was fortunate, for they both discovered when Mondragon tried to pull away that his legs were not up to holding him.

They staggered out the door, weaving back and forth, Raj sagging under Mondragon's nearly-dead weight. Out the double doors they wove, narrowly avoiding collision with an incoming customer, and down onto the lantern-lit front porch. Down a set of stairs were the tie-ups for small boats, only half of them taken tonight. And pulling up to those tie-ups was a skip poled by a dusky girl in a dark cap. Altair Jones, and no mistaking her.

They were just in time to see Denny catching the line Jones was throwing to him. Light from Moghi's porch-lantern caught her eyes as she stared at them. There was something of a mixture of surprise and shock—yes, and a touch of fear—in the look she gave them.

"I think we need to get this feller home, m'sera," Raj said loudly, praying Jones would keep her wits about her. She might not know him well, but she knew that Mondragon had trusted them to spy for him, and guard his back, and that more than once. He just prayed she'd trust him too, and follow his lead.

She did; playing along with him except for one startled glance. "Fool's been celebratin'?" she snorted, legs braced against the roll of her skip, hands on hips, looking theatrically disgusted. She pushed her cap back on her head with a flamboyant and exaggerated shove. "Ought to let 'im walk home, that I should. Ah, hell, hand 'im over—"

Mondragon was in no shape now to protest the hash they were making of his reputation. He was shaking like a reed in a winter storm, and his skin was tight and hot to the touch, as Jones evidently learned when she reached up to help him down the ladder onto her halfdeck. "Look—you—" was all he managed before another coughing fit took him and Jones got him safely planted. She gave no real outward sign that she was alarmed, though—just a slight tightening of her lips and a frightened widening of her eyes.

"Think we'd better come along, m'sera," Raj continued in what he hoped was a bantering tone of voice, for though they seemed to be alone, there was no telling who had eyes and ears in the shadows or above the canal. "Afraid m'ser is likely to be a handful. Won't like being told what to do." That last was for Mondragon's benefit. While he talked, he stared hard into Jones's eyes, hoping she'd read the message there.

Go along with this—he tried fiercely to project. *I can help*.

"Ye think so?" The tone was equally bantering, but the expression seemed to say that she had understood that silent message. "Well, guess it can't hurt—"

"Right enough then—Denny, give the m'sera a hand with that line—" Raj climbed gingerly down into the skip to where Mondragon sat huddled in misery, as Denny slid aboard, the tie-line in his hand.

"What th' hell—" Jones hissed as soon as they were out of earshot of the bank.

"He's got fever—you got something to keep him warm?"

Without the need to guard her expression, Raj could read her nearly as well as one of his books. First there was relief—*Thank God, it could have been worse, he could have been hurt*—and that was quickly followed by anger and resentment. He couldn't guess at the reasons for those emotions, but that expression was chased almost immediately by stark, naked fear. Then she shuttered her face down again, and became as opaque as canal water. At her mute nod toward the hidey, Raj ducked in and out again, and wrapped the blanket he'd found around Mondragon's shaking shoulders.

Mondragon looked up, eyes full of bleary resentment. "I—" cough "—can take care of—" cough "—myself. Thanks."

Raj ignored him. "First thing, we got to get him back home and in bed. But we gotta make out like's he's drunk, not sick."

Jones nodded slowly; Raj was grateful for her quick grasp of the situation. "Because if people figger he's sick—they figger he's an easy target. Yey. Damn!"

"Will you two leave me *alone?*"

This time Raj looked him right in the eyes.

"No," he said simply.

Mondragon stared and stared, like one of the piers had up and answered him back; then groaned, sagged his head onto his knees, and buried his face in his hands.

"Right," Raj turned back to Jones, swiveling to follow her movements as she poled the skip into the sparse traffic on the Grand. She wasn't sparing herself—Raj could tell that much from what he'd learned poling his raft. Which meant she was trying to make time. Which meant she was worried, too. "Second thing is, we need money. I got some, but not much. How 'bout you? Or him?"

"Some. What fer?" Suspicion shadowed the glance she gave at him as she shoved the pole home against the bottom, suspicion and more of that smoldering anger and fear. *Touchy about money, are we, Jones?*

"Medicine," he said quickly. "Some we send Denny for; people are always sending runners after medicine, 'specially in fever season. Nothing to connect Tom with that."

Raj fell silent for a moment.

"Ye said, 'some'—"

"I'll decide the rest after we get him back—" Raj said slowly, "And I know how bad it is."

Petrescu at last. Up the stairs at water-level they went, stairs that led almost directly to Mondragon's door. Mondragon tried to push them off, to get them to leave him at that door. But when his hands shook so that he couldn't even get his key in the lock, Raj and Jones exchanged a *look*—and Jones took the key deftly away from him.

He complained, bitterly, but weakly, all through the process of getting him into his apartment and into bed in the downstairs bedroom—not even with three of them were they going to try manhandling him up the stairs to the room he usually used. Ominously, though—at least so far as Raj was concerned—he stopped complaining as soon as he was installed there; just closed his eyes against the light, and huddled in his blankets, shivering and coughing. Raj sent Denny out with orders for asprin, menthil-salve, and blueangel; not that he expected the latter to do any good. This wasn't *that* kind of fever. He knew it now; knew it beyond doubting.

"I hope you can afford to lose a night's trade, Jones," he said, pulling her out of the bedroom by main force. "Maybe more—I'll tell you the truth of it. M'ser Tom's in bad shape, and it could get worse.''

''It's just a cold or somethin', ain't it—?'' Her look said she knew damned well that it was worse than that, but was hoping for better news than she feared.

''Not for him, it isn't,'' Raj said, figuring she'd better know the worst of the truth. ''He's not _from_ here, remember? Our germs are gonna hit him, and hit him hard. I know—it happened to me.'' Raj paused in thought. ''Bet he was taking pills before this, ney?''

Jones nodded, slowly.

''And I bet his pills ran out not too long ago. You can't get 'em here, not without connections upriver. You need tech for medicine like that. Same thing happened to me, when I had to hide in the swamp. I caught every damn thing that you could think of.'' Raj shook his head. ''Well, he needs something besides what we can get at the drug-shops. Now listen; when Denny gets back, you rub the salve on his throat and chest, you give him the asprin and a dose of the blueangel. Then you mix him some hot tea with whiskey—make it about half whiskey—and lots of sugar in it—that should help him stop coughing enough to sleep. Looks to me like he needs sleep more than about anything else right now. You stay with him; don't leave him. That might be enough—right now he feels like he wants to die, but he's not exactly in any danger, so long as he stays warm. But—'' Raj paused to think. ''All right, worst case. If he gets worse before I get back—if his fever goes up more—if he starts not bein' able to breathe—''

That was an ugly notion, and hit far too close to home. He steadied his nerves with a long breath of air and thought out everything he was going to have to do and say. What he was going to order Jones to do wasn't going to go down easy. She didn't like being ordered at the best of times, and this was _definitely_ going to stick in her throat. ''—I know maybe more about our friend than you think I do—I'm telling you the best—hell, the _only_ option. If he starts having trouble breathing, you send Denny with a note to that Kalugin. You tell him if he wants his pet Sword alive he better send his doctor. And fast.''

Jones' eyes blazed, and she opened her mouth to protest. Raj cut her short.

''Look, you think *I* want my brother going up there? You think we're in any better shape than Tom is in this town? I dunno what you know about us, Jones, but we got as much or more to lose by this. I dunno if Tom's let on about us, but—''

God, God, the chance! But they owed Tom more than they could pay.

''Look at me—*believe* me, Altair. If Kalugin—any of 'em—ever found out about me 'n Denny, we'd—we'd wish we were dead, that's all. We know things too, and we got nobody but Tom keeping us from getting gobbled up like minnows by the hightowners. Tom they got reasons to keep alive—us—well, you can figure how much anybody'd miss two kids. So trust me, the risk's a lot more on our side; if he gets worse, it's the only way to save him.''

''Damn, Raj—'' she started, then sagged, defeated by his earnestness and her own fear and worry. ''All right. Hell, though—what ye been doin'—I dunno why we'd need a real doctor. Yer as good's any doctor I ever seen—''

''Like bloody hell I am!'' he snapped, more harshly than he intended. He saw Jones wince away, saw her expression chill a little, and hastily tried to mend the breach.

''Look—I'm sorry, I didn't mean the way it sounded— Jones, Altair, I'm scared too—for all of us.'' He managed half a smile when he saw the hard line of her lips soften. ''And you just—stepped on a sore toe, that's all. See, I'd give my arm to be able to go to the College, to learn to be a doctor. And I've got about as much chance of that as your skip has of flying.'' He sighed. ''That's the problem with having things get better, I guess—when I didn't have anything, I didn't want things, 'cause I knew I'd never get 'em. But now I got a little, seems like I want more. Things I got no chance for.''

He hadn't really expected Jones to understand, but to his

surprise, she gave a little wistful glance back toward the bedroom, sighed, and nodded. "I reckon we both got a notion how that feels—" she agreed. "But—I dunno, Kalugin—he's a sherk—that doctor could just as easy poison 'im as cure 'im."

"So I just gave you what to do in worst case, hey? Worry about that when the time comes. Tom's luck with skinning through, he'll be all right. But if not—I'll tell you now—you might just as well chance poison, 'cause if you want Tom alive, you get him a *real* doctor as soon as he starts getting worse—*if* he does-before I make it back."

"Back? From where?" She only now seemed to realize that he wasn't planning on staying.

"I told you, I know this fever—I had it once, too. And Tom needs more'n what we can get from the drug-shop. So I'm going to get the medicine he needs—the one place where I know I can—where I got what saved *me*. The place I spent the last five years. The swamp." He smiled crookedly at her stunned expression.

"How ye gonna get there?" She stammered. "I—"

"I said you had to stay here, didn't I? And keep Denny here to help when he gets back. I'll get in the same way I did the last time. Walk."

He could hardly feel his feet, they were so numb and cold. He was just glad that it wasn't quite egg-season for the dragonelles, or he'd have had to worry about losing toes, instead of just *feeling* like he'd lost them.

He was halfway out to Raver's territory, and he was already regretting the decision he'd made, with the kind of remote regret of one who didn't have any real choice. The pack on his back was large, and heavy; the kind of goods he meant to trade to old May for her 'weeds' tended to be bulky. Blankets didn't compact well, no more did clothing.

The cold was climbing up his legs, and his britches were misery to wear, wet and clinging and clammy, and liberally beslimed with mud and unidentifiable swamp-muck. He'd forgotten how much the swamp stank; it was far worse than the canals. The reeds rustled, but otherwise there wasn't much sound but the wind whistling and the water lapping against what few bits of solid stuff poked up out of the surface.

The wind was cold, and ate through his clothing. And there was a storm brewing, which meant that he'd be soaked before the night was out, even if things went well.

He was half-soaked already. Just because it was possible to walk into the swamp, that didn't mean it was easy. He was just grateful that his memory of the 'trail' was clear; so clear he could find his way in pitch-dark—he was only mud-caked to his knees instead of his waist.

Overhead the clouds blocked stars and thunder rumbled, cloud-shadows taking the last of the light. But now the swamp itself flickered with an eerie phosphorescence, making it almost like dusk out here. There seemed to be more of the glow than there had been before—and a kind of odd, sulfurous, bitter smell he didn't remember as being part of the normal odors. The thunder came again, accompanied by flashes of lightning, and the wind off the sea began to pick up, bending the reeds parallel with the water.

Raj had just enough time for his nose to warn him, then the rain came.

The first fat drops plopped on the back of his neck and trickled icily down his back, adding to his misery. This morning he'd been sure there was no way he could even up the karma between himself and Mondragon. At this point he was beginning to think that the scales just might be tipping the other way.

"Hee *hee* he-he-he! Well, lookee what th' storm washet ep—"

The voice that brayed out of the dark and the rain was one Raj had hoped never to hear again.

"I heerd ye gone townie on us, Raj-boy." The speaker was little more than a dark blot against the phosphorescent water—a *large* blot. "I heerd ye niver come back t' see yer old friends. I heerd ye figger yer better'n us now."

It was Big Ralf, and he had the next segment of the trail

completely blocked. To either side was deep water and dangerous mud—some of it bottomless, sucking mire-pits.

"C'mon, Raj-boy—ain't ye gonna run from Big Ralf? Ain't ye gonna give 'im a race?" Lightning flickered once, twice. The blot shifted restlessly.

Raj fought panic. "Get out of my way, Big Ralf," he shouted over the thunder. "Leave me alone. I never hurt you."

"Ye hurt Big Ralf's feelin's, Raj-boy," the hoarse call came back. "Ye wouldn't play with Big Ralf. Ye sent that Raver t' warn Ralf off, ye did. But Raver, he ain't here now. Now it's jest me an' you."

He could run; he could shed that heavy pack and run back along the safe path until he came to one of the branches. Then he could get into an area he knew better than Ralf, where he could outdistance him and get safe back to town—

Without what he'd come for. And it was just possible that without May's medicine, Tom Mondragon would die, fighting for breath, choking—literally drowning as his lungs filled. The way Raj had almost died.

His knife was in his hand without his really thinking about it, and he slipped the straps of the pack off his shoulders, dropping it to the reed hummock he was standing on. With the feel of the hilt in his hand, his breathing steadied. He wasn't eleven anymore—not thirteen, either. He wasn't armed with nothing but a scrap of glass. He had most of his adult growth now—and a good steel blade in his hands.

"I'm warning you, Ralf—get out of my way."

"Ye gonna make me?"

"If I have to," Raj replied unsteadily; Big Ralf had sloshed a step or two closer, and now his knife seemed all too small. Ralf stood as tall as Raj—and Raj was still standing on a hummock a good foot or more above the underwater surface of the trail.

And Ralf had a knife too; Raj could see the lightning flickering on the shiny surface of the steel. It was ribbon-thin, honed almost to invisibility, but Raj would bet it could leave bleeding wounds on the wind.

Ralf cackled again, and there was no sanity in that sound.
"Ye try, Raj-boy, ye g'won 'n try! Big Ralf don't care. He
c'n play wi' ye live—or he c'n play wi' ye dead."

Raj's nerve almost broke—so before it could give out
altogether, he attacked. Before Ralf had a chance to react, he
threw himself at the bigger man with an hysterical and suici-
dal leap. One thing only in his panicked state he remembered
from his rough-and-tumble lessons with Raver. *'If yer willin'
t' take hurt, boy, ye c'n take anybody's knife away from 'im.'*

So he slashed the open palm of his left hand frantically
down on Ralf's knife—aiming for the blade, not the knife-
hand—hoping to impale his hand on that blade and render it
useless.

His dive off the hummock caught the crazy by surprise.
Raj had always run before—Ralf's twisted mind wasn't ready
for him to attack.

So Raj's half-sketched plan worked better than he hoped.

The point of Ralf's knife sliced into his palm and he
rammed his hand right up to the hilt, the pain splitting his
arm like the lightning was splitting the sky. He screamed, and
closed his fist around the crossguard anyway, wresting it out
of the bigger man's hand. Then, as his feet skidded in the
mud, he fell forward, throwing all of his weight awkwardly
behind an impromptu lunge with his own knife.

Ralf's screams were a hoarse echo of his own as the knife
sunk up to the hilt in his gut. He beat at Raj's head with both
hands; Raj slipped and slid some more, and fell to his knees,
but held to the knife-hilt, ripping upward with it.

Ralf howled and tried to pull himself off the blade, pushing
at Raj. But Raj slipped more, falling underneath the bigger
man, and he lost his balance on the slimy rock of the trail,
falling forward farther onto the knife blade. As thunder crashed,
he collapsed on top of Raj, screams cut off, pinning Raj
under the muddy water.

All of the air was driven from his lungs as the crazy fell
atop him. He tried to fight free but the slimy mud was as
slick as ice under his knees. Then he lost what little purchase
he had, and the knee-deep water closed over his head.

The surface was just inches away from his face—but he couldn't reach it!

He clawed at the twitching thing that held him there; tried to shove it off, but could get no leverage. Raw panic took over; he thrashed and struggled, his lungs screaming for air, his chest and throat afire with the need for a breath. He was caught like a swamp-hopper in a drown-snare. He was going to die, trapped under the body of his enemy—

The mud conspired to hold him down, now sliding under him, now sucking at his limbs. Sparks danced before his eyes, and he wriggled and squirmed and flailed at the air that his hands could reach, but not his head. He had a strange, crystal-clear vision of himself floating lifelessly beside the trail, touched by the morning sun—

Then a last frantic writhe freed him, and he felt himself slip off the trail into the deep water on the right side of it. His head broke the surface, and he gulped the air, great, sobbing heaves of his chest. He reached for and caught a clump of reeds, and pulled himself to the firm trail. He hauled himself back up onto the hummock where he'd left his pack, crying with pain and fear, and gasping for breath, while lightning flashed above him and thunder followed it, nearly deafening him. He clung there with only his right arm, for Ralf's knife still transfixed his hand.

"My *God*, boy—" Raver's eyes glared out at Raj from the shelter of his basket-like hidey. He and May had anchored their rafts and their hideys, side-by-side, on a bit of old wood Raver had driven into the muck of the bottom to use as a safe tie-up.

"Lemme in, Raver," Raj said, dully. His hand felt afire, he was shivering so hard it was only because he was holding his jaw clenched that his teeth weren't rattling. He swayed back and forth, drunk with exhaustion and pain. He could hardly use his arm, much less his wounded hand—it felt like a log of wood. He'd tied up his hand as best he could, but he hadn't done more than stop the bleeding. He knew he was probably falling into shock, but didn't care any more.

"Wait a sec." Raver propped the edge of the basket up with a stick, reached out, and shook May's hidey. "Wake up, ye old witch—it's Raj, an' he's hurt."

"What? What?" The edge of May's basket came up, and she peered out at Raj. For some reason, the sight of her struck him as funny, and he began to laugh hysterically—and couldn't stop.

He was still laughing when they propped the baskets together, like two halves of a shell, and helped him up onto their combined rafts—then, unaccountably, the laughter turned to sobs, and he cried himself nearly sick on May's shoulder.

May held him, wrapping her tattered old shawl about his shoulders and keeping him warm against her. Rain pattered on the baskets, and for the moment, there was no place Raj would rather have been. There was light in here, dim light, given off by some phosphorescent gook they both kept smeared on the inside of the baskets. May's wrinkled face and Raver's weathered one were a heavenly sight.

"Drink this, boy—" When the sobs diminished, and the shivering started again, Raver thrust a bottle into his good hand. "Let the old gal see t' yer hand."

He drank, not much caring what it was, or what germs might be lingering in it. It was harsh, raw alcohol, and it burned his throat and brought more tears to his eyes. He put the bottle down, gasping, then gasped again as May took it from him and poured it liberally over the wound. The clouds were clearing now, and the Moon emerged; you could see it under the edge of the basket. May propped up one side and held the hand in its light, examining it critically.

He had occasion to stifle a cry and seize the bottle back from Raver more than once before she was through with her probing.

"Should be stitched—but I got some stuff on it t' kill th' bugs an' the pain, an keep fever offen it, an keep it from swellin' too much. Ye tied it off right well, don' reckon ye lost too much blood. Ye'll do once I get 'er tied up good. Wha' happened?"

"Ralf," Raj coughed. His throat was still raw from screaming and crying. "He must've seen me; followed me in. Ambushed me." May was smearing something on the wound that first burned, then numbed the pain. Raj recognized it as numbvine sap. Then she reached back into the darkness behind her, locating rags by feel, and bound his hand tightly.

"I settle that one t'morrow." Raver's eyes narrowed.

"You won't have to, Raver."

May looked up into his face with stunned awe; Ralf was the legend of the swampies for viciousness. That *Raj* should have taken him out—

The alcohol had shaken Raj out of his shock, and he was beginning to take account of his surroundings again. The expression on May's face both pleased and obscurely troubled him.

"Well." Raver said. Just that one word, but it held a world of approval.

"Boy, you needin' t' hide again? Ye didn't come crawlin' out here in th' dark an' the' rain fer the fun 'a it." May came right to the point.

That woke him fully—reminded him of his purpose.

"No—no. I'm okay in town—May, I need something from you, one of your 'cures.' I got a sick friend in town, he's got the fever with the coughs and the aches—the one where you can't breathe 'cause your chest starts to fill up—"

"I know it," May nodded, her face becoming even more wrinkled with thought. "Only it don't gen'rally get that bad."

"Except my friend's not from Merovingen."

"Then that's bad, boy, that's *real* bad. He'll die, like as not, 'less ye can get 'im t' take my weeds."

"Look, I brought stuff to trade you—here—" He shrugged out of his pack and passed it to her. "Whatever you want—I got two blankets, a couple sweaters, fishhooks, a knife—"

"Haw, boy, haw! Ye got enough here t' trade me fer every last dose I got!"

"Then give it all to me, May. I got more friends; this fever is startin' to go through town like a fire—more of 'em may get sick. Janists came in town at Festival—been claiming there wouldn't be any plague this year—'' Raj noticed Raver stiffen at that, out of the corner of his eye ''—but I guess they were wrong. You can get more, can't you?''

''Yey, yey; stuff's jest weeds—know where there's a good bit 'a it, still good enuf t' pick. Ain't no cure though—ye know that— ''

''I know; it just keeps you from dying—and feeling like you want to! Remember? I got it first winter I was out here.''

''An' ye c'n get it agin—''

''So I'll keep some for myself. Deal, May?''

''Yey—oh yey, boy, 's a deal.'' She grinned, a twisted, half-toothless grin, as one hand caressed one of the damp blankets. ''This stuff'll make livin' right comfy out here, come winter. Tell ye what—I'll pick all I kin find, dry it up nice. Ye figger ye got need fer more, why jest come on out here—by *daylight* this time, boy!—an' ye bring old May more things t' trade fer.''

''You got yourself a bargain—''

''Ye gotta go back t'night?'' Raver interrupted.

Raj looked out at the swamp and shivered, but nodded reluctantly. ''Got no choice, Raver. My friend's bad sick, and you heard May.''

''Ney, ney—not soaked through like that, an' it gettin' chill. May, pack the boy's sack up. This old man knows the Harbor day *or* night. I got a dry blanket here—you wrap up in't; I'll pole ye back t' the Wharf.''

Raj accepted the shred of a blanket, speechless with gratitude.

Even with the ride to Dead Wharf, he was out on his feet by the time he got to Mondragon's apartment on Petrescu. Even if he could have found a poleboater at this hour, he had nothing to pay him with—all his money and Jones' had all gone into trade-goods for May. He stopped at Fife long enough to boil some tea and get into dry (if dirty) clothing; figuring that a half-hour more-or-less would make little difference in Mondragon's condition. Once dry and warm, he slipped on a waterproofed canvas poncho (the rain had begun again), cast a longing look at his bed, and went out again into the night.

He was ready to drop and staggering like a drunk by the time he got to Mondragon's door—a process that was not aided by the fact that he had to get *down* to water level and *over* to the water-stair (and convince Jones' friends tied up for the night that he was himself) before actually reaching the door. But there was no other choice for him to make; he was *not* up to an argument with the guard on the gated walkway. The stair seemed to go on forever, and the door looked like the portal to Heaven when he finally reached it. He leaned wearily against the lintel and let his fist fall on it.

The door opened the barest crack. "Who's out there?" said a muffled voice.

" 'S me, Jones. Raj. Lemme in before I fall down."

The door opened so quickly he almost did fall in. "Ye get th' stuff?"

"How is he?"

"Sleepin'. Don't *seem* no worse, but I had t' pour a helluva lotta whiskey in 'im t' get 'im t' sleep."

Raj slogged the few steps into the sitting room, let his pack fall to the floor, peeled his poncho over his head and dropped it beside it. "I got the stuff. Where's Denny?"

"Sleepin' too, upstairs. I figgered if I needed 'im I could wake 'im up. And it's no bad idea havin' him bedded down across the door up there, ney? The least, somebody forces it, he c'n scream his lungs out. May kill a boarding party by scarin' 'em to death!"

Raj made his way lead-footed into Mondragon's bedroom (you *don't* try and walk silently around an ex-assassin!), and stood in the dark listening to the sound of his breathing. A little wheezy—a little bubbly—but not bad. He'd gotten back well in time; there would be no need for a "real" doctor.

Satisfied, he dragged himself back out. "Boil me some tea-water, would you, Jones? I gotta get this stuff measured right—"

As she trotted back to the kitchen, he sat right down on the soft, warm carpet beside the pack and began taking out parcels of herbs wrapped in rags, identifying them by smell, eye, and sometimes taste. One or two could be tricky to use—too much and you got unwanted side-effects. Although—

He chuckled a little, and set aside a particular bundle. Wiregrass was to bring down fever; but a double-dose was somewhat narcotic. One danger was that Mondragon might get to feeling *too* frisky and try to get out and about before he should. A double-dose would take care of that problem— Mondragon would be seeing fuzzy—and be more than a little happy—for as long as Raj wanted.

"Jones," he called softly, "Think you can find me a couple big jars or bowls or something? I need something to put this stuff in besides a rag."

"Lemme look." She clattered down the stairs a moment later. "These do?" She brought him a pair of canisters, the kind tea came in, with a vermin-proof lid.

"Perfect."

May had gone by "handful" measurement—but it was a very precise handful. Although it was a little awkward to work one-handed, Raj weighed the herbs in his palm, adding or subtracting a few leaves at a time, until he was satisfied, then crushed what he'd selected carefully into the tin, trying to get it as fine as possible. Wiregrass for fever—and to keep Mondragon in his bed; there wasn't any redberry bush bark— but that was all right, it was the same as asprin and they had that. Marshcress for the cough; jofrey-leaf for the chest (the important part); tinwisle for the sneezing. And two others, amfetida and threadstem; May would never say what they were for, just swore they were important. Raj shrugged and added them—they wouldn't hurt, and May might be right.

He crushed the resulting canisterful yet again, until he had a mixture as fine as the best tea, then crushed a second bunch of wiregrass into the second canister. "Jones, that water ready?"

"Yey." She must have seen how tired he was, and brought the pan of hot water and spoon and cup to him. "Show me—"

"I intended to—you're going to have to do this from now

on. Look, exactly two flat spoonfuls of this for every cup of water—you can put it in the cup or the pan, don't matter which.'' He measured two spoonfuls into the cup and poured the still-bubbling water on it. ''This stuff—'' He picked up the canister of pure wiregrass ''—it's for fever, but a bigger dose gets you higher'n the Angel. Makes you happy and tends to keep you where you've been put. I figure we want to keep Mondragon where he is, ney?'' She grinned a slow, comprehending grin and nodded. ''Right, so I'm taking another half a flat spoonful of this stuff and adding it. You want to keep him down, you do the same. Now you let it sit for as long as it takes you to count to a hundred—''

He concentrated on the dull throbbing of his hand to keep from nodding off while the mixture steeped. He noticed with a tired little chuckle Jones's lips moving silently as she marked off the time.

''It ready now?''

''It's ready. Here—'' He handed the cup to her while he got himself slowly and painfully to his feet. ''Let's wake him up.''

Jones brought a candle with her, and lit the oil-lamp beside the door across from Mondragon's bed. *Some* of his instincts, at least, were still holding; he was awake and wary as soon as the light touched his eyes.

''Got som'thin' fer ye, layabout,'' Jones said cheerfully— real cheer; Raj was touched at her implied trust. ''Raj here says it'll fix ye right up.''

''Oh—'' Mondragon blinked, but before he could continue, began coughing, great racking coughs that shook his entire body.

''Tom—'' Raj had never used Mondragon's first name to his face before, but it slipped out. ''I mean, m'ser Mondragon—''

''Tom is fine,'' Mondragon said wearily when the coughing fit was over.

''Tom, I've had what you've got—honest, this will help. And if you *don't* drink it, you could get a lot sicker. Believe me—I almost died. I swear to you, it'll help. On Takahashi Honor, I swear.''

Mondragon gave him a long, appraising look—then wordlessly took the cup from Jones, and drank it down in two gulps.

''*Feh*—that—is—*vile!*'' he choked, face twisted in distaste. ''This better work fast, because if it doesn't, I'm not drinking more!''

''That's more words in a row without coughing than you've managed yet tonight—'' Raj pointed out. ''We'll sugar it next time.'' Without being asked, Jones brought the whiskey and a pair of asprin tablets, and looked inquiringly at Raj.

''Good notion—'' he approved, thinking that a bit more whiskey wouldn't hurt and might help the wiregrass keep Mondragon in his bed. ''Tom—I hate to ask, but is there anything around here I could use for a bandage? I love old May, but I hate to think where her rags have been.''

''Bathroom,'' said Mondragon around the asprin, and: ''I'll get it,'' said Jones.

Mondragon sagged back against his pillows, eyes going unfocused again. Raj carefully unwrapped his hand. The numbvine was working quite well—and May had included a bit of it and some other things in his pack for when this dose wore off.

The wound looked bad, red and swollen, but it was sealing shut and Raj knew by the look that it wasn't infected yet.

''That's a knife-wound.'' Mondragon was staring at the wounded hand, surprised and shocked alert.

''It is. Tom—I know you think I'm a kid, and you're right sometimes—but you're not right all the time. I had to go into the swamp for that stuff—May was the only place short of a real doctor where I was going to find what you needed. A man tried to stop me—''

Now Mondragon looked alarmed and wary, and Raj could have kicked himself for not thinking. Of course, Mondragon would suspect those enemies of his of trying to follow Raj—

''No, no,'' he hastened to assure him. ''Nothing to do with

you, he was a crazy. I had to fight him to get through. That's
where I got this, and lost my own knife."

"Was?"

"Was. And don't you ever tell Denny I killed a man. He
wasn't the first—but I don't want Denny to know about
that."

"You have a reason?" Mondragon was staying focused,
which rather surprised Raj, given the amount of whiskey and
wiregrass he had in him, not to mention the fever.

"Because—" Raj looked up from his hand, and he knew
his eyes and mouth were bitter. "He'll think he has to be like
me. Next thing you know, he'll go out looking; he'll either
get himself killed—or he'll kill somebody, and for all the
wrong reasons. And that would be worse than him getting
killed. I remember more than just you from home—I remember what some of the younger Swords were like when they
were my age, and Denny's. They started like that—first each
one trying to out-risk the other—then it got worse. I don't
think he'd ever turn out like them—but I'm not taking any
chances on it."

Mondragon nodded, slowly; relaxing and letting himself
give way to the drugs and the alcohol. "I think maybe I have
been underestimating you."

"Only sometimes. You getting sleepy yet?"

He coughed hard again, then got it under control. "Getting
there—and feeling a great deal less like death would be
welcome."

"That's the whole idea—Tom—" An idea occurred to him,
and he decided he wanted to broach it while Mondragon was
in a generous—and intoxicated—mood. "Could you do me a
favor? When you feel more like talking?"

"Maybe," Mondragon replied wearily, obviously wishing
Raj would leave him alone, as Jones came in behind Raj with
clean bandage, salve and tape. "What's the favor?"

Raj felt his face flame with embarrassment. He hated to
ask in front of Jones, but this might be his only chance.
"Could you—could you tell me some time—how to—how

to get a girl—to—to like you?" *And what to do with her after you do*—, he thought, but did not say.

"Oh, mercy—" Mondragon shut his eyes and leaned his head back on his pillow, his mouth twitching. Raj had the uncomfortable suspicion that he was trying to keep from laughing.

"If you'd rather not—"

"Later, Raj. We'll see about it later." Mondragon opened one eye, and gave him a not-unsympathetic wink, then coughed again, harder this time, and lost his amusement as a shudder of chill shook him. "Surely it can wait?"

"Sure—sure—" Raj hastily backed out of the bedroom, taking the bandages from Jones as he passed her. By the time she joined him, he was sitting on the couch, trying to rebandage his wound one-handed.

"Here, ye fool, let me do that." She took the things away from him and undid his clumsy work. He leaned back into the soft upholstery and allowed her to do what she wanted. "How much of this stuff of yours he gonna need?"

"Just what's in the canister."

"Ye brung back a lot more'n that—"

"I know. I could catch it again, or Denny, or you. There's likely to be a use for it before a cold snap kills the fever. May says I can come trade her for more, anyway."

"Ye know—this *could* be worth somethin'."

"The thought crossed my mind—but I was mostly doing it for Tom."

"I owe ye one, Raj," she said softly, earnestly.

He relaxed and shut his eyes, feeling tired and bruised muscles go slack. "Don't go talking karma at me, you renegade Adventist."

"Damnfool hightowner," she jeered back.

"Not any more. Just one of Gallandry's clerks." Fatigue made irrelevant thoughts swim past, and one of them caught what little was left of his attention. A thought and a memory of a couple days past.

What the hell. "Jones—it's 'aren't' when you're talking about 'you' or more than one person, and 'isn't' all the rest of the time. Exept when you're talking about yourself, then it's 'am not.' Got it? Think that'll help?''

He cracked an eyelid open to see her staring open-mouthed at him. ''How did ye—''

''Noticed you fishing for it the other day, figured nobody'd ever given you the rule. Hard to figure things out if nobody tells you the rules. Rat could help you better'n I could. She was an actress for a while, and she knows all the tricks. She could make—'' (yawn) ''—Kalugin sound like a canalsider, or a canalsider sound like—'' (yawn) ''—Kalugin.'' His lids sagged, and he battled to stay awake.

''Ain't nobody put it quite that way before—'' she said thoughtfully, while Raj stifled another yawn and a giggle. ''Huh. Damn, this's a bad 'un. Looks like it hurts like hell. What'd ye do here, ram yer hand down on the point?''

''Had to, he outweighed me by about twice; was the only way I could think to get it away from him.'' He ran his right hand up to check the knots on the back of his head and encountered his not-too-nice hair. And remembered—

''Oh, *hell!*''

''What's the matter? I hurt ye?'' Jones looked up, startled.

''There's no food in the house, I need a bath worse than I ever did in my life, all the clothes are filthy and *have* to be washed and I don't have a copperbit for any of it! I spent every last coin I had on trade-goods for May! Oh, *hell!*'' He squeezed his eyes shut to stop their burning, but a few, shameful tears born of exhaustion and frustration escaped to embarrass him. To have gone through this whole night only to have run up against *this*—

''Ne—not to get aslant—'' Jones still had his hand, and he managed to get enough control of himself to crack open his eyes to look at her. She was smiling broadly, and pointedly not looking at his tears. ''I reckon Tom owes ye a good bit—we got food here, we got hot water an' soap. Ye want, I can pole ye back to Fife when Denny wakes up, get yer things, bring it all back here. Given that hand, I reckon I could help ye with the clothes, even. Ye just be damn sure not to waste nothin'. That suit?''

Relief turned his muscles to slush and he sagged back. "More than suits—"

"Ye got that thinking look again."

"You get most of your work at night, right?"

She looked more than a little uncomfortable, but nodded.

"We work days. So—if you wanted, we could stay here just long enough for him to get better. Or—hell, half the town's sick; you could take a note to Gallandry saying *we* are, and we could even spell you in the daytime that way. Ancestors! The way I feel right now it wouldn't even be a lie! I figure he should be getting better in four, five days, a week, tops. We watch for trouble while you're out, whenever. We can feed him too, make sure he takes the medicine; keep him from going out when he isn't ready to."

"And you get?"

"Food and hot baths. I know damnsure Tom can afford to eat better than we can." He grinned; wearily, his bruised facial muscles aching. "You'll have to talk him into covering the pay we'd lose, though. Hell, Jones, you know we can't afford losing pay any more than you can."

"I know he trusts you." She looked back to the hand she held, and finished taping it up carefully. "I 'spect after tonight ye've proved it out. We got weapons enough, 'tween the two of us. An' if I don't show up for too long, it's gonna look funny. We don't dare let anybody guess he ain't okay. All right; ye do that." She sniffed, her mouth quirking a little contemptuously. "Hell, the way he throws his money around he'll cover ye if I say."

"We'll cook and clean up after ourselves."

"Ye damn sure better, 'cause I ain't gonna—" She looked up from her bandaging to see he'd fallen completely asleep, wedged into the corner of the couch. His head was sagging against the couch cushions, and he'd gone as limp as a loaf of watersoaked bread. She chuckled, and went to find him a blanket.

Rif glanced around at the crowd in Hoh's. It was pretty satisfactory for a weeknight. Tomorrow the place should be packed. She grinned at her partner, and Rat grinned back, throwing in an unexpected descant harmony.

Damn! Been practicin' that on th' sly! Rif grinned harder in appreciation. *Sounds right fine—* She glanced around the bar to see how the customers were taking it.

Well, "Fever Season" was a weirdling enough tune, and with that lost-soul wailing added to it—the marks were shivering, pretending it wasn't getting to 'em, and gulping down their beer like it was last chance before Retribution. Hoh was gonna love it. Probably ask 'em to do it every set from here on in. And Rat would nod and say something hightown and noncommittal, and they'd sing what they damned well pleased, same as always.

Then over Rat's shoulder, she saw Hoh's boy, Mischa, standing in the hallway and signaling frantically. *Cut it short— trouble, and it's got your name on it.*

She nodded understanding, and passed the signal on to Rat with a quirk of the eyebrows and a jerk of her chin.

They wrapped it up; packed up their instruments and headed for the back hall, Mischa uncharacteristically silent.

"What—" Rat began, then saw.

Just inside the back door stood Black Cal, all six-odd feet of him—wheezing and nearly bent over with coughing, and glaring like he was ready to bite Rif in two.

"I thought you said you'd taken care of this!"

FEVER SEASON
(REPRISED)

C.J. Cherryh

Jones waited, that was the only thing to do, perched herself on a straight chair in the corner and shut her eyes, half-sleeping, the way she would on canalside, waiting on a fare . . . only it was on toward dawn and Del and Min, who would have come in after her to tie-up last night, would be casting off to go about their business in an hour or so and leaving her skip to whatever came along—couldn't expect a thing else. Had to get moving soon.

But whenever she looked at Mondragon in the lamp-light, whenever he waked her with one of his coughing fits, she liked the look of it less and less.

The last one he got choked on, and when she handed him a cup of water, he was too far gone to manage it himself, slopped it all over and got the sheets wet when she tried to help him and he broke out coughing in the middle of a drink.

"Damn," he had tried to say, but it had come out half-strangled. And after that he just sort of fell back and was gone again.

And the boys went on sleeping, Raj done in with his hand and Denny sleeping like a lump, whatever. *Could've damn well choked,* she thought in panic. And then thought back to a time she had had the coughs and managed, that was all; a

body just managed. If it got no worse it was all right, and Raj
had him drugged, that was why he couldn't fend for himself,
damn heavy dose and all that whiskey.

"No," he murmured then. "No."

And broke up in coughing, deep, painful-sounding coughs
that were doing no good. It hurt all the way to her gut.

But it stopped after a moment. He lay there with his eyes
half-open, made a weak movement of his hand. Let it fall.

"You need something?" Jones asked.

"Home?" he asked.

"Yey, you're home. Right." Her heart sped in panic. She
got up and carefully, because Mondragon could knock her
right across the room, put her hand on his forehead. "Oh,
damn, you're *burning*."

"What day?"

"What day is it? Wensday. No, Thursday. Why's it matter?"

He grimaced strangely as if he was facing into the sun.
Coughed and muffled it.

"You want a drink?"

He shut his eyes. There had gotten to be a rattle in his
breathing. She brushed back the hair that was stringing down
into his face. Patted him helplessly and went and sat down
again, hands clenched between her knees.

Her own nose ran. She wiped it on her sleeve. But that was
what a body got from being a damn fool, out in the harbor,
an ache like fire across her shoulders and up her arm where
she had worked the fuel pump, and bruises about the armpit
where the tiller had battered her and down her leg where she
had had her foot braced against the strain. Ordinary aches.
What had got its claws into Mondragon was what Raj said,
the hard stuff.

Her mama had died of fever. Retribution Jones, that nothing else could stop, not weather, not the harbor waves, not
any no-good in the dark ways . . . had choked her life out in
her arms. And there had been no cure. No blueangel, not a
thing else she had tried, a scared kid and caught between her
mama's order not to leave the skip and the knowledge that
her mama was dying, in a place where the two-legged scav-

engers might not wait till a body was dead before moving in.
She had known the danger to her mama if she left her. She
had known that for sure. And made the wrong choice, followed her mama's orders and ended up trying to keep her
mama breathing all one long, long night. And lost.

Leave her skip down there with no one to watch it, that
was asking to get it pilfered. Lose the gun . . . that was damn
near as bad as all the rest of it put together.

Stay here with her skip below—that was saying to everyone on the canals that Mondragon was here, that something
was odd. And gossip got sold, by them as had no scruples.

Have her skip tailed off with Del Suleiman— Possible,
but the same problem: every one of Mondragon's enemies
who knew they were linked would start wondering and asking.

Safest thing for him, dammit, was her on the canals, every
day and dark, same schedule, close as she could make it.

But if the fever got worse, if he went off his head— If he
went crazy like in the nightmares—

The boys might not be able to handle him. *She* might not.
Her mama had split her lip for her, and loosened a tooth, and
never known it. Retribution had had a good right hand. But
mama was nothing to what Tom Mondragon knew how to do
if he woke up *not* knowing where he was.

She wiped her mouth with a sleeve that smelled of oil and
harbor, and stared at Mondragon with a despair that did not
want to reckon of the worse possibility—that the situation
was more than they could handle.

She went over to him again and knelt down by him and
shook at him. "Mondragon," she said. "You was with
Kalugin. You was on that boat. What did Kalugin say t' ye?
What was ye doing, that ye didn't come home?"

Because there was Kalugin in the middle of it somehow. It
was from Kalugin's hands that her partner had come back like
this, desperate and fevered, having sent a message, Raj had
told her, to them and not to her.

It was not the first time she had asked him those same
questions. But Mondragon had sworn there was no problem.
Between trying to cough his lungs up. It had been an errand
he wanted Raj to do.

After he had damned well been missing through the night and most of the day.

"Mondragon? Ye going to tell me?"

"No," he said, but not like he was talking to her. His arm came up, hard, and she flung herself aside and down below the rim of the mattress for a second, till the arm fell and he twisted aside, making havoc of the sheet and blankets. She grabbed them on the retreat and pulled them back again, him with them, and tucked the edges under. Which caught one arm, if not the other. "No," he said.

"You shut up!" she snapped at him. "Damn ye, lie still, ye damn fool, ye damn near hit me!"

"Jones?" he mumbled, as if he knew where he was again. "Jones?" And the coughing bent him double again on his side.

"What'd Kalugin want, damn ye? Where you been, ye come home like this?"

More coughing. He could not get it stopped. Jones reached after the cup and held it for him and held his head up, heart pounding in fear.

He managed to drink. The spasm eased, and he lay still when she let his head down, all curled up and quiet. She wanted the answer, dammit, but talking made him cough and the spasms put her all too much in mind of how her mother had died.

" 'S all right," he managed to whisper finally, staring off past her, eyes half-closed. " 'S all right, no trouble."

"Ye're a damn liar! Are ye *safe* here? Is anyone looking for ye?"

That jolted him into thinking. She saw the rapid flicker of his eyes in the lamplight, glassy as they were. "Be all right," he whispered. "Be all right, Jones."

"You want me to go ask Kalugin?"

"No!" That came out harsh, out loud, and he coughed again. "Oh, damn, let me die."

Joke, that was. She was sure. She sat back down in her chair and clenched her hands till they ached.

WAR OF THE UNSEEN WORLDS

Leslie Fish

It was coming on night as Jones tied up outside Moghi's, fingers fumbling in the chill shadows that fell early this time of the year. Cold, and due to get colder, and after steaming hot all day. The sky threatened rain for the night, probably another steam-bath fog tomorrow. Rotten weather, rotten season, rotten Merovingen anyway.

A familiar whistle tickled quietly at the edge of hearing.

Jones lifted her head and looked around slowly. Aw, not again. Not now.

It was.

Long dark hair held back with a kerchief-headband, big dark eyes, sharp features, hungry-hawk look and all. Rif leaned against a wall, half fading into it in her dark hair and cloak, points of metal twinkling faintly at her belt and boot-tops. She looked as if she'd put in a hard day or two, but she was smiling. Damn that smile.

"Go 'way," Jones snapped. "Don' want none o' yer business t'night."

"Ain't for tonight," Rif promised, gliding away from the wall. Her voice was shaped to that quiet, carrying pitch— aimed at Jones' ears only. "I wanta take you up on that offer from Festival. Take me an' my harp an' some . . . little things . . . around town tomorrow.''

Jones hitched her shoulders higher, remembering that little trip last Festival, and her too-reckless promise afterward. "Sure, an' how many holes 'm I gonna get shot in my boat this time? No thanks. Go 'way.'' Besides the risks—and with Rif, who could tell what those were—the work might take all day. When would she sleep, or keep watch on Mondragon?

"Hey, I paid all right, didn' I?'' Rif crouched beside the skip, her cloak making a pool of darker shadow on the wharf. Her trained singer's voice coaxed so sweetly, it was hard to see the hidden hooks in the words. "It ended up right, after all. Why'd ye change yer mind?''

Jones glared at her, angry with raised and dashed hopes, tired enough to be a little reckless. "All that damned trouble— the hole in my boat an' the stink after, an' I don't just mean that stuff in the water—an' fer what? You said you were gonna kill the fever in the water, ney?''

Rif flinched, then rolled her eyes skyward. "This again?'' she muttered to herself. Then, louder: "Shitfire, all I said was 'no Plague'—an' there's *been* no Plague! It's just the Crud, for Ja— Lordsake. Nobody dies of the Crud!''

"Just my man, maybe!'' The words slipped out before Jones could catch them. She tried to snatch them back, and choked on a sudden, explosive sob. *Damn! Tired, worried, miserable—now I'm getting careless too!*

"Aww . . .'' Rif edged closer, voice gone soft and kindly. "How bad's he got it? How long? Y'had a doctor see 'em? Got medicine?''

Jones nodded quickly, gulping back treacherous tears. "H-he's no worse, maybe a little better . . .'' And maybe not. Raj was good at nursing, and May's herbs had proved good too—so far. Still, how much could they really do? *No worse, but no real change . . .*

"Well, there.'' Rif slid a comforting arm around Jones' bent shoulders. "So, he'll get over it soon. Just the Crud.''

"But it's been near a week!'' *Shut up*, Jones kicked herself again. Damn that woman's kindness, loosening tongues. ''. . .

An' he's from out o' town, not used to it . . .'' Yes, that was the worst: not knowing where his body's weaknesses were, whether he could survive the Crud, if May's herbs and Raj's care would help at all or had only slowed the inevitable.

"Hey, I know this really *good* doctor." Rif squeezed her shoulder, a bit absently. "She c'n cure damn-near anything. One more patient won't hurt . . ."

"What'm I supposed to' pay 'er with?" Jones muttered, gouging tears out of her eyes. A fool's question: it meant she was seriously weighing Rif's offer, asking the price.

"Don' worry 'bout that," Rif soothed. "Where's yer man staying?"

Careful! Jones froze, balanced on the knife's edge. Tell Rif where Mondragon was, and maybe she'd sell the knowledge. Then again, Rif most likely didn't know *who* Mondragon was, or would much care. Besides, she wanted a favor, some more work done—and wanted it bad.

Take her doctor, take her job . . . And you know what some of her work is.

''. . . *And who some of her friends are.*

Rif's doctor just might be good enough to guarantee that Tom Mondragon survived.

"Petrescu. South-east corner, top o' the waterline-stairs," Jones gave in. "Got a kid there, watchin' 'im . . . Hey, you know Raj?"

Rif laughed. It sounded like the first good laugh she'd had in days. "Right," she yukked and gasped. "Oh hell, yes, I know that kid. Hell yes, everything's gonna be all right."

"Ye wouldn' laugh if it was *yer* friend sick," Jones grumbled, covering her retreat.

"Could be worse, believe me." Rif sobered instantly, eyes looking on something far off, out of sight. "You could have a sick enemy. Or . . . ally."

Jones barely heard, digging out her coins and counting them. Plenty there: enough for whatever was on the fire tonight at Moghi's. Her belly rumbled at the thought. Eat now, go to work after. Maybe buy some punk-charcoal and run another batch of fuel-brew through the kettle tonight.

Bundle up beside the stove and keep warm, maybe catch some sleep by Mondragon's bedside in the slack hours after midnight. And tomorrow . . .

"When an' where do I meet ye tomorrow?" she asked, resigned.

Rif waited a moment, glanced back down the hallway, then rapped twice at the featureless door. Pause, then three knocks more. Wait and listen.

Footsteps within padded close. A pinprick of light gleamed for an instant through a tiny hole in the wood, then shadowed, then gleamed again. The door swung open.

"Come to help us pack?" Rattail asked, giving her partner a look that suspected otherwise.

"Not exactly." Rif slipped inside, pushed the door shut and relocked it. "Uh, m'sera, I got another job for ye."

In the room beyond, a short gray-haired woman paused with a half-folded shirt in her hand, and rolled a disbelieving eye at Rif. "Rafaella," she sighed, not quite yet in exasperation, "You know we have to finish this tonight."

"Well, there really ain't that much. Rat could do it up while ye'r out."

It was Rattail's turn to roll her eyes. "If you think you're gonna leave me with—" she started.

"It's important," Rif plowed on. "Y'know I wouldn' haul y'away from this if it weren't. Somebody's sick, bad."

The older woman finished folding the shirt and slapped it down on a pile of clothes. "I can't go to every sick person in the city. That's one reason why we started the school, remember? Go to Yarrow when she finishes class."

"Ah, this is more'n just a sick-call. It's gonna need a . . . good political eye, I think." Rif chewed her lip a moment, then looked to Rattail. "It's Altair Jones' man—and a friend o' Raj."

Rattail raised both eyebrows. "What's the kid's connection with Jones?" she asked. "I hadn't heard about this."

"Dunno yet, just that Raj's keeping watch on Jones' man. That's prob'ly where he's been all week. Besides . . ." Rif turned back to the older woman. "I been trying t'get you an' Raj together, ever since I found out he's got a secret wish t'be a doctor. This is yer only chance t' check him over, see if he's right for the school."

Rattail opened her mouth, then shut it again, shrugged, looked away.

The gray-haired woman rubbed a brown-sleeved wrist across her forehead, and frowned at Rif. "I really appreciate the recruiting," she grumbled. "But at this late date . . ."

"How long could it take? He's over at Petrescu. Old Min's skip could take us there fast,. nobody t'see." Rif flicked another glance at Rattail. "She's tied up under the bridge here right now, ain't she?"

"Yes," Rattail admitted. "I don't suppose anybody'd notice or recognize Doc in this light, not down on the water . . ." She grinned wickedly. " 'Specially not if you lent her that dark cloak of yours."

Rif shrugged, yielding the point. It wasn't worth arguing about. "Right. And you could finish the packin' and mind the store while we're gone."

The gray-haired doctor rocked back and forth on her toes, balanced, considering. "Suppose something goes wrong, any little thing that keeps me from getting back here, or on the ship tomorrow? We're so close now, Rif . . . There's so much more to this, to be honest, than one man's life or one boy's career."

"M'sera . . ." Rif raised her right hand as if taking an oath. "If ye're stopped somehow, going or coming back or whatever, I swear I'll take the package upriver myself. Just tell me where."

The woman looked doubtful, but stopped her indecisive rocking. "And what if you get stopped too? It has to be on that ship tomorrow morning."

"Then I'll do it," Rattail sighed, throwing a poisonous what-are-you-getting-me-into look at Rif. "I suppose I can get the details from Yarrow, right?"

"Oh, all right," the doctor yielded. She went to a cabinet and took out a large, dark, oilcloth bag. The contents clinked as she picked it up. "I just hope this man's better tempered than the last one you dragged me off to see. Such a bitching, bullying, mean-mannered oaf I never met in my life."

Rattail whooped with laughter.

Rif shuddered. "Could've been worse," she muttered. "He could've been . . . really upset."

Rattail was still laughing as the other two padded out the door and down to Mintaka's tie-up.

A little after midnight Jones tied up under the water-stair at Petrescu and climbed to the door at the stairs-end, walking slowly, saving strength. Not much sleep last night, long day ahead, nobody but the kids to watch Mondragon while she was gone, and even that meant that Raj or Denny had to miss a day's work. Excuses could be made, of course, this being fever season. Money was another problem, but remembering how well Rif paid she could make it up to the boys on her own. Persuading them shouldn't be too hard.

It was Raj who let her in. He rolled an eye at Jones, shushed her and pointed to where Denny lay asleep on a tangle of blankets in a corner. He padded back to the bedroom. A quick glance as she came in showed Mondragon likewise sleeping, near-buried under more blankets. At least his breathing didn't sound too bad.

Raj filled the cup with reeking herb-mix and set it aside, watching as Jones closed the door. "M'sera," he whispered, "Did you really send that doctor that came last night with Rif?"

Jones froze, hand still on the door. "When's that?"

"A little after dark. Rif said you'd sent her, so I let them in. Just the same, I didn't think I should use those medicines until I checked with you."

"Yey, I sent 'em." Jones pulled away from the door, tiptoed to the bed and spent a long moment looking down at Mondragon's sleeping face. No better, no worse. Damn, his hair looked so pretty, spread out on the pillow every which way . . . "That Rif moves fast."

"She's all right. Just her friends . . . I don't know." Raj

picked up a small dark glass jar and a smaller box of hand-pressed pills. "I can use these, then?"

Jones read the labels, shrugged. Probably just what they seemed to be, and expensive if so. Rif still wanted her work done. "Go ahead. Cain't hurt. What'd the doctor say?"

"That he'd be all right. That May's herbs are good for this. That . . ." Raj caught his lip in his teeth for a moment. "That I'd make a good doctor, and . . . and there's a way."

Damn again. Jones sat down on the chair and leaned her back against the wall. Damn that Rif, getting another hook into her, this time through the kid. Didn't have to threaten people, no; just find a way to offer their dearest dreams. "Say it."

"There's a school for doctors, very new, very quiet. Won't even cost much. I'd just have to . . . take an oath, and no breaking it."

To the Janes. Jones closed her eyes, seeing where this led. No, the Janes hadn't been idle these past weeks. A new medical school, and Ancestors knew what else, and now they were recruiting. *Raj, and maybe even me.*

If so, they worked with a light, deft touch.

"Jones?" Raj's hunger stood in his eyes. So did a solid fear of what he could be touching. "You know it's what I want, what I'm good at. But I don't know . . . these people."

He'd said it. He'd guessed. Jones took a deep breath and opened her eyes again. "They done no harm as I can see. Maybe some good, even. Lord knows, there's worse ye c'n fall in with."

Raj ducked his head, shivering. No need to mention what worse, or who. "I know. Believe me, I *know*. And I don't want to deal with religious fanatics, ever again. But . . ."

Jones felt obliged to add: "I ain't seen 'em push hard on anyone yet. Ye could always back off, draw the line, if y'wanted to." *Like I could've backed off this job. And won't.*

"Well, that's one more thing to keep quiet from . . . hightown." Raj smiled a too-old, cynic grin. "Snatching up a few fish, right under Kalugin's wing."

"Shit," Jones whispered, seeing what the boy had guessed

before she did. Blackmail could work both ways. She could sell Rif, and Rif's friends, to Kalugin. And she hadn't thought of it.

Then again, Rif—and her partner—could be very bad enemies to make. Lord and Ancestors only knew what kind of enemies the Janes could be.

Or what kind of friends, if Anastasi Kalugin should ever decide, for some reason, that he no longer had any use for Tom Mondragon. Or one Altair Jones.

She badly wished that Mondragon was awake, and well enough to deal with a long serious talk.

But that just wasn't the case now. "I cain't stay. Got a job this mornin', an' it may take all day. C'n ye stay here, miss a day's work? I'll make it up t'ye."

"I know. Rif already told me." Raj shrugged. "I'll have Denny tell them I'm sick. Enough people are, they won't think anything of it."

Damn Rif! One step ahead of her again. Jones rubbed her forehead in exasperation and levered herself to her feet. *Is everybody else here super-smart*, she wondered, *or am I just a fool?*

Altogether, Jones was in a sour mood as she came poling through the dawn-pearled mist to Fife corner. The thinning fog revealed Rif's familiar silhouette coming toward her tie-up—and then a second figure, behind her. Jones watched, pole held cautiously ready, as the two came onto her skip.

There was Rif, dressed in middling-good musicians' work-clothes—dark red with a little tinselly jewelry—under her familiar faded-indigo cloak, along with the same shoulder-slung bag that might contain anything. It certainly contained seeds today, and most probably her gun and flat-harp.

There was a chunky little woman dressed in brown, carrying a big cloth bundle and a small bag of knitting, gray hair tied in a simple bun, kindly unremarkable face behind wire-rimmed spectacles.

"Who's this?" Jones asked, trying not to sound rude, as

Rif helped the older woman into the skip. "Thought the deal was f'r just one passenger."

"This is m'sera—" Rif started.

"Fern Johanssen," said the little woman, holding out her hand. Kindly, unremarkable voice too. "We'll pay extra."

"Going upriver to catch a ship," Rif explained. "North Flat, east bank docks."

Jones stopped to wonder about that. The only docks on North Flat were three plain piers designed for grain-haulers; boats that serviced the wetland-rice farmers on the long river island north of the city. She hadn't thought any passenger boats put in there.

She remembered that the last ship Rif had taken her to meet was up the Greve Fork again far outside Merovingen. Rif's friends didn't seem to want to come down near New Harbor at all. Maybe the docks there were a little too well watched for their taste.

"She's gotta board early," Rif went on. "That's why I wanted ye for a morning-job. . . . Besides, I gotta work t'night, too."

"Sit down, then," Jones shrugged, turning to pull out the ties. There was cold comfort in knowing that Rif wouldn't get much sleep either. There was uncomfortable familiarity in hauling Rif straight upstream to the river again. "We goin' t'pick up any cargo this time?" Careful, careful.

"Ney, just leave some off." Rif settled in the bow and fumbled in her bag, raising a twang of flat-harp strings.

Jones hesitated a moment, considering the full jerry-can of homemade engine-fuel sitting in the hidey. She could make more, cheap enough, but not quickly; her brew-kettle could hold only so much at any one time. She preferred to save it for emergencies if she could. "I c'n pole up there in less'n an hour. Traffic's light, and so's the load."

Rif glanced pointedly toward the engine, gave Jones a hard look, then a questioning glance at the other passenger. M'sera Johanssen shrugged, reached into her small bag and took out a nearly-finished sweater, a ball of coarse brown yarn and a crochet hook. Rif shrugged too. "Try to make it less," she said, leaning against the gunwale.

Jones stabbed the pole into the water and jigged the skip out into the Grand. There was a lot she wanted to ask Rif about, maybe yell at her about, and she couldn't do it with this nice little old lady sitting here crocheting a sweater. Damn. Well, there was always the return trip. Meanwhile, she took it out on the pole and the water, and the skip made good headway against the current

The sun rose gamely, hoisting the mist into a barely-clouded sky, and a light wind nipped through the canals without snapping. It looked fair to being a decent morning: bright, almost cool, not too windy. Not too noisy, this time of day, either, and the breeze from uptown blew away much of the canal-stinks. Maybe the weather would hold all day.

Between the good wind, good time and heavy effort, Jones felt her foul mood sliding off. Hell, Rif wasn't so bad. Paid well, anyway. A quick trip upriver and a leisurely voyage back, no weight but two passengers and then one: not such hard work for good money. She could complain later.

"Rif! M'sera Rif!" yelled demandingly from a dock at Mantovan corner. A man, carrying a sheaf of papers, well-dressed, waving urgently.

Oh, hell, what now?

Rif snapped her head up, looked, frowned briefly, then shrugged. "Damn. Put in there, Jones I know this dry-foot: won't take long."

"Sure," Jones grumbled, poling the skip over. Complications already. Best keep an eye on the man's hands.

Then she noticed a slight movement inboard. Johanssen had casually slipped her offside hand into her knitting-bag. Her land-visible hand kept working the crochet-hook, back and forth, back and forth: not actually catching the yarn, just keeping up that soothing, hypnotic movement. No fool, that old m'sera. Maybe a good bit more than she seemed.

The skip bumped at the narrow quayside. Rif quick-tied the bow and climbed out, looking expectant, hands resting on her belt almost-accidentally close to her visible knives.

But the well-dressed man made no threatening moves, only passionate ones. For all that he kept his voice low, his urgent look and stressfully flapping hand gave a good picture of his intentions. Rif listened, her frown deepening slightly, then shrugged and nodded. The man handed her the topmost sheet of paper from his bundle, clutched her indifferent hand for a moment, then scurried off. Rif climbed back into the skip wearing an absorbed expression, and pulled the quick-tie loose.

"Move on," she said. "Just some high-house flunky soliticin' fer a job."

"Not music, I'll bet," Jones commented, leaning into the pole. She noted that the old woman's hands were both back at her crocheting, filling out the last sleeve on the sweater.

Rif glanced at her companion, then opened out the paper and held it where Jones could see. "Ever laid eyes on that face before?"

Jones squinted at the paper. It displayed a printed hand-drawing of a man's face, followed by information about his size, weight, age and so on. Yes, it did look familiar.

"Seen 'im around, not lately. Not since . . . hmm, Festival. Ran a skip then, an' piss-poor at it. No born canaler, that's f'r sure."

"You know his name? Hangouts? Anything like that?"

"Hmmm, Chuz . . . No, Chud. Never seen 'im much, he just hung around a bit. Why? Who wants him?" *And for what? Money in this, or trouble?*

Rif gave her a long look, then hitched closer on the boards until she was sitting next to Jones' position on the deck.

"House Hannon," she said. "They got word this is the rat what killed that Hannon girl last Festival. They're offerin' a big reward for his head."

"Shit! Trouble!" Jones stabbed her pole hard into the water. *Smuggling, thieving, politics—and now you want to get into assassination, too?* "Leave me out o' that! Th'old Hannon-Gregori feud's pure poison, an' everyone knows it."

"It's good money," Rif wheedled. "Five big ones. I'm

not askin' ye to *do* anything; just keep yer eyes open. You see 'im, you tell me. I'll cut y'in fer a good share.''

"No chance! I'd as soon be caught in Kalugin House with them Swords runnin'— *Too much!* Jones bit off the last word, scrambled to cover it. "Uh, no way," she finished lamely. *Damn, short on sleep. Stupid.*

Rif hadn't missed it. *"Swords?''* she asked, very quietly, not looking away.

Johanssen, in the bow, kept her head down and crocheted at a furious pace—for all appearances oblivious to the world.

"Altair," Rif almost whispered, "If there're Swords rooted in at Kalugin House, then you an' me an' all our . . . connections are nose-deep in bilge-water. We all better know when, where an' how to jump.''

Jones said nothing, gritted her teeth, and sped the skip forward with hard, angry thrusts.

"Fer Goddess' sake," Rif insisted, "Don't keep me in the dark! I don't wanta get hit from behind.''

Jones flinched at that, remembering all the times she'd said as much to Mondragon. The not knowing was the worst. The not knowing could get you killed.

And Rif, with her connections, was an escape-way for Mondragon, herself, and maybe Raj too if Anastasi Kalugin went under or turned on them.

Snapping a short curse, Jones pulled in the pole, went to the hidey, brought out the jerry-can and started the engine. The motor coughed, belched a clot of smoke, caught and rumbled to work. The skip began to pick up speed.

Jones crouched at the tiller, glaring at Rif as she slid close and sat down.

". . . The new fuel seems t'agree with'er," Rif offered, glancing back at the engine.

"Yey," Jones admitted. "Runs cleaner." That too was Rif's—and the Janes'—gift. Fuel-alcohol did run cleaner than petro-fuel, smooth and strong and loud in the old engine. Loud enough to cover quiet conversation, anyway. "The Nev Hettekers . . ." Jones sighed. "The ones what got invited to that bombed-out Festival party uptown. A friend of mine spotted 'em, recognized 'em from back when, knew they was Swords.''

"Raj?" Rif whispered, wide-eyed.

Jones ducked her head and shrugged again. Let Rif think it was the kid who saw, not guess it was Tom. "I ain't sayin' who, an' don't ye go askin'. Point is, one of 'em's got in real cozy with Tatiana Kalugin . . .''

The islands of Fishmarket, Calliste and Foundry swept by as Jones told the whole Festival story, all she knew, had seen, had learned from Mondragon and elsewhere. Rif listened carefully, prodded little, took it all in, and ended gnawing her lip.

"That's bad. Real bad," she muttered. "Hightown rotten with Swords, Nev Hettek behind 'em . . . Hell, this time next year, Nev Hettek could be runnin' the town without a shot fired.''

Jones shrugged again, but shivered. Maybe Anastasi Kalugin could stop it, maybe not. A year ago she wouldn't have cared who ruled in Hightown; it made no difference to Merovingen-under, nothing to change life on the canals. But now there was Tom Mondragon. Nev Hettek rule meant Swords high and low, and they knew Mondragon was here. He'd have to run to Lord-knew-where, someplace where she couldn't follow or wouldn't know how to live—if he didn't wind up floating in the canals first. Politics mattered now.

"C'n yer friends stop it?" she asked, desperate enough to ask.

"Dunno. C'n find out, maybe." Rif glanced again at the chortling engine. "I'll pay ye back for the fuel." She got up and went back to her former place in the bow, and sat down beside the crocheting old woman.

Jones couldn't tell, over the engine noise, if they were talking or not. Maybe just as well. Just watch the water, mind the traffic—thickening now, out here on the Grand. Mostly skips and haulers, making morning deliveries. Mostly known faces, no danger anywhere—not yet, anyway.

They were almost under the Wex-Spellman Bridge when something hit the bow.

Jones instinctively snapped off the engine, grabbed her pole and stopped the skip, then turned to look.

On the bow sat a small stone. Not heavy enough to do damage, just enough to make noise. Rif and the old woman were staring up at the bridge ahead, not that Jones needed to see them to guess where the stone had come from.

Up on the bridge stood Black Cal, peering down at them.

Johanssen turned her gaze back to her crocheting. Rif kept watching, gone noticeably pale. Jones didn't move.

Black Cal pointed calmly at Rif, then jerked a thumb skyward. 'Come up,' clear as day.

"Why couldn't he just send a note?" Rif muttered. "Hell, pull over."

Jones did, carefully keeping her head down. Nobody wanted Black Cal for an enemy, but she didn't care for his friendly attention, either. Tie up, let Rif out—note that she didn't take her bag with her—squat on the half-deck and wait, trying to be as calm as that old woman with her crocheting. Wait, and try not to sweat in the rising morning heat.

Rif pattered up the bridge as if she were walking on eggs, hoping to high heaven that Black Cal was in a better mood than when she'd seen him last. "Hello," she chirped, trying to sound cheerful. "I see you're walkin' around again."

"Not much." Black Cal raked her over with eyes as cold as green gemstones. He sounded hoarse, still looked a bit pale, but he wasn't coughing.

"I told ye it wasn't the Plague," Rif grinned nervously, "Just the Crud. Told'ja you'd be up an' around in a couple of days, didn't I?"

"Mhm." His noncommittal gaze held her for several long heartbeats, then turned to the skip below. "Where's your doctor going with all that baggage?"

"Leaving town," said Rif, shivering in the sunlight. "It's gettin' a bit hot for her these days."

"Not from me," Black Cal said quietly, leaving her with the implications. Maybe he was fishing for news, and maybe not.

In any case he didn't sound happy, and that was bad news.

"Uh, I got a little something for ye," Rif offered, pulling out the paper. She unrolled it and handed it to him. "That's a slicer named Chud. He's the one killed that Hannon girl last Festival. Now he's back in town, House Hannon's offering big money for 'im."

Black Cal nodded absently, studying the picture. Then he snagged on a thought and turned a chill green stare on Rif. "I don't do extra-work," he said.

"I wasn't saying that!" Rif backpedaled fast. "I'm just tellin' ye what's afloat. You get 'im first, you do what ye want. You find 'im in the canal, you'll know why."

"Mm." Black Cal rolled up the paper, trapped it in the palm of his other hand. "No witnesses to the killing, no solid evidence." He frowned, eyes narrowing.

"Aw, cheer up" Rif offered. "Maybe y'can prod him into takin' a shot at you, and then y'can blow him away."

Black Cal rolled his eyes and snorted, not mollified by that, either.

"Damn," Rif muttered, playing her last card. *What the hell, maybe just as well now as later.* "I heard somethin' else interesting that y'could maybe use. Did you know that yer boss' new sweetheart is a big Sword of God agent from Nev Hettek?"

The old woman had very nearly finished the sleeve by the time Rif came back to the skip.

"Took ye long enough," Jones complained as Rif scrambled in. "Gonna have t'run the engine full-throttle t'reach yer ship in good time"

"Do it," said Rif. "I'm paying."

Jones restarted the engine, casting another quick glance up at the bridge. Black Cal hadn't moved. "He plannin' t'stay there all day?" she asked, ducking her head away from his gaze.

"So he says." Rif pulled her cloak around her and huddled in the bow. "He's gettin' over the Crud, and 'e's bad-tempered. Keep away from 'im if y'can."

"I try, I try." Jones set the throttle, and the skip chugged rapidly up the Grand. "Funny how I only run into 'im when ye're aboard."

Johanssen raised her head, smiling sweetly. "Maybe he likes you," she said, eyeing Rif.

"Goddess forbid!" Rif shook her head so fast that her hair flopped into her eyes. "It'd ruin my reputation!"

*   *   *

Another twenty minutes' wide-open running took them up the Greve fork to the farms depot and along by the piers where riverboats tied up. The place looked surprisingly busy, but then, this was shipping time for the North Flat harvest. Big ships put in here: grain-barges and steamers from up-Det, and little craft, some of which might not care for the public notice and the harbor-master's close attention, not so able to bribe inspectors as some.

It was not hard to tell which category Rif's ship fell into: a huge steamer with the high sides of a heavy cargo-hauler, passenger-decks above. Its smokestacks could have topped some of the lower islands in the city. Cargo— mostly farm supplies and bulk rice—was coming off and going on, pur poseful crowds busy. Nobody took parti-cular notice of Jones' skip pulling in at stairs-side.

Rif got out first, carrying the large bundle, and helped m'sera Johanssen onto the landing. "Wait here a bit, Jones," she said, sounding her old cheerful self. "Keep an eye on my stuff 'til I get back." She strolled away arm-in-arm with the older woman, looking like a harmless visitor seeing her mother off on a journey. The two of them disappeared quickly in the crowd.

Jones took the opportunity to check on the potful of slurry-mash yeasting quietly in the hidey. Maybe tomorrow she could brew off some more fuel, but it wouldn't be ready by tonight. Maybe just as well. Carrying a fare all day, real public, she wouldn't have to work late tonight, could spend the night at Tom's place, keeping watch on him, catching up on sleep. It wouldn't hurt to take a nap right now, in fact, with the day getting warmer and all. She set the pole and hook close, spread out a blanket and curled up in the hidey, and shut her eyes.

It seemed only five minutes later that someone shoved her, not too hard, in the ribs. Jones came awake blinking and gulping, reaching automatically for the barrel hook.

"Haw! 'T's only me," Rif laughed. "Wake up, lazy. We got work t'do. Oh, an' I got something for you." She planked down two sloshing jerry-cans on the deck, and sat back grinning.

Jones blinked at them, sniffed, recognized the smell. "Is that alkie-fuel? Here?"

"Yey, cheap as water." Rif beamed. "Word's got around, and the yeast too. Plenty of vegetable-trash t'grow it on up here. Folks're just a little more open about sellin' it, this far outta sight of the College." She snickered. "If yer own yeast dies out on you, the best price in-city's at Mantovan—north slot, under. Buy raw slurry-mash, cheap, do yer own distillin' and get the yeast too. Neat, hey?"

"C'n we get out o' here, ne?" Jones took the side-tie loose and skipped up on the half-deck. "Time's passin'."

"Right, right." Rif thought a moment. "Get into the Grand, then west at the Signeury. No point wasting this stuff north'a Spellbridge."

"No point usin' fuel up there, either." Jones cranked the engine over and eased the skip out into the current.

*   *   *

After all the buildup, the work was easy. Jones poled the skip into the lazy backwaters of Yesudian, Torrence and Eick, heading for Capone. Rif, her coin-catching basket set out on the bow played her flat-harp and sang sweetly under the windows and bridges, chirping at passers-by and collecting coins while anyone watched. She sang requests if asked, but generally came back to one particular song.

"There's a wheel turnin' on muddy ground,
    Gains an inch every time it goes around.

> Come on, let's make another revolution.
> Turn, turn, turn . . ."

For all its vaguely-subversive words, the tune was slow, meandering and hypnotic.

> "There are wheels that turn through all of our lives
> And we sometimes see them clear.
> When the night comes down, when the first snow
>   falls,
> We can mark the day or the year . . ."

Snow. First frost. End of fever season? Jones fixed her mind on the words, needing to concentrate on something, or the sleepiness would catch up to her. *Do all Rif's songs have secret messages in 'em?*

> "The circle's end we can tell too easy;
> The beginning is hard to see.
> And the wheel whose seasons no one knows
> Is the turn of the tide that can make us free."

Tide? Free? That had to have some meaning, but what? And to whose ears? Did Rif have friends this far uptown who might be listening in, picking up signals?

Occasional small coins pattered down, sometimes hitting the basket, sometimes dropping into the well. Rif duly picked them up between verses, not missing a beat.

> "There are wheels that turn in the natural world
> And there's some in the heart of man.
> Your will moves them, your hand proves them,
> So turn them the best you can . . ."

Back east now, past Deva, Novgorod and Bent, stopping once under an outdoor restaurant to play for a handful of diners until a complaining wine-steward shooed them away. Then on under Kass Bridge, still singing.

"When you see your wheel you can add your
    shoulder—
Or wait 'til it's rolling high.
You can slow it down or speed it around,
But you can't make it stop—even when you die."

Between songs, between ends and beginnings of that same
sleepy-strange traveling song, whenever nobody was looking,
Rif quietly licked her fingers, dipped them into the open bag
beside her, pulled out fingertips darkened with clinging seeds
and trailed them in the water. No one who wasn't specially
watching for the gesture would have noticed it.

"There's a wheel that's moving fast through our time
And we've seen the track it made.
I believe you know where it has to go,
And the way that the game is played . . ."

After a time Jones saw the pattern of the scattering: always
done in backwater corners, places where the current was slow.
The seeds could sink there, root and grow undisturbed. A few
mixed weeds grew already in such out-of-the-way corners;
newer ones would scarcely be noticed, surely not cared about.

"So night's come down and the turn is hidden,
But it never stops rolling 'round.
So lay on your hand, 'cause we're coming to land.
Just another strong pull, and we're on hard ground."

Jones decided she was getting tired to death of that song.
Talk to Rif, then. Quick, before it started up again.
"What'll they look like?" she asked, poling slowly between Bent and Kass. "They gotta break surface sometime."
"Thick flat leaves and pretty yellow flowers," Rif smiled,
trailing her laden fingers in the water. "Clusters of flowers
on one stalk, even smell nice. Nobody'll mind, not unless
they spread so thick as to block the canals. That ain't likely,
not with the steady traffic."

"They good f'r anythin' besides cleanin' garbage out o' the water?"

"Oh, sure. The leaves'll feed yer yeast, good as any other weeds. Dry 'em, if ye can, an' I suppose they'll burn too. I don't know if the flowers're good for much, besides being pretty, smelling nice—an' spreading the seeds. They'll drift downstream, wind up in Dead Harbor probably, after everywhere else." Rif dipped and trailed her fingers again. "Might even make this town smell downright good . . . Hey, what do I see?"

Rif sat up and peered ahead at a figure running madly along the Kass-Borg Bridge. He was tall, skinny, dressed in the rusty blue-black colors of a College art student—and running with a flapping, wobbling, exhausted desperation. The sight was laughable, but Rif only wore a faint, intrigued, calculating smile.

"I know him," she said. "Pull over there, and let's catch 'im."

Jones sighed, and poled over. The customer was always right, sure. But when the customer was Rif, anything could happen. She didn't trust that calculating smile.

Rif, following the running student with her eyes, hopped out of the skip and scurried up the stairs toward bridge-end to intercept him. The chase passed out of Jones' sight. She jury-tied aft and sat down to wait.

More of Rif's damn games. Can't she do anything simple?

The sun was approaching zenith, the wind had died and the day was heating up considerably. Jones yawned in the seductive warmth and studied the water, noted that wisps of mist were rising again. Damn, if the sun kept up like this, the fog would be blanket-thick by sundown. Cautious poling through that, even in the slower-trafficked side canals.

Then again, in a thick fog nobody could see them, either— nor see what Rif was doing. They could just pole around, scattering the seeds, not have to play-act at singing for pennies under the windows. Maybe Rif would prefer that, and maybe not. Gain cover, lose the extra money. Then again, somebody was paying Rif well for this work . . .

Footsteps came rattling back: Rif, with the tall skinny student in tow. They hurried onto the skip, and Rif shoved him back into the hidey, out of sight. Without a word, Jones cast off and poled southeast, toward French

Once they were well clear of Borg, the student began talking, babbling thanks at Rif. "—can't thank you enough, m'sera. That Krish, he remembers he owes me when he's sober, but when he's drunk he resents it. I swear, I thought he'd run me through if he caught me. He's that drunk."

"Krishna, hmm?" Rif purred, smiling thoughtfully. "Yey, I remember him, all right. You too, from those gigs around the College. When I passed the basket, you put a good bit in. Him, he took somethin' out."

"I'm really sorry," the student panted.

"Hey, don't be." Rif smiled, smiled. "Ye don't have to be a Retributionist t'believe in justice."

"It's *Justus!*" the young man insisted, sounding anxious. "And I've converted."

"Shh, don't worry." Rif craned her neck back and called up to Jones. "Hey, pull up under Porfirio-Wex Bridge, can ye? I've a friend there can put up Justus here for awhile."

"Lord and Ancestors, another game." Jones sighed and looked heavenward, but poled duly east around Cantry.

"Now go up to the fourth floor," Rif explained to the panting Justus, "And ask for Scarritt's studio. He's a portrait artist, has lots'a work, needs help preparing canvases, he says. For a few hours' work he'll give ye some good money, also show ye some tricks'a the trade. Good as any College lesson, I guarantee. You keep outa sight 'til Krishna's cooled, and won't miss any learning from yer classes. Right?"

"Oh, yes. M'sera, if there's any way I can thank you . . ."

"Yey, sure. Talk me up at the better-paying places around College, see if y'can get me some work there."

Jones almost whooped at that, held it back to a barely audible snickering. Trust Rif to twist money out of this, profit out of anything. Had to admire a mind like that, devious or no.

They let Justus off on the Wex side, nestling in between

two poleboats, and he scampered away toward the stairs. Rif smiled again, watching him go.

"Did ye notice," she purred, "How much he resembles Black Cal, seen from the back?"

"No more damn games!" Jones snapped. "Not now, not on my skip! Let's get done with business, cain't ye?"

"Right." Rif looked back to port, eyes half-closed, calculating smile turned subtly ruthless. "Go back up past Borg. We didn't seed there yet."

The customer's always . . . What the hell is she up to? Jones wondered, poling back out into the water. Well, whatever it was now, it hadn't threatened her skip or her hide yet.

Back under Borg, through the rising mist. Rif dropped seeds with a casual, practiced hand and studied the passing island. Between polings Jones watched too, wondering what Rif was looking for. Nothing but hightowners, walking to and fro, some in College dress.

"Hah, there!" Rif sat up sharply. "Pull under."

"What, again?"

"Pull under an' wait. Won't take long."

"All right, but this better be the last damn stop . . ." Jones tied up under Borg-French Bridge and watched while Rif hopped out. This time she could follow the woman's progress up the stairs, up onto first level. There: she was hurrying after someone, some swaggering student with a sword clanking at his side. He looked more than a little heavy with drink. Jones held quiet and strained to catch the words, couldn't make them out but could watch.

There came Rif, shoulders hunched and head bent, looking amazingly like a hightowner's doting footman, plucking at the drunk student's sleeve. He tured his flushed face toward her, half-eager, half-wary. Rif said something fawning and held out one hand, clearly begging for a coin. The sword-wearing student frowned, but dug into a pocket and came out with a silverbit. He dropped it, with a contemptuous flourish, into her hand. She clutched it, bowed quickly, and said something close to his ear. Then she pointed southward, downstream. A distinctly nasty smile spread across the youth's face, and he hurried off southward, pushing past her.

Watching him go, Rif straightened up—no longer looking like anyone's servant. She tossed the coin in her palm, stuffed it into her purse, and trotted quietly back down the stairs to the skip.

"That anythin' important?" Jones grumbled, poling back toward Bent and Ciro.

"Worthwhile, anyway." Rif smiled, reaching for more seeds. "He was looking for Justus. Well, he'll find Justice, right enough. Heh! 'Specially if this fog thickens a little more. Oh, that he will!"

Jones didn't ask anything more, not until they'd gone past the West Canal and under Bruder-Hendricks Bridge. The smell of swamp-grass from beyond Bruder and Golden reminded her of Raj.

"Tell me one thing," she prodded. "This doctor-school you told Raj about: what's it goin' t'cost 'im?"

Rif didn't so much as twitch. "Oh, very little. Probably nothing, if he'd good enough." She glanced up, smiled reasuringly. "Seems the boy's got talent. The school prizes that. They'll want him much's he wants what they got."

"That ain't the cost I mean! What do they really want 'im fer, after?"

"Healing. No more, no less." Rif tossed another fingerfull of seeds into the water. "Ye may's well go all the way down to Racawski before turning back north. Be sure to get Hendricks' slot."

"Damn it, don't you hold out on me, Rif! They'll want 'im to turn Janist, won't they? Do their work?"

"Maybe turn Janist, if he's willing. If not, then just heal an' bless in the name'a Jane, spread the word around that Janes make good doctors for poor folk. Where's the harm in that?"

"He's only a kid! Thirteen, maybe fourteen— That's a little young f'r these games."

"He'll be a good bit older before he finishes school." Rif

looked up, catching Jones' eyes. "How old were *you* when y'first took to working this skip alone?"

Jones ground her teeth. *Twelve. Maybe less.* "All I had ter worry 'bout was runnin' my skip, keepin' alive. This is big trouble yer into. Ye know that."

"Jones, that boy was raised the son of a Sword agent, and a stupid agent at that. He's spent the last few years hidin' out in the swamp, surviving there. You think he can't handle this?"

There was no easy answer. Jones poled her way silently around Racawski Island and back up toward Hendricks, watching as Rif flicked doses of seed into the waiting, quiet water.

". . . Besides," Rif added, "It's what he wants. Where else's he gonna get that schooling? The College?"

"Shit," Jones sighed, seeing the sense of it. "Just take care o' that boy. Don't run 'im into deep trouble. That's all I'm askin'."

"No worry, Jones. I know that kid, an' I like 'im. I wouldn't drag 'im into something'd really hurt him."

"All right."

They steered back up into the West Canal, toward Bolado. The fog was thickening steadily.

By the time Krishna reached the foot of the Wex-Spellman Bridge, the fog was so thick it was hard to see more than two body-lengths ahead of him. Damn weather, anyway. Damn Justus for running like a coward, making him work the euphoria off of a good booze-buzz. Damn that woman and her informant—what was his name:—Chud?—if this turned out to be an empty chase.

Puffing with exertion, Krishna started up the bridge. The few pedestrians coming down it took one look at his tight-gripped sword and suffused face, and quickly got out of his way.

Ah, there, just at midbridge: tall lean body, dark suit, dark hair, generally slumped and weary look about him, gazing down into the canal, back conveniently turned. Oh, it was Justus all right.

Krishna started to draw his sword, then thought of something better. *Just push him over, into the water.* Yes, yes, that would be perfect; no mark of weapons, no suspicions, no new dueling-fines. Just an accident, nobody to blame. He suppressed a snicker as he lunged forward.

His running footsteps thudded softly as pattering rain on the boards.

At the last second, the tall man dropped low and spun away to one side. Fast, so fast he seemed to blur.

When'd he learn that?! Krishna wondered, scrambling to stop his forward momentum on the fog-wet wood. Justus was usually so clumsy . . .

Then his chest hit the top rail.

A heavy hand slammed between his shoulderblades, pushing him forward. Krishna's feet shot backward, out from under him, and his own weight sped him out to-ward empty air. He squawked and scrabbled for hand-hold on the rail, caught it, swung precariously balanced a full five meters above the sullen, fog-hidden water.

That hand again, too heavy, far too strong for Justus, pressed down on his back, pinning him belly-down, butt to the breeze, on the bridge-rail.

Krishna briefly considered kicking at his opponent, then thought better of it. He felt around with his feet until he found one of the lower rails, and tucked his toes under it. Only then did he dare to turn his head and look up.

Less than an inch from his nose, absolutely steady, was the muzzle of a huge, long-barreled revolver. The aperture looked as big around as his thumb.

Beyond the pistol was a long, lean black-clad arm and shoulder, and beyond that a face that Krishna recognized all too well. He'd never wanted to see that face this close, and surely not ever smiling like this, showing so many gleaming, perfect teeth.

''Punk,'' Black Cal smiled. ''You just made my day.''

*   *   *

Close upon sunset, between Ulger and Calder, the seeds ran out. Rif pulled the small oilcloth seed-pouch out of her bag-of-tricks, turned it inside-out and trailed it in the water just under the Ulger side of the bridge, then sighed and tossed it back in the bag. "Ah, hell, that'll do 'er. Drop me back at Fife, will you?"

Jones stifled another yawn and poled slowly eastward, arms tired, everything tired. "Y'got only half the town," she noted.

"Rat's takin' the east side again. Probably done by now." Rif stretched, rubbed knuckles into her back. "Gotta ask 'er if she's seen that Chud anywhere, or got a copy of that handbill."

Connections finally clicked together in Jones' sleep-slowed mind. "House Hannon printed those up, spread 'em everywhere, ain't they?"

"Right."

"So all o' low-town an' half o' High's goin' ter be out lookin' fer'im. Sure ye want ter swim in that kind o' competition?"

"Not really." Rif shrugged. "Still, Hannon's offering five sols. If I get a chance at that money, I'll grab it."

Jones stared thoughtfully at the spangles of low sunlight on the passing water. "I don' think I could kill anybody just fer money," she said. "Nor religion n'r politics, either."

"No more would I." Rif crackled the joints in her knuckles, then wrists. "Besides, it's not just the money. That's what this Chud killed that girl for, an' that's what makes him worth killing."

Jones chewed that over. So, Rif did a lot of things for at least two reasons, maybe more. Maybe she never did anything for just one reason. "Ah' this seedin' job t'day? There was more'n one reason fer that, too, ney?"

Rif flicked a thoughtful look at Jones, then pulled her bag-strap onto her shoulder, reached into a pocket for some coins and started counting them. "We did five good deeds today, if y'wanta count 'em up."

"Five?"

"We planted the seeds that'll clean up the water," Rif ticked off on her fingers, "Helped Justy get away from a nasty beating, got Krishna what he deserved, cheered up Black Cal a bit . . . and maybe even prevented a war."

Jones pricked up her ears at that last. "How'd we prevent a war, just floatin' around town?"

Rif half-turned, and gave Jones a heavy-lidded smile that made her shiver. "No harm telling ye that m'sera Johanssen's a Jane priestess, as well's a doctor."

Jones kept quiet as they passed under Mendez-Calder Bridge. Rif had left too much dangling; it didn't add up. "But we took 'er out o' town . . ."

"Mhm." Rif thought for a moment, then pulled open her shoulder-slung bag and drew out a crocheted sweater, now complete. "Here," she handed it to Jones. "That's for Raj, or 'is brother. Tell 'im what you like."

Jones took the thing as if it were made of thorns, looked at it carefully. It was small, made for someone about Raj's size—or a little bigger. *Meant for him, or me, from the start* . . .

The Janes had been keeping an eye on her, or Raj, for however long it took to hand-crochet a sweater. Maybe since Festival first-night. She shivered again, but didn't put on the sweater. Another thought connected. "She was that same Jane what made the speech from the bridge, first Festival night?"

"Right. Her work's done here, so she's goin' elsewhere." Rif kept back a small count of coins and put the rest away. "Pull up under Fife southeast, same's before."

"Yey." Jones poled slowly under the Calder-Fife Bridge, thoughts grinding like reluctant gears. "*She's* goin' ter stop a war? All by herself?"

"Not quite by herself." Rif glanced at the walkways above, listening for footsteps or breathing. There was none. "Y'know, those Nev Hettekers wanta take Merovingen, any way they can. Your Kalugin wants war with Nev Hettek, but he can't push it past his big sister. Tatiana wants no war, but she's got that Sword lover what just might sweettalk'er into opening more'n just her legs to Nev Hettek. Now maybe Black Cal knowin' about that might change things, but I wouldn't wanta bet the whole—''

He knows? How?! Connections made, fast.

Jones yanked the pole out of the water, braced her feet and whipped it up to ramming height, aimed at Rif. ''*You* told 'im?!''

Warring calculations struggled for balance: Rif had valuable connections, Rif was dangerous, Rif's friends were dangerous, and valuable—and now Rif couldn't be trusted.

''Lord an' Ancestors, first chance ye got after I told ye, an' ye spilled it all ter a blackleg!''

''To *Black Cal.*'' Rif turned to face Jones, both hands resting on her knees—plainly far from her knives and from whatever was in the big bag. ''Do you know anyone else could maybe do something about it?''

''Anastasi Kalugin,'' Jones whispered, lowering the boat-pole a fraction, already wondering.

''You think your friend hasn't told 'im already? A big piece of news like that?''

Raj. She thinks it was Raj that saw . . . Jones let the pole end sag. Of course Tom would have told Kalugin everything he'd seen, heard, guessed. Probably before—and more than—he'd told her. If Raj had known, he probably would have done the same. But if Rif were to question Raj about it . . . ''Don't ye go botherin' that kid on this. Don't even ask 'im. Ye got 'im pokin' inter enough trouble already.''

''I won't. I got no reason t'hurt the kid.''

Jones dropped her pole-end back into the water.

''I *like* that boy, Jones. He's smart as a whip, knows how t'keep his eyes open an' his mouth shut. Don't worry about him.'' Rif took her hands off her knees and eased back against the gunwale. ''Y'can bet he made good money selling that story to Kalugin, but he's left no sign that he's got it.''

''Yey,'' Jones shrugged, poling smooth around the upcoming Fife corner. ''He's smart, right enough.''

''So Kalugin knows,'' Rif went on, ''But that Nev Hetteker's still alive an' waltzing with Tatiana. That means yer Anastasi hasn't done anything yet. Y'can bet he would if he could, so that means he can't.''

"Well . . . not yet, maybe." Fife-Southdike Bridge slid overhead. Its shadow felt heavy and cold in the fog.

"Meanwhile, who do we know that can get close enough to Tatiana to maybe do somethin' about her Sword sweetheart?"

Jones chewed that over, not seeing any sense here. Black Cal? What did he have to do with Tatiana Kalugin? She shrugged.

"Aw, *think*, Jones!" Rif snorted. "Tatiana's in charge of the city law-keeping, which means the blacklegs. She's Black Cal's boss!"

"Hell!" Jones whispered, poling the skip to a halt. "He might get close enough . . ." No, stop right there. Best not to speculate on what Black Cal could do, if he wanted, on his home ground. "But still . . . that wouldn't hold off a war, would it?"

"Ney, not alone." Rif glanced again at the walkway, kept silent for a moment as a half-drunk couple tottered past, then reached for the tie-up. "That still leaves Nev Hettek, plotting war, pushing the Sword down here. Nothing to hold *them* back, 'cept for a little advance planning. Nothing 'til now, anyway."

Jones waited, silent. *She wants to tell me. Why?*

Rif flashed that chilly smile once more. "Jones, you got a lead t'Anastasi Kalugin, one he'll believe if word ever has t'be got to 'im.''

Jones nodded understanding. Rif had guessed that her connections could work both ways. And also knew that Jones had someone to protect and worry about, though she didn't really know who it was. *Maybe knows my hin and haw, but uses a light touch.*

"I'll leave it t'yer judgment when and how t'use this, just in case I'm not handy for advice." Rif tossed a quick look over the water, then back. "The Janes don't want war either, nor Nev Hettek to take over. And now they've got a way t'stop Nev Hettek cold. You helped deliver it, in fact.''

"That Jane doctor?" Jones guessed, keeping her hands busy with the aft tie-up. "She's . . . goin' ter Nev Hettek?"

"Not empty-handed" Rif slid smoothly off the skip, and held out her hand. Five lunes twinkled there. "You want?"

Jones hesitated, knowing there was more here than she'd earned just ferrying Rif around all day, more passing to her than hauling fees. But she took the coins, all five. "Say it."

Rif hitched closer, voiced pitched to that low, carrying, tight-beam range. "She was carrying some . . . 'cultures,' they're called. Breeding-stock, like with the fuel-making yeast—only they're not for yeast. They were taken outa Dead Harbor."

It took Jones a second to understand, and then there was only one question left to ask.

"Before or after we dumped them barrels o' Plague-killer?"

"Before"

"Oh." Jones edged away, feeling the hair lift up on her neck. "Breedin'-stock fer . . ."

"Right." Rif smiled somberly into the thickening shadows. "There's no plague in Merovingen. But there will be—in a few special places—in Nev Hettek."

FEVER SEASON
(REPRISED)

C.J. Cherryh

Del and Min were not at tie-up yet. It was no safe place to leave the skip, at Petrescu, with so much wrong in the world, but Jones had no patience for waiting. The front room lamp was on in Mondragon's apartment, the signal she had arranged with the boys, left side of the couch one night, then right, then left, more complicated than with Mondragon, but then, things were, lately. Complicated.

She skipped up the stairs and onto the landing, breathless, knocked the special knock, and stood and fretted in the chill while she waited on one of the boys inside to see who it was.

Denny. The eye had a little to do to reach the garde-porte grate inside. The grate snapped shut again and the latch rattled back. Jones dived in and shut the door herself.

"How is he?"

Denny pointed at the back room and she went with a sense of panic, down the short hall by the stairs, to the open bedroom door where the oil-lamp burned.

Raj was there, sitting on Mondragon's bedside. He twisted around as she came in. And Mondragon had his head propped up, his eyes open.

She stopped her hurry. Made a nonchalant stroll into the room, hands in pockets. "Well," she said while her heart

settled down. "You look some better." "Doing all right,"
he said. It was hardly his voice. It was weak and it was half a
whisper. He needed a shave, bad. His hair was a mess. His
eyes being open and full of sense was the prettiest sight she
had seen in days.

"He ate some," Raj said.

"God, Raj's cooking," Denny sneered from the doorway,
and swung past the doorframe to stand in the room.

"Out," Raj said, waving a hand. "Man's *tired*, Denny.
Lord!"

Denny dived out again. Jones hardly noticed till the thought
of her skip flashed across her mind and she shot out a hand
and grabbed a fistful of sweater before Denny quite cleared
the door. "Go out an' watch. I got my skip out there. Get
aboard and sit. Penny in it f' ye."

"Two."

"Git!" Raj hissed, and Denny got. Raj turned round again,
and got up carefully. "Sorry," he said to Mondragon. "You
just rest quiet. I'll let m' brother out."

Jones stood still, hands in pockets while the room cleared.
Then she went over to Mondragon's bedside and stood there.
"All right, huh?"

"Jones," he muttered in that thin voice, and rolled his
eyes, looking up at her. "Jones, there was this crazy woman
here— Damn woman—"

"She done ye some good."

"For God's sake, Jones, she's a damn *Janist*—"

"Ain't *we* particular?" She sank down on the edge of the
bed.

"—in my bedroom," he muttered, and his eyes fluttered
shut. "No more crazy people here—"

"Mondragon."

But he was asleep, till the door opened and shut in the
front room, and his eyes few open again. She patted his arm.

" 'S all right, that's just Raj letting Denny out."

"Fed me this damn stuff," he complained. "'Sang songs
at me. For God's sake, Jones—"

He was gone again. But it was just sleep. She felt of his

face and it was cool, even if the whole room smelled like fever and sweat.

She stood there and wiped her nose with her sleeve, and one eye with the back of a knuckle, and shrugged when Raj came in, managing to keep her back to him. "Guess I'll get me somethin' in the kitchen."

"Sandwich on the table," Raj said.

There was. It could have been live eel and she would have eaten it. She could not remember *when* she had eaten. She gulped down beer and hiccupped down huge bites of sandwich, and wiped her eyes and her nose from time to time.

Which was the change in temperatures from outside. Sure.

She went back to Mondragon's room where Raj kept watch.

"Go sleep," she said. "My turn."

"Yey," Raj said, and went.

She pulled the chair over near the bed and just sat and looked at him, that was all, looked at him breathing without a rattle and his coughing just occasional, while a meal was steady on her stomach and friends were watching outside and in.

She had no inclination to move or shut her eyes or do anything but just sit there, to catch every little flicker of his expressions that meant better news than she had expected for a week.

Finally he drew a large breath, coughed and opened his eyes, confused-like.

"What're you doing here?" he asked.

She could have hit him.

Instead she said, "Well, you ain't been breathing real good."

He blinked and lay there staring into space a moment. Then he seemed more *there* than he had been, just a little twitch of his face, a focusing of the eyes. "Is it Friday?"

"Friday, damn, it's Tuesday."

"Still Tuesday?"

"No, *Tuesday*. Tuesday week. Ye been *out*, Mondragon."

"Oh, my God." He reached for the edge of the bed, tried to put his foot over. And broke into coughing, which gave her a chance to stop him. Not to push him flat. He was resisting that with a stiff arm.

"Raj!" she yelled.

Raj pelted in at speed, and Mondragon surged to his feet till his legs went out from under him and she pushed him back as Raj got after him from the other side and sat him down. A coughing fit decided it. He fell back into the pillows and Jones threw the blankets over him while Raj got him a cup of water and helped him get the coughing stopped.

He was quiet then. Just lying there on his side, breathing hard. Raj melted out of the room, with remarkable good sense. And Jones sighed and sat down on the bed and folded over him, just held onto him and tangled her fingers in his dirty hair.

"Jones," he said. "You have to get me uptown."

"Sure. You want t' try for the Moon whiles we're going? Never poled there before."

He shook his head slowly. Caught a large breath. "Jones. Kalugin—"

Worse and worse. Her heart picked up its beat. "Yey? What about Kalugin?"

"Told him—Monday, that's all. Already a day late. Oh, God, I can't remember—what I told him."

"Damn! why couldn't you have told me?"

Long silence. She answered her own question, inside, and shook her head. " 'cause ye think I'm a damn fool," she said sorrowfully.

"Don't want you in this. Don't want you near it." Cough. "Get me to Boregy."

"The hell!" She sat up. "I'm going to turn you over to those sherks? No chance, *no* chance."

"They'll take care of me."

That flat knocked the breath out of her. She sat back in outrage. "I ain't got no doubt they will, right to harbor bottom they'll take care of ye! Lord and my Ancestors! Who ye think your friends are, ye damn lunatic?"

He lay there on his belly a moment, staring off the edge of the bed. "Jones, this is serious."

"Thanks. I could'a missed that."

He rolled over. Stared at her with that stubborn, jaw-set look of his. But there was a lot of the desperate about it. "Jones, —"

"Yey?"

"There's this man—" Another coughing fit, and he had to turn. She offered him the water again, and he leaned back into the pillows with tears of pain running down his face. "Jones, all you have to do—" The voice was fading away in strain. "—Just get me downstairs, take me over to the Trade offices, over on the Spur—"

"Yey?"

"That's all you need to do."

"Need to know where you're going. That ain't no address. You want my help, you got to let me figure this."

"Dammit, Jones. You aren't going to get into this. It's already gone sour. I don't even want to use your boat . . ."

"'At's all right. I got no worry. What's the office? I'll just tell 'em you took sick. Fever ain't no news in town."

"*These aren't people who take excuses!*"

"Fine. You write 'em a note, all the same, you tell me where, and I'll get whatever you got to do."

"You can't, dammit, Jones. He won't cooperate for you. He's a scared man—"

"Fine." She grinned her widest and meanest. "We'll all do right fine. You just tell me the whole game."

He was quiet for a long time, staring at something else. Then he reached after her hand and squeezed it, hard. "Jones, you're a fool."

"Mama said. What's the thing I got to do?"

The stairs down from Petrescu loomed like a fall to infinity, for a sick man. Or a raggedy old canal-rat on her way down to her skip at dawn. Mondragon clutched the rail, kept his back turned to the rattle of foot traffic on the walkway, a lone passer-by at this hour, and coughed in the chill, limping his way step by slow step down toward the skip waiting blow. Denny had his elbow, Raj walked just in front of him.

Jones waited down below, steadying the skip, pulling the tie-rope tight through the rings as the boys helped his bulky person down into the well and toward the half-deck.

Damn tall old woman, he thought, trying to slouch. The rags stank, and his head spun as the skip moved. He hunched over, head down, elbows in his lap, trying to get his breath; and finally he slid down and sat in the well where he was out of Jones' walk-path on the deck.

"Yoss," was Jones' cheerful comment. "Hey-hass, ne."

They owed old Mintaka for this one. If they lived through it.

His fault, dammit. He had dragged Jones into it. He had dragged the boys in after. And they had to hope a whole bottle of Jones' whiskey had old Min so happy she would not get her story straight; all she had to do was take the bottle of whiskey and take one of Mondragon's pots over to the tin-smith over by Knowles, and wait around till it was fixed; for which favor Jones was so grateful she wanted to trade Min a good three blankets for Min's spare clothes and one of Min's knit hats.

Powder on the hair then. A lot of padding. Furniture polish on the skin. Keep the head down. Slouch.

He had suffered worse damage to his pride. But he had never felt more the fool. Keeping his head down took no urging at all, as Jones poled steadily along the canal, meeting traffic, hailing folk she knew.

"Somethin' took wrong wi' Min?" someone yelled across.

"Ney, she's fine," Jones yelled back cheerfully. "Drunk as any sailor!"

Jones set great store by the truth, in her dealings with the Trade.

Toward noon, and Jones walked up the stone steps of the Justiciary itself—barefoot as any canaler, right into the hall of justice: up the steps, turn right, down the hall . . . not the main steps, be sure. The only steps any canaler ever *wanted* to use, the ones that led off toward Licensing and Trade.

And the office of one Constancy Rosenblum, who had

gambling debts. "Tell 'im it's his Monday appointment," she said to the secretary. "He'll remember."

The secretary sniffed and left his desk, not without a backward glance to see if Jones was going to snatch something, Jones reckoned.

The secretary came back sober and thin-nosed with disapproval. "M'ser will see you."

"Thank ye." Jones lifted her battered hat and re-set it. And did a little bow as she walked on into the fancy wooden-walled office.

The man inside, an ordinary office-sort, looked up in stark alarm.

"You m'ser Constancy Rosenblum?" Jones asked. "I'm the Monday business."

"Who in hell are you?"

"Friend." Jones walked up to the desk as Rosenblum got up. "You got them papers ready?"

"I don't know anything about—"

She slipped the hook from belt to hand. "He said you'd be nervous. You want to turn 'em to him, you and me got to take a little walk, all right, just to Borg and Kass. Broad daylight. Ain't no harm going to come to you. I got this—" She pulled out a lock of blond hair from her pocket. "Right?"

Constancy Rosenblum's eyes followed all the little movements while his hands stayed poised on his desk like he was going to shove off straight for the window behind him.

But he looked a small bit relieved when he saw the lock of hair, looked at it, and her, and the hook, and at her again. "The note—"

"Ain't no trouble. My friend's got it. You got the papers?"

"Yes." Rosenblum moved suddenly, reaching for the drawer. Jones brought the hook down by his fingers. "Careful." She gave him a big smile. And drew the knife with the other hand. "You and I don't want to startle each other."

"I wouldn't think of it." Carefully, very carefully, Rosenblum opened the drawer, lifted a set of papers out. And backed up. "You know your chances of getting out of here with these."

"That's why you're carrying 'em, ain't it? Come on, broad

daylight, right in public, ye're safe as in services, ain't ye?
An' you don't got the chance t' snatch my friend, like if *he*
walked in here, do ye? 'Cause your note's out there.''

"Shut up." Rosenblum shifted his eyes nervously toward
the door.

"Right." Wide grin. "You got to walk along with me."
She hung the hook back at her belt, slipped the knife into
sheath, and flipped it out again. "Hell, I'm fast with this
thing, ain't I? Have to be sometimes. I c'n throw it fast, too."

Rosenblum nodded. She motioned to the door. And let him
walk her to the outer office.

"Appointment," he said to his secretary.

Out the other door then, down the hall, man in silk and
corduroy and leather shoes; a canaler in knee-britches and
bare feet, friendly as could be, down to the landing and up
the steps to the bridge over to Borg.

The skip was waiting here, Raj and Denny minding things
and an old woman dozing in the well.

Rosenblum balked. "I don't see him," he said.

"C'mon." She drew the knife and encouraged him with a
prick in the ribs. "Just like I said. You got the right papers,
you ain't got a problem in the world."

"The deal—"

"No problem. Hey."

As Mondragon lifted his face and smiled cheerfully at
Rosenblum, who balked again.

"Lord."

"Papers," Mondragon said.

"My note," Rosenblum said.

Mondragon held up a slip of paper, that fluttered perilously
in his fingers, with the water not far away. "We trade.
You're worried about *these* people. Let me tell you—cheating
mine is worse. The papers had better be real."

"They're real," Rosenblum choked. He dragged them from
his pocket. Leaned and made the simultaneous trade.

"Ware!" Raj gasped of a sudden, and the whole skip
jerked, Rosenblum staggered back and forth on the rim as
men came running down from Borg's walk.

Jones kicked the official from behind, right into the canal, jumped for the boat and started for the boathook, while Mondragon scrambled after the bow-tie and Denny for the side.

She fended off the bank with the hook, leaving the pursuers in midjump toward a boat that was suddenly moving away.

And poled with the long hook-pole, smooth and steady, around the corner of Kass by Bent, headed for Spellbridge. No hurry, no good thinking whether the bullylads had a gun, whose they were, whether there was ambush set.

"We scatter," Denny panted, crouching low in the well, while Jones looked back. Not all of the pursuit had fallen in. Some of them were headed down the walk and up onto the bridges. "Gimme the papers. They ain't knowing who's got what."

"Jones!" Mondragon breathed, and coughed, leaning on the well. "Jones, use the damn engine—"

"I can't pole and start 'er! Lord!" She leaped past her passengers and fended off a wall, trick turn, around Spellbridge leftward. "Lead 'em off! Meet ye later!"

Denny took his measure and jumped for Kass. She laid the pole down and pulled the pin on the tiller-bar, to set it to use, while they lost Raj, where, she did not see.

She cranked the engine over. Once. Twice.

"*Damn* this thing!"

It caught, as the bow scraped the side of Spellbridge.

She made the Spellbridge corner and headed into Archangel under power, around by the Spur, then south again by North, through the tight ways—dodged a poleboat whose owner and fare screamed curses after her for the shakeup of the wake.

"We've lost them," Mondragon said in a faint smile. "Circle back, see if we can pick up the boys."

She thought about it. Hard. And kept going as she was, by Yesudian headed for West.

"Jones, —Raj's got the damn papers."

"Lord and my Ancestors! Mondragon!"

"I didn't want the damn papers caught on your boat!"

She pulled out onto West, pulled the circle around a barge and in at Ciro, and came back again, by Bent and French and Cantry. Made the run slow now, the engine popping and sputtering.

"Damn, cut that thing!" another poleboater yelled as she came up into traffic by Wex's side.

"Sorry," she yelled, and kept going.

No sight of them. No sight, on the most direct course that might lead to Moghi's, over on Ventani.

"Ain't no way they can find the boys," she said finally. "Ain't no way *we* can. We're going."

"Damn," Mondragon said, and leaned on the deck-rim and coughed. "Not a good week, Jones. Not a good week."

Home, she reckoned, home by way of Moghi's, where they could wait for the boys to report in. *If* they could.

NIGHT RIDE

Nancy Asire

When Justice entered Hilda's tavern on the back side of Kass, it was to the hum of voices. The usual folk had gathered around noon for lunch: students, mostly, who sat clustered at the tables, some expounding on lectures they had attended (midterm exams being only days away); other men and women sat closer to the doorway—shopkeepers and the like.

The interior of the tavern was only a bit less damp than the air outside and a good deal cooler. Justice saw his table standing empty save for the ubiquitous golden-furred Sunny who lay sprawled in feline ease on one of the chairs. Nodding to Hilda, who moved her considerable bulk lightly back and forth between the kitchen and the common room, Justice passed the bar and threaded his way among the tables to his place.

"Ah, Justus! Back from playing the great artist, I see."

Justice cringed and turned slightly toward the voice. Krishna Malenkov (youngest son of The Malenkovs of Rimmon Isle) sat at a table to the immediate right, two of his hightowner friends seated with him. Lately, Krishna had taken every opportunity to bait Justice, belittling his chosen study of art, calling to mind Justice's less than noble heritage . . . anything that might anger him. Justice was usually able to ignore

Krishna's cutting remarks, but today had not been one of the best, and Justice had no desire to spend his lunch sitting next to his tormentor.

Today did not appear to be one of Krishna's better, either. The stocky hightowner's eyes were red, as was the tip of his nose. But if Krishna was feeling unwell, that fact had certainly not slowed down his tongue.

"Nice to see you, Krishna," Justice said and looked away, feigning total disinterest.

"You been back to see your aunt and uncle?" Krishna asked. He coughed—a raspy sound—and wiped his nose. "Can't see why you'd want to, what with that tiny place of theirs. Huhn. So tiny you can barely turn around, eh Justus?"

Krishna's two companions sniggered quietly, and Justice struggled to ignore them. Ever since he had placed Krishna in karmic debt to him, Justice had found his fellow student sour of mood and quick of temper. Krishna Malenkov was obviously not taking well to the fact he owed money and all the attendant karmic obligations to someone he considered his inferior.

"You've been busy lately," Krishna pushed on. "Haven't even see you babying Sunny."

Justice glanced down at the sleeping cat, and bit back a scathing retort. The sword that hung at Malenkov's side was not there for show: Krishna was one of the young rowdies (they liked to call themselves duelists) who hung around the bridges, picked fights, and generally made a nuisance of themselves. Unlike most of them, Krishna was an accomplished swordsman and, armed though he was with his own sword, Justice had no desire to let Krishna push him into a fight. Malenkov was too damned good.

But today it would not come to swords. Something had happened to Krishna recently, besides coming down with a cold . . . something that made the young hightowner less eager to physically bully other people. Justice smiled slightly. Perhaps Krishna had run into someone who had taken him down a notch or two.

Or, a situation that even his father's money could not handle.

And, if the priests at the College heard that two students had been dueling, expulsion for one or both of the offenders loomed as a frightening possibility.

Rising to his feet, Justice left his table and headed toward the door.

"Something bothering you, Justus?" Krishna called. "You're leaving so soon."

"The air," Justice said over his shoulder. "It's getting rather foul in here and I don't like my lunch ruined."

Laughter came from behind, punctuated by Krishna's coughing. Justice nodded to Hilda again as he went out, answering her unvoiced question with a roll of his eyes toward the rear of the room and Krishna's table.

Damn. Now what? I've let Krishna chase me away from lunch. Don't have many choice places left. Justice walked to the edge of the wooden walkway, leaned on the railing and stared down at the foggy canal below. Lunch. Though he had a good allowance from his aunt and uncle, Justice was, in a word, frugal. Since he lived in Hilda's rooming house attached to the tavern, he and the other students got a discount on their meals. Now that Krishna had made eating in the tavern unbearable, Justice had few places left to get a wholesome meal he could afford.

He straightened and considered the alternatives. There was a small tavern called John's on Spellbridge canalside that students frequented. Somewhat dangerous, that tavern, but the food was good and cheap. He started down the outer walkway of Kass toward Spellbridge, sniffling a bit himself as he walked. Ancestors keep him from getting whatever Krishna had. Some kind of bug was loose in Merovingen, likely brought in by the Falkenaer ship.

When Justice reached the Kass Bridge, he was able to see workmen rebuilding the Signeury. He frowned and walked on, lost in the noontime crowd. The less he knew about dark goings on in town, the better he felt. As it was, rumors ran everywhere, including some tale of crazy Janists dropping something in the canals at Festival time.

A steep set of steps led down to canalside from the second level of Spellbridge. Though it was high noon, visibility on this cloudy day would be very low in the manmade twilight below. Justus kept his eyes moving over the crowd as he descended the stairway, alert for anyone who looked intent on causing trouble.

The stench of canalside hit him as he exited the steps. Taking care for his footing on the damp stone walkway, Justice turned leftward toward John's. The foot traffic canalside was less than on second level, most of the lower level denizens being at lunch. Justice stepped around a suspicious pile of something in his path, then angled back toward the buildings again, approaching the first of the Spellbridge cuts. John's sat right on the corner of that cut: Justice saw the tavern's gaily colored sign now, and heard the muted roar of its customers from within.

And from the cut that ran darkly off to his right, just beyond John's, the sound of taunting voices.

Justice stopped, cursing himself for a fool, edged to the corner of the cut, and peered into the deeper twilight. Five— no—six figures were backing a slighter figure farther into the cut. *Damn! It's none of my business. Get back to John's . . . don't get involved.* Justice snorted. He no more could do that than jump in the canal and think to come out dry.

Unsure as he was of his footing, he hurriedly pulled off his shoes, clutched them both in his left hand, and with his right drew his sword. No duelist, Justice was still a capable swordsman and, if he played this right, surprise would be on his side.

After a quick look around to see if he was noticed, Justice carefully walked forward, testing the soggy walkway with his stockinged feet. The six figures resolved in the dusky light: shabbily dressed toughs, carrying knives and clubs. Facing them, white-faced in the gloom, stood a young boy of no more than thirteen.

Such odds made Justice's stomach turn.

And curse himself doubly as a fool.

Lifting his sword, Justice took a deep breath and ran toward the toughs. His stockinged feet made no sound as he rushed forward—the thugs' taunts and the boy's shrill cries would have drowned out his coming anyhow.

He took the first tough on the side of the head with the flat of his sword; the second he caught in the temple with a heavy shoe heel; and the third he shoved off toward the canal with a sharp kick to the kidney. Justice heard a startled yelp, immediately followed by the rewarding sound of a splash. Now the thugs turned, confused, their attention distracted from the youth they had cornered.

"Run, dammit!" Justice yelled. "Get us some help!"

But the boy merely wiped at a trickle of blood running down into one eye and hefted the heavy stick he had been carrying. Justice cursed, and smashed his sword flat against the face of the tough who stood closest, spinning him off to one side. Blood spurting from his nose, the thug yowled and fell heavily to the damp pavement. The boy grinned, his teeth bared, and jabbed the stick he carried up into another tough's groin. Justice stopped being so concerned for the lad's safety: fighting like that was learned in the hardest of all schools—the canalside.

"Behind ye!" the boy yelled.

Justice spun in time to dodge the sixth man's knife stab. A cold chill ran through his gut: this was for real. Death stalked the slippery walkway, unconcerned who would wind up at the bottom of the Det.

"Lord and Ancestors!" Justice breathed. He had never killed anyone before and the prospect unnerved him. The fellow he faced was an accomplished knife fighter; his stance and the way he held himself showed that. But Justice stood at least four inches taller and wielded near three feet of gleaming steel.

Another thump and a groan came from behind, but Justice dared not take his eyes from his opponent. He circled to his right, away from the knife blade, all too aware of the murky waters of the canal at his back. The tough lunged, knife coming up in a disemboweling stroke, and Justice dodged to one side. His stockinged feet betrayed him: he lost his footing and slid to one knee. Instinct took over—he slashed out where he thought the thug's legs were, trying to hamstring him. His opponent jumped back, then came in again, knife held low and aimed for Justice's chin.

Lord! It's over now! Justice tried to scramble to his feet, but the walkway was too slick. In total desperation, he flung up his sword, his shoes held out as a shield, lurching to one side at what he sensed as being the last possible moment.

A sudden meaty whack. The thug wavered on his feet, then fell heavily onto his side. Justice blinked the sweat from his eyes and glanced over his shoulder. A youth near manhood, with distinct Oriental features, stood a few paces behind, a slingshot in his right hand.

"Ware!" the young boy cried, and Justice turned in time to see one of the men lurch to his feet and run toward him. He rolled to one side, saw the thug rush past and knock the newcomer with the slingshot right off his feet.

The youth yelped in pain, and the thug disappeared out of sight around the corner of the cut.

Justice stood up as the young boy ran to the newcomer.

"You all right?" the boy asked.

The young man nodded, his face tight with pain. "You, Denny?"

"Aye." Denny ran a hand through his curly hair. "Wouldn't be 'cept for this 'un. Saved my skin, he did."

"Get, Denny! Now! Get back!"

"But. . . ."

"I'll be fine. This fellow's all right. Look at his sash, Denny . . . he's a student. Now get!"

The boy glanced up at Justice, his eyes narrowed, then nodded, sprang to his feet, and bolted out of the cut.

Justice stared after the fleeing boy for a moment, then looked around and assessed the situation. He had knocked three of the attackers senseless with his swordblade and shoe heel (though one had revived in time to beat a hasty retreat), and kicked one into the canal; the boy had taken the fifth in the groin: the man now lay unconscious, more than likely put out by another application of the stick. Justice looked down at the unconscious thug at his feet, at the pool of blood that had formed under his head—a sling and rock had done that deed.

The newcomer youth rose to his knees, cradling a bandaged left hand to his chest; lines of pain scoring his face, he shoved his sling inside his shirt and stood. A few steps brought him to the still body of the man he had brought down with his sling; he stooped, reached out and touched the fellow's throat as if searching for a pulse. An expression of relief relaxed his face, and with a small sigh, he turned and faced Justice.

"For what you've done," he said, the hint of hightowner accent, mixed with some other speech pattern, odd coming from one so plainly dressed, "my thanks. Are you hurt?"

"No." Justice sheathed his sword and dropped his shoes at his feet. The next time he came canalside, he would definitely carry a dagger as well as his sword. Overheated in the clammy air, Justice stuffed his wet feet into the shoes and looked up at the young man who faced him. "I'll be fine. Just need some fresh air."

The fellow darted an anxious glance up and down the cut; his face tightened again. "Damn!" he muttered, holding his left hand with his right. He looked up at Justice. "Do you know somewhere we could go sit down?"

Justice started at the young man's hand: a faint trace of what must be blood had stained the bandage. "John's," he said. "A tavern. Right around the corner to the left."

"Busy?"

"At this time of day, yes."

The young man grimaced, either in pain or in response to Justice's answer. "I'm Raj Tai," he said, introducing himself.

"Justice Lee."

Something flickered behind the young man's black eyes. "Adventist?"

"No. Name's confusing. It's J-U-S-T-U-S."

"Huhn. Let's get out of here."

Justice let his companion lead the way back out of the cut. "You know the young boy?" he asked.

"My brother."

The terse reply shed no more light on what had happened than what Justice already knew, which was a sum total of nothing. Raj hesitated at the edge of the cut, looked quickly up and down the canal, then hurried toward John's. Justice shrugged his shoulders, and followed.

Raj had already set off across the crowded room, aiming for a corner booth that sat far to the rear. Justice spotted John, the owner of the tavern, and wound his way through the tables and chairs toward him.

"Friend of mine's got a cut that's opened up. Could we get a bowl of hot water and a clean cloth?"

One of John's bushy eyebrows rose, but Justice had been coming here to eat long enough that what he said would not be questioned. "Sure. Where you sitting?"

"Booth in the far corner. We'll order in a few minutes."

As John turned away, Justice walked back to the booth. It was dark enough in this corner that he despaired of reading the menu, but since he knew it by heart, it hardly mattered.

He seated himself, noticing that Raj had taken the place that allowed full view of the door and anyone who entered. Not that John's dealt with ruffians; today's gathering was quiet ordinary—a clientele consisting of an even blend of students and canalsiders, with a few small shopkeepers from second level thrown in as an aside. The roar of conversation and laughter was nearly deafening.

Justice looked across the table at his companion, seeing the young man's face hidden by shadows, for John, like other canalside shop owners, tried hard to conserve on fish oil for the lamps. A chorus of greetings to some newcomer made Raj glance up in startlement. Justice took a deep breath, wiped at his runny nose, and looked at the noisy diners around him: why the hell was the young man so jumpy?

John himself brought a bowl of hot water and a freshly laundered cloth to the table; casting a wary eye at Raj, the tavern owner set the two items before him. "Ready to order yet?"

"The usual," Justice said, watching Raj watch John.

"And you?" John asked Raj.

"I'll have whatever he's having."

John snorted something and turned away.

Raj looked quickly at Justice, then down at the bowl of steaming water. He carefully stretched his hand out on the table and began unwinding the bandage.

"Your idea?" he asked, nodding toward the bowl, teeth clenched against the obvious pain.

"Thought you'd need it."

"Huhn." Raj finished unwrapping his hand and dipped the cloth in the hot water.

Justice could see why the young man was in pain: the hand was slightly swollen, the fingers bearing old bruises. But the puncture wound in the palm of Raj's hand made Justice wince in sympathy.

"How the hell did you do *that?*" he asked.

Raj glanced up from under his eyebrows, then looked back at what he was doing. "Gutting a fish. Damned clumsy of me. Knife went clear through my hand."

Like hell. Justice kept silent, watching as Raj cleansed the wound, then wrapped it again in the bandage.

"I owe you," Raj said suddenly. "Saving Denny's life like that isn't something I can lightly forget."

Dignity permeated those words, direct and unfeigned. Justice shrugged. "I couldn't very well turn my back on the boy. No one should face odds like that alone."

"And for bringing me here. . . ." He gestured with his good hand. "Like I said, I owe you." Raj's eyes flicked from side to side as if judging how much attention he and Justice were receiving from their nearest neighbors. He shoved the bowl and bloody cloth away, and leaning closer to Justice, he spoke in low voice, nearly lost in the noise.

"You're Adventist."

Justice stared back, trying to keep all expression from his face; the abrupt change of subject threw him. "I told you I wasn't, outside in the cut. Why should I change in here?"

"No Revenantist would get into somebody else's trouble unless they had karma in it," Raj said, his eyes very steady.

Justice looked sidelong across the crowd. *Damn! Slipped out of character and this smart one sees it. What's he want, this Raj? He's either out for something, or he's trying to discredit me and Father Rhajmurti. Whichever—I'll have to be more careful next time.*

The touch of Raj's hand on his arm brought Justice's attention back to their table.

"I'm not after anything," Raj said softly, as if reading Justice's mind, "or at least not after anything you can't give me freely. And I owe you, like I said . . . owe you a lot for saving my brother, *and* helping me."

"Then what can I give you?" Justice asked, allowing a hint of coldness to enter his voice.

"First, I can give *you* something," Raj replied, digging inside his shirt pocket. He extended a medium-sized packet to Justice. "Couldn't help noticing your sniffles. There's something going around town, and this will cure it if you've got it."

Justice took the packet, his eyes never leaving Raj's face. With mid-term exams coming, this medicine could be invaluable. "You a doctor or something?"

A look bordering on wistful yearning crossed the young man's face. "I only wish I could be. But to become a doctor I'd have to enter the College and I've got about as much a chance of doing that as walking across the lagoon."

"Huhn." Justice laid the packet down on the table. "So?"

"You're a student," Raj pointed out, eyeing Justice's saffron sash emblazoned with the College seal worn over the black shirt and black pants he favored. "And you're an Adventist. Somehow, you've managed to fool all the priests or you wouldn't be studying at the College."

Justice motioned for silence as a waiter came to their table and laid out a simple meal of silverbit, greens and beer. He dug in his pocket and came up with two pennies for the price of his meal; Raj produced two pennies of his own, and the waiter walked off.

"All right." Justice began cutting up his fish. He leaned forward again, lowering his voice to a near whisper. "For

sake of argument, we'll say I'm Adventist. What does that
have to do with your getting into the College?''

''You pass,'' Raj said quietly, lowering his beer mug.
One-handed, he attacked his meal, using his injured hand as
little as possible. ''I want to know how.''

Justice stopped chewing long enough to stare at Raj. He
swallowed, took a drink of beer. ''It's not that simple.''

''Then you admit that you *are* Adventist. Look, Justice.''
Raj's face was openly earnest. ''I don't want you thinking the
wrong thing about me.'' He glanced around, and quieter yet:
''I'm Adventist too.''

''With a name like Raj?''

''Rigel.''

Rigel turned into Raj . . . Justice corrupted to Justus.
Huhn. Not much difference.

''Truth?''

''Truth,'' Raj said, with the same open expression. A long
pause. ''And, even more damning—from Nev Hettek.''

Justice knew his face must have shown some surprise, for
Raj smiled, a thin, bitter smile.

''So you want to get into the College,'' Justice said, taking
another bite of fish and following it with a forkful of greens.
He met Raj's eyes. The young man's head had jerked up
again as a group of four students entered the tavern, but he
had looked back again; a subtle relaxing of Raj's shoulders
told Justice the newcomers posed no threat. ''Even if you're
Revenantist,'' Justice said, ''you'll need a patron. Or more
money than I think you have.''

Raj chewed and swallowed. ''A patron, most likely. You're
right. I have hardly enough money to live on.''

Justice shook his head. ''I wish I could help you,'' he said,
''and I really mean that. But I'm studying art, and don't
know anyone who's planning to become a doctor.''

''You have a patron?''

''Yes. But he's not. . . '' Justice stopped. What this young
man wanted was beyond reach of most aspiring Merovingens,
yet something about Raj made Justice trust him. And judging
from the short conversation they had shared so far, Raj was

hardly stupid. "I suppose I could talk to Father Rhajmurti. He knows the other priests." His locked eyes with Raj. "But you'd have to convert, you now. *I* had to. That's the price I had to pay to get Father Rhajmurti as a patron."

"You must be damned good at what you do," Raj observed, "or Revenantist or not, he wouldn't be backing you. And as for conversion—" He made a quick gesture with his unhurt right hand. "I don't think you're *really* a Revenantist, for all you say, or you wouldn't have charged into that slip to rescue Denny." The black eyes hardened. "You ever see any of those thugs before?"

"No. Probably some gang. Lord knows there are enough of them canalside. Prey on anything weaker than them that won't fight back."

Raj stared a moment longer, then nodded slowly. "Bit off more than they could chew when *you* showed up." He laughed coldly, a sound strangely old and cynical coming from one of his comparative youth. "Found themselves a Revenantist who's not afraid to get involved."

"Huhn." Justice sought his beer, found the mug near empty and considered ordering another. What was one more pennybit? This meal was far cheaper than what he got at Hilda's, though it stood as proof of the old adage that you get what you pay for. "I guess I'm *not* Revenantist at heart," he admitted softly, "but I did have to convert."

"So can I," Raj said, the earnest look back on his face. "Look, Justice . . . I can pay you for this. I can pay your patron for his attention." He gestured at the packet Justice had laid aside. "That's a cure for the sickness that's running through town. Trust me . . . it works. I have access to more, and I can keep you supplied with it. You can pass some along to your patron. All I ask in return is that you speak to him. Tell him you've found another convert. *That* ought to interest him."

Justice raised his mug and waved it at the waiter. Pennybit be damned, he was having another beer. He looked back at Raj and pointed to the packet. "What's in there, exactly?"

"Herbs, mainly," Raj said. "Keeps the fever down and

dries up your head and lungs. I've got it divided up into doses. Don't take more than one, or you'll be floating.''

''And not give a damn *how* bad you feel.'' Justice grinned. ''All right, Raj, I'll take the stuff. You mix it with tea?''

Raj nodded. ''And sugar it. Tastes vile as lagoon water.''

The waiter threaded his way to their table through the crowd, set the new mug on the table and went off with the old one, along with Justice's pennybit. Justice looked at Raj: the young man sitting across from him had all the earmarks of becoming a friend. He seemed smart, capable *and* desirous of making more of himself. Now, if he was as good a street doctor as he thought he was, he would have little trouble convincing the College of his potential.

Justice laughed. Perhaps it was the beer, but he felt a damned sight better than earlier in the day. ''I'll talk to Father Rhajmurti I can't *promise* anything, but I'll try.''

''That's all I can ask for,'' Raj said. ''It's a hell of a lot more than I could ever get on my own.''

''Where are you living in case I have to get in touch with you?''

There was a slight hesitation. ''Fife,'' Raj said in a very quiet voice, after having looked carefully around the room. ''Two doors down from Fife Small Boat Repair under the studio.''

Trust given—trust returned. ''I'm on the backside of second level Kass, in a boarding house behind Hilda's Tavern.''

''Long ways off,'' Raj observed. ''My brother and I work at Gallandry's: he's a runner, and I help doing their accounts. If you need to find me, try there . . . it's closest.''

''It's a deal.'' Justice motioned toward the packet of herbs. ''How many doses in there?''

''Enough to get you through the fever . . . more than enough for you since you haven't really got it yet.'' Raj leaned forward on the table again. ''I'll try to stop by Hilda's day after tomorrow with more packets.''

''When?''

Raj's face clouded—the dark eyes became opaque. ''Hard to tell. Sometimes difficult to get away. What's your schedule?''

"Midterm exams will be starting. I'll be studying, so I should be free most of the time."

"I'll try to be there." Raj looked up at the door, around the tavern at the boisterous diners; he drew a deep breath, shoved his chair back and rose to his feet. "I've got to get back to Gallandry's, or they'll think I got dumped in the canal."

Justice stood. "Come on over to Hilda's after work," he said. "We can have a beer or two."

Something dark and haunted slipped across Raj's face again, but the black eyes were still open and honest. "Can't. Got something I have to do."

Justice knew enough not to pry. "Sometime else, then."

Raj nodded and led the way toward the door. Looking quickly left and right, he led the way into the twilight of canalside.

"See that you take care of that brother of yours," Justice said. "Warn him against getting trapped in dark cuts."

"Ha! I can warn Denny all I want, but he'll listen only when he wants to." Raj glanced around, then gripped Justice's arm with his good hand. "And take *my* advice, Justice . . . keep to well-lit walkways."

With that, the young man trotted off into the semi-darkness, headed for the stairs to second level Spellbridge. Thrown into a darker mood, Justice followed.

He saw nothing wrong with speaking to Rhajmurti about Raj attending the College, and nothing wrong about promising a new convert. If he and Raj were alike, Justice knew Raj would learn all the creeds, the rituals, the proper words, and still keep on *being* an Adventist.

But there was something hidden about Raj . . . something Justice could not guess at. From Raj's speech pattern, he was a hightowner, but a hightowner who had fallen on bleak times. And from Nev Hettek? That fact complicated already complicated impressions Justice had received from Raj.

And the way Raj had acted: furtive, anxious . . . jumpy hardly defined the young man's reactions to his surroundings. His parting words—keep to well-lit walkways—made sense, but Justice sensed a warning in those words, not just prudent advice. A momentary tightening of his heart. *Damn! I could be getting myself into something here . . . something I might not like.*

He shrugged, started off toward the stairs, the packet of herbs carried carefully in one hand.

Twilight was not far off, and Raj increased his pace as he crossed second level Spellman Bridge over to Sofia. Traffic was still heavy—people going home after work, going to taverns, or picking up last minute essentials for the evening— but soon the crowds would disperse from the bridges and walkways. After dark, travel afoot became dangerous, if not deadly.

After his lunch with Justice, Raj had found himself a dark nook in North-Spellbridge's pilings; tucked up and hid out. Waiting. With the papers underneath his shirt.

Now he had to try it. All the way to Boregy. As he walked, Raj felt his heart thumping behind his ribs, the heightened state of alertness brought on by a heavy adrenalin flow. Though he did not know the contents of the papers he carried, he *did* know that lives rode on those papers . . . Mondragon's, Jones', Denny's, his . . . and God knew how many others'.

Raj jogged left on the second-tier Sofia walkway, headed toward Sofia-Bucher.

It was just before he crossed onto the bridge that Raj knew himself followed

Instinct? Perhaps; or a skill he had picked up in his youth, a skill that had served him well in the swamp. If pushed to it, Raj might have turned around and pointed to the men who trailed him. Two . . . thank the Ancestors there were only two.

Keeping in the mainstream of traffic, his eyes flicking from side to side as he walked, Raj again increased his pace. His only hope was to outdistance his pursuers until he reached Boregy, and the comparative safety of the House. What happened after he made the delivery he left for the future—he had enough problems in the present to think all that far ahead.

Raj trotted through the crowds the shortest way around Bucher, headed toward White. From White, it was a straight shot up to Boregy. Provided he made it without being stopped.

A woman carrying a packet of freshly caught fish collided with him. In one motion, Raj bent down, caught up her package, and handed it back to her as he trotted on. Damn! The two men following him were still there, persistent as a cat after cream.

Lord and Ancestors! Are they after me *or do they know I'm connected with Mondragon?* Raj resisted the urge to look over his shoulder, and hoped for heavier traffic on White.

His shod feet joined the hollow thuds made by the the other people around him as Raj crossed the bridge over to White. He made to turn to his right, to take the straight way around to the White-Boregy Bridge.

Two more men loitered on the walkway before him, out of place in the hurrying crowd. Faces he had seen once this day.

Raj cursed, did an about-face, nearly knocking over a man and woman. *Damn! Damn! They're blocking the way to Boregy.* His eyes scanned the people around him, alert for other suspicious figures.

Now he was headed the wrong way on White, toward Junction Bridge that spanned the Grand, the Signeury on one hand and Borg on the other. Raj considered his options. Safety . . . he had to get to some place where he could hide out.

The second bridge on Borg's south side led to Cantry; he need only make it across diNero to Gallandry's. Once there, he would have to answer innumerable questions, but the grilling would be small price to pay.

Raj was trotting so fast now, he was near a lope. A quick glance behind: the two men who had started following him on Bucher had joined the two loiterers who had blocked his way on White. Raj cursed again and kept his eyes forward. The twilight was deepening around him.

He dodged left and onto the Cantry Bridge, aware that he

was now quite visible as he loped along through the lessening crowd. The shadows of the bridge might hide his face from passers-by, make his Oriental features hard to recall. He glanced ahead toward the Cantry-diNero Bridge.

Two more men stood by the edge of the bridge, equally as sinister looking as the four who followed.

Sweat chilled Raj's forehead: his armpits were already slick. The way across diNero to Gallandry's was blocked, and he had four men coming straight at his back.

The only escape was the Cantry-French Bridge, and that led him off from any protection he might have sought. He considered going canalside but gave that idea up, imagining more men intent on stopping him waiting below. Where could he go? French led to Bent, and Bent led to—

Justice! Bent led to Kass and Justice had given his address as Hilda's boarding house which lay on the back side of Kass. Raj cursed as he darted aside onto the Cantry-French Bridge. Seeking refuge with Justice was something he would never have considered if he had anywhere else to go.

He did not. There was no choice. Besides, the traffic around Kass and the other islands known for their student population would be heavier than elsewhere.

Heedless of the attention he drew, Raj ran through the crowds on French, seeking to lose himself from sight of his pursuers. Sidestepping a fellow homeward bound from market, Raj crossed the bridge to Bent. He still sensed the men who chased him behind, but not as close as before. A small hope flared in his heart—perhaps he could outdistance them after all.

Feet pounding on the wooden bridge, Raj crossed from Bent over to Kass. Hilda's Tavern. He had never been there before, but he knew where it was. Luck, for the first time since he had left Spellbridge, seemed to be with Raj: the Kass walkway was full of students. He slowed his pace a bit, darted in and out between them, his eyes fixed ahead, searching for Hilda's sign.

There! Hilda's lay only a short way ahead. Raj took one last glance over his shoulder, and this time he did not see the men who followed. Certain now that he had momentarily lost his pursuers, Raj brushed aside two students, offering hasty apologies, and entered the tavern.

To stand panting in the doorway, his eyes adjusting to the lamplight. He looked from table to table, seeking the only face he was sure he would recognize. Few people had looked up when he entered . . . another stroke of unforeseen luck. A surge of panic started to well up in Raj's heart. What if Justice was not here? If the men who followed were persistent (and having chased him across half of Merovingen they *must* be) they would search any public place they could find.

Then, from across the room, Raj saw Justice lift his head and stare. Murmuring a prayer of thanks to whoever had guided him here, Raj took a deep breath, tried to assume a normal expression, and walked across the crowded room to where Justice sat.

Justice met Raj's eyes across the room and sat up straighter, awakening Sunny who had been asleep on his lap. Gone was the young man he had eaten lunch with—now the black eyes looked haunted in a face unnaturally pale.

"Raj," he said softly, indicating the chair next to him and waiting until Raj had sat down. "What brings you here? I thought you had something to do tonight."

Raj licked his lips. "I did. I—Justice, can we go to your room. I need to talk to you."

A chill ran up Justice's spine, a feeling he tried to ignore. "Sure. Have a beer first?"

"*Now*, Justice," Raj said, and darted a glance toward the doorway leading outside. "Please."

Justice lifted one eyebrow, nodded, and lifted the sleepy cat from his lap. Standing, he gestured for Raj to follow, and started off to the door that led back to the boarding house.

"I haven't made you miss dinner, have I?" Raj asked at his elbow.

Out of place, that comment, from a person so obviously upset, unless Raj was trying to cover his unease, *and* confuse anyone who might overhear. "No. I usually don't eat until later." Justice walked down the hall, turned left at an alcove, and—juggling Sunny on one arm—slipped his key into the lock. "Come on in, Raj."

Justice went first, knowing the way, and lit a large lantern. The room was small; against one wall stood Justice's narrow bed, cluttered with books and papers, an old wooden standing closet at one end. The table across the room was heaped high with sketches and drawings nearing completion. Other artwork hung on the walls, some pen and ink, and some oils. Justice pointed Raj toward the chair in front of the table, shut the door, threw the lock, and sat down on the bed. Sunny yawned, jumped down from Justice's arm and curled up on the pillow, determined to finish his nap.

"What's the matter, Raj?" Justice asked, leaning back on his elbows.

Raj swallowed. "I was supposed to take some papers somewhere for a friend of mine who's ill. I was followed by six men. They cut me off from where I was going and started to chase me. I wouldn't have come here, but I had no other place to go." Raj leaned forward on the chair. "On my honor, Justice . . . they didn't see me come into the tavern."

But why were they after you in the first place? Justice silently asked. His mind sorted through everything Raj had told him. Adding the fight in the cut and the way Raj had acted at lunch, Justice felt certain now that Raj was caught up in something ominous . . . something better left unknown.

"And. . . ?"

Raj met Justice's eyes squarely. "I can't go out again. Those men aren't going to give up easily. And Denny and—" He shook his head. "I've got to get these papers back to my friend, along with the message that I'm all right or they'll think I've been dumped in the canal."

Or worse. "Fife's a long ways from here," Justice said aloud. "And I'd have to take a boat. I wouldn't want to be walking the bridges at this hour."

Another uncomfortable silence. "Denny's not on Fife. He's staying with my friend."

"Where?"

"Petrescu," Raj said and gave an address.

Justice hitched himself forward, sat with his elbows on his knees and stared at Raj. "I don't want to know anything more about this. In fact, I think I might know too much as it is."

Raj's black eyes glittered in the lamplight. "It's not what you suppose, Justice. Believe me."

And what is it you think I suppose? Some crazy cult? Is that it, Raj? Could you be caught up with them? You say you're from Nev Hettek, and Adventist. And what did those men who followed you want? You or the papers you carry? O Lord and Ancestors! I hope I'm wrong! Justice matched Raj stare for stare. "Don't tell me any more, Raj. Just give me the message."

"Then you'll go?"

"Yes." *Idiot! I'm an idiot!* "Petrescu isn't all that far away. I know a couple of honest boatmen who'll take me there."

Raj started digging in his shirt pocket. "At least let me—"

"No. I can afford it better than you can. Now what's the message?"

"Justice." Raj leaned forward in the chair. "You *do* realize this could be dangerous, don't you? *Very* dangerous."

"The thought crossed my mind," Justice replied, somewhat amazed at his own calm.

"Then for Lord's sake, go armed. You're no mean swordsman from what Denny says. And tell the boatman to take the most direct route."

Justice visualized the ways to Petrescu. "Down Archangel to the Grand, I'd think."

"Go past Foundry, then up Fishmarket." Raj's face tightened. "And when you get to Petrescu Cut, be especially wary of the Hagen Cut opposite."

"Ambush?"

"It's a possible place for one."

"You think I'll be followed?"

"I'm not sure. Damn! I wish you had some kind of cover. Then you'd—"

A sudden inspiration. "I've got one," Justice said, and smiled slightly at Raj's expression. He pointed to his desk and the packet of medicine Raj had given him at lunch. "Your friend's sick. I could be making an after-hours delivery—"

Raj shook his head. "No. You said you don't want to know anything more about all this, but you've got to understand . . . such a delivery wouldn't do my friend any good. In fact—"

"So he's being watched too?"

Raj shifted in his chair. "Possibly."

Possibly? What the hell am I getting into? "Damn. Then what could I be taking?" Justice looked around the room, seeking anything that could make his trip seem legitimate. "Got it!" he said, and pointed to the floor beside the desk. "Books."

"Books?"

"How many people would pay attention to some student out making a book delivery from the College?"

Raj nodded slowly. "I see what you mean. Now if you were carrying something that looked like drugs or food—"

"I'd be prime target for anyone to take on."

"But books are so expensive. I can't imagine you taking some out on the canals at night."

"Those books cost me next to nothing," Justice explained. "They're old, dog-eared, and thoroughly marked up. And, if necessary, I can always get more."

"All right," Raj said. "Books it is. I can put the papers inside one of them."

"What's your message?"

"Once you get to Petrescu, you'll have to give a password to Denny, or he'll never let you in the door. It's simple: Rif just sings cute little ballads. Have you got that?"

Justice' stomach had knotted at the mention of a password. Now, he was *sure* he was into something he very much did not want to know about. "Rif just sings cute little ballads," he repeated. "I've got it."

"Good. When Denny lets you in, you'll meet another one

of my friends, Altair Jones. she's a canaler . . . operates a
skip. She and my friend are—'' He waved his right hand and
looked somewhat uncomfortable. ''You know. . . .''

Justice kept silent, waiting for Raj to go on. A canaler, a
message runner, an accountant who longed to be a doctor.
What Raj's other friend was, Justice did not want to know.

''Anyway . . . tell Denny and Jones that I couldn't get the
papers through and that I'm holing up here for the night.''
Raj stopped suddenly. ''That *is* all right with you, isn't it? If
not, I'll try leaving sometime around third watch.''

''You can stay here. Don't worry about it.''

Gratitude showed in every line of Raj's face. ''I owe you
again, Justice.''

''Anything else?''

After a prolonged silence, Raj nodded. ''Tell Denny and
Jones that assassins might be loose and may try to make a
move tonight, or very soon.''

Justice stared. *Assassins?* He had second and third thoughts
about the trip to Petrescu and nearly voiced them. But Raj
needed help and, for good or ill, Justice could not ignore
such a request.

''Don't ask,'' Raj said. ''If you don't want to know any
more about things . . . don't ask.''

''You needn't worry. Now, tell me if I've got it straight,''
Justice repeated Raj's message and the young man nodded at
the end.

''You've got it. And for Lord's sake be careful, Justice.''

''Huhn.'' Justice stood, reached out and scratched the
sleeping cat, then walked to the standing closet. He took
out a heavy black sweater, pulled it over his head, then
sought his sword. Buckling the swordbelt around his waist,
he considered taking his dagger, rejected the thought, then—
remembering the fight in the cut—picked the dagger up from
the floor by the head of his bed.

''Here.'' Raj stood and picked up the pile of five tattered
books, handling them as if they were gold. He opened the
book halfway down the pile, reached inside his shirt, and
pulled out a rumpled sheaf of papers. Glancing once up at

Justice, Raj slipped the papers into the middle of the book. "You might want to tie the books together," he said, "to keep the papers from falling out."

Justice nodded, shoved the dagger into the swordbelt at his left side, took a heavy poncho down from the hook behind the door and wormed into it. He knelt, reached under his bed, and pulled out a ball of twine. With Raj's help, he tied the pile of books firmly together. "If I were you, Raj," he said, standing, "I wouldn't go out into the common room. I'll have Hilda bring you something to eat."

"I can't let you—"

"You can pay me back later." Justice walked to the door, unlocked and opened it, then turned to face Raj. "Now stay put."

"Justice," Raj said, as Justice turned to go. "If anything happens . . . if you *are* attacked, throw those books in the canal and go in after them!"

It was not fully dark yet when Justice left the stairs leading down from second level front-side Kass to canalside. Across the way, hidden now in the fog, the Signeury loomed up, looking ominous in the gloom. Poleboats always gathered at the landing: traffic here, as in other student areas, was good and frequent. Justice scanned the three boats that had tied up to the pilings of the landing, and breathed a sigh of relief as he spotted the boat tied at the far end. Sergei.

The small, compact poleboatman looked up as Justice walked out to the end of the landing. "Good evening, m'ser," he said, his white-toothed grin visible in the fading light. "Chilly night, no? Might snow soon, I'm thinking."

Justice lifted his head and sniffed the air. Sergei could be right: there was a change coming and the air smelled of it. Thankful that he wore his heaviest socks with his soft-soled shoes, Justice nodded.

"Don't like to think about snow," he said, "but if it comes, it comes."

"Where ye be going?"

His heart pounding, Justice flourished the books so that

anyone watching could see. "Making a delivery from Father Rhajmurti—semi-official College duty." *Lord! If Rhajmurti finds out I've used his name, he'll skin me alive!* He grinned at Sergei. "A little extra money never hurt anyone."

"Huhn." Sergei waited until Justice had climbed down into the coat, then unloosed her from the piling. He jumped lightly into his place at the rear, and took up his pole. "Where to?"

"Petrescu," Justice said over his shoulder. "The most direct route."

Sergei nodded, set his pole and the small, narrow boat nosed out into Archangel. "Heard ye sniff some, m'ser," he said, guilding his craft along close to the shore. "Something's going 'round. Could be bad."

Justice nodded, not really in the mood to talk. Sergei was one of the poleboatmen he had known the longest, and it had been a stroke of luck to find him waiting this evening. "Maybe. The change in weather might stop it."

"Could be," Sergei replied, planting his pole and letting the boat slide across the still water toward Borg.

It was never truly dark on the canals at night—water held light and reflected it amazingly well. And with tonight's fog, the poleboat glided through a close, luminous cloud.

Lord and Ancestors! What the hell am I doing out here? I hardly know Raj, and now I'm off on some fool's errand Lord knows where with something Raj considers highly dangerous. What's in those papers, anyhow? He snorted quietly to himself. *Best not even ask* that *question. What I don't know could save me if I'm caught and questioned.*

"So, how ye been doing in yer studies?" Sergei asked.

Justice shook himself from his thoughts and looked over his shoulder. "Sorry, Sergei," he said, roughening his voice. "Got a sore throat. Hurts to talk."

"Understand."

The trip proceeded in silence from there on. Palms sweaty despite the chill, Justice carefully watched the shoreline. Past Borg, under Junction Bridge and into the Grand. The buildings on either hand loomed up, oppressive in their dark bulk.

There was little traffic now, save other poleboats and a few skips. Sergei hugged close to the buildings where the water was shallowest, the steady rhythm of his poling sending his boat along in practiced smoothness.

Bucher passed, nearly unseen in the fog; then Spellman, though there were a few more lights shining from windows at canal level. Justice tried to keep from looking up as the poleboat slid under the bridges—a quick glance under his eyebrows would have to suffice. Ambush, Raj had said. Maybe.

The Foundry stood to their left now. Justice had seen the canalers tied up in small groups around each of the bridges the poleboat had passed; the Foundry-Pardee Bridge was no different. Five or six skips had clustered about the edge of that bridge and, in the silence with aid of the fog, Justice could hear the canalers talking. Their presence meant nothing: if an ambush did take place, he and Sergei could expect little help from the canalers. Sergei seemed to sense the urgency Justice felt, for he poled along at a pace a bit faster than what was normal.

As the poleboat glided under the Nayab Bridge, Justice could have sworn he saw several figures leaning over the bridge, watching as he went by. He drew a deep breath, surreptitiously loosened his sword in its sheath, hoping Sergei had not noticed.

Sergei pulled a hard left at Fishmarket, fighting against the stronger Grand current. Justice sat up straighter, his eyes straining to see through the fog. He shivered, felt the sweat beginning to run down his sides. Hagen was coming up in a short bit to his right, and Raj had said that an ambush could come from Hagen Cut that lay opposite Petrescu.

But, no. Petrescu Cut opened before them, and Sergei brought the poleboat to an easy stop at the landing. Justice heaved a sigh of relief, stood, wobbled a bit, and reached out for the piling.

"Be a while?" Sergei asked, nimbly jumping up to the landing and securing the rear tie.

"Shouldn't be." Justice kept his voice rough. "Be out shortly. Wait, if you would."

"Ye got it."

Justice looked for the set of stairs he sought and walked toward them, the books he carried held in plain sight. Knees trembling, trying to appear to be only another dull student making a College-related delivery, he took the stairs two at a time, shivered once in the chill, and came to the second level landing.

To face the door that led to the apartment Raj's friend occupied. Shifting the books to his left hand, Justice knocked softly on that door.

For a long moment nothing happened—no sound, no sense of movement on the other side. Justice's heart sank: what if no one answered? He could not even use Raj's password then.

He lifted his hand for a second knock, but a voice spoke from the other side of the door.

"Who's there?"

"Delivery from the College," Justice said loudly. He leaned closer to the door. "Rif just sings cute little ballads," he said in a hoarse whisper.

Another long moment of silence. Then Justice heard the squeak and rattle of locks. The door cracked open a bit, and Justice had a glimpse of Denny's dark-eyed face.

A look of recognition flooded that face, immediately replaced by an expression bordering on fear.

"Who?" asked another voice, a female voice, from close beside Denny.

"I know 'im," Denny said. "He's okay. Gave the password. 'Sides, he's the one who saved my skin t'day."

Another pause. "Let 'im in, then."

Justice waited until Denny had opened the door wide enough for him to slip in. The interior was dark, lit by only one small lantern. Facing him was Raj's brother and a dusky-skinned woman clad canaler-style, who must be the Altair Jones Raj had spoken of.

Another Adventist, with a name like that. Lords! What had he stumbled into?

"Raj?" Denny asked, shutting the door, and throwing the series of locks. "Where's Raj?"

"Back at my place," Justice said, all too aware of the look he was receiving from Jones. He felt the weight of the sword at his side, remembering that these people might be as dangerous as the men who had followed Raj. "He asked me to bring you a message. He's all right. He was on the way to deliver some papers for a friend of his who's sick, and was chased by six men who kept him from his destination."

"Damn!" That was Jones. She shifted her compact body in the semi-darkness. "Never got through?"

"No."

"Where's them damned papers? He still got 'em?"

Justice extended the books. "Raj put the papers inside the book in the middle of the pile."

Jones snatched the books, stood holding them to her chest. "Why'd he come to ye?"

"We had lunch today. I guess after I beat the thugs off Denny, he trusted me. He remembered where I lived, momentarily lost his pursuers, and came to me, looking for a place to hide. He knew you'd be worried about him, so he asked me to let you know he was all right."

Denny's face had brightened as Justice told his story. "He's all right," Denny murmured. "He's all right."

Justice looked at Jones. "Raj had more to say. He wants me to let his sick friend know that—" He licked his lips. "—assassins might be loose, and they may try to make a move tonight. If not tonight, then very soon."

"Dammit all!" Jones' voice shook and she darted a glance over her shoulder into the apartment. She looked back. "Ye followed by anyone?"

"Not that I can tell."

"Come by poleboat?"

Justice nodded.

"Who brung ye?"

"A fellow named Sergei."

Jones thought for a moment, then nodded. "Good man." She hefted the books. "Papers is small. What'd ye bring *these* for?"

"My cover. I wanted everyone to think I was making a delivery from the College. That's what Sergei thinks too."

Denny was staring at the books. "Ye'd leave 'em here?"

"Raj said he'd return them." He met Jones' eyes. "And if anyone *is* watching me, I can't very well leave with books I'm supposed to be delivering."

Jones stared at Justice. "Where d'ye live?"

"Backside of Kass." Justice gestured to the books. "My address is inside."

"Anything more? When's Raj coming back?"

"He asked if he could stay all night at my place. He's afraid to go out. He'll leave in the morning."

"Huhn." Jones' dark eyes flickered in the lantern light. "When ye going back home?"

"Sergei's waiting for me."

The silence stretched out until it felt uncomfortable. "Ye mind me, now. Ye've done us a favor, an' ye done Denny one t'day. Raj, he'll pay ye back. An' me 'n. . . ." She gestured briefly "Ye take the straightest way back, hear? Don't stop for nothin'. Ain't nothin' worse'n t'be caught canalside when ye don't know the territory. Hear me?"

Justice nodded, his heart beating faster. "I planned to do just that."

"Good. Now, git . . . 'fore the traffic clears off the canals."

Justice met Jones' eyes for a moment, saw the unspoken thanks there, and nodded again. A touch came at his hand.

"An' thank ye again," Denny said, "for savin' me t'day. When y'see Raj . . . tell 'im we'll figure out what t'do at this end."

"Git," Jones said in a friendly voice, brushing Denny aside to unlock the door. "Go safe!"

Justice slipped out the door, heard it shut firmly behind him, the rattle and squeak of locks loud to his ears. Drawing a deep breath, he trotted back down the stairs toward the landing where Sergei waited. The damp fog hit him in the face again and he shivered in the chill wind. Snow. The orderly change in seasons. Maybe snow would make things seem normal gain. Normal? Justice snorted a laugh, and looked carefully around, alert for the slightest hint of trouble. After tonight, he doubted he would ever take anything at its face value again. Sergei stood up as Justice walked out on the landing and began untying the poleboat.

The water slapped against the side of the boat as Justice crawled in. He drew the poncho closer, sneezed once, and thought of the medicine he had left at home. Sergei guided the poleboat back out into Fishmarket; Justice peered ahead into the murky darkness, and smelled a new rawness in the wind.

FEVER SEASON
(REPRISED)

C.J. Cherryh

The front door opened and closed again, and Mondragon leaned against the bedroom door frame, the pistol fallen to his side as Jones came down the hall toward him, waving a battered set of papers.

"Raj's all right, he couldn't get 'em through, but he's all right." As Denny arrived in her wake.

Mondragon let out a breath, felt the hall spin round, and held onto the doorframe until he had got another to steady him. Good news and disaster all at once. He had not killed the boy. Thank God, he had not killed the boy.

Jones held his arm, pulled him loose from the door, guided him back to the bed and sat him down. He put the pistol back into the reading rack of the nightstand and swung one leg up onto the bed, leaning back against the pillows, trying to think past the ebb and flow of blood in his brain.

"Could be worse. Denny, get out of here. I've got to talk to Jones."

"I don't want to."

"Denny, —" Jones clenched a fist, grabbed for the urchin, and Denny ran.

Mondragon coughed and recovered himself while Jones sat down on the bedside and pulled a blanket over him. It had been

hell getting home again—pick up a couple of Moghi's bullylads
to ride with them and see him up the stairs and watch the boat
till Del and Mira showed, and Min came back with the
damned pot, drunker than a sailor for sure. Thank God he had
shed the knit hat and the padding and sopped off the powder
with canalwater by the time they got to Moghi's, and looked
no worse than a poor fool in a smelly sweater and pants three
times too big and full of holes—with his face and hands and
feet all splotchy with brown stain. He had had a bath since.
He had had to have a bath. He was covered with bites from
something in the clothes.

"I c'n try—" Jones started out predictably. She would,
too. He had known that when she tried to worm his situation
out of him. *Raj* was supposed to have gone into the Justiciary. Raj was supposed to have delivered a quiet message.
Jones had double-crossed him, and said, cheerfully: *Ain't no
problem. What's he going to do? You got that paper out here.*

"No," he said.

Odds were high it was a setup. That someone had gotten to
Rosenblum. And God knew whether the papers they had
risked their lives for were forged.

No, gut-level instinct said. If the men who had sprung the
ambush were Tatiana Kalugin's, they might well have been
blacklegs. If arrest with state papers was the game, if the
game was hauling a band of fools into the Justiciary for
questioning that would turn up the name of Anastasi Kalugin—
then best those papers be real. And Rosenblum might or
might not have been in on it. It was even possible that it had
been House Rosenblum's own hired muscle, commanded by
Constancy Rosenblum, trying to save his reputation at both
ends—get the note *and* the papers back. Mondragon had
feared some such move and tried to dissuade it with threats:
the Families, and Rosenblum was from one of the Families,
ran their own police actions.

Mondragon took the papers from Jones. He spread them
out on his knees and looked them over. There was the Trade
Ministry seal on them, that he had insisted on, though they
were copies. There were the activities of the investigating

arm of the Ministry. There were the warehouse inspections, and the name of the inspector. There were the waivers granted regarding Nev Hettek shipments. And who had granted them.

If they were not real, whoever held these pages could force a comparison with the official record.

And there was, damningly often where it regarded waivers, the name of a certain inspector Nadya diNero. Who also had invested to the hilt with one Sulie diNero, who was into speculative investments on which one Anatoly Kuzmin, *the* Kuzmin, *had* had the notes, but Boregy's banking operation had done a lot of note-buying lately, offering the holders a small profit a month ago when liquid assets meant a chance of bigger profits on pre-winter cargoes.

Even a Merovingen gaming house was quite happy to sell a note. Or two. A little purchase no Boregy banker could have made, but a slightly raffish Boregy adherent might, without rousing alarms. Even a foreigner-Boregy might look to investments, of the slightly seedy sort his small allowance and duelist's resources made reasonable.

So the gambling house would reckon.

Rosenblum to diNero, diNero to a list involving inspections of cargoes, *and* the corresponding warehousing records, including Megarys. And all those waivers and variances, with names attached.

The Justiciary could be very rough in questioning, once it got on the track of evidence.

Even where it regarded high names.

And God knew, only those who knew what the connections were, knew how to doctor this list. *If* it was doctored. If Rosenblum had known how. If someone had instructed Rosenblum how, Rosenblum would be a dead man before winter, as they covered their traces. And he had told Rosenblum that. He had told him that if that started happening, Rosenblum had only one hope, and that was in going home to House Rosenblum, locking the doors, and admitting only a messenger who would give him a certain password . . . because his living to testify was desirable only to the side who wanted these papers.

He thought that Rosenblum understood that. It was worrisome that someone had been watching Rosenblum. But it was still possible that Rosenblum had run for home. Boregy had to have the papers. Boregy had to know what had happened. Boregy had to have the other gambling note, in case.

And have the papers yesterday, that was the damnable problem. By now Anastasi Kalugin might well be moving to find out why Thomas Mondragon had betrayed him and to whom. Or moving, having decided in his own mind that Thomas Mondragon was about to betray him: Anastasi had everything to lose if Mondragon talked, and the Thomas Mondragons of the world were always replaceable.

"What d' they say?" Jones asked.

"You don't want to know. But I think they're real enough." Cough "That part doesn't matter. Boregy can still use them."

"Ye let me run 'em t' Boregy. I c'n make it fine."

"No."

"Well, you ain't in no shape."

He ran a hand through his hair and let his head back on the pillows, trying to think.

"Look, I can do 'er. No problem."

"Jones, —I'm a day late. With men who get panicky when people don't keep their schedules. I don't want you out there alone. I don't want you in this apartment. God, I don't know where's safe. Look, I want you to go downstairs, get Tommy to run over to Grand, up to Boregy, get Boregy to send the launch down. I can take the papers over. In person."

"Ye think it ain't likely Anastasi heard about the fracas over on Archangel? Ain't heard how ser Constancy Rosenblum got kicked into the canal?"

"God." His head was throbbing. He noticed the pain finally. He was not thinking down all the tracks. He knew he was not. Focus kept coming and going.

"I figure," Jones said, "he knows damn well you made pickup today, not yesterday."

"Damn noisy. Everything was damn noisy."

"Well, that ain't bad."

"It ain't bad—except the papers haven't gotten to Boregy,

dammit, and by now Tatiana and Iosef and Magruder and Rosenblum and every other damn interest in town know *somebody* just made a delivery here. Who was it?''

"Student name of Justus. Same that saved Denny's skin. Raj come back to him—"

He thought that was what he had heard from the hallway. Strangers in this thing gave him cold chills. He entertained the lightning-flicker of a suspicion that Raj was in deep trouble, the papers a ploy, the student a decoy, everything set up by their enemies. But there was the reality of the papers in his lap to tell him that somehow, someway, St. Murfy had worked on their side.

Or a resourceful kid had handled himself like a professional in this, which was just about as likely as the Angel's personal intervention——handled himself like a professional until he had run into ambush and then found a way to leverage a perfect stranger into risking his neck. If the student had known.

But the student must have known—having fended the attack off Denny—that Raj was not in any ordinary kind of bind.

Damn, he distrusted charity. It all led in circles. It scared hell out of him. But there were the papers. Which meant that every assassin of every faction in Merovingen might have marked the boys, the student—it was the one thing Raj might not have thought of. It was a shadow-war. And someone was always watching.

Watching—for something to leave again.

"Someone will come here," he said, "looking for these papers."

"Who?"

"Make a list. Half the damn town's on it." He had a mental flash of the roof over on Hagen, the walks and bridges around Petrescu, as a battlefield of spies, littered with detritus, one faction and the other trying for position, and winced. Of himself outright throwing up the window and yelling at all and sundry that he was throwing them the damn papers and they could swim for them. But he was wandering. His face

was hot again and his focus kept coming and going. *This* was
the mind trying to think its way through a maze of cross and
double cross. "If we just stay put, *someone's* going to come.
If they try shooting their way in, that brings the blacklegs. . . ."

"Which is Tatiana's bullylads."

"Damn!" He shut his eyes and figured the best thing was
to go down there, himself, be the target, take the hit. But that
left Jones. Who knew too much for Anastasi to let her alone.
And the boys. Everyone. It kept coming back to himself and
Jones, making the run to Boregy. Best chance they had.

"Look, I c'n make it."

"Boregy won't like the racket. If you live to get there."

"I c'n do it," a higher voice said. Jones twisted around
and he flattened his knees and looked in consternation at the
urchin who put his head in the door—listening on hands and
knees, he had been. Denny scrambled up and stood in plain
view. "I c'n go right over the roofs."

"Out of the question," Mondragon said.

"Ain't no problem," Denny said, and fished in his back
pocket. Pulled out a folding grapple and a wad of cord. "I do
'er all th' time."

"Why, ye little *thief!*" Jones exclaimed. "That's a filch's
line!"

Denny shuffled and put the evidence behind him with a
little wince. "I ain't no filch, I'm a runner!"

"Come here," Mondragon said, folding up the papers.
"Come *here*." As Denny hesitated. Denny came, with a
wary look at Jones, still with the grapple behind him.

"As happens," Mondragon said, "a *thief* would be more
useful."

Denny winced and lifted a shoulder. "Well, if I was, I
could do it, couldn't I, get right over to Boregy—"

"There's likely men on Hagen's roof."

"Yey. Blacklegs've laid traps too, but they ain't never
caught us."

"You little sneak," Jones said. And: "I'll go with 'im."

Denny looked her up and down and sneered. "You're too
big. You couldn't keep up. No way."

"Denny," Mondragon said. "They'll shoot at you."

"They done that before too." Denny pointed straight up, looked toward the imagined roof. "Ye got a little tower up there. Got a lock-door. Tower down t' the other end. They got this beam ties Petrescu up with Vaitan, 'bout that crack on the north side—"

"You know it all the way to Boregy?"

"Sure." Denny gave his hair a toss, grinned as it fell back into his eyes. Mean-looking and impish as any canal-brat. "What table ye want me t' lay them papers on?"

"Listen. They're going to have Boregy watched."

"Boregy's got a lot of windows. Ye mind if I break one?"

"I don't mind."

Denny's eyes lit.

Vega Boregy lifted the teacup, perusing the market reports, meticulously penned by the House copyist, and sipped.

Something in Boregy exploded, with a racketing clank of massive shards of glass hitting the ground, that sound unduplicatable and unmistakable in timbre, which sent Vega Boregy's heart to a lurching double-beat, the teacup banging onto the table in a puddle, and the market reports sliding every which way as Boregy headed for the drawer and grabbed a pistol.

Retainers and poleboatmen and every member of the house who remembered the Sword attack up the watergate-stairs, that had rendered the elder Boregy an invalid and killed two of the Family and wounded a dozen of the staff—were headed toward the sound with guns and swords and knives and every other weapon at hand: when Vega Boregy came into the great dining room he had a half dozen retainers in front of him and a dozen more behind—

—to face black night and a free-blowing wind through the ruin of the great hall window, tall as three men. Shards of glass were everywhere, the whole central pane having come down and showered over the polished dining table, the chairs, the tesselated floor.

"Did they get in?" his chief of security yelled. "Search the halls! Fan out! Ware of gas!"

But Vega Boregy crunched his way through the wreckage to the agent of the ruin, a single brick, a very substantial brick bound about with cord.

There was an envelope bound to it.

Addressed to him.

The awful part of it was, Denny mourned, that he could not *see* the end of the matter. He was busy running, among the chimneys and the flues and vents, down over the copper plates of the big gable, eeling his way over the lumpy ridge-cap, and down the other side, down the guttering to grab a tall chimney, swing round and over to White on the top of the covered bridge, flat as he could make himself, and shinnying along fast and light as one of Merovingen's multitudinous cats, *far* side of the slope, because if there were watchers who had seen that big window go, they were on White, and he was going right by them.

Just as slick as ever he had done it: he heard the uproar, heard the thief-bell tolling, the whole town in upset, and himself with a glorious view of the Signeury itself right across the Grand.

Alarm, alarm, alarm!

The big Signeury bell took it up, thundering its moral outrage.

And Denny drank it all in with a thrill of absolute and passionate delight.

Jones paced, paced the bedroom till she was aware she was doing it, back and forth so often her feet stopped being cold; and then forced herself to stand still, which felt stupid; and then to sit, which was damned near impossible, while Mondragon lay silent and followed her with his eyes, as if he would do much the same if he had the strength in him.

She imagined a sound in the all-too-silent apartment. She went upstairs again with the gun. She came down again and padded to the front and listened with her ear against the wall, then went back and paced the bedroom again till she knew she was driving Mondragon mad. Then she just stood where she was and shoved her hands into her pockets and confined her pacing to smaller, rocking movements.

"Takes a while," she said.

But all the while she was thinking of that roof up there, and the way the kid had lit out the way Tom had told him, out that rooftop door like a shot, with a tumbling roll right to the cover of the chimney; and she had not bothered to see anything else. She had shut that door and thrown the deadbolts and listened for a long time, hearing running then. Light and quick.

She had dived right down and closed the trap that was Mondragon's second line of defense, bolted it, and come on down the stairs.

To pace and fret.

But of a sudden a thief-bell rang out somewhere far away, nothing unusual in Merovingen. And hard on that, the deep voice of a different bell.

"The Signeury," she said, her heart leaping up. She exchanged a look with Mondragon, listening, listening, as the pealing went on.

"Could be," he said. Then she knew how afraid Mondragon had been, because there was so much and such desperate hope in his eyes as he looked toward that wall. Like he could see through it all the way to Boregy.

She came and sat down by him and held onto his hand.

"It isn't over yet."

No. A very young boy had to get away. Had to take a devious route all the way over to Kass, where Raj was; pick up his brother and get over the roof-ways to Moghi's, to the shed where a couple of boys with a purseful of money and Mondragon's note: ("This should pay for them. —M.") would find shelter not even blacklegs could crack.

"Them out there," she said, with a jut of her jaw toward the canal, the general vicinity of Petrescu, where their enemies watched quietly. "I dunno if they're onto him, but they got to know something's happened up there."

"They'll know," Mondragon said. "They'll know real soon. Whatever's happened."

"They going to hit us?"

Mondragon shook his head slowly, against the pillows, his eyes wandering to the other, the front wall, as if his thoughts were down on the canal, out there on the roofs. "No. Whoever's out there, they're professionals. If they lose, they lose. Revenge *costs* too much—generally. No. We'll smile at each other—in Boregy's drawingroom. Or when we meet on the walkways."

It was something like what he had said about Min and the Suleiman skip being down there on the canal: *No. Too noisy. Too uncertain. You don't murder canalers wholesale in this town. They don't need a quarrel with the Trade.*

She had halfway understood that. Even if they were foreign. *Mondragon* had understood it right well.

But the business about drawingrooms baffled her.

Waiting did.

Mondragon held onto her hand, and squeezed it. While the Signeury bell fell quiet. "If Boregy gets the papers, they'll know, that's all. Publicity is what these people have to dread. It'll go all quiet again. Boregy will get the word to Anastasi. And Rosenblum. And Tatiana will regroup. That's the way it works. The boys hide out a day or two. Moghi won't let them out till it's safe. Then everything goes back to normal. If those papers got through. You aren't going out on the water tomorrow. Hear?"

"Huh," she said. "If that Denny got through, if he gets to Moghi's, I got somebody coming t' get t' Del. Del's going to take my skip down to Moghi's. Moghi'll keep 'er at tie. Like we was in the Room. I set it up with Denny."

He looked a little surprised. "Good," he said.

And in due time, there was a to-do out on the canal. A thumping on the water-stairs then. And a voice singing:

> "There's a wheel that's moving fast through our time
> And we've seen the track it made.
> I believe you know where it has to go,
> And the way that the game is played. . . ."

*   *   *

"He made it, he made it, he made it," Jones cried. And hugged Mondragon hard.

Three days on, Mondragon got out of a hired poleboat and rang the bell at Boregy. He was still short of breath, still prone to chill, and carried no sword, first because it was daytime in a high-class neighborhood, and secondly because he reckoned he would be doing well just to walk. He had thought of taking the gun, highly illegal, but he had to surrender the cloak to Boregy servants, and Boregy was a nervous man. He went without, having told Jones to stay at Moghi's for the morning— (*"Please,* Jones. —Jones, shut *up,* don't fight me, just do this one thing for me. A few hours. Say I'm hiring you to *sit,* all right?")

In fact it was Jones' fretting and pacing that stirred him out earlier than he might have tried it. Sitting still was eating her gut out; and he had come finally to the conclusion that there might indeed be protection in waiting till he was solidly on his feet before putting in an appearance at Boregy's, in the case there was trouble waiting; but there was more percentage in letting Boregy see that he had come there as soon as he could physically make it.

Jones was fretting to get back onto the canals, there were two boys fretting in Moghi's shed, and if he was determined on one thing, it was that none of them were going to probe the way for him: if it was safe, *he* would find it out, he would feel out the temper of things uptown, and in the hightown, and if he was wrong in his estimation, Jones would take the boys and take the money he had left with her, everything he had, and get herself and them whatever safety his money could buy.

He hoped. God, she was stubborn. She had listened very quietly at the last, when he gave her the purse full of gold and forcibly wrapped her hand around it; and Jones listening quietly was either an uncommonly good sign or a very bad one.

He exchanged a pleasant good morning with the servant

who answered the door, walked up to the main level, surrendered his cloak and scarf to the servants who met them there, and was advised ser Boregy was anxious to see him.

In the dining room.

He walked in. And stopped at the sullen, angry figure of Vega Boregy, standing firmly in his path with hands behind him; at the instant realization that there was something very *wrong* with the dining room, something was obstructing the light—a large panel of wood instead of the glass—

Denny—

Oh, my . . . God . . .

"*Good* morning, Mondragon. You look surprised. What did you *think* you hit?"

He felt dizzy. He walked aside and sat down uninvited on a straight chair by the door. "I'm sorry. I'm truly sorry."

"We gave out that it was an assassination attempt. That we drove off the invaders. I appreciate your necessity to make it clear to Rosenblum's agents that the package *had* been delivered. We assume you were aiming for one of the side panels."

"M'ser, I—assure you that was the case. I'm mortally sorry." Coughing overtook him. He got his breath back.

"Now you bring us the local misery."

"I didn't plan to stay long." He stood up carefully. "I only wanted to be sure you did get the packet. That you understood my note. I've been—as you see—rather well done in by this stuff. I hope you'll tell our friend—I did everything I could, as soon as I could. I hope it *was* adequate."

Boregy's mouth made a thin line. His eyes raked Mondragon up and down. He went to the sideboard and poured two brandies, which action Mondragon followed with gathering hope. Brandy, Mondragon thought. And thought of a small ship and dark waters. And who sold it at the best prices in town. He took the glass from Boregy's hand, sipped and felt its fire on his raw throat.

"Let's go into my study," Boregy said, indicating the door with his glass. "I have some additional details to ask you.

Your own estimation of m'ser Rosenblum, for one. You seem to have a fine grasp of mercantile affairs. . . ."

"Tool of the trade, m'ser."

"Of many trades, m'ser. I do not ignore ability. Especially when it is there for me to use. . . ."

LIFE ASSURANCE

Lynn Abbey

The Ramsey Bell looked no different from any of the dozen or more taverns tucked into the nooks and crannies of Ramseyhead Isle. A faded shingle swayed in the tidal breezes, proclaiming both name and brew; a plume of damp sawdust spread out from the doorway proclaiming that the previous night's tailings had been swept away and today's business could begin.

Inside, the owner, a burly man who looked as if he could stop or start the occasional barroom brawl, supervised the simmering stewpots while empty kegs clattered down a ramp to the canalside cellar. A scene no different from that in any Merovingen tavern as it prepared for an ordinary day in the fire-wary city where a home with a legal fireplace or kitchen was a luxury.

No, the Ramsey Bell took its personality from its patrons, the first of which arrived not long after the wharf bells (situated on the tavern's roof and from which it took its name) echoed the noon peal from Signeury. A regular, Franck Wex, nodded at the chalkboard menu and needed no further word nor gesture to place his order. He settled into a hard-back seat at the large left-side front table and appeared to doze off immediately.

It was unlikely that anyone else who frequented the Bell would have taken his favored table, but habit and a certain type of caution was bred deep into Merovingen's wealthy mercantile houses. Someone always arrived early to assure that the appropriate places at the afternoon gathering place for trading heirs and second sons were properly reserved.

"G'day, ser Wex. Ships in?"

Dark eyes opened and examined the questioner with perfect alertness. Dao Raza, scion of the corn merchant, and not a casual question, considering the Wex traded mostly in corn themselves.

"Some."

"Unloaded?"

"Most."

"Same," Raza acknowledged, shuffling chairs at the opposite table.

Franck Wex shut his eyes again and wondered if Raza had lied as well. Likely. No dock crew had been spared by the seasonal fever; everyone had to be short-handed and scrambling. And no house had been spared the economic anxiety that had sprung up in the wake of the *pathati* attack on the Signeury. Indeed, that malaise was spreading beyond Merovingen to her trading partners and though there was nothing so formal as war along the River Det, the city's merchantry cloaked themselves more and more in an atmosphere of siege.

Having long feared the wrath of Kalugin within Merovingen's Signeury, the disorganized merchants had looked there now for leadership against real, if still generally faceless, enemies. And old Iosef Kalugin, who had passed his life confounding all around him, kept his record intact by doing nothing the merchantry recognized as useful. For a census—whatever else its civic merits might be—did nothing to grease the wheels of commerce.

But their offspring and journeymen came still to the Ramsey Bell after their morning's work along the wharfside, in the markets and at the warehouses had been completed. They took a late lunch as their parents and grandparents had done before them and engaged in the discreet art of gossip without which no mercantile culture could function.

The outer door repeatedly slammed on a broken hinge, stifling the beginnings of conversation at some of the back tables. The owner, muttering that once broken nothing on Merovin was ever truly fixed, hastened to prop the door open. His more important customers—those who would in time be among the more important men in the city—would be arriving soon and they had no need of grand entrances. Besides, the day was close enough that a breeze was welcome despite the inevitable flies. He placed a tray of glasses and a pitcher of pale ale on the Wex's table, then took a page of orders from less familiar faces.

Gavin Yakunin, looking hot and tired in a sweater that should have been appropriate for autumn but wasn't, slumped into the second seat at the table.

"Pour me one, while you're about it," the newcomer asked.

Wex did so silently. The time was not yet right for conversation.

Some distance away, Richard Kamat threaded across the narrow bridges that connected one isle to the next and Kamat, ultimately, with Ramseyhead. He had the longest walk of any of the regulars at the Bell and, since the death of his father, no real reason to go. He was househead now, without the narrow directives of a house's dockside agent. He could have—perhaps should have—dined in his own quarters or in intimacy with his peers, the scant eight dozens of househeads who stood at the top of Merovingen's pyramid.

That thought, frankly, still set his innards twisting. At twenty-five he was the youngest major househead in the city and could not yet sit across a table from his peers without thinking of Nikolay Kamat—of his father and of himself as untried son. The image of his suddenly mortally-stricken parent rose unbidden to the forefront of Richard's memory. He could not shake it away, but in the months since the

funeral he'd learned to modify the scene and the mood it
invariably brought.

He'd approve, the young man thought as he waited for a
pushcart to clear the entrance of Fishmarket Bridge. *I'll
always be your son to the men who were your friends and
enemies, but at the Bell I'm the first who's jumped. Not fish
nor fowl, but they look up to me, and I'll be their spokesman.
Karma. Not balanced, but it will serve.*

A shout rose up from beneath the bridge: Damn you to
Megary—or some such. Richard pushed his way to the side
and stared down. A poleboat had gone broadside in the
current, fouling a canaler as it went. The poleman, woman
actually, was scarcely into her teens and short on skills as
she recovered her course. The insult had shaken her—Richard
could see the sweat on her white face from the bridge—or she
was fevered. More likely the latter, he considered as he
started walking again; no one who lived canalside, not even a
child, was unaccustomed to insults.

Megary, though, flew in the rumors these days and Kamat,
which had better ears in Merovingen-below than many, was
sensitive to the sound. Kamat had a score to settle and word
had come back it might be settled at Megary. Sword and
slaver—an appalling sort of partnership if it were ever proven,
but a logical one for all that. If there were Sword of God in
Merovingen then Megary would be working with them as they
had with every other shadowy or illicit enterprise for a
generation or more.

Richard was almost positive he could prove it. Prove it
through the person of Rod Baritz who was certainly from Nev
Hettek and almost as certainly an operative of the Sword. If
there was karma then it weighed against Kamat each day he
delayed—but interrogation in the Justiciary wasn't Baritz'
destiny—yet. No one there would care that he had drugged
Marina Kamat, Richard's sister, and left her for dead at
Nikolaev. And since Kalugin and the city would kill him for
the crimes they did care about, Baritz would have to answer
for Marina before he went to the Justiciary.

Vengeance was an unpracticed art in Kamat. Nikolay Kamat

had had few enemies and none whom he didn't respect or mingle with socially; he'd brought up his son the same way. It was measure of the depth of the Sword's cut, of the damage it had already done to Merovingen's delicate structure, that Richard cherished vengeance in the coldest regions of his heart.

And kept it hidden there, for no one at the Ramsey Bell, not even his cousin Gregory who was now Kamat's agent wharfside, suspected it as he took the last vacant seat at the table.

"How goes the war, Dickon?" Gavin asked, using the nickname that went far back into Richard's childhood.

"Holding our own," Richard replied with a laugh as he poured the last of the pitcher into his glass.

"Ah, but how long could you hold if the city shuts down?" Franck asked morosely. The Wex trade in perishable food-stuffs was more vulnerable to day-to-day shifts in the city's mood than that of Kamat, whose dyestuffs and textiles were durable and more easily stockpiled. "And who has the power to shut down Merovingen?" Richard replied with another laugh, but one that was less sincere.

"Our own governor, for a start," Krespin Balaci muttered.

So they were into it without a mouthful of food among them yet. And Richard, feeling his way in his new role as elder statesman here, sat back to listen.

"A census—by all that's sacred, what does he hope to accomplish with a census?"

"If there's outsiders in the Below, then no nose-counter's going to smoke them out. And as for religion, saving the lunatic Janes, who's going to say they aren't precisely what they're supposed to be?"

"And who cares—save that the Below's riled and there's no business with strangers . . ."

"That's not the census . . . that's something else again."

Richard's table froze into silence; the last remark had come from Raza's table, though not from Dao himself. Angel knew these men listened to each other and often spoke for the room rather than their closest companions—but actual con-

versation between tables was rare enough to raise eyebrows.
Richard felt the dynamic pendulum swing his way.

"What else, ser Martushev?" he asked, giving the unseen
pendulum a shove.

Martushev shared Rimmon Isle with Nikolaev, among others,
and knew more about the deaths and destruction there than
had ever officially been put out.

"Nothing you don't know of yourself, ser Kamat."

Richard drummed his fingers lightly against the side of his
glass. He didn't doubt he knew more than Martushev imagined. "Safe to say. Who knows what the Sword of God will
do? Or what the Janes have already done."

The taproom grew closer as every man drew his breath in.
Not even Kalugin, in his commands and proclamation, had
said what the census was supposed to isolate and expose.
Now Kamat, not the highest of the mighty, but a respectable
source all the same, had put its name in front of the rumors.
The silence broke like a storm surge.

Trade balanced its risks with intrigue. A little disorder, a
little uncertainty in the world beyond the counting-rooms,
was the oil that kept the machinery running smoothly. Too
much chaos, though, and the mechanism slipped out of control.

"I pay an out-city agent a silverbit a hundred-weight as
surety." The softly spoken words came from Dao Raza, and
the grain surety he quoted amounted to nothing less than
extortion.

Franck Wex pushed his stew aside. "Same here," he
admitted, "give or take a copperbit."

Richard knew the House Wex balance sheet better than he
knew House Raza. In his mind he calculated how much the
corn traders would have to raise their prices, then he made
another guess of when Merovingen-below would erupt in
food riots. It could make for a very long winter—and it could
make the diplomatic niceties of war completely unnecessary
for Nev Hettek.

Other voices emitted brief tales of up-river pressure. Richard retreated into silence as the scope and pattern of Nev
Hettek meddling emerged. He had supposed, owing to the

blood-tie between Nev Hettek and his mother, that Kamat was alone in receiving thinly veiled threats; that his house was uniquely vulnerable to economic blackmail.

He was wrong. Someone in Nev Hettek knew the city's traders better than they knew themselves. Someone had tailored the blackmail to each house's particular weakness. Someone understood the habitual secrecy with which each house shrouded its inmost affairs. And someone had been willing to stake everything that no househead would turn to the Signeury for help.

It had happened before. Famine or glut had tipped the balance too far toward the side of disorder and chaos reigned in the shops and warehouses of Merovingen. Fortunes were made and lost in a season. The Adami, who had lent their own name to Kamat Isle not two generations past, had crumbled into poverty in just such a tumult. But their downfall had been the result of a season-long failure of northern timber (the organic skeleton of Merovingen which must be constantly restored and replaced). This cycle would be driven by the Adventist expansionism of Nev Hettek into the far-flung trade of the Det River delta.

Everyone knew the Sword of God could be relentless and brutal; Richard had contemplated his vengeance in that same spirit. The face of Rod Baritz floated square in Richard's mind. He took a new measure of the man—his physical softness contrasting with his hard, porcine eyes. Such a face, such a man, could plot a city's downfall through riot and starvation. The young Merovingen househead had never before imagined how subtle the Sword might be in using Merovingen against itself.

"They must be stopped," he muttered.

"And how would you stop the Kalugins?" Franck inquired.

Richard shuddered as he came back to the tangible reality of the Ramsey Bell and sought the context of the question. The census—everyone was still griping about the city census while his thoughts had wandered down more twisted pathways. "The way we always have," he said, sounding more casual than he felt. "Obey and ignore."

"What? Ask his prying list of questions and hand out his filthy scraps of paper? Canalside will run wild," that from Balaci.

"Forget canalside—what business is it of Kalugin's who resides in our house or on our isle?" That from Martushev again, at the other table.

"No business—unless he gets so curious he sends his own eyes over for a look. Kamat will tell Kalugin what Kalugin needs to know—nothing more, nothing less—but Kamat knows more about Kamat than Kalugin will ever *need* to know." He gave them food for thought to accompany the steaming bowls appearing at their places. It would have pleased them even more if Richard had told them that Kamat had already refused to use its First-Bath dyes to tint the identity-card paper. Those cards were going to be hated and forged out of all proportion to their effectiveness, and Richard would not see the words "First-Bath" associated with them. Not even at the price Iosef Kalugin had offered.

The excitement which had bound the tables together had almost completely faded when Pradesh St. John, whose lips were twisted by a childhood scar, spoke up in his slow, careful voice: "It's not the foreigners who need separating out. We shut our eyes to our own."

That meant Megary—everyone knew it, and no one meant to acknowledge it. So Desh, who was not accounted much power here anyway, lowered his eyes and said nothing more.

His words stung, though. They haunted Richard throughout the meal, inhibiting his conversation and causing him to invent a pretext for leaving early. Then they led him up the far side of Grand Canal, to the canalside slips of Calliste and a dark, tilt-angle alleyway no man of property ought dare to walk.

Richard didn't know the names and homes of every man who drew Kamat pay, but he knew most of them who'd been there any length of time. He knew Jordie Slade for a hard working, god-fearing man. It had been five days since Jordie had picked up his sack and sweater and headed for home— and nary a word since. Probably nothing more serious than the fever, which was serious enough down here. But Jordie was a member of what Hosni Kamat, who started the Kamat fortune, called the greater family. Richard would give him a lune for medicine; more if the crud had spread through his family.

Karma. It was the least a house could do . . . should do.

He rapped on the door and listened with growing curiosity as furniture was shoved aside. The door opened a crack—not enough to cast light on the room or its occupants.

"What're you here for?" a voice more hostile than female demanded.

"M'sera Slade?"

"So. Who're you?"

"M'sera, I'm Richard Kamat—your husband works for me. He hasn't been to work for several days. We're worried about him, it being the fever season and all. Has he taken sick?"

"M'ser *Kamat*?"

The voice changed its modulation away from hostility toward something Richard could not immediately identify. More furniture was quickly shoved aside. The door swung wide.

"Come in, come in. I didn't know . . ."

Richard ducked under the doorway. He stood still, waiting for his eyes to adjust to the dim light while the woman re-erected the barrier. He was used to hearing surprise and embarrassment in their voices when he entered their homes, but Jordie's wife's voice held only faint hope and despair.

There was no fever in this spotless, threadbare flat—and no Jordie Slade either. Only a woman no older than Marina and two small children who watched him in huge-eyed silence.

"Does he do this often?" the Househead asked.

"No, not my Jordie. He never done this before . . ."

Her eyes filled while she spoke, then released her tears down trembling cheeks. Richard wondered how many days she'd hidden behind her door, sharing her terror with none but her children. He guided her to the sofa where, once she was seated, the children immediately moved to her side. Richard asked what had happened, then offered her his handkerchief as the question brought forth more tears than words. The wise man of wealth and power knew better than to presume casualness in the homes of his inferiors; Richard stood at military rest while the young woman stumbled through her story.

Their youngest had been fevered and Jordie had cast about looking for quick work to get the medicines that would see the child to health. He'd found something five nights ago.

"He must've known something," the woman said, her voice suddenly steady as she stared into Richard's eyes. "He come back here with the coin first. Said he'd got less for the work, getting the coin first and all, but it was enough for the medicine an' that was all that mattered."

"Did he say where he was going, or who he'd be working for?" Richard asked, already certain that Jordie hadn't told his wife.

She hesitated then hid her face behind the cotton square. "He said he'd be back by third watch, and he just said he loved me. . . . Oh, m'ser, Jordie'd always say he loved me an' not to worry—but he just said he loved me."

Richard felt his blood go cold with karma. If he'd been his grandfather, who'd grown up working beside men like Jordie, he'd have taken the woman in his arms like a daughter and promised her that Jordie's vengeance was Kamat's vengeance. But Richard wasn't Hosni, and compassion pounded through his veins without ever breaking the surface.

"We'll look for him, m'sera," he said awkwardly.

"Not the blacklegs!" she hissed.

So she knew enough to know that whatever Jordie had done that night, it hadn't been legal. And even if it had, there was no love and less trust between the workers and the enforcers of Merovingen.

"No, not the blacklegs," he assured her. "My own men. Kamat men. We'll find out what happened."

He didn't offer her the false hope that they'd find Jordie and he was grateful that she didn't seem to look for it. He asked when she or the children had eaten last and was not surprised when she didn't answer. Canalside they had a phrase for people, events or days like this: Instant Karma, they called it. The upper classes generally preferred the more discreet *lifetide*. Jordie Slade's wife had crossed his destiny and there wasn't any use in fighting it.

"Gather enough for tonight. You'll stay at Kamat until this is over." He did not add that where karma was involved, nothing was ever over.

The young woman seemed to sense that her own karmic stream had sluiced into a different channel. With whispered instructions to the children, she gathered her life with Jordie Slade into three sturdy baskets. They followed Richard down to the Calliste slip where he hailed a poleboat.

"Where're we going, Mama?" the youngest, a girl-child of about three, asked.

"We're going where it will be safer."

"Does Daddy know?" the elder, also a girl-child one or two years older, asked in faintly distrustful tones.

"Daddy would want us to be safe."

Richard felt an unexpected twinge of admiration that she had reassured them without lying. "You'll be safer in Kamat. . . . I, I don't know your name, m'sera."

"Eleanora."

Andromeda Kamat, dowager of the house, had been persuaded to spend the foul-aired autumn at one of Kamat's indigo estates some one-hundred-and-seventy kilometers down the coast. She'd left more than a month ago and taken with her the remnants of the Adami—twenty-odd dispirited former aristocrats who had dwelt cheek-by-jowl with his family since Hosni Kamat's purchase of their island.

At the time Richard had rejoiced, seeing two of his nagging problems resolved: his fragile mother had been removed from Sword influence or observation and the Adami would finally have the chance to reverse their collective karma or disappear completely from Merovin geneologies. Now he had another reason: his mother would not return until the end of the week, and by then he'd have the remnants of the Slade family settled.

The Adami had vacated a half-dozen cavernous apartments and it would be easier to install Eleanora and her children in one of them while his mother was away. Richard might have inherited the Kamat business, but Andromeda still ruled the house. His mother would have asked questions he was not ready to answer; questions his sister would never think to ask.

"I would earn my way," Eleanora said, hesitating at the threshold, daunted by the ornate door with its wrought-iron straps and grill-work.

Richard repressed a sigh. "We can speak of that later . . . when all this is settled. But first I'll see you and the children fed and rested."

He pulled the bell-rope then opened the doors himself. In the absence of the Adami, Kamat was understaffed. Andromeda had charged her daughter with the hiring—thinking it would take her mind off the Nikolaev disaster. It hadn't. Andromeda would return to find they still needed new servants—from chars and porters up through butlers and cooks. Richard could easily say that Eleanora—if she could cook or sew—was a god-send, except that karma seldom involved itself in domestic service.

"Wait here," he instructed, indicating the scrollback chairs lining one wall of the vestibule. "My sister will know which apartments are ready. I'll be back after I speak with her and take you down to the kitchen."

Looking very young and completely lost, Eleanora nodded silently then took a firm grip on each of her children before perching at the very edge of the least comfortable-looking chair. Richard understood the futility of suggesting she relax, and hurried up the stairway to the drawing room where Marina was most apt to spend her afternoons.

He saw the pile of crumpled paper and heard her muttering as he slipped, unannounced of course, into the room. Three piebald kittens were noisily scattering the paper beyond even Marina's usual carelessness; a fourth was trying to climb a dark blond plait. Marina did not seem to notice any of that or her brother from the depths of the day bed in which she reclined.

"Having fun, Ree?" Richard asked innocently.

The kittens and Marina all jumped with surprise. The kittens slipped and fell in their attempts to find hiding places; Marina took a sheet of paper from her writing board and stuffed it between the cushions beside her.

"I don't know how mother manages," Marina said rather more quickly than was necessary. "There must be honest people in this city looking for work—but I can't find them. And if I'd known *that* I'd never have promised to hold a reception for her when she returned. *She* never seemed this *overwhelmed*. Well, she had the Adami, of course, but she had to write everything herself. A buffet for sixty people— what's sixty people?—and I've been writing invitations, menus and shopping lists *all* day. And I'm nowhere near finished . . ."

Richard ignored the details. He heard only the rapid rise and fall of her voice and her determination that he not notice the scrap she'd hidden away. So Marina had her little adventures going again. At any other time, Richard would have looked less charitably on his sister's penchant for schoolgirl romances and intrigues, but she had been shaken by the Nikolaev affair and he was glad to see her interested in anything again. He scooped up one of the kittens and sat at the foot of the day bed.

"There's been a problem with one of the workers. I've brought his family here to Kamat."

Marina's eyes brightened. She fancied herself more kindred to the workers than to the privileged elite of Merovingen society. She affected worn clothing which Eleanora Slade would likely have given to the rag-collector but, to her credit, Marina did keep herself informed about the ups and downs of the workers' lives. A House-gift of silver commemorated each birth, marriage and death without fail.

"Which one? Bolger? His wife was doing poorly . . ."

"No, Jordie Slade's gone missing and—call it a hunch, or karma—I don't feel good about it. I went to check on him after lunch and, well, I thought it would be just as well to bring them here. There's his wife, Eleanora, and two children—I forgot to ask their names.''

His sister chewed on the tip of her pen. "She isn't a cook, is she? Angel knows we *need* a cook.''

"I didn't think to ask that either—I mean, it's not certain she's staying very long. There could be any number of good reasons why Jordie's gone.''

"But you don't think so, do you, Dickon?''

Richard pushed his hair back from his forehead and shrugged noncommittally. Like almost every other member of his class, he'd been exposed to orthodox Revenantist teaching during his impressionable years; like almost every one else, the surface of his life seemed relatively undisturbed by religion or philosophy. But Revenantism flowed deep and he was dwelling on karma today more than he had in the previous ten years combined. Not even his father's untimely death had seemed so laden with destiny.

Marina shoved the writing board to the carpet and swiveled the length of the day bed to take her brother's hand between her own. *"Lifetide?''*

Richard met her eyes and saw the excitement, verging on envy, in them. Marina lived for lifetide, yearned for a manifestation of uncontrollable destiny in what she considered an unrelentingly boring life and mourned the fact that, even considering Nikolaev, lifetide had never caught her in its undertow. He squeezed her hand then released it with a little smile.

"I doubt it,'' he assured her gently, convincing himself at the same time and breaking the spell karma had woven over him since lunchtime. "More likely something I ate at dinner last night. You're absolutely right: we've got to get a cook before Mother comes home.''

He stood up and walked back to the door. "In the meantime, I'll be setting up m'sera Slade and her children in Ferdmore's old rooms—just so you'll know they're occupied again.''

*   *   *

Marina Kamat sat back on her ankles, a huge smile bursting across her face the moment her brother had shut the door again. She worried about him as he worried about her. Worried about the maturity which had overwhelmed him after their father had died. Worried about the grim determination that had marked his comings and goings since he'd rescued her. She wanted the elder brother she remembered back again—the brother who knew how to laugh and joke.

Besides, she had felt guilty this last week, keeping her own good fortune and excitement bottled up inside for fear that Richard would get hysterically cautious. Lifetide would loosen him up a bit—bring back a bit of his old spontaneity—especially if it involved a woman. If Dickon had finally fallen in love—for the first time, she reminded herself—he'd understand that the much-folded piece of paper she'd tucked between the cushions was truly the answer to all her dreams and prayers.

She retrieved the paper and smoothed it carefully against her thigh. It was cheap paper, already going brittle. The ink was cheap as well, and had spread through the cracks in the paper, further weakening it. Scarcely the vellum and india ink that the poetry deserved. It was understandable; Tom had enemies all over Merovin. He was undoubtedly hiding at this very moment—but he'd risked everything to tell her that he had seen her that night at Moghi's, that he did remember her and that he'd felt the lifetide between them, too.

She'd have to put the paper in her jewelry box for safekeeping—next to the other, similar sheet already stored there—but not until she'd gotten every word memorized. It was embarrassing that it had taken so long to commit the sonnet to her heart, but her imagination kept getting ahead of her. Her thoughts wrapped themselves more easily around handsome, mysterious Thomas Mondragon himself than they did around the obscure metaphors he'd used to describe her hair.

The first poem had taken her utterly by surprise. Worse, she'd almost discarded it unread thinking it was yet another useless inquiry for a domestic position now that it seemed the worst half of Merovingen-below knew Kamat was hiring. It was karma that had kept the message in her pocket until she was alone, in bed, in the privacy of her own room. She'd prayed that there'd be a second message, and promised herself she'd catch the messenger.

It hadn't been easy. The youth had plainly been terrified. White and shaking, he'd refused to give her his name when she'd offered him a silverbit in thanks. He'd absolutely refused to enter the house, but he had promised to come back today to carry her reply back to her beloved.

Marina rescued her writing-board from the kittens and read her latest attempts with a frown. Some people simply lacked the poetic flair—and she was one of them. She'd actually considered copying something from one of the books in her mother's rooms—Nev Hettek, oddly enough, had produced more than its share of romantics. But Tom was a Nev Hetteker and Marina's heart burned with the thought that he might recognize her borrowings and scorn her as unworthy.

So Marina's message was a mere seven lines of neatly written prose—unsigned as his had been. Indeed, she'd considered his precarious position and never mentioned his name at all—even to his messenger or in her diary. Mondragon's secrets were safe with her. She sealed it with ordinary wax and did not mark it with her ring. Then, suddenly aware that the messenger would arrive shortly, she raced to her room to dress.

Tom would undoubtedly want to know how she looked, especially if he could not see her himself.

She plunged deep into her wardrobe—past the canaler trousers and the worker smocks—to her real clothes: Kamat clothes in rich colors trimmed with jewels, lace and silver. It was afternoon—the most dramatic garments would be inappropriate; and it was a meeting by proxy—nothing too relaxed or intimate-seeming. The Mondragons had been powerful in Nev Hettek; their children surely knew the same etiquette Andromeda had instilled in her daughter.

In point of fact, Marina would have been grateful for her mother's advice at that moment. Andromeda shared her daugh-

ter's romanticism and would have known exactly how to cast
the proper mood. As it was, with primping time running
short, Marina settled for comfort and simplicity. She was still
arranging a strand of moon-gray pearls in the vestibule mirror
when she heard a tentative rapping.

"You're just on time," she greeted the youth, locking her
fingers around his wrist and pulling him in beside her. "I was
afraid you wouldn't come."

"No, M . . . Ma . . . m'sera Kamat."

"You should call me Marina. I feel like we're old friends
already. And I'd like to know your name. If that's not too
. . . dangerous." She could feel his pulse racing beneath her
fingertips and suspected that it was, indeed, dangerous.

"Raj, m's . . . Marina."

"Come upstairs, then, Raj. I have a message for you, and
some tea if you have the time to sit and talk."

He followed her meekly, stealing furtive glances at the
tapestries and hesitating an instant before setting his foot on
the stairway carpet. Marina paused until he was beside her
then put an arm around the narrow shoulders, hoping to
reassure him that he was welcome. It wouldn't do to have
him so nervous he wouldn't remember enough to answer
Tom's questions.

She got the vellum from the mantel and put it in his sweaty
hands. "I'll give you this now—so there's no chance either
of us will forget it."

"For me?"

His voice cracked and Marina despaired of setting him at
ease. "For our friend," she hesitated herself, not daring to
speak Tom's name. "Our friend, the poet."

Raj muttered something but put the vellum carefully in his
belt pouch. He was only a messenger, Marina reminded
herself. A student, she guessed, since the last time she'd seen
him he'd been carrying an armload of worn textbooks. He'd
probably never been inside one of the Merovingen's island
Houses before in his life.

"How are your classes at the College?" she asked, handing him a glass of fragrant tea. "Seasonal exams are coming up, aren't they? I always dreaded them myself."

She pointed him toward a chair. "Uh . . . I'm not really a student, m'sera," Raj admitted.

Marina set her own glass on a lacquer trivet and gave the lad a closer examination. "I thought we agreed you'd call me Marina." She was beginning to doubt that Raj was, in fact, Tom's messenger.

"Yes, m's. . . . Marina. I guess I should be going, really."

"I guess it's hard to get into the College if you're poor and Adventist both, isn't it?"

Andromeda Kamat would have blushed with shame for the rude presumption of her daughter's question, but Marina was serenely satisfied. Raj looked like the Angel of Merovingen had called his name. All Marina's doubts vanished.

"I'm no Adventist," he sputtered.

"Of course you are, there's no need to pretend. I told you: we're like old friends. I wouldn't expect . . . our friend . . . to trust anyone else. And we're Adventist here ourselves. Or my mother is, in a way. She left Nev Hettek to marry my father, but she stayed Adventist in her heart. The cardinals even asked some questions when my brother and I came of age. —So, you see, I *do* understand."

Raj finally sat all the way back in his chair. He was still breathing a bit heavily, but Marina thought she'd finally gotten through to him.

"Your mother, *the* m'sera Kamat, is from Nev Hettek?"

Clearly, Raj knew very little about the realities of House life. Not, of course, that a canalsider should know that much but it seemed strange that Tom would have left his messenger so totally uninformed. Surely there was a limit to the benefits of ignorance so Marina undertook to outline the systems of dynastic alliances that bound most of Merovingen's mercantile Houses to similar clans in other cities as far away as the Chattalen and the Falken Islands.

"When all is said and done," she concluded, "trade is more important than religion and politics combined."

The youth was speechless with disbelief and Marina, who

by reciting her father's dinner-table proverbs had exhausted her own understanding of Merovan realities, quickly shifted the subject. "The cardinals might run the College, but the Houses endow it. With the right patron—and the proper manners, of course—a student can believe whatever he wants."

"And the money," Raj added. Bitterness touched his voice and drew him away from his nervousness. "Money comes first, doesn't it? You don't get a patron or the manners if you don't have the money."

Marina grew defensive. She had always believed that Kamat did its part for the common good of Merovingen, and then some. But Marina had little experience with those who weren't already under Kamat's umbrella.

"Each term we get petitions from the workers and from people who live here on Kamat. We have three students now—not counting my cousins." The youth remained unimpressed by Kamat's unaccessible bounty. "What did you want to study at the College?"

"Medicine."

Nothing safe like music or literature. The cardinals were fussy about some things where the possibility of heretical progress existed. Still, what finer gesture could she lay before Thomas Mondragon than to see his confidant safe inside the College? Her personal income wouldn't be enough—not unless she wished to share Raj's poverty—but Richard could surely be persuaded to extend the family largesse.

"It would certainly make it easier for you to come here and visit me if Kamat were your patron at the College, wouldn't it?" Marina asked lightly—and watched as distrust settled across the youth's face. Too late she remembered all Richard's lectures about presuming friendship or equality where none could ever truly exist.

"I'm sorry, Raj. It sounds like I'm toying with you—or offering a bribe. I didn't mean that. But I don't think it's right that you can't study medicine. I mean, if you're good enough to get in on your own, then you should have a chance. The Houses aren't going to turn their sons and daughters into doctors . . ."

"I'm good enough," Raj told her bluntly.

It came to Marina then, that she knew very little about survival in this world. She couldn't comprehend the dangers that forced an aristocrat like Tom Mondragon to hide in the squalor of Merovingen-below. And she couldn't comprehend the determination that kept Raj's eyes level with hers.

She looked down at the carpet. "I'll do what I can, Raj," she promised.

Raj stayed a while longer—considerably longer than either he or Marina had expected. At first Marina had prolonged their conversation because she wanted Raj's memory to overflow. She imagined the youth would spend the entire evening with her beloved, telling him what they had said to each other. But by the time the sun was below the spires and she was lighting the oil-lamps, she knew she kept him because he listened to her in a rapt way that no one else did—not even Richard.

She found herself telling tales she'd never told before and, when the sky was night-dark, she offered to take him down to the kitchen and prepare a dinner for them both. He accepted and she found herself strangely complimented that he ate her cooking without complaint. When Richard did not appear— and she suspected they were alone in the family suites—she opened a bottle of her father's brandy and poured them both a glass.

It was well into the second watch, and the second glass, when common sense regained the upper hand in her mind. Raj could scarcely convey her message to Mondragon if she didn't let him leave. Even now it was late enough that the slightly built youth took some risk traveling alone—though he assured her that he felt more comfortable in the city after dark.

She gave him the rest of the brandy—to share with their friend—and a handful of coins—in case he was bluffing about feeling safe in the night and wanted to hire a poleboat from the Kamat slip. Then, as they said good-bye in the lee of the doorway, Marina rose up on her toes to kiss him lightly on the forehead.

"For the poet," she whispered, extremely grateful for the shadows that hid her schoolgirl's blush.

Raj fairly ran away from her then, dashing across the bridge to the abandoned bulk of a Wayfarer's hostel without a backward glance. She waited a while longer, wishing she'd thought to bring a sweater and hoping to catch a glimpse of him darting across the Foundry, but as the moments passed she guessed he was taking no chances with a direct route down to Ventani where Tom, she believed, had hidden himself.

Marina extinguished the watch-lantern and threw the heavy stop-bolts across the door when she finally went back inside. Anyone from Kamat left outside in the city had best be carrying keys for the canalside entrance. She was not, of course, the only soul in Kamat—not even the only family member. Light showed out under the door where Richard had placed the worker family, and her three cousins were playing music-charades in their own second-level suite. But no respectable person would approach a darkened doorway.

The heroines of the novels Marina and her mother read and reread never had problems falling asleep. Their thoughts were always filled with visions of their beloved and from the moment their scented tresses touched the pillow their dreams were filled with romantic idylls. Marina had no trouble conjuring Mondragon's image in her mind's eye, but the grinding of her empty stomach completely disrupted the passionate illusions that should have followed.

Hungry and disgusted, Marina found an old, comfortable robe, a lantern and her keys and scuffed along the hallways to the back stairway. The house was quiet now, or as quiet as any ramshackle Merovingian building ever got. There was always something clattering in the breeze or tide. Locals usually suffered a few sleepless nights when they left their city for some ordinary abode.

For Marina, the occasional shouts and crashes were the sounds of security. She moved confidently through dark warrens—though she locked the kitchen door behind her once she'd reached it. She had carved a pleasant heap of sausage

and cheese when the latch grated and began to turn. Leaving
the lantern shielded Marina grabbed the cleaver and hid in the
darkness beside the doorway.

"Who's there?" Richard asked, his eyes drawn to the
slivers of light on the table.

"Who's here, yourself," she replied, letting the cleaver
drop benignly to her side. "I thought *you* were a sausage!"

"Sorry. Is there any left—sausage, I mean."

Marina gestured toward the table then watched with some
concern as Richard wolfed down the lion's share of her
snack. He was dressed in workman's clothes and despite the
chill in the air, his hair was sweat-stuck to his forehead. She
figured he'd been down in the dye-rooms making First-Bath
until she realized she was watching him in moonlight. Kamat
mixed its First-Bath dyes only when the moon was new.

"What happened, Richard? Why've you been out so late—
and dressed like that?"

The kitchen echoed with the *thwack* of steel against hard-
wood. "No good reason," he muttered, raising the cleaver a
second time.

"How very unlike you, Dickon," Marina retorted, the
sarcasm and nickname an insufficient mask for the anxiety his
behavior brought her.

He raised the cleaver, then aborted the chop in mid-descent.
His hand was shaking as he laid the blade on the block. "I
can't tell her." Richard's arms were braced in a triangle
against the table, keeping him upright, though his neck sagged
and he spoke to the tiled floor, not his sister.

"The new woman?"

The shoulders hunched together as he nodded. Marina tried
to remember when she'd last seen her older brother cry. It
hadn't been at Nikolay's funeral.

"He was worried that his kids would get the fever, so he
took on extra work: gray work—loading and unloading at
Megary. Or that's the guess canalside; Jordie Slade isn't the
only one who's gone missing from Megary this month."

Marina took the unnecessary precaution of drawing the
cleaver to her side of the table and shoving it into the

deep-socketed knife rack. "You went to Megary?" The question was also unnecessary.

Richard managed a bitter laugh. "Hide in plain sight—that's an old one, isn't it? Why would they expect anyone to look for Jordie Slade? Why would ser Megary expect to see a face he recognized hauling his freight?"

"You took an awful risk, Richard. What if anything *had* happened to you?"

The ugly laugh surfaced again. "That would have been most worthwhile of all. They couldn't hide me; couldn't pretend I hadn't happened. The lights would shine in the shadows, Marina—and no man could ask a better karma. You'll never guess who I saw at the Megary slip."

"Kalugin?" She didn't like his tone or direction. He'd been in the grip of the lifetide all day and it no longer seemed benign, much less romantic.

"That's no answer, Ree. There're three Kalugins—four if you're counting bodies, not brains. But no, none of them were there. Someone else."

"I don't want to play games."

"Ser Rod Baritz."

Megary alone was a blot of bad karma across Merovingen's fate. Megary and the Sword of God was a combination so malign and yet so logical that Marina swayed sideways, barely catching her weight on the cook's stool. Her memory brought back the smell of gasoline in her hair.

"And Jordie Slade?" she asked in a hoarse whisper.

"One of two places: shipped out drugged and slaved or shipped out dead and dumped. I pray God the latter. That's what I'll tell Eleanora, I think. And the children. It's better that way."

"But why? If he knew where he was going—he must have know it wasn't square."

"I'll wager a guess. One of the crates I hauled tonight had a Kamat mark on its side. Maybe indigo, maybe salts we thought we were transhipping down to the Chattelen. I loaded it up without a question asked—I'll wager Jordie didn't."

The sons and daughters of Kamat took pride in status as

ethical, sensitive citizens of a world where such graces were often a luxury. They felt real pain for the loss of Jordie Slade. But they felt something colder, harder and far more enduring over the loss of their indigo. Morality was a hobby of the rich and Kamat would be rich only so long as it had a virtual monopoly on indigo in the Det Valley.

"What will we do?" Marina asked, her fingers absently curling over the knife hilts exposed at the edge of the table.

"First, I think I want to visit our warehouses with Uncle Patrik's account logs in hand. Second—well, second will take longer. But Megary and the Sword only have power because the rest of us don't stand up to oppose them. I think maybe it's time for the merchants who keep this place going to stand up together for a change."

"Do you suspect Uncle Patrik?" The words burned across Marina's tongue like treason.

Richard shook his head. "No, nor our cousins, nor—for that matter—anyone having to do with Kamat. Not that they are immune to conspiracy, but this doesn't have the marks of an inside job."

There was no reassurance in her brother's words. "So, you could suspect Uncle Patrik—or anyone else, if the situation were different?"

He shrugged himself erect. "Patrik is weak, but loyal. So long as he is not exposed to temptation there is no need to suspect him."

"He knows Baritz, and Baritz knows him."

Richard grimaced at a mote of knowledge he had not considered. "No," he repeated, letting the sound of his own voice convince himself as well. "It will not wash—not now. But it is something I must not forget again. He must be kept on a tight, but familiar and comfortable, leash."

"Then it will not do to take his accounts and logs and march through the warehouses checking after him."

There was an overlong pause in the conversation while Richard considered not only what his sister had said but—and more important—that it had been Marina who had said them.

Nikolay had never been able to rely on Patrik and, as a result, he had never advised his son to seek his sister's advice.

"You think there'd be a better way?"

"Go down to the warehouse right now and see if anything's amiss. It's *our* warehouse, after all. We don't need to make an appointment to inspect it."

The young househead considered the risks in a notion—it could hardly be called a plan—that would never have entered his mind. A part of him, the part that had known from childhood that he would someday be the head of a Merovingen house and a man of power, balked at sneaking into his own warehouse. But the risks? Well, the risks were negligible compared to gray work in Megary Cut.

"We?" he asked with the first honest laugh of their conversation. "Don't you think you should change your clothes first?"

So lifetide was making itself felt already, Marina realized as she sped up the stairs in front of him. She had her spontaneous elder brother back again, but hardly on the scale she had imagined. This was not an expedition to the bedrock beneath the house nor a romantic escapade such as unfolded in her novels. It wasn't romantic at all. Worse, sooner or later it was going to touch Nev Hettek and the Sword of God.

Without being consciously aware she'd made the decision, Marina postponed telling her brother that Thomas Mondragon had become her admirer and that Kamat was going to sponsor an Adventist to study medicine at the College.

"Bring your signet," Richard cautioned as they reached the branch-landing that separated her level of the house from the spire-rooms Richard called home these days. "And wear something appropriate."

And what was appropriate attire for breaking into one's own property? A signet ring, of course—such as Richard had not been wearing for his Megary adventure. A gold ring, with a House's intricate monogram or device etched across its flat surface, and a familiar face was the best security a Merovingen aristocrat could hope for. Identity, after all, lay not in chits of paper passed out by the recently formed census committee, but in objects and manners that were not so easily forged.

The ring, though, was only one aspect of the total image. There was also a serviceable sweater—identical with those worn by every canaler save for one detail: it was knit from dense merino wool and that wool had been carefully dyed First-Bath. After the sweater, canvas trousers: nearly indestructible but also in Kamat's trademark midnight blue indigo. The high lisle socks were also that special dark blue, but the high boots of tough but supple leather with flexible soles were sooty black. All of it had been made to fit Marina Kamat to the exclusion of all others.

In short, from a distance, as she sat in the prow of a nondescript poleboat the family used for shuttling the daily groceries between the market and the house, Marina could have been anyone from the less fortunate parts of Merovingen. Should her presence be challenged—examined at something less than an arm's length—any native of the city would know what, if not who, she was.

There was little enough traffic in the dead of fourth watch. The tide was running out, tugging at the boat as Richard guided it into the Grand Canal, but the moon was near full; Marina could have handled the boat had she been so inclined. Here and there a tavern glowed; voices could be heard at the more popular tie-ups. Richard had a ready reply for the comments they got: *Uptowner party. Kept us waitin' half the night, then passed out in the hall.* Their passage was observed but not noted.

Marina found a battered cap under the rails and stuffed her long blond hair into it. She passed for a boy the rest of the way and acquitted herself well when they tied up off the East Dike. Not that any one—male, female, rich or poor—who reached adulthood in Merovingen didn't know how to make a boat fast against the Det River tides.

The warehouses—squat, ugly buildings devoid of the whimsy and improvisation that marked the rest of the city's architecture—belonged, strictly speaking, to the Signeury, not the Houses. Kamat, like everyone else, rented only what it needed, but its needs had been consistent over the last fifty years. Not Iosef Kalugin, nor any of his children, would have considered exercising any theoretical right to break a family's padlocks.

Kalugin was, however, supposed to provide protection in return for the rents the Signeury received once a quarter. Blacklegs should have manned conspicuous platforms on the roofs and should have made it difficult, at the very least, for Richard to guide the boat into the shadows unchallenged.

Brother and sister glanced across the loading platform, each able to see nothing more than the other's silhouette, neither needing to see more. Richard fumbled with his keys beneath his sweater.

"No need to break the locks," he said in a normal voice, handing her one of the heavy iron keys.

A single person could enter the warehouse, unlocking one end of the bar at a time. But the beam would hit the dock and echo clear across the harbor. In the unaccounted absence of the blacklegs Richard wasn't concerned about the noise but he had a mind for the cost of the locks and beam. They lowered it carefully—silently, and were glad enough that they had when a light started flashing several bays down.

Four short, one long, then a repeat: not a recognized signal, but not an accident either. Richard gripped Marina above the elbow, very much regretting that he'd brought her along. He gestured to the doorway and she followed him in silence. As there was always some noise in Merovingen, no one—not even the mysterious signalers in the other bay— paid any attention to the single, sharp creak the door gave as Richard flung it open. To be sure, the others cocked an ear for another sound, but the Kamat siblings were motionless where they stood. It was less than a minute before the irregular crew went back to its tasks and Richard led the way through the Kamat crates.

"Wait here," he breathed in his sister's ear.

She shook her head. It was neither the time nor the place for an argument; Richard had no choice but to let her follow as he wove closer to the circle of light. There'd be time to count the Kamat inventory some other night. They were well out of the family's storage area before they were able to get a good look at what was going on.

Shaped pieces of steel and iron rested in partially completed crates. No two were alike, and no proper Revenantist knew much about the structure of steam engines anyway, but the simple presence of tech machinery in a Merovingen warehouse boded no good. The siblings glanced at each other with wide eyes, then looked back into the light, hoping some additional piece of the puzzle would fall into place. It did— though it merely expanded the problem. The crates were labeled as they were completed: shipper, destination and customs clearance. Richard saw that Kamat was sending an iron hemisphere clear across the Sundance Ocean; St. John was sending a similar piece to a different receiver in the same far-off port.

Kamat had been caught in smuggling scams before. At least once a year drugs or other illegal luxuries turned up in a bale of wool or cotton. It didn't take much imagination to piggy-back on the usual routes of trade. But a few kilos of psycho-active extract were considerably different from full crates of machinery.

No, this was directly related to the absence of the blacklegs and, by extension, to Megary and the Sword. That machinery, after all, hadn't been made in Merovingen's foundry. Richard would have dearly loved to drop a net over the crew boss and take him to some deserted spot for an interrogation. Failing that, he committed the man's face to memory and memorized those labels he could read.

That done, and well before the last crate was finished, he tugged at Marina's sleeve and pointed back toward Kamat's bay.

Marina pulled away when they were out of sight of the machinery. "Aren't we going to do anything?"

"Like what?" he whisper-shot back at her and grabbed her arm again.

"Stop them. Scare them away."

Richard said nothing until they were back on the Kamat

portion of the dock, then he locked his hands on her shoulders and forced her to look at him.

"Don't you understand what we saw in there? That isn't some canalside operator trying to make a back pocket lune. It couldn't be happening at all if someone hadn't bought protection in high places. And, Marina—people who have tech like that, they don't protect it with swords and knives."

"What was it?" she asked in a smaller, sober voice as they lifted the bar into place.

"Damned if I know. A machine, probably. An engine to make something bigger, or faster; to do the work of ten honest men, maybe." For Richard, as for many other merchants and workers, technological disdain, after nearly six hundred years, was more economic than religious.

"The Adventists don't see it that way."

"Technology is just another form of Adventist Melancholy," her brother replied, proud of his epigram and setting himself to remember it for other audiences.

There might even be some truth to it, he considered as Marina pulled the ropes back into the boat. Neither Adventist nor Revenantist, when in the grip of their more absurd teleology, ever considered the possibility that the grass was *not* greener on the other side of the atmosphere. And while the possibility of escape was very nice, the old texts said that most people never left the planet they were born on; they never left the planet their great-grandparents were born on, either.

For Richard, whose life, he believed, would be pretty much the same with or without space travel, it just didn't matter very much.

"But what about the sharrh?" his sister asked when they were well clear of the East Dike.

That was the final question, and answer, for everything on Merovin. What about the sharrh: unseen and implacable, beyond reason and appeal, the aliens stood between Merovin and its gods. Adventist, Revenantist and Jane—whatever they imagined their differences to be, they were bound primarily by their similarities and those similarities were contained in the single word: *sharrh*.

"There are no sharrh," Richard said after pushing hard on the pole. It was a revolutionary remark—a blasphemous remark—and he didn't need to look back over his shoulder to know the look on his sister's face. "Do you watch a roach nest after you've poured boiling water on it?"

"No," Marina admitted in a soft voice.

"Of course not. The job's been done. So why should the sharrh be hovering over us, watching our every move, making judgments about every little thing we do? It's our arrogance; *we* think they care."

Marina tugged the cap off her head. "Roaches come back," she admonished, tucking the cap under the rail again.

"So, the analogy isn't perfect. Yes, the roaches come back. Yes, the roaches will outlast everything on Merovin. But I think we're a damn sight cleverer than roaches."

Marina heard something unfamiliar in her brother's voice—something that sounded dangerously close to belief and commitment. "You won't be so clever if the College hears you say something like that," she cautioned urgently.

"I wouldn't say anything like that to the cardinals, Ree. I'm not about to do something stupid like start a crusade—but I'm not going to live my life worrying about myths, superstitions or the sharrh."

Marina said nothing more to him about the sharrh or the activities they'd witnessed in the warehouse—not in the poleboat nor in the days that followed. She had activities and worries enough of her own between the reception honoring Andromeda's return to the city and the failure of Tom's messenger, Raj, to reappear.

Of course, had the youth come to the door he would most likely have been draped in livery and dragooned into the temporary corps of domestics necessary to put on a proper occasion. Eleanora had been so imposed upon—though not quite to the point of donning livery. It was not uncommon for a House to provide genteel employment for those whose income had fallen far below their social station. Richard had suggested, in one of their fleeting conversations as the week wore on, that Eleanora be described as the daughter of one of Kamat's trading partners who had suffered irreversible losses.

Marina took note that m'sera Slade was *not* to be passed off as a Kamat blood relation. Then, remembering the sense of lifetide that had accompanied Eleanora's arrival, she gave the newcomer some of her more discreet clothes. No need to fire the rumors, or their mother's suspicions, before absolutely necessary.

"So you'll have her pouring tea?" Richard nodded as he asked the question. "Just the right place. I knew you'd think of something."

Marina managed a weak, harried smile. It was Satterday. Andromeda, who had disembarked at noon, was resting in her rooms. The kitchen swarmed with hired help, as did the entry-level salon and drawing-room. The first guests would arrive at dusk and it began to appear that the event might happen without untoward disaster.

"I won't be able to be here," Richard informed her, as if he didn't know what his casual words would do to her carefully arranged schedule.

"A joke? It's a very poor time for a joke, Dickon."

"Not a joke. I've spent the week wining and dining every man of influence I could put an arm around. They've managed to pry Anastasi Kalugin off the Rock. . . . I'd hoped he'd be willing to come to the reception for mother, but he wouldn't agree. Said there'd be too many people asking too many questions about the census and other things he'd rather not discuss."

"But he'll talk about the warehouses and Megary and the Sword of God with you—someplace else?" Marina slumped down into one of the armchairs, torn between her anger that he would abandon her this way and her fear. "Richard, don't do it. They control the blacklegs; they've got to be in on it one way or another."

"I don't think there is a *they* where House Kalugin is concerned anymore. Beside, Ree, it's not as if I'll be meeting him alone. None of the men will be here. I'm sorry," Richard backed toward the door as his sister's face darkened. "I truly am—but we have to take the opportunities that fall to us."

He pulled the door shut behind him. Marina's comments were lost to the sound of glassware shattering against the wood. He was well aware that he merited his sister's anger but events had, in fact, been ripped away from his control.

For three days he had met with househead after househead, breaking the codes of silence as he told them what he'd seen at Megary and the East Dike warehouse and what he knew of Rod Baritz and the disappearance of Jordie Slade. He challenged his peers to meet in Kamat's upper rooms on Satterday, during Andromeda's reception, and had been told, with varying degrees of politeness, to leave the conjunct realm of trade and politics to those who knew it better.

His failure had shown clearly in the averted eyes that had greeted him at the Ramsey Bell, Friday noontime. He'd wandered home slowly, wondering how he'd explain that he'd embarrassed Kamat in front of the entire city, and arrived to find a deck of vellum calling cards waiting on the vestibule table.

The old men would not take his word for anything, but their curiosity had been roused and they'd made their own investigations. Richard shuddered to think what skeletons had fallen out of which closets as afternoon became evening but only this morning he'd been informed that Anastasi Kalugin was taking a personal interest in the matter. Since then it had been a steady parade of negotiations, messengers and the occasional warning from a senior house culminating with a simple scrawl from the governor's younger son.

I will meet with you, and those of your choosing, at twenty-one hours, this evening in the meeting hall above the Fishmarket.

By then Richard had also been informed of whom he would be advised to choose and the folly of questioning the change in time and venue. Telling his sister was his last gesture before retreating to his octagonal office far above the entertainment level of the house.

Pacing from one wall to the next, Richard rehearsed any number of conversational gambits and discarded them all. He and Anastasi Kalugin were roughly the same age—but similarities ended there. They had known of each other all their lives but they were not peers, much less friends. By the time he was ready to dress for the evening, Richard more than half hoped one of the elder househeads would usurp control of the Fishmarket meeting.

He lingered at Kamat long enough to compliment the women of his family on their appearance and to greet the earliest guests—ranking women and a lesser assortment of men. Then he was off across the bridge to Wayfarer's and on to the Fishmarket.

"You're expected," a surly blackleg informed him as he entered the cavernous lower hall.

"I can't be late," Richard muttered to himself as his coat was lifted from his shoulders and the appropriate staircase pointed out. "I set my watch by the Signeury chimes just this afternoon—"

"'M'ser Kalugin," the blackleg interrupted, "does not use the *Signeury* chimes."

It would be a long evening if even the hired blacklegs were speaking with hidden meanings. Richard thanked them with a curt nod and hurried up the stairs.

The room above the Fishmarket was one of many large halls scattered throughout the city. The middle ranks of Merovingen society—those who had a bit of extra money but who still dwelt in tiny apartments—held their celebrations in such places. On rarer occasions they became the setting for meetings too important to be held in public and too delicate to be held in any one House.

After checking the lay of his collar and hair, Richard pushed through the double doors. He stood at one end—the empty end—of a large room which fell silent as his presence was noted. His heels echoed on the wooden floor; it took eternity to reach the dais where Anastasi Kalugin stood waiting.

"I understand you're the cause of all this," the governor's son said—a greeting carefully, and successfully, calculated to set Richard at a disadvantage.

The head of House Kamat felt a hastily eaten canape rattle vilely through his stomach. Kalugin seemed in control of everything; the notion of demanding accountability from any member of Merovingen's ruling family seemed utterly absurd. The smile spreading slowly across Anastasi's face, went a long way to confirm that impression.

Richard swallowed hard. "I suppose I am," he said, expecting to sound like a young fool. But the men, Nikolay's friends and competitors, who formed a ring around the dais didn't regard him as a fool. Kalugin's smile faltered and Richard had a moment to reflect that perhaps they did have much in common after all.

"I'm impressed that you travel with an escort, m'ser Kalugin. I'd have been more impressed on Monday last if I'd seen a blackleg or two along East Dike or at Megary slip where East Dike goods are exchanged for god knows what—and good men have died for asking the wrong questions."

The smile was gone completely now. "My sway over the blacklegs stops somewhat short of East Dike—as you're well aware."

"No, I am *not* aware; I should not *need* to be aware—"

"Don't be foolish," Anastasi interrupted.

"Foolish! I'll tell you what is foolish: sitting by idly while the business of your House and family is ripped apart—that's foolish, Anastasi Kalugin. Using the city as a battleground in your family wars—that's foolish, too. Or don't you care that none of this could happen if the Signeury weren't paralyzed?"

"I care."

There were murmurings in the ring of men beyond them. The sounds of new arrivals, of disagreement and surprise. Richard heard them but was not affected by them. Of course Anastasi cared; he was scared beneath his pallor and elegance else he would not have placed himself here in this room.

"Then you should do something, m'ser Kalugin. It will not be enough to sit back until the waters clears. The Signeury has certain obligations to this city, to the Houses that keep Merovingen alive—and your family isn't living up to those obligations." He paused, but Anastasi said nothing and he feared he had not been understood. "Merovingen is not a hostage in the battles within your House."

Richard became aware then of a collective intake of breath in the circle beyond himself and Anastasi. There was muttering as well, and in the lengthening silence the young Househead sensed approval as well as stunned surprise among the older gentlemen. Kalugin heard it too.

"That could be treason," the governor's son said.

While Richard wracked his mind for the right words, the circle parted and a third man joined them on the dais. Vega Boregy: a man about Nikolay's age, a man whose reputation in the city entitled him to join any gathering but, so far as Richard knew, a man who had not been invited to this one.

"I doubt that, m'ser Kalugin," Vega purred, easily displacing both young men from the center of attention. "Our mercantile barons are simply trying to remind you that they put your great-grandfather in the Signeury and they can pull you out of it—or keep you there."

"It would be treason—"

"The winners are never guilty of treason. I would have thought you'd learned *that* above all else at your father's knee."

"Iosef's more worried about you and your damned sister than he is about Merovingen." Richard and Anastasi snapped about to see who among the others had spoken, but the circle held its secrets.

"There, Anastasi," Boregy continued, "you should be honored. The barons prefer you to the rest of your infernal family. They think you can win it all."

Anastasi Kalugin glared into Boregy's face, giving Richard and his associates ample time to wonder what alliances had already been drawn between Merovingen's most powerful banking family and a Kalugin heir. A House's banker, like its lawyers and doctors, knew where the scandals and skeletons were hidden; and no merchant believed that anything was truly not for sale if the price were right. Yet Boregy's roots went deep into the mud of the Det delta; as a man and as a House they risked no less than any other in this room in any struggle with Nev Hettek.

"It will take time," Kalugin said to Boregy alone.

"We're setting our own men to guard the warehouses," Richard interrupted, obliquely telling Kalugin that time, as a commodity, was in short supply. "And we'll take other measures to assure ourselves that commerce moves unimpeded through Merovingen."

Now it was Kalugin's turn to wonder what else this collection of merchants might do to protect its interests and Richard's turn to pray that the men arranged behind him would not reveal how little had been discussed, much less decided. Kamat got lucky, for the men enjoyed the spectacle of a discomfited Kalugin in their midst.

But power is a heady wine and each man gathered in that hall above the Fishmarket had drunk deep. The merchant barons—acting in concert for the first time in living memory— had found within themselves a weapon of awesome power. Anastasi Kalugin studied that weapon and in faint expressions only Vega Boregy could interpret, compared it with others in the Kalugin arsenal.

Richard Kamat had drunk most deeply of all and, for the moment, saw the world with lesser clarity. Everyone wanted to have a word with him, to shake his hand and to tell him how much he reminded them of Nikolay. He left the hall awash in pride and amazement: the way he felt in those rare moments when his father's praise had erupted unexpectedly. He returned to Kamat expecting to celebrate and was surprised to find it dark with only Eleanora to greet him.

"It was very dull," she told him, "with only women, children and old men to provide the conversation. Your mother seemed not at all displeased, but your sister seemed in a fine rage when all the guests had left before midnight."

Intimate family realities dampened the glow of the evening. "She'll recover," Richard replied, suddenly aware of

the hours he had spent at the Fishmarket after Kalugin and
Boregy had left.

"Did you get what you wanted?"

"I think so—"

"Did you get what *I* wanted?"

Richard let his coat fall over a chair and put his arms over
her shoulders. Dressed in Marina's clothes, Eleanora seemed
like another younger sister but there was a burning fatalism in
her eyes that would never be assimilated into an aristocratic
house.

"It will not happen again—I can only promise you that; I
can't find Jordie or bring him back."

He felt but did not see the flicker of tension that raced
through her. "Karma, then," she whispered, meeting his
eyes again. "A beginning in every ending."

He could have taken her in his arms and made a most
spectacular beginning. Instead he gave her the same quick
hug he would have shared with Marina.

"Definitely a beginning," Richard assured her as he backed
to the stairway.

FEVER SEASON
(FINAL REPRISE)

C.J. Cherryh

Jones stared with apprehension at the little card the harried blackleg was making out for her at the table set up on Moghi's porch. *Jones,* it said, *Altair X.*

"I ain't no X," she protested.

"Ye're s'posed t' have three names."

"Well, maybe I *got* three, but my mama never told me. It sure as hell ain't any X."

"It's X," the blackleg said. And went on writing in the blanks. "Adventist."

"Ain't."

"Convert?"

"Ney."

"Adventist." That went in the blank. The most damning thing a body could *be* in Merovingen, except Janist. And the man went on writing. "Residence?"

"My skip."

"What's its number?"

"I dunno. It ain't got a number."

"It's got a number. It's on your license. Let's see it."

"I ain't got it on me. It's on my skip. It's supposed to be."

"Go get it."

Jones looked around at the line, that stretched clear off the porch. "I got to go through this damn line again?"

The blackleg set her card aside on the table. "Sorry. I need the number. Next."

"Ye damn—"

The blackleg looked up. Not without a certain anxiety. But Del Suleiman had her by the arm, and patted her shoulder. "Ye go. I save yer place. Mira, ye go get our license."

"No holding places," the blackleg said.

There was a mutter up front, all around. "Line ain't moving, then," yelled Libby Singh, and the mutter got uglier. "We can jest stand."

"Blacklegs ain't getting no ride in this town."

"Get the damn papers!" the blackleg yelled, his face reddening. "Every canaler in this damn line better have the damn papers when they get here!"

"Atterlad," Hen Fregit said, and waved a hand. "Ain't n'body movin' in this line till we all got back. Hear it?"

There was a shifting among the canalsiders, a little muttering, but partners and kids and family folded their arms and stood, still as monuments, exactly in place, and no lander moved up in line to fill the vacant spots, as canalers went to the skips and poleboats tied up along the porch and under Fishmarket Bridge, and all along the bank.

No one had moved when they got back either. And Altair Jones unfolded the waterstained paper that was her shipping license, and held it up in front of the officer's eyes. "That's the number on the paper. Ain't the number on my skip. My skip ain't got a number."

"It does now," the officer muttered. "*That's* the number. This is *your* number. What's your mail pickup?"

There was an ominous muttering in the line.

"We ain't got no numbers," Singh yelled.

"Throw 'at there bastard in the canal!" someone else yelled.

The officer looked up, clench-jawed and worried. "Look, I ain't got no more choice than you! This is the governor's law!"

"Then damn the governor!" Libby Singh yelled. "You write on there that that's a *license* number, ain't no numbers on the boats!"

"I can't do that!"

"You c'n write 'er right there," Jones said helpfully, pointing to the place on the card, and turned her head so she could see rightwise up as she indicated the blank. "See, ye just cross that there *boat* out and write in *license*."

"I've got a thousand of these damn cards to do!"

"Ye ain't going to get done any this way."

The officer glowered. "I'll remember you."

"Yey. An' canalers remember faces real good too, m'ser blackleg."

"Right," a dozen voices said, at her back.

"So ye write *license*. Ain't no boat got a number."

She came early to Mondragon's that night—Denny let her in, Denny still vastly satisfied with himself these days. The boys were back at work at Gallandry despite their two-week-long absence (ser Gallandry *owed* Mondragon in some way powerful enough that he would have hired old Min herself if Mondragon asked it) but Mondragon still worried enough about the pair that he insisted they stay another week or so—ever since Raj had gone missing one evening and had had them damned near dragging the canals for him. Un-Raj-like, he had *not* told Denny where he had been, he had not been straight with Mondragon, or with her—

In fact it was, she reckoned, one of the prime reasons Mondragon had laid down the law with the boys: *You show up here by dark,* he had said, seizing Raj by both arms and glaring at him in a way that had Raj frozen stiff. *You and Denny both,* you go to Gallandry in the morning, you check in at Moghi's on your way home, and if it so happens I'm not here, you go straight back to Moghi's and you *sit* there, you hear me, till I come or Jones or Del or somebody you know damn well for sure Jones or I sent, and if you've got any doubts, you have one of Moghi's men go with you and them and put it on my bill. Do you understand me?

Whereafter Raj had nodded emphatically that he did, indeed, understand. Denny had sulked, Raj had hit him, and, Jones reckoned, Raj had enough to occupy him just making sure Denny stayed in sight.

But Mondragon was taking no chances with another of the Boregys' windows. And more worrisome, something that had occurred to Jones and something she was certain was in Mondragon's mind, it was clear that something had scared Raj and upset him badly.

" 'Lo." she said, meeting Mondragon in the hall that led back to the kitchen. She gave him a hug. "I got Min down there watching." Meaning the boat. It was safe enough, she reckoned. Min was content to tie up early and earn a copper, these chilly nights, and all Min had to do was bang on a pot with a spoon and raise hell, defense enough against the usual kind of pilferage, if somebody bothered her skip.

"Good," Mondragon said. "I'm doing soup."

It smelled like it. It smelled good. Mondragon's cooking had damn well *improved* in his staying in the apartment so much. "Going to wash," she said, and headed back around the stairs and up again to drop her little bag of personal stuff (like the gun and the ammunition, which she did not leave on the skip, along with clean clothes for the morning) up in Mondragon's bedroom upstairs.

Raj was not what she expected to find up there, Raj sitting there in the chair with the lamp lit and a book he snapped shut right fast and stuck into his pants as he scrambled up and tried to leave.

But she was standing in the door and she did not oblige him by moving.

He just stood there with a very un-Raj-like sullenness and finally got the presence of mind to step aside and wave her in.

"Thanks," she said dryly, and went to set her things by the bed.

Except she thought then about the gun, and the ammunition, and the money in that kit, and turned around and looked at Raj, who was standing there looking at her as if he had fishbones in his throat.

Damn, she had *trusted* the kid. Until he had gone secretive and peculiar.

"Close the door," she said, suddenly figuring that something had to get worked out. And Raj went from looking like he was going to say something to looking like he was going to run. "Shut it!"

Raj shut it, pressed it closed at his back and stood there with a cornered look. "What in hell're ye doing here?" she asked then. "Raj, you answer me. You answer me real plain. Ye got some trouble ye ain't told Mondragon?"

There was absolute hell in the boy's eyes. Panic. "I haven't done anything. I wish he'd just quit worrying about me."

"Something t' do with that brother of yours?"

"No."

"You sure? You real sure? I tell you, if you *don't* sit on that kid hard, there'll be something you can't pull him out of. *Mondragon* took the blame with Boregy, you know that. You know why. You know damn well why. Denny's enough to try the Angel Hisself. And here you stay out all damn night, you take to skulking round and sulking when ye're spoke to—I'm telling you, Mondragon's got enough on his mind! He don't need this! Now ye tell me, ye tell me what ye're into."

"It wasn't all damn night! I was fine! I don't need somebody hovering over me all the time!"

"Oh, sure, *sure*, ye don't. You got a hand all cut up, you got Denny to watch, you got some bullylads who seen your face right well—"

"They saw yours. And his. Same as mine."

"Well, I got a boat, don't I? *I'm* on the water, I'm in the Trade, and there ain't no way they cross the Trade in this town, friend. And if you ain't noticed, Mondragon's in by dark and watching his back all the time till this blows over. What in hell's the matter with you? What're you doing up here anyway?"

"Maybe I want a little time to myself."

"Ain't no law. Go on. Git! Ain't nothing t' me ye're an ingrate."

He turned then, jaw set, and opened the door.

"But I'd've thought," she said before it was halfway, "you owed Mondragon better."

Raj froze. Just stopped, with his hand on the doorknob, his head down.

"Ye want to say?" she asked. "You think we're stupid? Think we couldn't help you?"

"It's nothing to do with anything."

"Sure."

He walked out, and went on downstairs.

"Dinner," Denny said, putting his head into the sitting room where Raj had withdrawn to the farthest corner and tucked up in a chair, not interested in being bothered. Something in him pricked up an interest at food; his stomach said no and rolled over in queasy protest.

Denny had given him the news, Denny dived back into the hall and headed for the company of Mondragon and Jones in the kitchen.

Raj opened his book, on the folded note that he knew by heart. That said, in Marina's fine, beautiful handwriting:

My dear Angel:

I send this by your messenger—wishing I could see you face to face. . . .

I am so touched by the poems from your hand. I would not try to equal them. . . .

He hurt all over again. He traced the letters *her* pen had made, and knew that he was a fool. Knew that he had made a mess of things.

Even halfway through the letter, the first time he had read it, he had been blind to the cues. Then they had added up. Mondragon. *Mondragon.*

Everything had gotten twisted up. He had traced and retraced every mistaken move, everything he had said and Marina Kamat had said to him that he had taken and confused and believed in.

She had taken the poems for Mondragon's. She had taken him for an errand-boy. *Boy*— Just that. It was Mondragon, it had to be, Mondragon who looked like the Angel Himself, like Retribution who stood on Hanging Bridge. And he was a fool.

Oh, God, he *was* a fool, who had to tell the truth—to Marina, to Mondragon, all the way around. It was so damned hard. It hurt so much.

He *loved* her, dammit. For a little while he had believed she loved him.

And the man he owed everything to—he loved Mondragon, in a confused tangle of debt and need; and he had been so proud of what he had done, so overwhelmed by his failure to get the papers through, but proud all the same that he had worked everything out—and Mondragon had treated him like a grown man. Now Mondragon was mad at him, Jones was mad at him, Denny was too young to understand him and no little mad at him too. And Marina—

Marina was going to be more than mad at him. Marina was going to be his enemy, forever. And he still loved her.

House Kamat would despise him. Marina's brother might come looking for him—or for Mondragon. Who was a duelist, who would have to defend himself—

No. Mondragon was too smart. Mondragon would only break Marina's heart and apologize and maybe be polite to her, because Mondragon always knew how to smooth over a situation.

Then Mondragon would come home and grab hold of him and kill him. He had seen that look on Mondragon's face, that made him remember what Mondragon really was; and Mondragon was involved in things in hightown, a whole tangled mess on which everyone's life depended—dangerous, dangerous things, which meant Marina Kamat would be involved with him, and that mess, and he was—

Jones came padding in, barefoot and quiet, just the creak of the board floor to give her away. Raj shut the book with a lurch of his heart and hoped his face was not as pale as he thought it was.

Jones came over and leaned an arm on his chair. "Raj. What in *hell's* the matter?"

"It's a girl," he said. Choked out.

"Oh, Lord and my Ancestors!" Jones jerked back and stood up and set her hands on hips. "Is *that* it?"

In that way of someone Older and beyond understanding the knife twisting in his heart.

"Come on," she said, and took him by the arm and dragged him up. "That ain't a cause to miss a good supper." And when she had gotten him to the kitchen. "He says it's a *girl*," she said to Mondragon, with Denny right there to hear.

"Hoooo," Denny said.

Mondragon just gave him a bewildered look, a totally astonished look, that was far and away the most unguarded expression he had gotten out of Mondragon in a week.

"Who?" Mondragon asked.

"Oh," Raj said, thinking wildly, realizing he would be a fool to claim someone who *was* anyone, and unprepared to deal with the truth, "I saw her on this boat."

"Whose?" Jones asked, sitting down at table.

"I dunno." Raj found himself a way to go, a little lie that would give him time, and room to think, a little breath in a situation that had gotten narrower and narrower. "I didn't see them real clear."

Jones snorted. Mondragon laughed softly. Denny gave him a look that looked halfway mad and halfway betrayed, as if he saw something ahead that he did not want to happen.

The knot came back to his stomach. He sat down with the book in his lap, and ate the stew, spinning out the details they asked.

Lies, every one.

And that night in bed, in Mondragon's downstairs, while Mondragon and Jones were in bed upstairs, doing things that Raj imagined with all too much tormenting detail, Denny said:

"You going to go all stupid on me?"

"Happens," Raj said, staring at the ceiling. Thinking now he had to find new places to hide the letter, because now they might suspect about the book. Nothing seemed safe.

There was just a little more time, that was all.

INSTANT KARMA

Janet Morris

Magruder wasn't quite sure when the idea had come to him. Maybe as early as last week, when he'd said to a distraught Sword named Chamoun, *"We're here to win the hearts and minds of these Merovingians, and we're going to do it if we have to put the fear of sharrh in heaven into 'em."* Or maybe later that evening, when Tatiana was so obviously hiding something worrisome during dinner—and after.

But Magruder never let a good plan go unimplemented, so here he was, knocking on the slavers' door with Megary Cut behind him, and a killer named al-Banna guarding his back and the launch they'd brought.

Chance Magruder was in disguise, his face hooded, his Sword credentials hung at his waist—armed to the teeth, like you ought to be when you walked into a den of lions.

"Whaddayawant?" came a voice through a rusty grate once the peep was open.

"Heaven on earth," Magruder said dryly. Then, having given the recognition sign, set the plan in motion. "Brought Baritz's boat. Him an' Ruin al-Banna, back there, 'll wanna invite y'all to their party." Keep the accent heavy, keep talking while the alert code that had followed the recognition signal sank in.

It must have, because Magruder was told to wait while someone else was fetched to talk to him.

Which he didn't. He got into his own rented boat and left Ruin al-Banna to do the rest. The ride back from Megary seemed to take forever, in the small skiff whose pilot had taken a rich bribe to make the run to Megary and back to the Grand at Foundry, where Magruder had hired the boat. Chance could feel the pilot's nervousness, with the slavers' enclave still close behind and Magruder closer; he could nearly see the man's back twitch in anticipation of foul play.

Like Magruder's own muscles were twitching. Ruin al-Banna had done his part like clockwork; the gunpowder and the other necessities—ceramics, metals, saltpeter-soaked cord and instructions—were now safely in the hands of the Sword operatives based out of Megary. Not that there was anything safe about giving that much explosive to the kind of men that served the Sword here in Merovingen.

Magruder could only hope that Ruin al-Banna got the job done. The plan was . . . one of Magruder's better ones; if not brilliant, then at least serviceable. There was going to be one hell of a show tomorrow night, climaxing in the sky over the Signeury, if Magruder had done the math right and al-Banna followed his instructions to the letter. Instant Karma, you bet.

It was risky, but so was reaction, or inaction. Magruder needed to take the initiative, the upper hand. If this worked, Iosef Kalugin would have his wrist slapped for decreeing the census. If it didn't, at least some of the traitors who'd wormed their way in among the Sword would be flushed.

Magruder needed, as much as anything else, to find out whom he could trust among the riffraff he'd inherited from Romanov. What was going on out at Megary? If the plan aborted, or word leaked, Magruder would have a lead on Romanov's killer.

It wasn't that he minded Romanov being murdered, but he minded like hell not having time to give the damned order. And he minded more not knowing from what quarter the assassin had come. He knew the Sword didn't have a corner on violence, much less assassination, in Merovingen, but he didn't know much more than that about Romanov's death. And since he was living with the opposition under deep cover, he needed to know who his enemies were; whether he was in bed with any of them.

Figuratively speaking, of course. Since he knew one of his enemies, and was in bed with that one, literally: Tatiana Kalugin.

Come on, son; you've been over all of that a dozen times, he told himself as the launch headed sluggishly toward the Grand. Tatiana couldn't have been responsible for Romanov's death. Not the way she'd almost bought the farm at the 24th Eve Ball—would have, maybe, if Magruder hadn't saved her.

So that left only the rest of her family, the Boregys to boot, and half of ambulatory Merovingen. For all anyone could prove, Michael Chamoun was seeing warnings where none existed. For all Magruder knew, Romanov's death was just a nasty coincidence—a robbery attempt that got out of hand, random violence. Any of the *Detfish's* crew had plenty of reason to dislike Romanov; there were factions among the Sword, here as well as at home in Nev Hettek.

And now Magruder was without Romanov's guidance, such as it had shown itself to be. Whatever else Romanov was, he'd been an expert on Merovingen. Without him, Magruder was having to play everything by ear—to improvise, to operate in a theater of the unknown.

And like this trip to Megary, made in person because there wasn't anyone Chance could trust, the unknown was becoming increasingly dangerous. Therefore, the plan. If you don't know the rules, Magruder always said, then change the game.

Cardinal Ito was a man who cleaned up his own messes. It wasn't like him to tell tales out of school, or to go outside his own power structure for help. But this was an unusual circumstance, and permission, of a sort, must be sought outside the College for the executive action Ito wished to order.

So he went straight to the top. It was the only way. And

Iosef Kalugin was the only authority Ito Tremaine Boregy was answerable to—beyond the ultimate authority of karma.

In Iosef Kalugin's Signeury offices, the flick of his cardinal's ring at a worried secretary gained him instant admission to Iosef's presence.

The Kalugin patriarch took one look at his Collegiate visitor, checked his appointment book to make sure the meeting hadn't been scheduled, and told his secretary that he wasn't to be disturbed until further notice.

Then Kalugin opened the doors to the balcony, letting in the rising mists of night, and stepped outside without a word, motioning Ito to follow.

"What brings you here, Cardinal, in person?" said the wolfish old ruler of Merovingen, with a show of yellow teeth.

"I felt the need to . . . consult with you, Your Excellency," said Ito mildly, knowing that his presence here spoke urgently enough.

"Yes. About what?" asked the Revenantist patriarch carefully.

"The College has a student whom it wishes to expel . . . permanently."

"So? Is this all?" Iosef Kalugin's voice sounded in no way relieved. His guard was up; he was looking for the catastrophe; or, if there was none, for the trap. "Who is this student? Or should I not ask?"

"Cassiopeia Boregy's new husband. And when I say expel, I mean from more than just the College. He is an evil influence. In his heart he carries seeds of destruction—as you well know."

"Ah, I see. You mean *permanently*." Kalugin turned from Ito and leaned his hands on the guardrail, looking out over the Signuery and the mists beyond, rising so thick that they nearly masked the Justiciary and the bridge connecting it to the Signeury itself.

"I do. And we know—the College has its ways of knowing—that you might have . . . dealt . . . with this Chamoun previously, and decided to content yourself with sending a message in the form of one, ah, Romanov . . .

instead. So we wish to know whether this office has any
objection to . . .''

"To Chamoun's karmic debt being paid in full?" Iosef
Kalugin supplied. And turned back to face Ito again.

"To the College making its own determination on the
fitness of this student, yes." It didn't do to say things in a
more straightforward manner. It didn't do to even allude to
irrevocable actions taken temporally by a spiritual college
whose putative concern was the immortal soul. Normally, the
College would have dispensed such karma without consulting
a secular authority. And Kalugin knew it.

But this was a special case, because for some reason, Iosef
Kalugin had blessed the union of Cassiopeia Boregy and
Michael Chamoun; blessed it perhaps because of Tatiana's
interest in Chamoun's patron, Magruder, but blessed it none-
theless. Ito needed to know that the reasons were not tactical—
that if the College dispensed with the problem Michael
Chamoun represented, it would not be guilty of interfering in
Kalugin's own plans.

If Chamoun were some agent of Kalugin's, some carefully
inserted spy sent into the nest of Merovingen's enemies by
Iosef Kalugin himself, Ito needed to know that now.

"We favor this boy, as you have guessed." Kalugin's eyes
were deep in shadow; Ito couldn't read them.. But Ito could
read the tone: even Iosef Kalugin walked carefully around the
College. "So does your family, Ito Tremaine *Boregy*. But do
what you must; just don't botch things. Nothing public,
nothing clumsy, nothing that will shame either Vega's house
. . . or Chance Magruder. Not publicly, at least."

"I will do only what karma decrees," said Ito with a
tongue suddenly thick and unwieldy. So there *was* something.
Something special about Chamoun. Some place that the Nev
Hetteker and his patron fit into Iosef's plans.

"If karma could decree that all my children stop fighting
among themselves," said Iosef Kalugin; "or that one be
declarable the obvious winner, most competent and deserv-
ing, I would be exceedingly grateful to the College." Sarcasm dripped from the patriarch's tongue. "Be careful, Ito,

that you don't lose more than you gain with this. I do not forbid or decree the actions of the College, but I must warn you: these are difficult times, and any misstep can come back to haunt us. Do nothing that will compromise yourself, your station, or the College.''

But I already have, you old fool. Why do you think I'm here? "We will proceed as karma dictates,'' said Ito unhappily, having been put on notice that, if anything should go wrong, the College would take any ensuing blame—or scandal—alone, with no help from the Signeury.

"Now, if that is all?'' Iosef Kalugin wanted to end the audience. The not-quite-respectful prompt made Ito even more nervous as he began his farewells, blessing Kalugin and his family and the stones of the Signeury as he went.

Only when Ito was back at the College, after he'd climbed the familiar steps and was seated in his deep dark sanctum with his prelates washing his feet in warm water and attending to his before-dinner drinks, did it occur to the Cardinal that Iosef Kalugin might be bold enough to use the Chamoun matter *against* the College—whether it succeeded, or even if it failed. Ito should have thought of it before, but he hadn't. He'd been too worried about the young man named Michael Chamoun, who held true memories of the alien sharrh in his oft-reborn soul. Memories that would have remained forever dormant if Ito Boregy, in an attempt to acquire the boy as a pawn, hadn't used illicit techniques to awaken them.

When Ito called for his favorite boy and his thorn switches, everyone in the College dorm below the rank of acolyte scurried for cover.

There was nothing worse than a cardinal who felt the need of discipline. When Ito had finished having himself whipped, the prelates would beat the novices, and the novices would beat the choir boys, and the choir boys would beat the cooks. . . .

It was going to be a long night at the Revenantist College. And in the midst of it, a single acolyte slipped unnoticed out the water-gate, bound for Merovingen-below on a mission

of mayhem so foul and so important that Ito sweated under
the whip even as it began.

Tatiana Kalugin had eyes and ears everywhere in Merovingen,
including her father's office. Thus she was already gone
when Magruder arrived at the embassy, having left him a
note that she'd be back.

And she would. But now, wrapped in a heavy cloak and
standing at the Boregy high-door, where the wind was fierce,
she had more important things to deal with. At the sight of
her, the servants scurried and scraped.

It was not often a Kalugin came unannounced to Boregy
House, unless it was her eel of a brother, Anastasi.

"No, no, don't bother Vega," she told a worried Boregy
retainer. "It's Cassiopeia I've come to see—a woman's
matter."

There was too much silence in this house. The household
was unwilling to believe the fiction Tatiana had concocted.
She didn't care if they did or not; she didn't care if Vega bit
his nails to the elbow because his patron's enemy had come
to his house to see his daughter.

Tatiana had her reasons. So she told the worried Vega
Boregy when he came down the stairs, arms outstretched to
greet her, saying how glad he was to see her and asking what
he could do for her.

"Nothing, as I've said. It's Cassie I wish to see. About the
census—you know her husband's working for us diligently in
the matter of the census. Cassiopeia may be of service also.
And she may already have earned a commendation. Now,
Vega, if you'll take me to her . . ."

"She's up with Gregory—with her grandfather."

"Ah," said Tatiana, not able to resist the opportunity.
"And is he awake, your father?" Gregory spent long periods
of time comatose or sleeping, no one outside the family quite
knew which. When he was awake, control of Boregy House
was unconditionally his. No wonder Vega looked so pale
beneath his black hair.

"Awake. Alive and well," said Vega with just a hint of challenge in his smile.

Long ago, there had been an attack by unknown persons on Boregy House; the old man's infirmity was whispered to be a result of that attack, but not even that fact could be determined for certain by outsiders. As Boregy House's sympathies could not be.

Which was why Tatiana had come here: perhaps Anastasi, her brother, had Vega's ear, but now there was Michael Chamoun, Chance's young protégé, and Cassie. And so much at stake. Any ill befalling Chamoun could destroy the new embassy more completely than earthquake, lightning, or the sinking of the entire Spur into the canals.

If Chamoun were assassinated by the College, and word reached Magruder, and through him Karl Fon, it might be just the pretext Fon needed to declare Fon's sort of war on Merovingen. Even if war didn't result, Fon might easily call back his new ambassador, since the whole trade agreement was predicated on the merger of Boregy Shipping and Nev Hettek's Chamoun Shipping. And then Magruder, and all the opportunities he represented, would be gone like a thief in the night.

Tatiana couldn't risk it. Nor could she confront the College directly, or go against her father's (admittedly vague) permission in this matter. Nor would she dare tell Magruder what she'd learned: she'd have to tell him *how;* she'd be forced to explicate her motives. And she didn't want Magruder going up against the College.

So using Magruder to stop the College's attempt on Chamoun was out of the question. That left only unorthodox avenues of procedure, and Tatiana had chosen an audacious one.

"Your daughter," she reminded Vega, who was still staring at her owlishly. Tatiana had cultivated a rude manner; it was not flattering, but it was an effective tool. "Take me to her, now. I haven't time to stand around chatting with you, Vega, until my brother shows up and it becomes a threesome. Unless that's what you want? Perhaps a political debate this evening. . . ?"

"I . . . m'sera Secretary, you cannot go up there. My father isn't— I'll have Cassie sent down to you. If you'll wait in the green room?"

The green room, where a servant led her, was a reception room for guests to eye with envy. It was meant to cow. Its ceiling was high and its gilding excessive. Tatiana hated gilt. She was a prisoner of pomp and circumstance; she knew it for a curse, not a privilege.

High position must be guarded; she was always in danger of losing grace, face, power. Every material item in her care had upkeep, valuation, maintenance. The pure wealth of Kalugin power had made Tatiana vulnerable. She had so much to lose; she'd made so many enemies; there was no way to judge whether her work was good enough, her mind quick enough, her skills honed enough to make her equal to the tasks before her. As she got older, she became more practiced, yes, but more skilled? She wasn't sure. She'd been bolder in her youth, more optimistic.

Once she'd thought she could remake the world; when she'd held those dreams, she'd always assumed that by now, facing her fourth decade, she'd have done it: be recognized as a power on her own; be respected for more than her bloodline; be fulfilled and happy. She was none of those. She was uncertain and frightened.

She'd tasted failure too often; and success, when it came these days, was only a relief, not a reason to celebrate. She was expected to succeed; she was a Kalugin. Someday, the unstable perch on which she rested would bend or break. By then, she had to have a safety net in place—even a safety net such as Magruder's ambassadorial ties to Nev Hettek was better than no safety net at all. She had to find a way to weather the storms coming, storms she could smell in the new odor wafting up from the canals.

Had to. Or she'd lose Merovingen to her brother, Anastasi; or to Mikhail—even that was possible. She was fighting for life, watching power pass her by as her father grew closer and closer to retirement age—or to death.

When Cassie Boregy finally arrived, preceded by three

servants with a pastry tray and tea in vermeil pots, Tatiana was sunk in thought.

She didn't notice servants; they were all around her every day. She didn't notice Cassiopeia Boregy until the girl blurted out, "M'sera Secretary Kalugin, I'm so *excited* that you picked Michael to help with the census. So *honored!* Even daddy's proud, he just can't admit it." And the girl was pumping her hand, all youth and expectation.

Yet Tatiana could see through the gloss to the fear, the uncertainty that Cassie's father must have put there. The eyes behind the smile said, *What do you want? My father says you're not to be trusted. He acts like you're an enemy in this house, yet you can't be, can you? Have I done something wrong? Please don't let me do anything wrong.*

"Shoo the servants, child," said Tatiana, and Cassie Boregy's face went white.

When the girl had obeyed, Tatiana drew her toward the window and opened it. "Look out there. Your husband is out there somewhere, on an errand for me." She put her arm fleetingly around the younger woman's shoulders because, if not until now, then at this moment Cassie was a true Merovingen woman of high estate: in politics up to her neck.

"This is about . . . Michael?" Cassie's tone was hushed with foreboding and shock.

"It is. We think Cardinal Ito might be very upset. We think your husband should be careful. We think you should tell him so."

"I *told* Michael we should tell Daddy what happened. I told him. He wouldn't listen." Cassie's face worked with conflicting emotions. "You know what happened, then?"

Tatiana didn't tell her no.

"It's so wonderful, and everyone's acting as if it was an awful thing. To remember a past life—I wish I could. Michael's promised to teach me, to show me, but Ito made him swear not to, so it's hard. . . ." Cassie's hand flew up to cover her mouth. Above it, her eyes went wide.

It must have been the look on Tatiana's face as the pieces clicked:

"Oh, *no,*" Cassie whispered. "You *didn't* know, then. I'm sorry. Oh, I'm sorry. Promise you won't tell—"

The girl was backing away, panicking, and Tatiana had to grab her arm and squeeze. "Shush, girl! Don't be a fool! If I were your husband's enemy, would I have risked coming here personally, where your father was bound to find out? Do these things: Tell your grandfather, if he's still awake, what happened to Michael at the College, as well as what I've said to you. If your father asks, tell him only that I advised you that your husband's life is in danger—that we have good information that there may be an attempt on his life, but that, nevertheless, we expect him to keep on with his commission as officer of the census. Nothing more, do you understand?"

"Yes, yes. But is it enough? Will Michael be—"

"Karma, my dear. We don't know the future, any of us. But we help make it, every day. You do what I say, and make sure that if your father inquires, you tell him enough to grant m'ser Chamoun a bodyguard. Or order one yourself. You're a woman of a great house. Act like one, not like a child."

"I will. I promise I will," said Cassie as Tatiana let her go and strode to the couch to get her wrap.

"Tea?" said the child to the woman as Tatiana brushed past her. "A pastry, m'sera Secretary?"

When Tatiana strode out the door, Cassie Boregy was still holding the vermeil teapot in her hands helplessly, and her huge eyes were sparkling far too brightly.

Michael Chamoun was down in Merovingen-below, on Grandside near Fishmarket, looking for someone named Alvarez, who was said to be of Nev Hettek descent. Chamoun had separated from his three Nev Hetteker teammates, all handpicked by Magruder because they weren't Sword of God.

The night was veritably steaming as the warmer waters of the canal met the chill evening air and gave off a sulfurous mist. Here deep in the belly of poverty, picking his way along a quay slimy with fish guts and bloody fins, Chamoun was buoyed by the sense of mission that had been with him, like an ineluctable tide, ever since he'd found out he'd once been 'Mickey,' once fought the sharrh to the death. Sometimes he felt the power of the vision more strongly; sometimes it was like a half-remembered dream. But tonight it warmed him against the cold and he fancied it even armored him against the mayhem of the dockside.

So he wasn't worried about having parted company with his teammates. They had so very much of Merovingen-below to cover, they couldn't stomp around like a street gang or a group of slavers on the make. They couldn't skulk, either, or shrink from the rougher areas. They were on a commission from the highest levels of government. It should be enough protection.

The real reason, Chance Magruder had explained to him, that the Sword was going along with this census-taking, was more than the simple one of it being impolitic to refuse Tatiana Kalugin, or her father. Chamoun's job was to register as many Nev Hettekers as possible—twice. The ensuing extra green cards, some of them made out in assumed names, would make subsequent Sword infiltrations easier by providing false identities and covers. Some of these fisher folk and poleboaters and barmaids had agreed to sign two forms, to go twice to the Nev Hettek embassy (after shaving or dying their hair or changing their clothes) in return for a bit of the embassy's petty cash. Others, less trustworthy, didn't know they were being used; they knew only they were called back a second time, to fill out duplicate forms or correct errors.

Chamoun's job was to sort out the subornable, the bribe-worthy, and the coercible from the rest. This was easier when he was alone.

He'd meet his three cohorts at Ventani Bridge in two hours; until then, he had Nev Hettekers to recruit.

He was just about to try a dark bar Alvarez was said to frequent when three men came up behind him, walking fast, totally silent but for the crack of their heels upon the quayside.

Chamoun was Sword-trained. His shoulder muscles stiffened; his gut contracted; his hand went to his fishknife in its sheath, wishing he'd brought a longer blade into Merovingen-below. Or brought a gun.

There were muggers aplenty down here, and that was what the three coming up on him sounded like—because they made no sound at all, beyond the sound of their boots and their breathing.

Michael Chamoun quickened his pace. Only a dozen more strides to the bar's dark door; if he made it inside, he could pull out his credentials . . .

A passing boat slowed, going by, and someone in it called his name.

Chamoun stopped.

The men coming up behind him stopped too.

What was unexpected was that the boat stopped, someone jumped up on the quayside and made it fast, bow and stern, while two other crewmen scrambled Chamoun's way.

The three behind him were in a huddle, talking together in low tones.

The two newcomers strode straight up to Chamoun, one of them calling out boldly, "M'ser Chamoun, your esteemed wife sent us to keep you company on your rounds." And then Chamoun could see the Boregy livery, the long, dangerous blades at the men's hips, and the gunbutts stuffed in their waistbands.

So could the three on Chamoun's track, even in the dim light of Merovingen-below at quayside. They turned on their heels, grumbling churlishly, and melted into the mist.

Michael Chamoun said, "I don't need—" Then stopped. These men deserved better. And he *had* needed them—or thought he might have. "Thanks for coming. We're spread so thin. I can use all the help I can get." *Not that kind of help, boys. Don't worry, I won't recruit any double-card candidates, not outright, not tonight, thanks to you two . . . three.* But he'd tell Chance, and Magruder would handle the rest.

Then the leader of the household guard whom Cassie had dispatched started explaining what he'd been told to expect:

that Cassie feared an attack on Chamoun's life and her father had told the three to "'humor the lady.' None of us is presumin' that y' need any help, m'ser; we's just doin' our jobs."

And there was a plea there that Chamoun didn't mistake. These men couldn't very well go home and say they'd been rejected. It would lower their status; they'd have failed.

Michael said, "The more's the merrier, m'sers. As long as you'll let me buy you a beer or two: this officering the census is thirsty work. Now in here, we're lookin' for a fella named Alvarez. He's on my list as being about six foot . . ."

Magruder watched the Nev Hettekers, in their rags and stinking fishing boots, straggle into the Nev Hettek embassy all morning. When he saw one who looked likely, who matched a dossier alert-flag, or who was already prepped, he'd step forward and handle that case personally.

He'd show the poor bastards around the embassy, and watch eyes pop in undernourished faces. Once he got a woman with three teenaged children and he wanted to ask her to move in right there and then, so poor and downtrodden were these people of his homeland.

In fact, he did say, "M'sera, you've forgotten your incentive payment," and gave her a lune for herself, and one for each child.

Then he had to make it right, and add the silver give-away to the whole process. Which was going to dent his petty cash drawer. But it could have been worse; he could have given in to his initial impulse and asked the woman if she could cook. She probably couldn't, not from the way those kids' bellies were distended. She hadn't had anything to cook better than rice and garbage, fish guts and heads and seaweed and moldy cheese, for far too long. Not the sort of chef you needed for state dinners. Still, the woman's plight haunted him, and he sent somebody around later that day to see if she'd like a job doing washing or making beds at the embassy.

Truth be told, the whole head-counting enterprise was having an unexpected result, deep in the armored soul of

Chance Magruder. He'd kicked a lot of butt in his time, butt resoundingly in need of kicking, for the faceless masses of the oppressed. It was a rote catechism to him. He'd been through one revolution and it had taught him that the best you could do was rotate the oppressors and the oppressed: there was always an underclass. That was lots easier to accept when you didn't see the gummy eyes of hungry waifs and the hopeless ones of their mothers. Maybe Magruder was getting soft, but it bitched him to see the way refugees from the revolution he'd helped make in Nev Hettek had fared in Merovingen.

Another reason to bring this anti-tech, pro-superstition regime crashing down, he told himself. And that was fine; that was his job here. But it was a deeper unrest he felt, an impossible urge to do something for these people here, these people of *his*—as if he were a real ambassador and the Nev Hettek embassy was here for some real purpose, besides the fomenting of a revolution, if not the start of an out-and-out war.

Which he wasn't. Charitable works were no part of his job. He was a professional, and as one, he was professionally uncharitable. So maybe what seemed an uncharacteristic impulse was an intuition of another sort: maybe he could put together some "program" to aid his supposed constituency here; one he could use against the establishment. He was still thinking about it when Mike Chamoun came in, demanding an audience with an abrupt handsign.

There were offices and offices in the embassy. It was a big place and the staff was almost entirely Revenantist Merovingian. Magruder had taken to having his real meetings in the stairwell leading to the water-gate, where all sounds were magnified and he could be sure there wasn't somebody listening at a door.

On pretext of taking Chamoun down to look at the new boat that the embassy had been given by the "grateful House of Kalugin for services rendered under fire during the 24th Eve Ball," Chance led the infiltration agent halfway down the steps. And then it hit him: Magruder could, and would,

fire all the help that had come with this place and hire Nev
Hettek nationals to do the work—give his own people better
paying jobs, and himself a little more security. Sure, the
displaced and the descendants of the displaced, who'd fled
Nev Hettek for reasons better left undisclosed, might not be
the most loyal of staffers, but they beat people handpicked by
the Kalugin administration. Beat them to hell.

"—and then the damnedest thing happened," Chamoun was
saying.

"What thing?" Magruder rerouted the conversation back
to its beginning.

"Well, I was down near Fishmarket and there were three
guys following me, I'm almost sure, when out of nowhere
comes a boatful of Boregy retainers, sayin' Cassie sent 'em.
Climbs up and swaggers over, and *whoosh*, the guys followin'
me disappear into the fog. And these guys, they say they
come down t' keep me company on account of the House has
heard there's to be an attempt on my life—they're on me like
flies on a carcass. So I had kinda mixed results . . ."

"You've got to watch your accent, Michael," Magruder
growled. "Really watch it. You've been hanging around with
the bodyguard for just one evening, and you sound like one
of them." Magruder had to keep the young Sword on track.

And he had to think. Cassie Boregy trying to prevent
Chamoun's assassination? Boregy nerves? Or something real?
In the bad light of the stairwell, Chance couldn't tell much
from Chamoun's expression. Was the youngster spooked? Or
just making apologies for a wasted night's work?

Chance said, as gently as he was able, "And you? What do
you think it means? Besides the obvious, that your wife's in
love with you." Give the boy a bit of approval to hold onto—
Chamoun's main mission here was to make a good marriage;
let him know Magruder hadn't forgotten.

But Magruder's mission included keeping the boy alive,
unless he had good reason not to. And the mess Chamoun
had gotten into, carrying messages back and forth for Tom
Mondragon and Vega Boregy, Anastasi Kalugin's people,
wasn't good enough reason not to. Yet.

"You didn't answer me," Magruder reminded Chamoun after too long a pause. You couldn't let things like this fester. The boy had come to Magruder with this, so there was still hope. "Come on, Mike, what do you think it means?"

"I don't think anything." Chamoun's voice was dark and tight, recessed deep in his chest. "I'm askin', that's all." He raised his head. "You finished with me, Chance? 'Cause I'll leave—go back to Nev Hettek, fake my death, anything you say. I just don't think one mistake's reason enough to—"

"That's what I thought you'd say. But you don't really believe I'm behind this attempt on your life—if there was one, and we don't know that for sure—or you wouldn't be here asking me about it. Am I right?" *Talk to me, kid, before it's too late.*

"I don't know. Yeah, I'm here. So I guess I don't. But I don't know what to believe . . ." Chamoun took a step back, as if he could step into the stone wall behind him.

"Well, neither do I. But you can believe that if your bodyguards came from Vega Boregy, he saw something in it for himself, sending them. You're his boy, he thinks. He doesn't want you dead. Or he does, and he's setting up a smokescreen behind which a later kill will disappear . . ."

The boy's eyes gleamed in the dimness now as he stared straight at Chance. "What do you want me to do?"

"Act like a good trapped spy; do what Vega tells you. Thank him for the protection, but don't let on that with his men there, you couldn't do what you were supposed to in Merovingen-below. He's got dogs on you, Mike, and he wants to be sure that whatever Tatiana has you doing, he knows about. So you don't do anything about the double cards, you just mind your manners and leave the rest to us. And you come back to me, tomorrow night, same as usual, with your paperwork and your day's report."

Was it enough support? Enough reassurance? Magruder couldn't risk much more. At any point, the kid could turn over for real, become an Anastasi/Vega agent instead of his. And all Chance would have, to tell the difference, was his own instinct.

"Right. Thanks," said young Chamoun, and pushed away from the wall wearily. Magruder didn't move back; they were so close that he could feel Chamoun's rapid, warm breath puff against his face. "I'll see you then . . ."

Magruder still didn't move out of Chamoun's way. "Wait a minute, son." A friendly slip of the tongue. Chamoun paused, licked his lips, and looked at Magruder for a moment with a naked plea for help on his face.

Magruder said, "It's going to take time to get you out of this mess—a tight spot's not too harsh a term. But I'm working on it." Magruder shifted and Chamoun fell in beside him. As if he had the younger man on a leash, Chamoun paced Magruder as he started to slowly climb the stairs.

"I'm glad to hear that, si—m'ser," Chamoun said, his voice shaking just a little.

"You're going to do more than hear it. You're going to see it. In a couple of hours, if not sooner. I'd like to explain more. I'd like to have you stay here with me and watch while the Sword teaches this bunch of fanatics a lesson about Instant Karma. But I can't risk it—can't risk you. So you go home."

"I understand."

"No, you don't. But you'll do it because I'm telling you. You go home and take your wife and spend some time looking up at the sky tonight—if possible, in Vega Boregy's presence. If not, make sure you're up when all hell breaks loose."

"An attack? If there's going to be trouble—"

"No violence. No bloodshed. Psychwar, Mike. No way of telling what the result will be, beyond the fact it'll be interesting, and to our advantage. I want to know how Boregy reacts to what I've got in store for Merovingen tonight. If you can find a way to be with Vega, so much the better. But don't push it. And I want to know if any midnight messengers come from Anastasi—or from the College, to Boregy House tonight."

"I don't understand."

"I know. You will. You know all you need to—all I can

tell you without screwing up your reactions. You've got to trust me, Mike. If I wanted you dead, you'd be floating in the Grand by now. We'll turn all this around—you, me, and their own karmic debt.'' Magruder bared his teeth.

Chamoun tried to return a wolfish grin, managed only a patently uncertain smile. ''I'll let you know, then. Tomorrow night.''

''Good enough. And watch your back—there's no guarantee that there *isn't* somebody trying to take you out.'' *And I don't want you feeding the fish, and the murder blamed on the Sword of God. When and if it's necessary for you to get dead, I'll do it. Until then, even if you don't realize it, you'll have better protection from now on than Boregy retainers can provide.*

And that was a promise, albeit an unverbalized one, that Magruder could make good on: he called his best man in and ordered a covert escort for Chamoun, to make sure the youngster got home. And to capture and return to the embassy for interrogation anybody caught following Chamoun who so much as picked his teeth with a fishknife or even smelled of foul play.

There was no reason for Anastasi, or Vega Boregy, to eliminate Michael Chamoun, not while they considered him a compromised player—their player. There was no percentage in scaring the kid, or his wife. At least, not to Magruder's way of thinking, there wasn't. Therefore, either Boregy believed that Chamoun was in danger from another quarter, or didn't believe that Chamoun was successfully compromised. Either way, right now Michael Chamoun was a trouble spot.

Whether he'd still be one after midnight remained to be seen.

Ruin al-Banna, agent of the Sword of God, was out in a skiff in deep water, as far out in New Harbor as he could get and still keep Rimmon Isle in sight.

The skiff had to be positioned so that al-Banna could keep Rimmon in sight, Magruder had been implacable about that.

Ruin al-Banna hated Chance Magruder, but he loved the Sword of God.

Sometimes, al-Banna thought he *was* the Sword of God, incarnate. Especially now, since his twin brother had died in the attack on the 24th Eve Ball, the Sword's aims and his own seemed indistinguishable. And these days, Chance Magruder was Karl Fon's representative in Merovingen; Karl Fon was the man in whose worthy hand the Sword rested; therefore, Chance Magruder must be obeyed. For now.

But only for now. There were other malcontents among the Sword in Merovingen, and al-Banna knew them all. Men who knew direct action was the only way to conquer the Kalugins, who must be wiped out like vermin in a cleansing bloodbath. . . .

Al-Banna shook his head to clear the muddying thoughts of vengeance from his mind and the accompanying snarl from his lips. Later. Later, Romanov would be avenged—Magruder must have done it; everybody in the Sword cell based at Megary knew that. Nobody, however, could prove it. Eventually, they would. Eventually, they'd supplant Magruder. Baritz was sure of it. Baritz wanted to be Fon's new Magruder in Merovingen. So did Ruin al-Banna. But the Sword ran on discipline. The Megary Sword cell also ran its own reporting chain, and that chain was letting itself be used by Anastasi Kalugin to discredit Magruder.

Soon, Magruder would be no more. Soon, the Sword in Merovingen would rise up and destroy every Kalugin, the entire Boregy House and all the other aristocrats on the Rock and on Rimmon Isle. Soon, Ruin al-Banna would have the blood of Chance Magruder, in exchange for the blood of Ruin's twin brother. Blood that Magruder had shed during the 24th Eve Ball.

Soon. But not yet. Until the time was right, Ruin al-Banna would follow Magruder's orders. Even when those orders were as obscure as tonight's.

The skiff rocked gently in the water, pulling on its sea anchor. The night was cold and the fog out here was as thick as cheese. Magruder's ways were inscrutable, but al-Banna knew this was the time for following those orders to the letter.

The task at hand was dangerous, and al-Banna was proud to be the man entrusted with so difficult a job. He had gone over everything in his mind until he knew the procedure by rote. Now there remained only the execution.

Before him in the skiff, between his wide-flung legs like a lover, was a great ceramic pot, tilted away from al-Banna, pointing skyward and inland. In the pot was the formula.

In the pot, Magruder had said with his mirthless grin, was the sharrh. At first al-Banna hadn't understood. Eventually, he had. Magruder had run al-Banna through the drill until the Sword man could have performed his tasks in his sleep.

He had filled the ceramic pot with gunpowder; he had angled it away from himself so that flying gobbets of sulfur would be less likely to set him afire. He had mixed smaller paper packages of gunpowder, some with copper (for green fire); some with iron (for red fire) and stirred them into the larger mass of powder. He had made the fuse from thick cord, soaking the cord in saltpeter; he had concocted his slowmatch, a long stick of it.

Now there was only the danger, which al-Banna was proud to endure. Magruder had looked through the roster and realized that only Ruin al-Banna had the intestinal fortitude for this job, the raw courage and the overriding commitment to follow through at great personal risk. Many things could go wrong. A fiery death was not one al-Banna craved.

The pot of gunpowder could flash and explode in his face; the force of the crude rocket he'd mixed could send packets jumping onto him while they burned. The sulfur gobbets would stick to him like glue.

Or he could be found out. A patrol boat might come across him. He might have to abandon ship, or sink it with himself and the evidence aboard. Al-Banna was not a marathon swimmer. The shore was far, the water cold; visibility at the water-line would be next to nil.

But none of these risks were too great to take. If all went well, the sharrh would appear in great flaming ships of red and green, arcing through the sky over New Harbor. The fireworks would shoot as far as forty or fifty feet into the air, above the fog and the mist. From shore, their height and distance would be impossible to determine.

It would be as if the sharrh had returned. Instant karma, Magruder had said, and even al-Banna, who was slow with words, a man of deeds, had understood.

So the most important single action taken against the Revenantist oppressors was in al-Banna's hands. His brother would be proud of him. The technophobic, superstition-mongering Revenantists would never figure out that the sharrh were just a chemistry lesson; they had no logic in their souls, just fear and karmic debt.

With a final look around, al-Banna set to work. He reached over the side and scooped up water, dampening his sleeves and his arms to the elbows—not much protection, but a little. Then he took from its place the slowmatch, still smoldering where he'd wedged it under the gunwhale near the stern, and blew upon it until he had a bright flame, which he shielded with his palm.

There was no more time to waste. The explosive power of the tilted pot before him was now daunting. The pot was a dragon's mouth, and he was about to plunge a sharpened stick into it . . .

But he had accepted this assignment; he must follow through. The sharrh would appear over Merovingen tonight, and the Revenantist College would find itself forced to explain the sharrh's return in terms of karma. Terror was its own reward, all men of the Sword knew that.

With a sudden, quick motion, Ruin al-Banna plunged the slowmatch into the tilted mouth of the deep pot. Into the loose gunpowder and the bags of powder and metal sprinkled through it.

There was a blinding flash, a roar like a waterfall, and the surface of the mixture was a sheet of fire. Then the fire began to rise, and to spit. Packets leaped into the air and exploded, some high, some so low that al-Banna screamed.

He dropped the slowmatch. He shielded his face with his hands, then his arms.

Thus he missed the seeing spout that thrust upward, and the balls of colored fire that arced into the air.

He missed them because more than one packet had exploded too low: he was on fire.

He was screaming and batting himself, panic-stricken as the sulfurous fire burned him.

And he was overboard, in the water, by the time the packets that had been rocketed fifty feet in the air started to cascade like the wrath of heaven, exploding the very night and rendering al-Banna and his skiff in sharp relief, culprits against the fog.

But then an unexpected thing happened: the skiff, burning, began to founder. And as it sank, the fire below was put out.

The fire above in the heavens seemed to go on forever as the burned and half-blinded Sword operative tried to save himself. First he swam away from the sinking skiff, then he swam toward it, hoping to find a timber to hold onto, hoping to find a way to shore.

Somehow his feet got tangled in the sea anchor, but by then he was already too exhausted to swim any farther. He was only half aware that he was bound up in the rope, tied to a piece of the skiff's bow, and being dragged with the current. He'd swallowed too much water, breathed too much sulfur, been burned over too much of his body. But he'd seen the sharrh flaming across the heavens, and he'd seen that the evidence was destroyed.

Unconsciousness came so stealthily that he never wondered whether he'd drown, trussed to the spar with the anchor rope, or be washed ashore. It didn't matter. He'd made the sharrh return to Merovin, made the very sky into an Adventist testament.

"Come on, Cassie," Michael pleaded to the trembling woman weeping against his chest. "It's not Retribution, it's just—"

"The sharrh?" said Vega Boregy bleakly, an interrogatory

eyebrow raised, as the last tails of red and green faded into wisps in the moonless sky.

Chamoun didn't answer, but he knew what he'd tell Magruder tomorrow night. And he was no longer afraid that Chance was trying to kill him. Even if Cassie hadn't explained that it was Ito she was worried about, some ill will from the College, the fireworks display would have eased his mind.

Chance, you crazy bastard . . . thanks. Michael Chamoun kissed the top of Cassie's head and ran his hands slowly up and down his wife's back and looked over her shoulder at her father.

Vega Boregy's face was composed, but then, Boregy had been to Nev Hettek. He might well have seen fireworks before. Nowhere in the house was there an echo of his calm. Servants were screaming and sobbing and praying and begging forgiveness. People streamed toward the House's small chapel. Beyond, even through the fog, one could see lights in the Signeury and black dots like a mass of ants, headed for the Revenantist College.

Up from the water, on foot, and over the high bridges they hurried. Beyond the balcony, it was as noisy as midday in Merovingen tonight.

"When you get her calmed, Michael, I'll see you in my office," said Vega, and stomped away, slamming the balcony doors shut behind him.

There was time to deal with Vega; there was time to deal with Ito; there was time, even, to find Rita and console her, if she were as shaken and as guilt-ridden as Cassie seemed to be.

But right now, Michael Chamoun knew exactly what he had to do. He had to take his wife in his arms, carry her up the stairs, and help her find a previous life in which she wasn't afraid, a life which would help her deal with her present.

When that was done, Michael Chamoun could get back to helping the Sword of God. Not that Chance Magruder needed anybody's help now that the sharrh had come back again.

*   *   *

Cardinal Ito Tremaine Boregy had been personally punishing his failed assassins when the ruckus began. So it seemed to him at first that the flaming sky was some personal Retribution visited on him by an angry God for his failure—or for his foolishness at attempting to change fate.

But now, with people streaming into the great chapel in search of salvation, with all the faithful crying out for guidance, their trembling hands outstretched with gifts of atonement they begged the College holy men to take, Ito was once again composed.

If the sharrh had come, so be it. If this was some other manifestation—Instant karma for the attempt on Michael Chamoun's life, or for any other failing of Ito's, including failing in the attempt on Chamoun's life—then Ito would make the best of it.

The sharrh had not destroyed anything, the churchmen were telling the faithful as they logged in the gifts of gold and silver and oil and gasoline, of fish and textiles and ceramics and glass. It was a test of faith.

"Look around you," Ito told his multitude of aristocratic faithful, in the chapel reserved for the most wealthy and the most karmically flawed. "These are your brethren, the true believers. Whoever is absent this night, is lacking in faith, is a part of the reason we are huddled here together in prayer. Fail not to cleanse yourselves, and fail not to notice who is absent. For the absent are the guilty ones, who are not true believers, who do not pay the price of karmic debt, and who have brought this evil upon us all."

And just as Ito was finishing his lecture, in strode Vega Boregy and Anastasi Kalugin, shoulders brushing.

Which, in the long run, mightn't be so bad an omen: if no representative of the ruling house, or of Ito's own house, had arrived to share the guilt and do penance, then the College might have had an opportunity to take power. But power was up for grabs tonight.

Tonight, all of Merovingen, for perhaps the first time in

history, truly believed. And true believers were what the College loved most.

"Perhaps we should go to the College with the others," Tatiana Kalugin whispered into Chance Magruder's neck.

"Like this? I don't think your family would ever get over it, m'sera Secretary." Her Excellency was lying under Magruder, naked, her legs wrapped around him.

She hated it when he got formal with her in bed. But in bed was where he'd made sure to have her when the fireworks started. And in bed was where he'd kept her, because if he could ever make the earth move under her, it was tonight.

She cursed him like a soldier, and then her ire dissolved into nervous laughter.

He simply stroked her, waiting for her distress to pass. She was tough, and before him she pretended to be tougher still. He knew she was frightened; he'd considered telling her the truth, but he couldn't risk it.

He looked into her hungry eyes and saw an urgency there that only fear could spark. She said, "Tell me it isn't the end of the world," in a voice hardly louder than a sigh.

"It isn't—not our world. I promise, if the sharrh come, I'll use all my influence to get you whatever tech protections you'll accept from Nev Hettek. Just you, of course, not your brothers."

"And if the sharrh don't come?"

Then, honey, I'm going to use you to get the same result. Just you, the way I said—not your brothers. Relax, lady; play me straight and I won't let you lose. Out loud: "If they don't, we'll hear a lot about what it all means, and things will go on the same as before. We'll have to watch those cardinals—or you will. They could interpret this . . . event . . . to their advantage. But so can you."

Then she chuckled, and locked her arms behind his neck. "You're a monster, Magruder. But you know that."

Despite her words, she was pleased. And beginning to pay attention to what he was doing to her. Which in turn pleased him.

There wasn't a place more dangerous in Merovingen to the health of Chance Magruder than Tatiana Kalugin's bed. And there wasn't a place, for that reason as much as despite it, that he'd rather be.

He'd told her the truth, tonight: he was going to do his damnedest to hand her Merovingen on a silver platter. And when it came time to hand her, in her turn, to Karl Fon. . . . well, that was a long time off.

Right now, he had all the trouble in bed with him that any man could handle, even a man like Chance Magruder.

And outside, tonight, Merovingen had all the trouble it could handle: Merovingen had just met the sharrh, courtesy of the Sword of God.

APPENDIX

Merovingian Songs

FEVER SEASON

Lyrics by Mercedes Lackey
Music by C.J. Cherryh

The night is hot and starless
And the moon won't show her face.
The walkways and the bridges
Seem as frail as half-burnt lace,
And if the city holds its breath
In silence, there's a reason—
Fever season.

She drifts along the bridges—
Or canalside she will go.
She's on the prowl for lovers
And this lady don't take "no."
Her lovin' leaves you burnin' hot
Her lovin' leaves you freezin'.
Fever season.

Now if she comes to take you
You will never see her face;
You'll only hear her laughter
As you melt in her embrace.
And if you wake next mornin'

Thank the Angel she was teasin'—
Fever season.

She takes 'em rich and hightown
And she takes 'em low and poor.
It don't matter—when you hear her
You cannot escape the lure.
The priest in all his holiness
The rebel steeped in treason—
Fever season.

The night is hot and restless
And the clouds hang dark and low.
You'll never see her shadow
But she'll take you even so.
And if you feel a breath of chill
Be certain there's a reason—
Fever season.

MIST-THOUGHTS
(A WALTZ WITH A LIMP)

Lyrics by Mercedes Lackey
Music by C.J. Cherryh

I have no reason to hope—I have no license to care—
It is no more logical far not to trust
Anything, anyone, anywhere.
Just taking each hour as it comes—and grateful to have one
  more day
Letting my guard down no more than I must
Never seek—never touch—never pray.

I should be watching my back—I should be just marking
  time—
Go through the motions, and know it is worth
Slightly less than a badly-made rhyme.
Why do I let myself wish? Why do I hear myself laugh?
Where is my reason for longing or mirth,
Who is helpless as wind-scattered chaff?

Who is this slip of a girl that touches the soul I thought dead?
What did she do when she saved me to share
In her life and her heart and her bed?
Making a wreck of my pride—or what little pride I had left—

Binding me up in the loom of her care.
Where bright hope is the warp and the weft.

I say I've nothing to give. *She* will not leave me alone—
She sees through evasions and futile disguise
As I try to seem harder than stone.
She searches for a way out; *I* give myself to despair—
Yet when she is done with her tricks and her lies
Then somehow an escape will be there.

What could I give her but pain? Or dreams that could never
  come true?
But—God help me—in unguarded moments I see
My traitor heart's dreaming them too.
I'll make no bonds I may break—or promises I might deny—
But—despite what has been—and for all that *might* be—
And my dear, foolish, Jones—I will try.

PARTNERS

Lyrics by Mercedes Lackey
Music by C.J. Cherryh

My mother worships money
And my father worships work.
My sister says that I'm a whore,
My brother, I'm a sherk
With such a loving family
There's no need to wonder why
At sixteen I determined that
I'd break away or die.

Well, die is what I nearly did—
Out singing for my cash;
They threw a little money
But they threw a *lot* of trash.
I tried a little acting
'Cause the bug was in my soul,
But acting couldn't keep me fed;
I starved, and then I stole.

Her name was Rif; she sang in bars;
Her hat was full of coin;
And she caught me quite red-handed
With what I tried to purloin.

Index of Isles and Buildings by Regions

THE ROCK: (ELITE RESIDENTIAL) LAGOONSIDE

1. The Rock
2. Exeter
3. Rodrigues
4. Navale
5. Columbo
6. McAllister
7. Basargin
8. Kalugin (governor's relatives)
9. Tremaine
10. Dundee
11. Kuzmin
12. Rajwade
13. Kuminski
14. Ito
15. Krobo
16. Lindsey
17. Cromwell
18. Vance
19. Smith
20. Cham
21. Spraker
22. Yucel
23. Deems
24. Ortega
25. Bois
26. Mansur

GOVERNMENT CENTER

27. Spur (militia)
28. Justiciary
29. College (Revenant)
30. Signeury

THE TEN ISLES (ELITE RESIDENCE)

31. Carswell
32. Kistna
33. Elgin
34. Narain
35. Zorya
36. Eshkol
37. Romney
38. Rosenblum
39. Boregy
40. Dorjan

THE SOUTH BANK

THE RESIDENCIES

Second rank of elite
41. White
42. Eber
43. Chavez
44. Bucher
45. St. John
46. Malvino (Adventist)
47. Mendelev
48. Sofia
49. Kamat
50. Tyler

Mostly wealthy or government
51. North
52. Spellbridge
53. Kass
54. Borg
55. Bent
56. French
57. Cantry
58. Porfirio
59. Wex

WEST END

PORTSIDE

Upper middle class
60. Novgorod
61. Ciro
62. Bolado
63. diNero
64. Mars
65. Ventura
66. Gallandry (Advent.)
67. Martel
68. Salazar
69. Williams
70. Pardee
71. Calliste
72. Spiller
73. Yan
74. Ventani
75. Turk
76. Princeton
77. Dunham

Middle class
78. Golden
79. Pauley
80. Eick
81. Torrence
82. Yesudian
83. Capone
84. Deva
85. Bruder
86. Mohan
87. Deniz
88. Hendricks
89. Racawski
90. Hofmeyr
91. Petri
92. Rohan
93. Herschell
94. Bierbauer
95. Godwin
96. Arden
97. Aswad

② MEROVINGEN
(second quarter — frontispiece map)

DET

THE FLAT

ESHKOW

ROM-NEY

DORJAN

Grand Canal

CHAVEZ

EAST DIKE

DOCKS

EBER

MENDELEV

MALVINO

41

45

SOFIA

KAMAT

TULER

NAHAR

VAI-TAN

SARD-JIN

FOUNDRY

109

110

114

HAGEN

MASUD

KNOWLES

119

❋ NUMBERS INDICATE ISLES AND BUILDINGS LISTED IN INDEX

③ MEROVINGEN
(third quarter — frontispiece map)

EICK
81
82
NOV-GOROD
55
56
CANTRY
WEX
Branch
DEVA
61
62
63
65
Veit
83
87
MARS
GALLANDRY
West Canal
Port Canal
West Canal
68
BRUDER
Greve
88
PAULEY
ARDEN
ASWAD
HAFIZ
72
78
89
ARDEN
93
HOFMEYR
ROHAN
HERSCHELL
Tidewater
102
PETRI
SOUTH DIKE
BIER-BAUER
GODWIN
Marsh Gate
GHOST FLEET
OLD PORT
Marsh
Old Harbor
FLOOD ZONE
ANCIENT SEAWALL
Sea
RIM

✳ NUMBERS INDICATE ISLES AND BUILDINGS LISTED IN INDEX

④ MEROVINGEN
(fourth quarter—frontispiece map)

65
Port
Grand Canal
WILLIAMS
PAR-DEE
CALLISTE
FOUN-DRY
NAYAB
FISH MARKET
MASUD
118
GOSSAN
Snake
SALEM
VEN-TANT
TURK
YAN
75
DUN-HAM
Gut
MANTOVAN
RAVI
101
MEN-DEZ
DELAREE
EAST DIKE
ULGER
FACTORY
CALDER
107
Old Grand
SALVATORE
RAMSEYHEAD
102
Tidewater
105
SOUTH DIKE
WHARF GATE
POGY GATE
New Harbor
DIKE
DEAD
WHARF
RIMMON ISLE
124 125 120
127 128 129 130
GHOST FLEET
Dead Harbor

RIM

Sea

* NUMBERS INDICATE ISLES AND BUILDINGS LISTED IN INDEX

② MEROVINGEN
(second quarter — frontispiece map)

DET

THE FLAT

ESHKOW

ROM-NEY

Grand Canal

DORJAN

CHAVEZ

EAST DIKE

DOCKS

EBER

MENDELEV

MAL-VINO

41

45

NAHAR

SOFIA

KAMAT

TULER

VAI-TAN

SARD-JIN

FOUNDRY

109

110

114

HAGEN

MASUD

KNOWLES

119

✱ NUMBERS INDICATE ISLES AND BUILDINGS LISTED IN INDEX

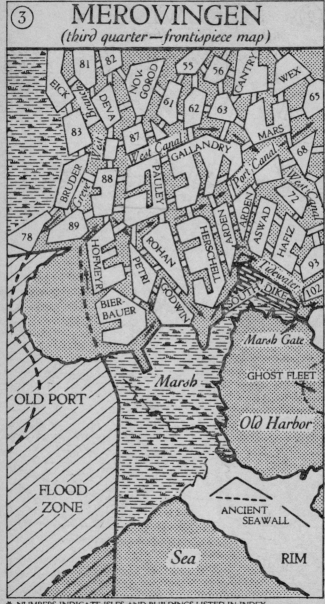

MEROVINGEN
(third quarter — frontispiece map)

③

EICK
81
82
NOV. GOROD
DEVA
Valmarsh
Breuk
83
55
56
CANTRY
WEX
61
62
63
65
West Canal
87
GALLANDRY
MARS
BRUDER
Greve West
88
PAULEY
Port Canal
68
West Canal
89
78
ARDEN
ARDEN
ASWAD
72
HOFMEYR
ROHAN
HERSCHELL
HAFIZ
93
PETRI
Tidewater
SOUTH DIKE
102
BIER-BAUER
GODWIN
Marsh Gate
GHOST FLEET
Marsh
Old Harbor
OLD PORT
FLOOD ZONE
ANCIENT SEAWALL
Sea
RIM

✳ NUMBERS INDICATE ISLES AND BUILDINGS LISTED IN INDEX

MEROVINGIAN EPIDEMIOLOGY 101 OR "THIS TOWN IS MAKING ME SICK."

There is only one thing keeping the entire city of Merovingen from being decimated—if not removed entirely from the map—by disease. That is that even the lowliest inhabitants have a thorough and practical working knowledge of the germ theory of disease. They all know to boil suspect water before drinking; to scald or sear dishes and implements before cooking; to throw out suspect food; to disinfect wounds however possible.

Nevertheless, there are still plenty of "bugs" to lay the unsuspecting low.

INFLUENZA:

By far and away the most common diseases in Merovingen are the upper respiratory influenzas—the *true* 'flu,' as opposed to what is commonly referred to as 'flu'—viral-born gastrointestinal afflictions. For the native, these are usually non-fatal—only the old, the very young, or those weakened by something else are liable to become statistics. For the native, the symptoms include running nose, clogged sinuses, irritated throat, coughing, and low-grade fever.

For the non-native, however, the consequences of catching 'Influenza-M' can frequently be fatal. Within a few hours of the onset of the first symptoms, fever can be high as 104° F, congestion in the lungs can be life-threatening, delirium is a possibility and pneumonia is little more than a breath away.

VIRAL PNEUMONIA:
Without the drugs available to the rich, this disease is invariably fatal. The virus appears to be native to Merovin, and is probably the first to have 'crossed-over' to non-native hosts.

BACTERIAL PNEUMONIA:
Usually survivable, provided the victim is not allergic to whatever antibiotic is available. Bacterial pneumonia is known to hit whole islands, causing the priests to declare a quarantine.

TUBERCULOSIS:
Human stock is less susceptible to TB than in pre-Ship days, but the bacillus thrives in the damp, polluted air of Merovingen. While humans are less susceptible to the disease, the bacillus is far more resistant to antibiotics.

BACTERIAL DYSENTERY:
This is the 'fever' that commonly carries off those who drink canal-water; it is extremely resistant to penicillin, the most commonly available antibiotic for the canalers and canalsiders.

AMOEBOID DYSENTERY:
Another of the first 'cross-overs' to non-native hosts. Was invariably fatal until a vermifuge was discovered that killed it—ethyl alcohol. One of life's little ironies. . . .

TYPHIN:
True 'fever,' one of two; a mutated form of the typhus bacillus. Has the same symptoms as typhoid fever. Vector is the water. Resistant to most antibiotics. Can sometimes be survived with the help of blueangel.

BUBONIC PLAGUE:
Somehow this managed to make it into space; so far however it has been only a few isolated cases since the majority

of citizens manage to avoid both the rats and the fleas that carry the disease. Canalers are uniquely 'immune' since they seldom come into contact with the above; the large number of feral cats keeps the rat population down and so helps prevent the spread of the disease.

HAKIM'S FEVER:

The other 'true' fever. This one appears to be either a mutated form of some otherwise harmless virus, or something entirely new; without electron microscopes it's impossible to say which. Vector is unknown, transmission is unknown. This is a real killer, and appears only in really hot weather. Symptoms are a dangerously high fever, delirium, hallucinations, insatiable thirst. This is a cyclic fever; if the first bout doesn't carry off the victim, the second, the third, the fourth probably will. Named for the first person to survive it; has a 90% fatality rate.

MEROVINGIAN PHARMACOLOGY 101 OR 'HI!—NOT YET."

It is something of a commentary on life in Merovingen that the majority of the available pharmaceuticals are either recreational or fatal.

Since *medicinal* drugs are by far in the minority, we will begin with those.

MEDICINALS:

The range of medicinal drugs in Merovingen varies wildly with the state of one's pocketbook—there are some fairly sophisticated drugs available to the very rich—from up the Det, where tech is better tolerated.

Chiefest among these are the *Immuno-system boosters*. These little lovelies are used chiefly when moving into a new area, and resistance to local diseases is nil. Theoretically they sensitize the immune system to operate at high gear and deal with *everything* that happens to waltz by. There are two dangers involved with taking these; one with taking them too short a period of time, the other for too long. When the course of medication is timed properly, the patient has acquired the same immunities as the surviving natives—may, in fact, have a superior set. If the course is not followed through, for whatever reason (and the average course is about six months), the patient will *not* have time to acquire his own immunity to the local diseases. If the course is followed for too long (a year or more) there is a possibility that the immune system will become too sensitive and begin attacking helpful organisms such as intestinal flora, or even cause severe allergies to food, drugs, and breathable proteins (pollens, mold-spores).

A better choice are the *prophylactic antibiotics;* less expensive and easier to manufacture (though useless against viruses) these can be taken as a precautionary measure against bacterial disease, and can be prescribed for an indefinite period without harm.

Whole Blood Transfusion is also available to the very wealthy. The cost involved is due to three factors: firstly, that it must be performed patient-to-donor directly, as it was originally; secondly, the difficulty of manufacturing hollow needles and flexible tubing (there is a small plastics plant in Nev Hettek proper which produces such specialties on a very limited scale; how long it will continue to do so is problematical); thirdly, although blood-typing is a relatively simple procedure, it is one few doctors or priests have learned; by the time the appropriate text is unearthed the patient may well have expired. When the paraphernalia is available, *fluid replacement* with some form of Ringer's solution is far more common.

Antihistamines and *decongestants* are common in the medicine-cabinets of the well-to-do; they are easily obtained, but the cost of producing them keeps them confined to the upper and upper middle classes.

Various painkillers available range from *Demerol* to *Synthetic Codeine*—again, cost of synthesis (although they can be produced in a lab the size of most sitting-rooms) keeps them limited to the upper classes.

Available to the middle class are several wide-spectrum antibiotics including *tetracycline*. There is an anti-viral agent, *Contradine*, which is not overly costly but has several nasty side-effects, up to and including death by asphyxiation (about 5% of the cases). A painkiller, *Comeine* (which is similar in effect to codeine but not as powerful) has been isolated from a native plant, the bloodbulb. *Actominophin* and *ibuprofen* are also available.

At the lowest common denominator, there are *contraceptives, antibiotics; blueangel* (a febrifuge of native origin) and *ethyl alcohol*.

Unofficially, there is also a growing 'pharmacy' of herbal medicines available to the lowest classes. In Merovingen resistance to change among the priests and priest-taught doctors and medics tends to keep these medicinals limited only to the lower classes who cannot afford the services of such lofty personages. One of the more common herbal concoctions is *menthil-salve* which has a very similar formula to the ancient eucalyptus and mentholated rubs used both for arthritis and aching muscles and as a decongestant for the common cold. The 'herb-doctors' tend to be secretive about their lore, which again tends to limit the spread of such knowledge. Things filter into town from time to time from the swamp, but up until now the proliferation of such medicinals has been limited to a scant handful of people at any one time. Usually it has been on a case-by-case basis—someone falls ill, and the desperate loved-one seeks help in the swamp; the crazies for unfathomable reasons give aid instead of the business-end of a blade. But as with all things in Merovingen, this, too, is subject to change without notice.

RECREATIONAL DRUGS:

By far and away the most common drugs used in Merovingen are the narcotics, intoxicants, stimulants, euphorics and hallucinogenics. Nearly all of these are derived from native plants or animal products.

Those ingested by smoking tend to be lumped under the name of 'tobacs' (usually spoken with a wink and a nudge).

Most of the tobacs are narcotics or euphoric in nature. Most stimulants are drunk in the form of 'cordials'—sweet, alcohol-based drinks with additional 'flavorings.' Most intoxicants and hallucinogenics are eaten. Due to the scarcity of hypodermic needles (the treasured possessions of the wealthy doctors) the practice of direct injection of recreational drugs has not developed.

Side effects: the 'tobacs' tend to nurture psychogenic dependence if abused; also evident has been loss of short-term memory and creative ability. Abuse of the 'cordials' is very low, primarily because of the protocol surrounding the ingestion of same; alcoholism is far more prevalent. The few cases of abuse have seemed to display violent withdrawal symptoms, however, indicating that abuse can bring on strong dependency. Side effects of the hallucinogenics include flash-back, unpredictable memory loss, and personality changes—up to and including severe mental disorder. Abuse of the intoxicants can lead to severe dependency, loss of interest in anything not connected with the drug, immunological depression, accumulative poisoning, severe mental depression, and death by a variety of causes.

There is some experimentation connected with combining two or more recreational drugs or 'boosting' the strength of the existing drugs by attempting to concentrate the active principle in one of several ways. Results of this experimentation are not generally known; however the morning following some of the wilder parties among the well-to-do not infrequently finds one of the invitees no longer among the living.

PRACTICAL MEROVINGEN AQUATIC ECOLOGY 101 OR "WHAT'S TO EAT?"

The aquatic ecosystems of Merovingen and its surroundings are influenced primarily by the following two factors: (1) the cold arctic current that travels down along the eastern coastline and cuts in through the Strait of Storms (which, cold current meeting warm, is why the Strait has so many storms); and (2) the relatively narrow continental shelf. These two factors give the area around Merovingen a climate a great deal like Northern California (as opposed to the Eastern Seaboard).

The current is fast and pretty much constant, carrying away silt and sand. As a result the shellfish and crustaceans found in the area around Merovingen are either of the 'rooting' variety (i.e., they anchor themselves and let food come to them), or they are large enough (around a meter in size) when full grown that the current can't pick them up and carry them off. They are intolerant of change in temperature and salinity, hence for the most part cannot live in the harbor or estuary. Because the continental shelf drops off so quickly, their preferred habitat is below ten meters—this makes them nearly impossible for anyone but trained drivers to retrieve. This keeps them rare, expensive, and prevents them from being fished out.

The one exception to this is a tiny 'crab' of about three inches in diameter that lives among the reeds in the swamp. These are edible only in summer when they emerge from hibernation in the mud. After the fifteenth of the Quinte they have ingested enough insect larvae to give them an extremely disagreeable taste—and worse, very powerful purgative properties. Favorite punishment among the swampy gangs is to force a malefactor to eat a double-handful of them after they've gone inedible.

DINNER TIME IN THE SWAMP

Spring (Prime, Deuce, Planting)

Edible are the very young shoots of reeds and marsh-grass (edibleness can be judged by the color), either raw or boiled. Fish, of course, provide protein—but the springtime staple is the 'mud-pup.' Mud-pups are the juvenile form of a remarkably ugly, tough, and vicious oceanic reptile called the 'dragonelle.' Dragonelles (not entirely reptilian as they are endotherms and do not hibernate, and have a warty hide instead of scales) are sea-going creatures that range from one to two meters in length, and are possessed of a mouthful of needle-teeth, long, tearing claws on webbed feet, and poisoned ventral and tail spines. Their flesh is very unpleasant to the taste, and quite poisonous. In late summer they mate at sea, and the gravid females take to the marshes to lay their eggs in the mud at the foot of reed-clumps. The mud-pups emerge all three months of spring. Mud-pups are plump, stupid, and easy to catch, having only the urge to get to salt-water on their tiny minds. Their flesh is fairly tasteless, but nourishing, and most of a mud-pup is edible. And there are *lots* of them, presumably to make up for their stupidity, as one adult dragonelle can produce up to a thousand eggs per season, laying them over a period of one to two months.

Summer (Greening, Quartin, Quince)

Some time in the beginning of Greening the crabs begin to emerge from hibernation. They are not overly large, and they are not as easy to catch as a mud-pup (they defend themselves) but again, there are lots of them. Fish, as usual, provides the rest of a swampy's protein. Vegetable material is provided by one of the few things seeded by the Ancestors; several varieties of edible deep-sea kelp. By Greening the kelp beds have grown up to reach the surface and long pieces are constantly being broken off and carried in to the beach. A hungry swampy need only stake out a section of beach for a few hours and sooner or later an oceanic salad big enough to stuff him and several friends will come floating in. If he's really lucky, clinging to the kelp will be one of the oceanic crabs, but he'd better keep such a piece of great good luck to himself. . . .

Fall (Sexte, Septe, Harvest)

These are the lean months for the swampy. The kelp beds have died back down, the mud-pups are gone, the crabs can't be eaten, and the reeds and grasses have all gone woody and fibrous. The only vegetable material he can get is the pith of certain rushes; knowledge of those rush-beds is carefully guarded. About all there is for the hungry swampy is fish and river-eels. Things can get very unpleasant in the fall. . . .

MEDICINALS AND OTHER RELEVANCIES:

Although most of the vegetation in the swamp is either poisonous or disagreeable in quantity, in small amounts quite a number of the plants have medicinal properties.

Redberry bush bark: contains salicylic acid and acetyl salicylate (locally called *asprin*). Useful for headache and fever-reduction.

Wiregrass: contains quinchona (quinine).

Marshcress: an expectorant.

Nodding Tom (a reed): seeds produce a mild tranquilizer; root, a sedative.

Numbvine: sap has a benzocaine-like-substance; a local anesthetic; also speeds clotting.

Potchbush: sap has a very powerful antibiotic effect, but only externally.

Rainbow weed: stimulant.

PRACTICAL MEROVINGEN ECOLOGY 102 OR "WHAT'S EATING YOU?"

In sober fact, most of the wildlife of Merovin finds human beings (a) inedible or (b) as poisonous as humans find the wildlife. This is fortunate for the humans, especially those in the swamp. However there are any number of things out there that are perfectly willing to defend themselves/territory by taking a bite out of you, provided they can spit it out afterwards.

JAWS 3, SWAMPY 0

The single largest dangerous critter a swampy is likely to encounter is the gravid female dragonelle. They are between one and two meters long, have short tempers (you'd be peeved too, if you had up to a thousand eggs to lay), are highly territorial and aggressive, and are possessed of poisonous ventral and tail spines and a mouthful of needle-sharp teeth. They swarm into the swamp in the winter months, coming in after dark with the high tide and leaving with the ebb (like grunion) before dawn. They have been known to take a whole foot off an injudicious swampy, and will certainly extract the proverbial pound of flesh if they get the chance. The main rule in dealing with dragonelle is, NEVER, EVER, PUT ANY PART OF YOURSELF INTO THE WATER AFTER DARK IN WINTER. While they are amphibious, they don't really like 'dry land' and much prefer to grumble down in the mud underwater. They will not climb up on rafts or into boats.

Moving down the food chain, we come to the smaller 'reptiles and amphibians.' Here the rule is, if it has teeth, it will usually bite. Nature has been a bit kinder to humans here—the poisonous ones advertise themselves with bright, vivid colors. The three most often fatal are:

THE BLOOD-SKINK: about ten to twenty centimeters long, and a vivid ruby red in color, the blood-skink is normally shy except in summer (mating season). Both sexes fight, both are poisonous. The venom is a neurotoxin acting on the autonomic nervous system.

THE ASP: named for Cleopatra's pet, this is actually a legless lizard patterned in brown and bright yellow. It lives in the center of reed clumps. It is normally shy but will bite if disturbed, frightened, or captured. The venom is, like that of the Indian krait, a catalyzing enzyme; it causes euphoria and vivid hallucinations, and death is usually due to heart-failure.

THE KOBRA: this is a true snake, rarely exceeding ten centimeters and pencil-thin. In color it is a vivid emerald green. It is most often encountered because it has climbed up onto a raft or boat to sun itself; it is incredibly quick, and can strike and be over the side almost before the hapless swampy has realized it was there. The venom is a respiratory system depressant; death is caused by asphyxiation.

A variety of other toothy denizens can be an indirect cause of death via infection of the wound.

WHO'RE YE CALLING VERMIN?

Along with cats, rats and mice went to space, made it to Merovin, and unlike the human colonists, throve. How they got here is uncertain; legend has it that they are all descendants of a shipment of lab animals whose cages broke during an earthquake. This may be at least partially true; there is a heavy preponderance of albinism among them; also about twenty percent of the population are piebald (Wistar) rats.

The indigenous critters to look out for are as follows:

SKITS: about the size of a large mouse, these things look like an unholy mating of crab and shrew; they have sharp hairy snouts with lots of teeth, a horny carapace, a long, hairless tail, and a voracious appetite. They are found in the swamp and in town, both. They are omnivorous, and the main reason why no sane swampy will try to store food; if more than ten assemble to chow down, it kicks off a feeding frenzy among them. If stored food attracted a swarm (a feeding group of a hundred or more) to a raft, the inhabitant stands a real good chance of ending up on the menu, literally nibbled to death.

MUDSUCKERS: the Merovingen leech; they will attach themselves to the unfortunate who happens upon them and will create a nasty sore before realizing that they've latched onto something inedible and drop off.

NARKS: the Merovingen cockroach; similar in habitat and indestructibility, they look rather like a silverbit-sized insect that couldn't make up its mind whether to be a spider or a beetle.

In addition, a number of the smaller lizards have made themselves at home in the canals and buildings of Merovingen. They're mostly shy and harmless; many of them actually provide a service of eating insects and insect larvae.

For the most part, Merovin insect life finds humans unpalatable; the one thing a swampy or canaler DOESN'T have to deal with is mosquitoes and flies, or the local equivalent. This is the one bright spot in an otherwise unpleasant existence.

MEROVINGEN OCEANOGRAPHY 101 OR "WHOSE FAULT IS IT?"

Merovingen has an overall climate much like that of Northern California, rather than New Orleans, which it otherwise resembles in continental placement. This is caused by the cold arctic current which flows down the coastline. . . .

What is wrong with that statement? you have five minutes.

Right. Cold arctic currents do not flow along eastern coastlines in northern hemispheres. Such currents would have to flow *against* the Coriolis forces.

Nevertheless, the current *is* there. And the reason is tied in with why Merovingen sits in such a geographically active area.

Not too far off the coast (geographically speaking) is what *should* (if the gods did not play with loaded dice) be a mid-oceanic ridge. It is a very young and very active ridge, and may someday grow up to be a continent if it is very, very good. It extends all the way up to the arctic circle and down three-quarters of the way to the antarctic before fading out. It has been the source of some wonderful displays just off the Falken Islands of the eternal antagonism of fire and water. It also is high enough that it literally cuts the arctic current in half, with one half taking the proper Coriolis flow past the Falken Islands—and the other half forced down along a surprisingly deep right valley (the Suvagen Rift Valley), trapped between itself and the eastern coast of the continent where Merovingen is. The current is forced all along that coastline until it gets itself untangled near the equator, and joins the warm upwelling off the Sundance which is behaving the way a current should. This warmed current travels up the opposite side of the ridge, meeting the cold current right at the Strait of Storms—which is why the Strait *has* so many storms. Being young and active, as well as out of place, this ridge is blessed with a number of fracture and fault lines, one of the largest of which runs—.

You have five minutes. . . .

Give yourself a gold star. Precisely underneath Merovingen.

Now since it's pretty hard to ignore a volcanically active ridge that is high enough to divert a major arctic current from Coriolis flow, a number of terms come to mind to describe whoever was in charge of the geologic survey of the area. "Criminally negligent" is one; I'm sure the inhabitants of Merovingen have a few more. Be that as it may, it would be difficult to have picked out a *less* suitable site for a major city, much less a spaceport. But we knew that already.

The one advantage this arctic current confers is that it is extremely rich in the Merovin equivalent of plankton. And where there is plankton, there will be fish. Lots of fish. Which makes the fisheries off Merovingen second only to those off the Falken Islands (which are rather like Greenland—cold, barren, and boring—thanks to the other half of that arctic current). And bad as Merovingen is, it is at least a far more interesting place to live than anywhere in the Falken Islands.

Provided you don't mind the house rearranging itself a couple of times a year.

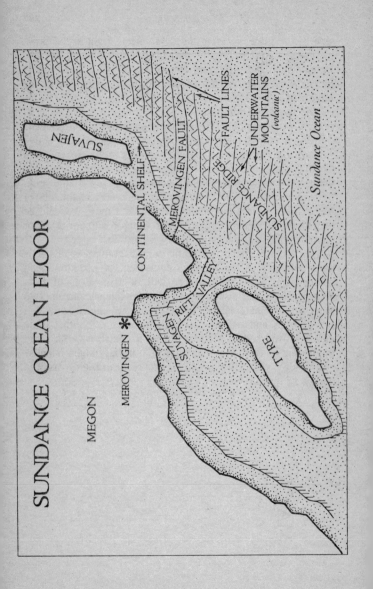

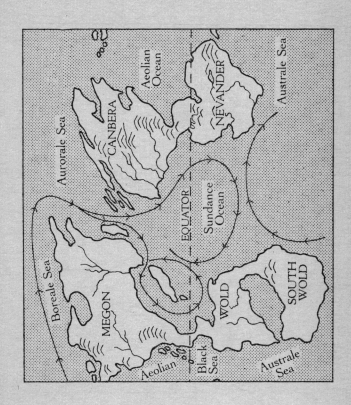

MAJOR EASTERN OCEANIC CURRENTS (affecting climate)

N

Aeolian Ocean

Australe Sea

Aurorale Sea

CANBERA

NEVANDER

EQUATOR

Sundance Ocean

Boreale Sea

MEGON

WOLD

SOUTH WOLD

Aeolian

Black Sea

Australe Sea

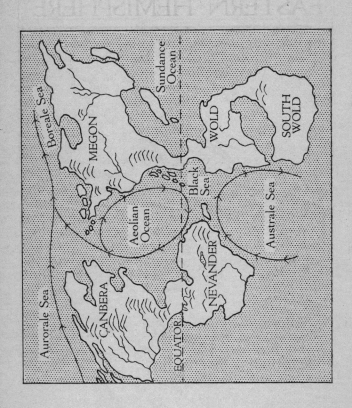

EASTERN HEMISPHERE

WESTERN

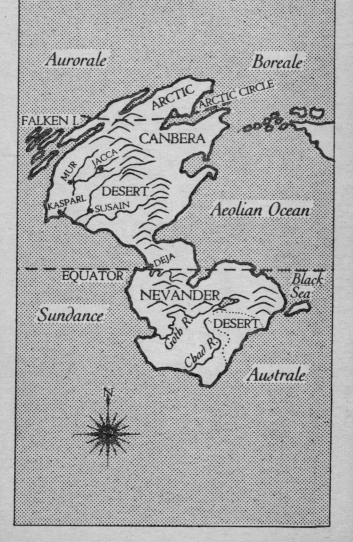

EASTERN HEMISPHERE

Aurorale

Boreale

ARCTIC

ARCTIC CIRCLE

FALKEN I.

CANBERA

MUR

JACCA

DESERT

KASPARL

SUSAIN

Aeolian Ocean

DEJA

EQUATOR

NEVANDER

Black Sea

Sundance

Goth R.

DESERT

Chad R.

Australe

N

WESTERN HEMISPHERE

Boreale

Bay of Winds

JET STREAM

MISTY
MTS.

Det R.

MEGON

NEV
HETTEK

MEGAR

Ligar R.

*KEVOGI

NEX

SOGHON

SUVAJEN

DESERT OF
GEMS

MEROVINGEN

SUTTANI

Strait of Storms

ISLES OF FIRE

TYRE

Sundance

CHATTALEN

EQUATOR

Black Sea

WOLD

Australe

TEMAJI
RAIN FOREST

Sea of Wold

PRAESI

N

WOLD
SOUTH

DAW

More Top-Flight Science Fiction and Fantasy from
C.J. CHERRYH

Merovingen Nights

ANGEL WITH THE SWORD
A Merovingen Nights Novel   (UE2143—$3.50)
FESTIVAL MOON: MEROVINGEN NIGHTS #1
A Merovingen Nights Anthology
(April 1987)   (UE2192—$3.50)

Ealdwood Fantasy Novels

THE DREAMSTONE   (UE2013—$2.95)
THE TREE OF SWORDS AND JEWELS
     (UE1850—$2.95)

Other Cherryh Novels

BROTHERS OF EARTH   (UE1869—$2.95)
CUCKOO'S EGG   (UE2083—$3.50)
HESTIA   (UE2102—$2.75)
HUNTER OF WORLDS   (UE1872—$2.95)
SERPENT'S REACH   (UE2088—$3.50)
WAVE WITHOUT A SHORE   (UE2101—$2.95)

Cherryh Anthologies

SUNFALL   (UE1881—$2.50)
VISIBLE LIGHT   (UE2129—$3.50)

DAW

SCIENCE FICTION MASTERWORKS FROM THE INCOMPARABLE C.J. CHERRYH